A THRONE OF SHADOWS

PROPHECY OF THE FORGOTTEN FAE BOOK ONE

TESSONJA ODETTE

A THRONE OF SHADOWS

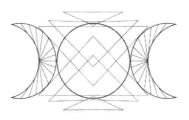

1

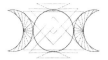

W hen Cora dreamed, she dreamed of castles. Not the storybook variety with shining turrets and glistening marble columns, but dark towers brimming with even darker magic. These castles held no masked balls, boasted no gilded statues or impressive tapestries. Instead of fancy footmen fluttering about the halls, the corridors were empty, black, and soundless. All that existed was a *feeling*, a deep and hollow knowing that something wasn't quite right.

In her dreams, Cora could do nothing but follow this sense of unease, this wrongness that existed outside of her, calling to her like the mythical sirens of fae lore. It was a silent song, one so chilling it made her hair stand on end. Still, she could do nothing but follow. Follow. Meeting dead end after dead end.

The feeling intensified, growing heavier, tugging her bones until it bore down upon her like a leaden weight. She knew she should stop following the feeling. Knew she should turn around and forget the dark pull. But even when she tried to forget, tried to turn around, the feeling only drew nearer. Soon the halls closed in, inch by inch, until they narrowed down to a single corridor, one that ended in the same door no matter which way she turned.

A rattling sound echoed around her. Glancing down, she found it was coming from the serving tray she carried. A teacup trembled against its saucer. Her hands were shaking even more.

The door loomed ahead of her, gaping like a hungry maw.

Against her will, her feet moved toward it. Too soon she stood in the dreaded doorway. As she saw what lay beyond, she felt as if she'd known all along. There was a bed. And upon that bed...

Blood. So much blood.

A scream shattered the air, piercing her eardrums.

She shook her head, trying to rid her eyes of the sight and her ears of the blaring shout. It grew louder. She blinked several times, but that only brought her closer to the bed. The blood was no longer just in front of her but all around, dripping from her hands. The sharp tang of it filled her nose, seared her throat.

Then a question filled her mind, the voice angry and familiar.

What have you done?

The scream intensified.

It was coming from her.

Cora opened her eyes but all she could see was black. Two weights pressed down upon her shoulders—hands

—and she flailed against them, fighting the unseen assailant who restrained her.

"Cora, quiet, you're safe."

The voice leached the fight from her bones. She went limp beneath her friend's touch, pursing her lips against the screams that still crawled up her throat.

"It's just me," soothed Maiya, stroking the damp hair away from Cora's forehead. "You're home. It was just a bad dream."

Cora gritted her teeth and breathed away the remnants of her terror. In its place, anger grew. Not at her friend but at herself. She was supposed to be stronger than nightmares. She was a witch, after all. Witches were meant to be powerful.

"I'm sorry," Cora muttered, finding her voice far weaker than she liked. Wiping furiously at a few errant tears, she rolled onto her side and buried her face in her blanket. Maiya gave her shoulder a light pat and returned to her cot at the other side of the tent they shared. Even in the darkness, Cora could feel the other girl's eyes burning into her.

"Did you take your sleeping tonic last night?" Maiya asked, caution heavy in her tone.

"Yes." She'd brewed it herself. Stronger than usual.

"Is...is something wrong?"

Cora remained silent because she had no answer. This was the third night in a row she'd woken screaming from this same terrifying nightmare. Such dreams plagued her on occasion but never with such alarming frequency. Her sleeping draught was normally enough to drive them away.

"Would you like to tell me about your dream?" Maiya

asked, trying to sound nonchalant but failing miserably. "Perhaps I can help divine its meaning."

Cora ignored her. Not because she didn't trust her friend. Maiya was probably the only person she trusted with her whole heart. She was like a sister to her, one of the very few people Cora had let herself grow close to ever since she was taken in by the Forest People six years ago. But Cora's burdens were hers to bear. Besides, Maiya was a witch too and growing proficient at dream divination. What if her abilities had grown beyond the realm of dreams? Cora couldn't risk her discovering any of her secrets. It was too dangerous for them both.

Without another word, Cora focused on slowing her ragged breathing until it settled into a gentle rhythm. Hoping Maiya would fall for her ruse and think she'd drifted back to sleep, she kept up the act until she heard her friend's soft snores. Only then did she let herself remember the dream.

A dream that felt like a memory.

CORA WOKE TO MORNING SUN KISSING HER EYELIDS. EVEN with just a sliver of light peeking in from the open tent flap, it was bright enough to tell her she'd slept in. She pressed a tattooed palm over her eyes, but it was no use. She was already awake. Not even the black symbols inked into her skin could ward away the evils of everyday responsibility. She rolled over and peered at Maiya's cot. Her bedroll was empty, and her wool blankets and furs were neatly folded on top of it. How late in the morning was it? Cora rubbed her eyes to rid them of grit, but nothing seemed to soothe them. Her throat too felt raw, and she was almost of a mind to go back to sleep. However, she knew there was no use lingering in bed all because of a bad dream.

With a stretch, she forced herself to rise from her cot. Her arms prickled with gooseflesh beneath the cool spring air that drifted into the tent. Dressed only in her linen shift, she peeked outside and found her freshly laundered clothes hanging on a line. The smell of lavender wafted on the air, mingling with the earth, woodsmoke, and pine scents of camp. All at once, Cora felt a sense of calm. Of safety. She was protected by the Forest People. With their proficiency at wards and subterfuge, her enemies couldn't find her here.

If only her dreams couldn't either.

She tugged her patchwork petticoats and bodice off the line, then brought them back inside to get dressed. She'd have Maiya to thank for the clean clothes. Her friend had clearly been up working hard while Cora dozed.

Once dressed, she strolled between the tents of varying shapes and sizes, each structure draped with oiled hides, and tried not to look anyone in the eye. Her screams had to have been loud enough to wake half the camp, and she dreaded knowing what everyone thought of her. Did they think she was crazy? Or did they feel pity? Cora wanted neither sentiment and preferred no one thought much of her at all. Luckily, it seemed most of the Forest People were too busy with their daily tasks to pay her any mind, whether they were hunting, cooking, weaving, brewing tinctures and salves, or practicing the Arts—magic, in other words.

Magic was the lifeblood of the Forest People, infusing their way of life. The nomadic commune was once comprised of the last living Faeryn, ancient fae who practiced the Magic of the Soil. Nowadays, there wasn't anyone left of pure Faeryn blood, as most had eventually mated with humans, but some within the commune still bore obvious signs of their heritage—petite stature, the slightest hint of a pointed ear, skin and hair in the richest earth tones.

In recent decades, those with human magic came to live amongst the commune too, making the Forest People an eclectic group. Most citizens in the Kingdom of Khero didn't believe in magic, but they had no qualms about ostracizing anyone who possessed uncanny senses or an unusual fondness for nature. Whenever the Forest People came across these individuals, they welcomed them with open arms. They did the same when they found Cora, an orphaned girl wandering alone in the woods.

Cora nearly fit in with the Faeryn descendants with her dark hair, brown eyes, and warm tan skin, but she wasn't of Faeryn blood. She was a witch. Even though this made her welcome with the Forest People, it didn't make her feel like she belonged. She'd been with the commune for six years, but she didn't think she'd ever stop feeling like an outsider. Probably because her new family might very well revoke their welcome if they knew who she was.

She made her way to the heart of the camp, her stomach growling at the smell of roasting meat and vegetables being heated over the cook fires. Once she reached the common area, a clearing surrounded by brightly painted wagons, she found Chandra on cook duty. The middle-aged woman was of stout build with dark eyes and a bronze complexion. Her hair was black with the faintest hint of dark green—a sign of her Faeryn heritage. Inked designs extended from her palms to her shoulders. Cora stared at the woman's tattoos with longing. Unlike the cook, Cora's ink only marked her palms and forearms, indicating the levels of the Arts she'd proven herself accomplished in. She wished to one day be covered to her neck with ink. Maybe then she'd be strong enough to banish her nightmares.

"Twenty-five years," Chandra said.

She frowned. "Pardon?"

"That's how long I've worked to get my *insigmora*."

Insigmora was the Forest People's name for the tattoos —a tradition passed down from the ancient Faeryn. The thought of spending two more decades honing her Art left a pit in Cora's stomach. She didn't want to wait that long. "They're beautiful," was all she said, forcing a smile to her lips.

Chandra's expression turned wary as she eyed her. Cora held her breath, hoping the cook wouldn't bring up her nightmares. The cook was known for her bluntness, and the last thing Cora wanted was for her to ask about the screaming that shattered the peace of the camp last night. She bit the inside of her cheek, resisting the urge to open her senses to the woman so she could read her feelings.

As a witch, Cora's talent was clairsentience. Every witch had an affinity for at least one of the six senses— feeling, knowing, seeing, hearing, tasting, or smelling. Sensing the feelings of others had been a bane since she was young, but after she was found by the Forest People, they taught her to shield against constant outside stimuli.

Now she could use her Art at will, but it didn't always go undetected. Not when used on fellow witches or the descendants of the Faeryn.

"Stew or porridge?" Chandra asked, finally breaking eye contact and nodding toward the cook fires.

Cora let out a sigh of relief and turned her attention to the simmering cauldrons. The smell of root vegetables made her mouth water. "Stew."

Chandra went to the nearest pot and ladled a hearty serving into a clay bowl.

Cora nodded her thanks as the woman handed over her breakfast. As she went to turn away, Chandra spoke. "What are they about?"

Cora paused. "What do you mean?"

"The dreams that make you scream at night. What do you dream of when that happens?"

Cora's muscles tensed at the question, but there was only one answer she could give. "Death."

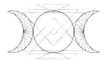

2

A bow in Cora's hand always felt like home. And a belted dagger at her waist felt like safety. Strength. Practical defense to fill the many gaps in her magic. There was only so much a clairsentient witch could do. Cora was determined to do more. To *be* more.

She donned her cloak and gathered her weapons from inside her tent, shouldering her bow and quiver of arrows, then securing her belt with its sheathed dagger. There was no doubt Cora had missed the day's hunt, considering she'd slept in so late, but she could at least practice her archery. She rarely missed a day using her bow. Besides, she needed to harvest more valerian root for her sleeping tonic. She knew she could get some from the potions tent, but the Forest People kept up a stringent inventory of their ingredients during harvesting, stocking, and brewing. If Cora asked for yet another pouch of valerian, people would start talking. They'd know just how strong she'd begun to brew it. Which was why it was even more frustrating that her nightmares had become so persistent.

She left the tent but only made it a few steps before she pulled up short. Maiya stood just outside with her arms crossed. She was dressed in her most brightly patterned skirts and had pink cherry blossoms woven through two long black braids. An amused smile danced over her lips as she assessed Cora's much plainer ensemble. "Really, Cora? On Beltane?"

Cora grimaced. "I forgot it's Beltane."

"Some witch you are," Maiya said with a chuckle. She hesitated then, some of the mirth leaving her eyes as she shifted from foot to foot. "So...did you sleep all right?"

"I'm fine, Maiya," Cora said with what she hoped was a reassuring grin. "You can stop looking at me like I'm made of glass."

Maiya gave Cora's shoulder a playful shove. "I just worry about you, that's all. I'm here if you want to talk. My mother is here for you too. Salinda's an elder. She has more wisdom than anyone."

"I know she does." Cora started off toward the edge of camp. Maiya shadowed her every step, silent although Cora knew she was dying to say more. From the corner of her eye, she could see her friend opening and closing her hands—Maiya's telltale anxious gesture. The girl's palms were inked with only a single tattoo at the center of each, a design made from several overlapping circles and triangles that vaguely resembled a flower. She was a year younger than Cora and only just beginning to explore her talents with the Arts. While Maiya's mother was half witch and half Faeryn, Maiya's magic seemed to favor her witch heritage. She was claircognizant and used her keen knowing to divine meaning from dreams.

"You could let me practice on you," Maiya said, voice brimming with innocence. "It would be good for me. And...and I think it would be good for you too."

Cora halted and faced her friend. She knew Maiya meant well. Knew in her deepest heart that Maiya's prying was done with nothing but love. Still, it had to stop. Maiya didn't understand what she was asking to get involved in. "Just drop it, all right? Please."

Maiya nibbled her lip. "I only want to know that you're really okay. I know something is bothering you."

"It's nothing."

Maiya reached for her hand. As soon as their fingers made contact, Cora was overwhelmed with a sense of worry and desperation—Maiya's feelings. Her breath caught in her throat at the sudden onslaught of emotion. Wrenching her hand away, she took a stumbling step back.

Maiya's eyes turned down at the corners, her sympathy palpable. "Cora—"

"You are not going to believe it!"

Cora startled at the voice, but it was a welcome interruption. It severed her involuntary connection to her friend's feelings. Her breathing eased as she faced the figure darting their way.

Gisele stopped before them, bouncing on the balls of her feet. "It's Roije. He's back!"

Maiya's face went blank, her preoccupation with Cora's wellbeing instantly forgotten. The name Gisele had mentioned was probably the only word in the history of the spoken language that could wipe all prior thought from Maiya's mind. Her voice turned wistful. Anxious. "Roije...he's...he's really back?"

"I thought you'd want to know," Gisele said with a wink. "Come on!"

Before Cora could argue, Gisele linked her arms through both of theirs and dragged them across camp. They came upon a crowd gathering near the picket line where the Forest People's horses were kept. A familiar young man stood at the far end, hitching his horse. Cora's first glimpse at Roije showed he'd grown at least three inches taller since he'd left the Forest People a year ago. His hair had grown too, no longer cropped close to his head but in black waves that fell over his dark eyes. She turned her attention to his clothes and discovered more changes to admire. Instead of the leather britches and wool tunic most of the men wore around camp, he was dressed in a fine linen shirt and black trousers. His sleeves were rolled up to reveal inked forearms—proof of his skill in the Arts. But as Cora drew closer, she noticed something else about his shirt—a haphazard spatter of rusty reddish brown. Blood.

Strange appearance aside, Cora was surprised Roije was back. He'd grown up with the Forest People, but his father was not of their commune. When his mother took ill and died a year ago, he left to find the man who had sired him. His loss was felt by many, especially since his tracking skills were second to none. His Art was the Magic of the Soil, thanks to his Faeryn heritage, and he used it to speak to the earth. Before he left, he was considered the most marriageable bachelor in the commune. Now that he was back, Cora was curious to know why. She wasn't the only one, based on the size of the crowd.

Cora expected to come upon giddy conversation, but the closer she and her two companions drew, the more obvious it was that something was wrong. It was too quiet. Roije had never been a frivolous man by any means, even before he came of age. He was never one of the youths who snuck off to the nearest towns to drink at pubs or steal kisses from farm girls. He took his tracking duties seriously and had gone to great lengths to care for his mother in her dying days. Even so, the look in his eyes was unlike anything she'd seen in them before. They seemed...haunted.

He unsaddled his horse with slow motions, wincing now and then as if he were injured.

"Roije!" Gisele released Cora's arm to wave frantically for his attention, clearly unable to read the mood. "Where did you go? Did you find your father?"

Roije paused his ministrations and ran a hand over his face. He gave a solemn nod. "I found him. Turns out he...he was a butcher in Kubera."

"What's Kubera like?" Gisele asked. "Is it a large village? A wealthy one?"

It took all of Cora's restraint not to stomp on the girl's foot to quiet her. A single word nestled within Roije's answer said everything she needed to know. *Was.* His father *was* a butcher. She held no optimism that his usage of past tense suggested a change in occupation. His emotions were written clearly on his face, in the tilt of his eyes, and the dark circles beneath them.

Even if his expression had been blank, Cora would have known, for his emotions were so strong they slipped past her shields, much like what had happened with Maiya minutes ago. Grief flooded her heart, followed by shame. It made her feel heavy. Dizzy. Disconnected.

Breathing deep, she turned her attention to her own emotions, her own body. She focused on the cool spring air against her skin. The smell of earth and pine. Soon the unwanted emotions began to fade. She breathed deeply again, imagining the air around her growing thicker, gathering roots from the soil beneath her feet, soaking up water from earth, from the molecules in the air, then absorbing the bright light of the sun, the warmth of its fiery rays. Welcoming all four elements, she imagined them dancing, weaving, forming an invisible wall that hummed with energy all around her.

With her mental shields strengthened, she returned her attention to Roije.

"I'm so sorry," Maiya said, her voice barely above a whisper.

His gaze cut to her, and his expression softened. Their eyes held for a heated moment that made Cora want to look away.

Gisele glanced from Maiya to Roije. "What? I don't understand. What happened?"

"My father accepted me into his home," Roije said, his eyes finally leaving Maiya's. "When I tracked him down, I knew there was a chance he'd turn me away, but he didn't. He remembered my mother and was eager to get to know me. Then *they* came."

"Who's they?" asked one of the men in the crowd.

"King Dimetreus' soldiers. They came to Kubera."

Every muscle in Cora's body stiffened at the mention of the King of Khero. A spike of anger burned her blood, but she tried not to let it show on her face. She wasn't the only one who seemed unsettled by the news, however. Some stared with hard looks while others exchanged wary glances. It wasn't hard to understand why. The Forest People may have resided primarily in the Kingdom of Khero, but they served the land, not its king. They owed their allegiance to no monarch and avoided royal politics like a plague.

Roije continued. "They were recruiting young men to join the army by force. Father begged me to hide, said they wouldn't know I'd ever been there. Two soldiers came to the shop while I hid in the cellar. Rumors about me had spread. Father refused to give me up so they… they killed him." His expression hardened, taking the breath from Cora's lungs. She knew that look. Terror meets a thirst for vengeance. It was as familiar to her as her own skin.

"Oh, Roije," Gisele cooed, "that's so terrible. But I'm glad you made it out alive."

"Barely," he muttered. "I had to take the two men out with me." With that, he turned back to his horse and began brushing him down, a silent dismissal of his audience.

The tension was heavy in the air as the crowd dispersed. Gisele remained in place with a pout on her lips, but Maiya tugged her arm. "We should give him some space."

Gisele cast one more longing glance at Roije before obeying. Cora was more than happy to follow, but before she could take a step, Roije's voice called out. "Cora."

With a frown, she turned back to face him, her cheeks burning beneath the sudden scrutiny of her companions.

Gisele looked scandalized while Maiya's expression flickered with hurt. Maiya had always held a secret affection for the man while Cora had never been close with him at all. It made little sense why she'd be the one he wanted to speak to after returning. She gave Maiya an apologetic smile and then approached him. Dread filled her stomach as a terrifying possibility occurred to her. Could his summons be romantic in nature? Goddess above, she hoped not. But why else would he single her out? It was Beltane, after all. Then again, why would he harbor romantic thoughts when he was clearly grieving?

Cora sent out a silent prayer that there was a perfectly reasonable explanation for his summons that had nothing to do with courtship. It wasn't because she was unattracted to him. He was without a doubt the handsomest young man in the commune. But she knew how Maiya felt. Besides, romance was something Cora sought to avoid. Love needed to be built on trust and honesty. And for a girl with a past shrouded in blood and secrecy...

"What is it?" she asked, trying to smile but managing only a grimace.

He continued to brush his horse, keeping his voice low as he spoke. "I just wanted to tell you to be careful."

She frowned, not sure how to respond to that. "All right." When he didn't say more, she took a step away. "Welcome back—"

"Avoid the villages."

"Excuse me?"

"I know you normally stay at camp when we trade with the local towns, and...that's smart. You should keep doing that." He paused and met her eyes. The gravity in his expression sent Cora's heart hammering against her ribs.

All she could think was, *He knows. Goddess above, he knows who I am.*

Before he could say anything more, she turned away, once again haunted by dark castles and blood. And a question. The question that haunted her mind, twisted her heart.

What have you done?

Her footsteps quickened until they kicked up into a jog, then a run, as she made a beeline for the edge of camp.

She didn't stop until she disappeared into the shadows beneath the trees.

3

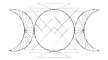

Teryn Alante, Crown Prince of Menah, tried his best not to scowl at his fiancée. It was a difficult task considering the woman he'd been engaged to for three years was publicly courting eight other men before his very eyes. It was under the guise of accord with neighboring kingdoms, but Teryn knew what was truly happening, as did everyone around him.

Princess Mareleau was keeping her options open.

Not that he blamed her. And not that he didn't wish he could do the same. The Princess of Selay was beautiful, but he felt not an ounce of affection for her. How could he when they'd hardly exchanged more than a few letters over the years? Her first letter to him had been uncomfortably ardent while the rest were icy enough to assure Teryn they held each other in the same unfeeling regard.

He stared at Mareleau standing stone-faced upon the balcony two floors up, watching some northern prince spout poetry from the garden courtyard below. Her expression looked more appropriate for someone attending an execution than a Beltane festival. Teryn was grateful his scowl could at least be blamed on the sun beginning its descent behind Verlot Palace—home of his betrothed.

The princess' long hair shone a silvery blonde in the waning sunlight, adorned with pearls and lace flowers, while her dress was a confection of silvery blue brocade trimmed in white fur. Her skirts were so wide, they nearly spanned the length of the balcony floor. Her parents, King Verdian and Queen Helena of Selay, stood just behind, looking equally as ostentatious. Although, come to think of it, pompous was probably a better word. The king wore a powdered wig and an overly ruffled lace shirt beneath his crimson jacket, while the queen bore skirts that were twice as wide as her daughter's, her graying brown hair assembled in an enormously tall updo. Selay was known to be a fashionable kingdom, and if that meant ridiculous clothing ensembles and a hefty dose of snobbery, he could see why.

Teryn gritted his teeth as the prince continued to serenade his fiancée. He was fully aware that his glower was growing deeper by the moment. He'd once hoped his engagement would be dissolved before it could come to fruition, but that was before he knew how badly his kingdom needed the marriage. Back then, he would have felt only relief at seeing his fiancée entertain another suitor, but now it gave him no small amount of anxiety.

One of nine. That was all Teryn was to Mareleau now.

When he'd been invited to Verlot Palace for the Beltane festival, he'd assumed it was to solidify plans for his and the princess' upcoming nuptials. Ever since their betrothal was arranged by their parents three years ago, the plan had been for the two to marry in 171 Year of the Hound, which it was now. So he was quite surprised when he arrived at the palace and found he was one of nine men who held the same marital notions as he. What followed was a week of dinner and dancing—occasions the princess was mind-bogglingly absent from for the most part—and now culminated in a spectacle called the Heart's Hunt. The nine princes would read the princess poetry from under the garden balcony like some idiotic storybook hero. Afterward, Mareleau would select her three champions whom she'd then send on a scavenger hunt. He who returned with her requested prize would win her heart. It made sense for Beltane, he supposed. As for his pride...

"This is humiliating," he muttered under his breath.

His half brother, Larylis, leaned in and whispered, "I told you she was cruel."

Teryn nodded with a shrug. Larylis *had* warned him. Several times. And if anyone knew the princess' true nature, it would be Larylis. His brother had met her a time or two when he'd lived as a ward to Lord Ulrich, Mareleau's uncle.

Teryn's father stood at his other side, posture tense. "Grin and bear it," he said, demonstrating the feat himself. His grin, however, looked more like a snarl.

Teryn knew his father's humiliation must be equal to his own. Mareleau's public defiance of her engagement to Teryn wasn't just a slight on Teryn's behalf. It was a direct affront to his father, King Arlous of Menah. If their kingdom had been in better financial standing, the rulers of Selay would never so blatantly insult an ally, especially not in such a public manner. Wars had been started over far less. Either Mareleau's parents were well aware of Menah's state of financial ruin, or King Arlous' sinful reputation had made the match between Teryn and Mareleau unsuitable in her parents' eyes.

Another thing he couldn't blame them for.

His father had made a mess of his kingdom, all in the name of love. The thought alone made Teryn's blood boil. He respected his father as king, but he didn't think he would ever forgive him for trying to replace his mother— Queen Bethaeny—with the king's mistress. It nearly resulted in war with the queen's home country, a dispute that could only be settled by taking out a hefty loan from the Bank of Cartha to make amends. In the end, Teryn's mother kept her crown and a good portion of his father's finances, not to mention a newly built palace of her own. Teryn applauded her for it, for she had every right to defend her place as queen. But after the attempted-divorce scandal and a year of bad crops, his kingdom now stood on the brink of bankruptcy.

Leaving Teryn to pick up all the pieces.

He *needed* this marriage alliance. To do that, he had to stoop so low as to become a poet.

Larylis must have sensed Teryn's unease, for he grasped him by his shoulder. "You can do this. You only have to read it once."

His only answer was a tightening of his jaw. Why did this farce have to be public? The audience consisted of more than just the nine princes and their families. While the royal guests stood around the courtyard beneath the balcony, there were leagues upon leagues of festival spectators filling the lawn behind them.

The northern prince finished his lengthy poem with a smug grin. Teryn forced himself to bring his hands together in applause along with the rest of the audience, but the gesture felt more violent than friendly. The young man returned to the edge of the courtyard, and the Master of Ceremonies took his place. "Thank you, Prince Nadris of Charsony. Next, please welcome Prince Teryn Alante, son of King Arlous and Queen Bethaeny Alante of the Kingdom of Menah."

The blood left Teryn's face at the sound of his name. He stood frozen for a moment, the loud hammering of his heart drowned out by the new wave of applause. His brother gave his shoulder another encouraging squeeze and his father leaned in close. "Just woo the spoiled brat," he whispered.

His father's voice steadied his nerves and reminded him what was at stake. If Teryn didn't secure a favorable marriage with a wealthy kingdom, he'd have no crown to inherit. The Bank of Cartha had already sent pirates to sabotage Menah's trade routes in warning. Next, they could send war.

With a deep breath, Teryn strolled to the center of the courtyard and lifted his face to the balcony. The sun was now fully behind the palace, casting the princess and her parents in shadow. Good. If he couldn't see her, he could pretend she was someone else. Someone he loved. Someone who deserved the words he'd agonized over for the last week.

He tilted his lips in a crooked grin and relayed the poem with a ridiculous flourish of his hand. He knew he was about to make a complete ass of himself. But it seemed only an ass had a chance at wooing his bride.

"Oh, what beauty shines from my love fair!
'Tis greater and beyond any to compare,
Her eyes, they glisten like the sea so blue,
She is as sweet as my love is true,
Her lips are rosebuds, her skin like a dove,
Her smile is what my dreams are
    made of,
Her voice rings like bells so sweet,
I ask one thing; will you be my queen?"

It was over both too soon and not soon enough. His poem wasn't nearly as long as Prince Nadris' sonnet, but it was better. Wasn't it? Or had he just royally screwed up? He blinked at the backlit balcony, now wishing he could see the princess' face. A small part of him hoped she'd hate his poem. Hoped his words were enough to sever the tie he'd never wanted.

But a greater part of him knew he needed her to love it. To love him. To choose him and his bankrupt, scandal-ridden kingdom over all the others there today.

Polite applause erupted behind him, snapping him back to attention. Keeping his head held high, he returned to his brother and father while the Master of Ceremonies announced the next prince.

Teryn's stomach turned as he caught a glimpse of the princess. He hoped he'd find her eyes on him, hoped he'd find some sign of her favor. But she seemed as unmoved as ever.

He leaned toward Larylis. "She hated it, didn't she?"

Brow furrowed, his brother hesitated before answering. "No, I don't think she did."

"Seriously?"

Larylis met his eyes then, and there was something pained about his expression. "She smiled."

Teryn tilted his head back in surprise. "She did?" He hadn't seen her smile at anyone yet.

His brother's throat bobbed. Once. Twice. The pained look still heavy on his face. Then, in the blink of an eye, it was gone, replaced with a jovial grin. Larylis slapped Teryn on the back. "Yes, brother, she smiled. It seems you stand a chance with the Thorn Princess after all."

Teryn snorted at the nickname. Thorn Princess. A woman known for her prickly demeanor and even pricklier heart.

A woman who would—hopefully—soon become his bride.

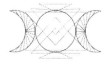

4

Princess Mareleau Harvallis thought her face would crack from the effort it took not to guffaw at the ridiculous spectacle she'd just forced herself to endure. Nine poems she'd pretended to tolerate from nine princes she'd wanted only to sneer at. Thankfully, she could rely on what she liked to think of as her *magic trick*. It was a way to present a carefully curated outer composure no matter how she stewed inside. Only once did it crack, and that was when Prince Teryn, her fiancé, read his awful poem. She'd wanted to glower at him but instead, she'd grinned, knowing she'd soon be free of their engagement. She'd been trying for years to sever it, but this time she was finally close to getting her way.

With the poems read, it was now time to choose her three champions for the Heart's Hunt. Mareleau and her parents left the balcony and strode into the foyer. The low heels of her silk shoes clacked against the white marble floors as she made her way to the tea table and took a seat across from her mother. Their wide skirts fanned out around the table in an array of silk, fur, and lace. Her corset kept her back straight as she leaned forward and took up a freshly poured cup of tea. Her father, meanwhile, took a seat in his favorite wingback chair, a glass of brandy quickly placed in his hand by a servant.

"I'll choose first," King Verdian said, then took a hearty sip of his drink.

Mareleau brought her teacup to her lips to stop herself from releasing an irritated groan. Unfortunately, Mareleau's parents had insisted they choose two of the three champions. She already knew who her father would pick before the words left his mouth.

"Prince Teryn."

"Of course you choose him," she said, setting her cup back down. "Even though you know I don't want to marry him."

"You're already engaged to the man," he said, tone barbed. "You have been for three years despite your every attempt to get out of the arrangement."

She planted a pleasant smile over her lips. "Don't forget to mention *your* every attempt to try and sell me to the next highest bidder."

"And yours to undermine my decisions." He burned her with a sharp look. Despite his powdered wig and elegant white-and-gold silk coat, King Verdian was anything but the pretty monarch he appeared to be. He was fierce. Cold. Calculating.

Probably where Mareleau inherited the same traits herself.

Her father shook his head. "Your marriage to Prince

Teryn will give us access to their trade with Brushwold. Additionally, once you inherit my throne, Selay and Menah can merge as one kingdom. Even though this marriage sets you up as the future queen of what could become the greatest seat of power in southern Risa, I've tried to find you an alternate match. All to stop your incessant whining about how much you despise Teryn Alante. So don't act like I've done anything but the best for you. You're too spoiled, Mareleau."

"Spoiled." She scoffed. "Is it spoiled to not want to marry a man from a kingdom that was recently embroiled in a divorce scandal?"

Her father took another drink, unfazed. "You fought me on this engagement long before that came to light."

She opened her mouth but didn't know what to say. He was right. She'd wanted out of her engagement to Teryn the moment she'd learned of it. Not that Teryn had done anything to deserve her scorn. His only crime was not being his half brother, Larylis.

The same was true for Larylis, she supposed. He too suffered from not being his brother. Had he been a prince and not the illegitimate progeny of the king and his mistress, he'd have been an acceptable match for a princess. She would have loved him regardless, of course. She couldn't have cared less about his unfavorable parentage and could even forgive his kingdom's scandal. What mattered was that Larylis was a liar. When it came to acting on pretty words, he'd failed her. Abandoned her. Broke her heart until there was nothing left but brambles and thorns in her hollow cavity of a chest.

Were she a crueler woman, she'd marry Teryn out of spite, if only for the chance at wounding her former paramour. Then again, perhaps he didn't care. She'd seen Larylis in the audience today. While she couldn't handle meeting his eyes for fear of shattering her composure, she'd stolen a few covert glances. She'd seen him smiling with Teryn, laughing, encouraging. As if watching his brother marry the woman he'd once professed to love was nothing.

Nothing.

"Come now, my darlings," her mother said from the other side of the tea table. "Let's not talk of scandals."

"Then speak some sense into her, Helena." Verdian stood from the divan and threw back the rest of his drink. "She doesn't know what's for her own good. She doesn't want to marry Teryn. She doesn't want to marry King Dimetreus. She doesn't want to marry Prince Augustine. She doesn't want to marry Prince Frederick."

Fire burned through her blood at the mention of those names. She stood from her seat, her skirts bumping the table and sending the teacups rattling. "Oh, don't get me started on them! King Dimetreus is a widower—"

"Of six years," her father interjected.

"—who lives in a creepy kingdom where everyone dies. Prince Augustine was twice my age and had his hand up my skirt within minutes of our first meeting alone." She said the last part through her teeth.

Verdian at least had the decency to blanch at that, but he quickly steeled his shock behind a stony mask. "And what of Prince Frederick?"

Mareleau took a few steadying breaths, knowing it was time to utilize her *magic trick* again. She forced her lips into a trembling frown, let her shoulders droop. Her voice came out small and quavering as she brought her hands to her chest. "You know he broke my heart, Papa."

Prince Frederick was the most recent royal her parents had paraded her before. After she'd caught him dallying with her former lady's maid, she'd bullied him into ending their engagement. It served to garner pity from her parents when she pretended to be hurt by his abrupt end to their courtship and softened their ire enough to put her current plan into motion.

Beltane. The Heart's Hunt.

King Verdian huffed, but she could tell she'd drained some of the fight from him.

"We're talking nonsense again," Queen Helena said, rising gracefully from her seat to stand next to Mareleau. "Talk of the past isn't worth our breath. We must speak of the present instead."

"I said my piece," the king grumbled. "I choose Prince Teryn as one of the three champions and I won't change my mind. If the both of you want to dance about selecting the remaining two, have your way. I'd like to get this farce over with." With that, he marched past them and left the foyer.

Queen Helena faced Mareleau with a glowing smile and took her hands. "Don't fret, darling. Just because Teryn is one of the champions doesn't mean he'll win the Heart's Hunt. It could very well be your choice or mine."

Mareleau said nothing. If all went to plan, there wouldn't be a winner.

The queen's voice took on a serious tone. "However, if Teryn wins, you must honor that, just as we've promised to honor the winner as your betrothed. This was your idea, remember?"

She gave a reluctant nod. It had been her idea. After she'd claimed a broken heart following Prince Frederick's rejection, she'd appealed to her mother's romantic side, saying she needed to marry for love. It was almost too good to be true when the queen fell for Mareleau's insistence that the Beltane festival held the perfect solution, that a poetry contest and the Heart's Hunt would prove a suitor's true love. Pathetic. But that was the kind of girl her parents thought she was. A starry-eyed fool who dreamed of storybook romance and epic declarations. That wasn't her at all. She was practical. Sharp. While she'd once entertained notions of love, back before Larylis proved himself unworthy, she now wanted no husband at all.

As her parents' only child, she was set to inherit the throne, something the king and queen thought possible only if she married a king or prince. Otherwise, her uncles would fight for the throne. While she understood the implications of having her right to rule contested, she railed against the assumption that a woman must have a man at her side to be a proper queen. It fueled her rage to no end, but royal succession was a game of well-placed maneuvers. A game she could play. For now. This time, she'd be the one moving the pieces.

"Fine," Mareleau said, forcing her face into an agreeable smile. "Who is your choice of champion, Mother?"

Queen Helena clapped her hands in front of her chest, crystal blue eyes—the same shade as Mareleau's—alight with excitement. "I choose Prince Helios of Norun. He's wealthy, handsome, and...dare I say a perfect match?"

Mareleau nodded along, pretending she had even the

slightest inkling whom her mother was referring to. She'd done her best to ignore the visiting princes all week and learn as little about them as she could. That often included their names. "Oh, yes, I'm sure you're right."

The queen beamed at that. "I knew you'd think so. Do you recall his poem? It was quite moving. I particularly liked the part where he compared you to the Goddess of the Sea."

Had he known her, he would have chosen the Goddess of War. Or better yet, the Goddess of Death. But Mareleau kept that to herself. "Yes, that was lovely, wasn't it?"

Queen Helena released a dreamy sigh, eyes distant for a moment. Then, with a shake of her head, she said, "Now, who do you choose, darling? If I haven't already stolen your choice." She said the last part with a wink.

Mareleau opened her mouth, realizing she'd made a grave error in her attempts to keep the princes at a distance. She had no one to select as champion. Not that it mattered. These princes were all the same, bandying about words like *love* to a stranger they knew nothing about save for the fact that she was pretty and had a dowry that rivaled their own kingdoms' wealth. With a simpering smile, she said, "Uh, Prince Thomas, I think it was?"

Her mother's expression hardened. Mareleau knew there hadn't been a Prince Thomas, but she couldn't resist sparking her mother's ire just a little. "Mareleau Harvallis, don't you dare tell me you aren't taking this seriously. It was *your* plan—"

"Pardon, Your Majesty," said a small voice. Lurel,

Mareleau's fifteen-year-old cousin and newly appointed lady's maid, approached. Mareleau hadn't noticed when the girl had entered the foyer, but her other three lady's maids followed in her wake, clustered together as they gossiped behind their hands. The three girls stopped their chatter to curtsy for Mareleau and the queen, then went right back to it. Lurel dipped low, bowing her head far longer than necessary. Showoff. When she stood, she lingered, smiling and wringing her hands awkwardly.

Mareleau gave her a pointed look. "What is it?"

"Oh, yes!" Lurel blushed. "I was going to say, could the princess be referring to Prince Lexington of Tomas?"

Mareleau quirked a questioning brow.

"When you said Prince Thomas."

Queen Helena's mouth fell open with a light laugh, her previous irritation gone in a flash. "Darling, is that who you meant?"

"How silly of me," Mareleau said with a forced chuckle. "Yes, that's him. Of course it's him. Prince Lexington of Tomas." She said the name slowly, enunciating each word, certain she hadn't heard it uttered even once this week.

Her mother furrowed her brow. "Odd. He doesn't seem your type. And the only line I remember from his poem was, *You are graceful like a deer and smart like a fox*."

It took all her restraint not to snort a laugh. She kept her expression serious as she said, "Oh, he's exactly my type."

Suspicion flashed in Queen Helena's eyes, but she only said, "Very well. Are you ready to award your champions and announce the object of the Heart's Hunt?"

"I am."

"And you have selected an object for the Hunt, correct?"

"I have."

Another suspicious look. "What have you chosen?"

Mareleau did her best to keep her malicious grin at bay. "You'll see. It's a surprise."

After the queen left to find the king, Lurel spoke again, her voice rich with excitement. "Oh, I can't wait to find out what the object is. Will you give me a clue?"

Mareleau's eyes dipped to the pair of white earrings dangling from her cousin's ears. They were delicately pointed at one end and rounded on the other, with just the hint of a spiral pattern. Mareleau had been bitten with envy the moment she'd spotted them. She'd asked Lurel about them and learned the earrings were a gift from Lurel's father, Lord Kevan. And if Lurel was to be believed, they'd been carved from a piece of bone.

A rare piece of bone.

One belonging to what was a presumed-extinct fae creature.

And if her uncle was to be believed as well, he'd seen it with his own eyes on a hunt up north.

Mareleau's lips pulled into a smirk. "You, cousin. You're the hint."

HALF AN HOUR LATER, MARELEAU STOOD BACK ON THE balcony with her mother and father. The nine princes once again surrounded the marble courtyard, their upturned faces alight with hope. A hope she'd soon crush.

The Master of Ceremonies addressed the audience from below. He thanked their guests and the royal families in attendance, then announced the three champions.

Prince Teryn Alante of Menah.

Prince Helios Dorsus of Norun.

Prince Lexington Quill of Tomas.

Mareleau was particularly curious to learn who she'd chosen as champion and was rewarded with a chubby young man with ruddy cheeks and messy blond hair. His elegant silk coat was buttoned askew and his white neckcloth was tied all wrong. As he made his way to the center of the courtyard next to the other two champions, he looked about as thrilled as he'd be at a funeral. That made two of them. She reined in the laughter that bubbled in her throat and settled on trying to appear moderately pleased instead.

The queen stepped closer to Mareleau and whispered in her ear, "Are you certain that's the young man you intended to select?"

Mareleau glanced over her shoulder at her mother. "Of course it is." She caught her father's grunt of disapproval from the other side of her, which made her smile grow wider.

The crowd applauded, and the Master of Ceremonies called for an encore of the poems. Mareleau made no effort to listen—because why torture herself a second time?—and instead compared her three champions. Prince Lexington was the shortest of the three and the only one who wasn't smiling. Prince Helios was the tallest, standing about two inches over Teryn. The former was a brute of a man with a barrel chest, tanned arms roped with muscle, and a smug confidence that made Mareleau want to take him down a peg. His hair was bronze and cropped close to his scalp, the planes of his face hard, his jaw shadowed with stubble. If she were to guess, he was at least five years her senior.

Teryn, on the other hand, was just a year older than she was. She knew this because he and Larylis were the same age, both born by their separate mothers the same year. Despite only sharing a father, they looked almost similar enough to be twins. Both were annoyingly handsome with their father's green eyes, sharp cheekbones, and dark hair. Teryn's tresses were shorter on the sides and wavy on top, lightly touched with gold, while Larylis' hair was overlong, curling at the nape of his neck, and glinting copper when touched by light. Larylis was the leaner of the two, although both were tall and broad of shoulder.

Larylis suddenly met her eyes from across the courtyard, making her breath catch in her throat. Her heart hammered as she averted her gaze. She hadn't realized she'd been staring. It took a few moments longer than she cared to admit to gather her composure, but by the time the last of the three poems were read, she'd replaced her cold countenance.

The Master of Ceremonies congratulated the three champions, then gestured toward the balcony. She knew what came next. His voice took on a dramatic tone. "It is now time for Princess Mareleau to announce the object of her Heart's Hunt."

The crowd went quiet and all eyes focused on her. Despite her outward confidence, sweat began to bead at her neck. She hated attention. Hated crowds. But she knew what had to be done. Better yet, she was glad to do it.

Tapping into her make-believe magic, she took a deep breath, doing her best to settle her nerves. She lifted her chin, her chest, standing tall as she focused her intent on shaping an outer persona that radiated poise. Demanded respect. Inspired awe.

She knew her so-called magic trick wasn't really magic at all. It was only a matter of controlling her demeanor in a way that shifted the perceptions of those around her. Still, people always seemed to respond the way she wanted. Sometimes it curried favor. Garnered sympathy. Won her friends. Other times it brewed hate and discord. The latter was how she'd escaped so many prior engagements. As she took in the audience before her, she saw reflected back that which she intended now. She saw awe, respect, desire, admiration.

She had command of the crowd.

Stepping closer to the rail, she placed her hands on the balustrade and projected her voice out over the garden. "My three champions have been chosen for their love for me," she said with a false smile. "In one week, the three of you will embark on a dangerous mission in search of my heart's desire."

Her mother gasped behind her. "One week? The Hunt was supposed to start tonight," she whispered furiously, but Mareleau ignored her.

"The champion who returns first with what I demand will prove he loves me most and will, in turn, receive my hand in marriage. What I ask for is rare and will put its seeker in grave danger. You must accomplish the Heart's Hunt without the aid of hired help, professional hunters, or the accompaniment of servants and guards. He who has the determination and skill to persevere is the one worth my hand. Listen carefully to what I ask, for you must bring me exactly what I demand."

"Mareleau," King Verdian drew out her name in a whisper laced with warning, but she ignored that too.

"For the Heart's Hunt, you must find me three unicorns. From the first unicorn, I require a horn. From the second, its pelt. And the third will be my pet. No item shall be purchased or traded for. It must be freshly harvested by your own hand. I wish you three the best of luck, and may the worthiest man win."

Stunned silence followed. She assessed the faces of the crowd. Some looked mortified while others bore half smiles, as if they expected her to laugh and take it all back.

She put their hopes to rest with a wave as she said, "Goodnight, and thank you for joining us for Beltane." With a triumphant grin, she turned on her heel, only to find her father's fingers winding around her upper arm.

"Unicorns, Mareleau? Is this all a game to you?" His face burned beet red.

She blinked back at him with an innocent expression. "Of course not. I told you, I'm only marrying for love and this will prove which man loves me most." Lies. Delicious lies.

"I'm of the same mind as your father," Queen Helena said, voice quavering with suppressed anger. "This is ridiculous, not to mention offensive to our guests. You cannot send three suitors on a fruitless quest for creatures that don't exist."

That was precisely the point, of course. Send the

three men on a mission that had no expiration, only an impossible goal. And she had the perfect person to blame for her absurd request.

"Oh, they exist. Just ask Uncle Kevan." With that, she brushed past her parents into the foyer. There, she found her cousin staring wide-eyed at the three royals. Mareleau gave a light flick to the girl's dangling unicorn-horn earring, sending it swaying back and forth. "Lurel will tell you all about it."

Her parents burst into a heated argument, which was Mareleau's cue to make a hasty exit. Mirth bubbled in her chest with every step she took, but she swallowed it down. Only when she reached the quiet halls outside the foyer did she finally let herself erupt with victorious laughter.

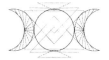

5

Cora nocked an arrow into her bow and pulled the fletching back to her cheek. Her heart thumped heavy in her chest, her mind still reeling with the echo of Roije's words. It was sundown—several hours since he'd delivered his cryptic warning—yet she still couldn't shake what he'd said.

She released the arrow and heard the beautiful strum of the string snapping forward, a sound that normally settled her nerves. Now it did nothing to calm her, especially when the arrow missed her target and struck an innocent cherry tree standing just behind the pockmarked stump she'd been trying to hit. Pink cherry blossoms rained down to the forest floor in protest.

She cursed under her breath and withdrew another arrow from her quiver. As she nocked it, she replayed Roije's warning for the hundredth time.

Avoid the villages.

What had he meant by that? Was she simply imagining the darker implications of his statement? His warning must have had something to do with what happened to his father...

Murdered by King Dimetreus' men.

But had the warning been given out of general worry? Romantic favor, like she'd first assumed?

Or because he'd learned why she'd really been stumbling through the woods six years ago when the Forest People found her?

Her fingers trembled, sending her aim wildly askew as she shot her arrow. "Damn." She nocked another one, willing her hands to remain steady, her grip easy on her bow as she shot her arrow. This time it struck the rotting half-felled tree, but nowhere close to the circle she'd carved as a target when the Forest People first settled camp at the beginning of spring. This little pocket of isolation was her safe space. Her private training ground. Not that it was doing her any good at the moment. She was normally an adequate archer. But today...

With a grumble, she threw her head back and closed her eyes.

Breathe, she told herself. *Breathe. It was nothing. His warning meant nothing.*

Releasing a slow exhale, she forced her worries aside and tried focusing on her inner sensations instead. As a clairsentient witch, *feeling* was the source of her power. She knew this, and yet it wasn't always easy to remember in practice. But as the Forest People liked to say, magic was strengthened by challenge. Often that meant doing the very thing that felt the hardest. Right now, Cora's greatest challenge was getting out of her head and into her magic. The last thing she wanted to do was abandon her attempts at logic, but she could at least admit her current state was doing her no favors. Not where her sanity was concerned, and certainly not for her archery practice.

She breathed in again, narrowing her attention down to the sensation of air moving through her nose, filling her lungs, then warming her nostrils as she released the breath. Shifting her focus to her skin, she felt it prickle beneath the cool evening breeze, then warming under the blush of the setting sun, diffused beneath the canopy of trees overhead. Next, she brought her attention to her feet, to the feel of solid earth beneath her leather boots, and imagined she could sense the Magic of the Soil the way the Faeryn descendants could.

Calm replaced her racing thoughts, settling her heartbeat into a steady rhythm. She took several moments to relish that calm, to feel it with every fiber of her being, before she opened her eyes. Drawing another arrow from her quiver, she nocked it in place and assessed the stump with its carved target, saw in her mind's eye her arrow soaring straight to it. She drew her arrow to her cheek, felt calm radiate down her arm, her hand, felt her tattooed palms tingle with magic.

Everything inside her felt her next shot wouldn't miss.

She released the arrow and watched the arrowhead strike the center of the circle. Exactly how she'd seen it in her mind. Exactly how she'd *felt* it would hit.

Her lips flicked up at the corners, but her smile faded as soon as she heard the crack of a twig behind her. Nocking a fresh arrow, she whirled around and aimed her weapon.

"Salinda," Cora said, tone full of apology as she quickly let down her bow.

The other woman didn't so much as flinch at having been momentarily targeted. In fact, there was a good chance that snapping the twig had been intentional. A test. Salinda nodded at the stump that still bore Cora's arrow. "You shot that arrow with clairsentience, didn't you?"

"I did," Cora said and went to retrieve her numerous arrows that were scattered around her practice area. It was considered disrespectful to turn one's back on an elder when approached, but Cora had a feeling she knew why Salinda was here and hoped she could end the conversation before it began. Besides, Salinda was Maiya's mother, as close as Cora had to a mother herself, which meant the woman expected less formality from Cora than the others.

"Maiya told me about the nightmares," she said.

Cora sighed as she tore an arrow from the stump and tucked it into her quiver. "Of course she did."

"That's not why I'm here, though."

Cora slung her bow over her shoulder and turned back toward Salinda. "It's not?"

With slow steps, Salinda closed the distance between them, stopping a few feet away. She and Maiya looked similar with their petite stature, dark eyes, brown skin, and warm smiles. Salinda, however, had the slightest point at the top of her ears. Even being half witch, she still might have had the most Faeryn blood of any of the Forest People. Salinda also had more tattoos than most, with black ink trailing from her palms to her inner forearms, disappearing beneath the sleeves of her green linen dress, only to peek up again above her bodice. From there, geometric shapes adorned the sides of her neck, ending in a single tattoo at the tip of her chin—the sign of the triple moon. A symbol only the elders' chins were marked with.

Salinda gave Cora a warm smile, one that made her eyes crinkle abundantly at the corners, and took another step closer. "I think you should take the path of elders."

Cora stared back at her, stunned silent. Taking the path of elders was a high honor, as one could only begin training by invitation of another elder. Thirteen Forest People comprised the council of elders. Aside from Nalia, the High Elder, there were six witches and six Faeryn descendants on the council. The six witches represented the strongest in each of the six senses, while the six Faeryn performed a separate vital task. Unlike Maiya, Salinda's magic favored her Faeryn side, although she understood witch magic just as deeply as the Magic of the Soil. She was so skilled in her Art that she'd earned herself a place as one of the Faeryn elders, tasked as the commune's Keeper of Histories. It wasn't just Faeryn lore she kept either. She also recorded anything relevant to the witches of the commune. With how intermingled the two people had become, the distinctions between the witches and Faeryn were growing less stark. New traditions were being created every day, new spells, tonics, and rituals that combined witch magic with the Magic of the Soil. It made Salinda the perfect candidate for the job of Keeper of Histories.

Cora knew she should feel triumphant. Proud. To be singled out as a witch worthy of one day becoming an elder...it should have been a dream come true. The way her heart raced, cheeks warm under Salinda's kind gaze, made it seem like Cora's body knew exactly what kind of honor it truly was.

But her mind...

Her mind filled with echoes of her nightmare. Echoes of Roije's warning. A reminder that being singled out for anything could be dangerous. And not just for her. For the Forest People.

Reining in the joy that begged to fill her chest, she took a step back. "I don't think I'm the right choice for the path of elders."

Salinda reached for Cora's hand and cradled it in hers, Cora's palm to the sky. "You've only been with us for six years, yet look how your *insigmora* has grown."

Cora's eyes dipped to her inked palm, taking in the pattern of overlapping shapes. The tattoos were a Faeryn tradition, the process itself meant to represent the elements—minerals from the earth to form the pigment, water to turn it to liquid, fire to transmute it into ink, air to aid the tattoo's transformation from a wound to a permanent marking of the flesh. The symbols themselves were thought to help connect one to the elements as well as direct one's magic. Another high honor Cora wasn't sure she was worthy of.

She slid her hand from Salinda's. "There are other witches stronger than me who've earned far more *insigmora* in a shorter time."

"Time isn't everything, Cora. And I promise you, you're stronger than you think. You came to us fully clairsentient."

Cora chuckled. "You mean plagued by it."

Salinda's tone softened. "You didn't understand it. Yet you learned so quickly what your powers meant after we took you in. You learned to put up mental shields within your first three months of being with us. The way you can feel what others feel, sense outside emotion...not all clairsentient witches can do that. Most simply connect to their magic through feeling, bodily sensation, and personal emotion. What you do is no small thing."

It felt like a small thing, but Cora didn't say so. She was grateful she'd learned to control her Art, but even after six years, being clairsentient didn't make her feel powerful. Or safe. Archery, on the other hand, made her feel at least somewhat capable. Strong. That was all she wanted—one thing that could make her feel like she could face the horrors of her past and overcome them.

Instead of being destroyed by them.

Cora's hand went to the bow slung over her shoulder. She closed her fingers around the solid wood wrapped in smooth leather. "I think I'd rather take the path of hunters."

Salinda's smile fell, revealing the full weight of her disappointment.

Before the woman could reply, Cora rushed on to add, "I've been practicing. You saw me use my magic to make that last shot. I've been joining the hunts."

"And do you enjoy them? The hunts? Do you honor the process of taking life from an animal, blessing its spirit and its sacrifice for the good of the commune?"

Cora bit the inside of her cheek, trying to form a proper response. The truth was, she cared little for the hunt itself, only for the opportunity to learn how to use her weapons in a practical manner. She hated the act of killing. Hated skinning rabbits and carving hides. The other hunters didn't relish such acts either, but she could tell they honored the process, held it in high regard. Cora didn't have a sacred connection to hunting. If there was a path of warriors, she'd prefer that.

"Cora, I'm proud that you've learned to use clairsentience with your bow, but your magic has more potential than you've been giving it. If you let it flourish, you could step fully into the role of empath."

Again, Cora knew she should feel honored. An empath was the strongest kind of clairsentient witch, much like a seer was the strongest clairvoyant or an oracle was the strongest claircognizant. An empath had the power to do more than read feelings. According to legends, she could use the power of sensation to accomplish many magical feats, and most were too fantastical to believe—use another's emotions to read their mind, control physical material using touch. Cora wasn't sure she *did* believe any of those things were possible. The commune had one empath, an elder. Her greatest feat of magic was taking on the pain of the ill or wounded so they could be more easily healed. But that would always leave her recovering from the pain she'd taken on, and the actual healing was left to those skilled in brewing tinctures and salves or setting bones.

Salinda released a sigh. "You don't value the role of the empath."

"I'd rather be more useful."

She placed a hand on Cora's cheek. "Magic is so much greater than you know. You don't believe in its power because it leaves very little evidence to the naked eye. That is the way of things. True magic is quiet. Unassuming. Easily explained away through logic. But remember, just because magic is quiet doesn't mean it isn't strong."

Cora wanted to argue. She'd seen magic before that was neither quiet nor unassuming. It was dark. Terrifying. How could she value the gentle power of the empath when she'd witnessed something so much darker?

"Sit with me at the Beltane ceremony tonight," Salinda said. "*Feel* what it's like to be amongst the elders."

Her heart sank. Part of her yearned to make Salinda proud, to be the person Salinda thought she was.

If only she knew the truth...

"I believe in you," Salinda whispered, then took her leave.

Cora watched her go, stomach sinking under Salinda's faith in her. Part of her wanted to run after the woman, take all her doubts back, profess that she really did want to take the path of elders. That same part of her craved the future the opportunity offered.

Prestige.

Respect.

Family.

But it would all be a lie. Cora may have been a witch, but she wasn't truly one of them. No matter how much she wished it, no matter how much she yearned to bury her past, it haunted her.

With the resurgence of her nightmares and Roije's mysterious warning...

She felt more than haunted.

She felt hunted.

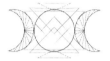

6

Night had fully fallen and Cora still couldn't bring herself to return to camp. The Beltane ceremony would soon commence, something she dreaded in and of itself. During her first few years with the Forest People, Beltane had become one of her favorite holidays. She loved dressing in her brightest skirts, wearing flowers in her hair, dancing around bonfires, weaving ribbons around the maypole. However, now that she was older, she was acutely aware of the deeper themes that came with the holiday. Fertility, primarily. Or, to put it bluntly, lovemaking.

Not long ago, Cora had entertained the idea of taking a lover from the commune, but it had culminated in nothing more than heated kisses and a few experimental trysts. That was all it took for her to learn what risks came with romantic pairings. Not the usual dangers the young women whispered about during their monthly moon cycles, but ones personal to Cora. Intimacy. Honesty. Questions she couldn't answer. The discomfort of being courted into a deeper relationship than she was capable of having.

And after what happened with Roije earlier today, Cora wasn't sure she was ready to face him. Especially not at Beltane. There was still a chance her first instinct had been correct. That he favored her. Romantically.

Cora shook the thought from her head and collected her latest bunch of arrows from her target. Her aim had significantly improved since her conversation with Salinda, but it was too dark to practice any longer.

As much as she wanted to avoid what came next, she knew it was time to face it. Beltane. Salinda's offer. Roije.

With her quiver full, she made her way back toward camp, her steps purposefully slow. She was only halfway there when a light shone up ahead, revealing two figures behind it. They were too distant to make out, but when Cora opened her senses, extending them until she tapped into a much-familiar energy, she knew who at least one of them was. With a deep breath, she replaced her mental shields and closed the distance between her and her lantern-bearing friend. As she drew near, she realized the second girl was Gisele. Maiya still wore her colorful skirts and flower-laced braids while Gisele was outfitted in her finest floral-patterned dress, her golden-brown hair tied up in a ruby scarf.

"There you are," Maiya said. "Mother told me she found you practicing, but I didn't think you'd still be out here."

Gisele's lips twisted in a wry grin. "Oh, Cora. Always the overachiever. But enough work for the day. We're going to the hot springs."

Maiya gave Gisele a sharp look. "I said I'd only go if Cora does."

Gisele quirked a brow at Cora. "Of course she wants to go."

Cora frowned. "What about Beltane? The ceremony—"

"The ceremony is the same every year," Gisele said with a roll of her eyes. "Besides, the boys are extra ravenous tonight, if you know what I mean. Had I any magic, I'm sure I could smell the desire raging through camp already." Gisele's mother was a clairlient witch, her magic rooted in scent, but unlike Cora and Maiya, Gisele showed neither talent nor interest in the Arts. Not everyone born within the commune did. "And I don't know about you, but I've had enough of *boys*. They can come find me when they're ready to be men."

Cora suppressed a huff of laughter. Gisele had certainly made her rounds when it came to sampling the company of single men within the commune. She'd never complained about it before. Cora turned her attention to Maiya and quirked a suggestive brow. "What about you? Is there any reason you might want to enjoy the ceremony?"

Even under the warm glow of the lantern, Cora saw a blush crawl from Maiya's neck to her cheeks. They both knew Cora was hinting at Roije. "No," she said too quickly, her voice small. "But...but I'd understand if there was a reason *you* wanted to go."

Cora didn't need to let down her shields to understand the meaning behind her words. Maiya must have come to the same conclusion Cora had first entertained regarding Roije's earlier summons. More than that, she was giving her blessing. Giving Cora the go ahead to court the man Maiya had fancied for years. Her friend was always too generous. Too kind. A trait that would probably annoy Cora to no end were it anyone else. But with Maiya...that was just how she was. She was the best of them.

Cora gave her friend a pointed look. "No, Maiya, there's not a *single reason* I'd want to attend tonight's ceremony. I promise you."

Maiya's lips pressed into a shy smile while Gisele looked from one girl to the other, brow furrowed. "Does that mean you're both coming or not?"

Cora didn't immediately answer. Going to the hot springs would provide the perfect distraction both from Salinda's offer and the inevitable romantic overtures she was sure to receive from one source or another. But she didn't want to keep Maiya from enjoying what could potentially be a pleasant night, should she finally get the courage to speak to Roije about her feelings.

As if Maiya knew exactly what Cora was thinking, she lifted her chin in defiance. "I already told you, I don't want to go to the ceremony."

Cora shrugged. "All right. I suppose we're going then."

Gisele bounced on the balls of her feet and hefted a woven basket. "Good, because I already pilfered two bottles of wine."

THE HOT SPRING CAVES WERE LESS THAN AN HOUR'S WALK away. With the aid of one of the bottles and its intoxicating contents, Cora felt as if the walk went much faster.

She and her two companions were a mess of laughter by the time they reached the mouth of the cave. They huddled close together as they proceeded inside, their giggles turning to silence. Entering the cave came with both reverence and a healthy dose of fear. The antechamber was blanketed in a darkness so bleak, their lantern only lit the next few steps. Cora kept her breaths shallow as they made their way slowly forward, deeper into the cave. The antechamber narrowed to a corridor and soon the warmth of steam met her skin, bringing with it the telltale aroma of sulfur. Then light just ahead.

The three women quickened their pace, their steps now fueled with excitement as the corridor took them down a slight decline toward the belly of the cave. The sulfurous aroma grew stronger, and while it wasn't the most pleasant smell, Cora was more than happy to suffer it for the benefits that awaited. Finally, they stepped into the main chamber, the walls of the underground cave glowing with bioluminescence, lighting the surface of the three small steaming pools pocking the rocky floor. The heat alone had every muscle in Cora's body loosening, and she couldn't wait to slip beneath the warm waters.

Gisele looked from Cora to Maiya with an inebriated grin. "Ready?"

The three girls darted toward the largest pool, roaring with laughter as they stripped down.

"See, we're celebrating Beltane just fine," Gisele said as she pulled her shift over her head. "Skyclad. Naked as the day we were born."

Cora rolled her eyes as the girl sauntered into the pool without an ounce of inhibition. Still, Cora knew the hot springs were no place to try and maintain modesty.

Not when walking home in a sodden shift was far more uncomfortable than the brief moment of nudity she'd endure. Besides, Gisele was right. Going *skyclad*, as the Forest People called ritual nudity, was neither odd nor shameful. And yet, Cora hadn't been born under such freedoms. She was born into a world of strict rules and propriety.

Turning her back to her friends, she unshouldered her bow and quiver, tucking them next to a low boulder before removing the rest of her ensemble.

"Hurry up," Gisele called, sending a splash of water to the hem of Cora's shift. Squealing at the warm spray, she pulled her shift the rest of the way off, then rushed to the pool and plunged shoulder deep. Maiya was up to her chin in the water, the cherry blossoms that had once adorned her braids now floating wilted on the surface. Gisele lounged against the side of the pool, her arms outstretched and propped on the rocky ledge.

Cora tilted her head back and admired the blue-green glow lighting the pool from above. Peace settled over her, mingling with the warmth in her belly leftover from the wine. She felt every last bit of stress she'd picked up from her day dissolve. "This was the right choice," Cora whispered.

"I told you so," Gisele said. She reached for her basket and retrieved their bottle, taking a drink before passing it to Maiya, then she to Cora.

Cora took a hearty sip, finishing the remnants. Gisele was already opening the second bottle.

"Do you think it's true?" Maiya asked, turning her gaze to the glowing ceiling.

"What? The legends about the caves having once

hosted dragons?" Gisele said the last part with a sardonic look.

"It sounds silly when you say it like that," Maiya said.

"It is silly." Gisele took a sip from the new bottle. "Do you really think those," she pointed at the ceiling, "were once dragons?"

Maiya dipped a little lower in the water. "Maybe."

Gisele chuckled and passed Maiya the wine. "What do you think, Cora? Historical fact or faerytale?"

Cora shrugged. "Faeryn legends are faerytales, aren't they?"

"I suppose," Gisele said, "but are they true?"

Cora wasn't so sure. When the Forest People had first found the hot spring caves a month prior, Salinda had been adamant that the caverns had been left behind from days when fae still roamed the land, back when pixies, sprites, and unicorns were as common as squirrels and deer. Back before the Elvyn and Faeryn—the two races of High Fae—went all but extinct. No one knew why the fae disappeared, only that a terrible war hundreds of years ago had prompted it. The stories told how all fae creatures turned to regular animals after that. And Salinda was convinced the glowing worms that painted the cave walls in bioluminescence were once dragons. The hot spring caves, according to her, had once been home to the legendary fae creatures. There was no way to know if Salinda was right. She may have been the Keeper of Histories, but that didn't mean the tales of the past hadn't been skewed by the fancies of those who came before her.

"True or not," Maiya said, "this is the best place we've ever found."

"I can agree with that," Gisele said, taking the bottle of wine back. "I hate that we'll have to leave the caves behind soon."

Cora's heart sank. They all knew the Forest People would be gone by Litha—the summer solstice. They traveled to a new camp with every season, both to follow the most favorable weather in Khero and to ensure they never overburdened the land that nourished them. Even after six years with the commune, Cora still wasn't used to constantly moving around.

She'd been in one place the first twelve years of her life.

Before everything changed.

Before she became an outlaw.

Chased by dark magic.

Haunted by blood—

A sound coming from beyond the cave snapped Cora from her thoughts. Maiya, who'd been saying something Cora hadn't been paying attention to, cut off mid-sentence. She and Cora turned their gazes to the corridor from where they'd emerged.

The sound was slow and rhythmic. Footsteps.

"Someone's coming." Cora reflexively reached for her bow, but it was too far.

"Relax, Cora," Gisele said, looking completely unflustered as she took a deep drink of wine.

Cora narrowed her eyes at her friend, suspicion crawling up her spine. The steps drew nearer and nearer.

Gisele's lips curled into a guilty smile. "Don't worry, he's harmless."

"He?" Cora and Maiya said in unison as they both

dipped deeper into the waters. "Who the hell is *he*?" Cora said through her teeth.

There was no time for Gisele to reply, for the male figure striding into the cave was answer enough. The bioluminescent glow revealed an unfamiliar man a few years older than Cora. His hair was blond, his face handsome with a short beard covering his jaw. He was dressed in leather trousers, tall boots, and a travel-worn greatcoat.

"Gisele," he said, smiling when his eyes landed on her. "You came."

She batted her lashes. "I said I would."

His gaze briefly darted toward Maiya and Cora. "I wasn't aware you'd be bringing company."

"Neither were we," Cora said, not bothering to hide the bite in her tone.

He paused several feet from the pool, posture hesitant as his eyes strayed from Gisele to the pool's two extra occupants. "Should I..."

"Meet me in that pool," Gisele said, pointing to one of the smaller ones nearby.

His shoulders relaxed a bit as he gave her a nod, then made his way to the pool she'd indicated.

Gisele whirled back to her friends with a grimace. "Don't be mad."

"I'm not mad, I'm seething," Cora said. "I thought you said you wanted nothing to do with boys tonight."

"He isn't a boy," Gisele said, expression all innocence. "He's a man."

"Who is he?"

"His name is James. He's a hunter camped out close by. I met him yesterday when I was foraging for Mother. I promised to meet him here tonight, but I didn't want to meet him alone. He could be a murderer for all I know."

"That isn't comforting," Cora said through her teeth.

Gisele nodded. "Tell me about it."

"You said he was harmless," Maiya said, her tone far gentler than Cora's.

"I'm pretty sure he is."

Cora turned and started to get out of the pool, modesty be damned.

"Please don't leave," Gisele rushed to say.

Maiya tugged her arm before she could heft herself onto the ledge. "We can't leave her with him," she whispered.

Cora clenched her jaw. Of course Maiya would put her own discomfort beneath the safety of others. And if Maiya was staying...

"Fine," she bit out and settled back into the pool, "but you owe me."

"Always. Forever." Gisele's tone was more desperate than convincing. Without another word, she climbed from the pool and hurried to the one the man waited in.

"We should have known better," Maiya said with a sheepish grin.

"Yes, we should have." Had Cora's shields been down, she might have sensed Gisele's duplicitous intentions. But there was nothing to do about it now.

She eyed the two figures in the other pool, watched Gisele melt into the man's arm as she pressed a kiss to his lips. The kiss immediately grew heated, and Cora averted her gaze. It landed on a boulder between the two pools, one strewn with the man's discarded clothing. She was about to turn her back to the pool completely when something caught her eye—a small detail on the man's greatcoat, illuminated by the glowing ceiling. It was a symbol embroidered on his sleeve.

A black crescent moon on an indigo background.

The sigil of Duke Morkai.

The man who'd made her into a murderer.

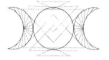

7

All the relief Cora had felt since entering the pool fled in an instant. Her muscles coiled, stiff with rage, her mind reeling.

This hunter, James, belonged to Duke Morkai. But he was more than just a duke. More than one of the most influential men in Khero, second only to King Dimetreus. He was a mage too. Not merely a witch, working quiet magic or the elements. No, he was something else. Something darker. Stronger. His Art was blood. His spell was death. Only Cora seemed to know the truth.

It brought her back to the dreaded bedroom of her nightmares. To the blood on her hands. To her screams. To the condemning voice, half anguish, half anger.

What have you done?

"Cora. *Cora*."

She jumped at the arm lighting upon her shoulder. She had to shutter her eyes a few times to clear them of the bloody tableau.

"What is it?" Maiya whispered, casting a quick glance

at Gisele and James. "Is it the hunter? Do you feel danger from him?"

Cora didn't know what she felt about the man. Her senses were too clouded with ghosts of the past. That and her shields were still firmly in place. With a slow exhale, she imagined a small window parting the elements that comprised her mental shields. Narrowing her focus to the two figures in the other pool, she extended her senses, let herself feel what they were feeling—she snapped the window shut faster than she'd formed it.

Desire was all she'd sensed. That and...arousal.

It was enough to steal away some of Cora's prior tension and send her cheeks heating.

Maiya snorted a laugh. "Did you just try to read their feelings?"

"I know, I know. It was a bad idea that I should have seen coming."

"Hopefully we won't see anything else coming, if you know what I mean."

It took Cora an extra second to understand what she was referring to. When she did, her mouth fell open and she gently slapped the surface of the water, sending a teasing spray to her friend's face. "Maiya! Did you just make a naughty joke?"

She sank down a little with a bashful grin. "I'm serious though. If they do anything more than kiss, I'll...I'll...throw a rock at them."

"Make sure it's a big one," Cora muttered. She risked another look at the couple, but thankfully they'd parted from their kiss and now chatted side by side. As she pulled her gaze away, her eyes lingered on the boulder where James' greatcoat was draped, that patch of indigo bearing a black crescent moon still watching her like an eye.

"Are you mad I told Mother about the nightmares?" Maiya said in a rush.

Cora wrested her eyes from the hateful sigil.

Maiya's grimace was laced with guilt. "I know she came to talk to you earlier today. Are you mad?"

"Of course I'm not mad, Maiya. I couldn't be angry with you if I tried."

Maiya gave her an apologetic smile. "Did Mother end up...helping at all?"

Cora bit her lip, debating whether she should tell her the truth. "She didn't talk with me about my nightmares."

"She didn't? What did she say?"

Again, Cora considered keeping the facts to herself. But she trusted Maiya. Besides, if she didn't know now, she probably would soon. Maiya and Salinda had an honest relationship. "She wants me to take the path of elders."

Maiya's eyes went wide. "That's amazing! That's the highest honor—"

"I told her I don't think I'm right for the position."

Her friend blinked in disbelief. "Why?"

Cora shrugged. "I'm certain there's someone better suited to the position. Someone who has been with the Forest People far longer than I have."

"Cora, when will you finally accept that you're one of us?"

Cora's eyes darted back to the sigil. She would never truly believe she was one of them. Not when her presence alone could put everyone at risk. Not when there was a chance she'd be banished if they knew the truth. And she'd been tempted to tell the truth. The closer she got to Maiya and Salinda, the more she wished she could be honest with them. But honesty had never proven to be on her side. Not when dark magic and murder were involved.

Maiya's expression fell. "Why do I feel like you're always one step away from leaving us?"

Cora opened her mouth but no words would form.

She was saved from having to reply, however, when Gisele hopped into the pool between them. "What are we talking about?"

Cora gave the girl a wry grin. "Oh, just how we can make you pay us back for subjecting us to your makeout session."

"Do you like him? James?" Gisele asked, a hopeful gleam in her eyes.

Cora glanced at the other pool where the hunter lounged alone, his gaze fixed longingly on Gisele. "What does it matter if we like him? You seem to like him well enough."

"He's sweet, isn't he? Kind. Funny."

"I didn't realize he had a personality, but I'll take your word for it."

Gisele rolled her eyes. "Oh, Cora. You're so droll."

"Who does he think you are, by the way?" Maiya asked, her voice barely above a whisper. "You didn't tell him..."

"About the Forest People?" Gisele's mouth fell open with indignation. "Of course not. What kind of fool do you take me for? I may not be all magical like you two but I know our rules."

"Then where does he think you live? If he's a hunter,

he should know the nearest village is hardly a casual stroll away."

Gisele frowned. "Well...he hasn't asked."

Cora gave her a pointed look. "Sweet and kind indeed."

"It's not like I'll see him again after tonight," Giselle said with a casual flip of her sodden hair. "Tomorrow morning he and his companions are leaving their camp and heading north to join the rest of their hunting party."

Cora's stomach knotted for reasons she didn't quite understand. She itched for something she couldn't name. The idea that the duke's men were so close filled her with a frenetic quality, an urge to move, to run. Not *away* either. But toward them.

That was when she realized what the uneasy feeling was. Vengeance.

Thoughts of finding the hunters' camp, sabotaging what she could, knowing whatever she destroyed was indirectly the property of the duke, filled her with the most delicious satisfaction.

But the longer she entertained the fantasy, the more ridiculous it felt. What could a girl like Cora do against a group of trained hunters? And how would it have any impact on Duke Morkai in a way that mattered?

Morkai was second to the king. He was King Dimetreus' most respected councilman. The hunters were likely on an errand to fell some great beast for a royal dinner. And what was Cora dreaming of doing? Breaking their spears like a child throwing a tantrum in hopes that her greatest enemy would be mildly inconvenienced. Gisele had said James and his men were joining the rest of their hunting party. If they too served Morkai, harassing this smaller group would do nothing of import.

She breathed her thirst for vengeance away. It was childish. Silly. Besides, acting on her fantasy went against the Forest People's most important rule—never get involved with royal matters or attract the attention of agents of the crown.

"Gisele," James called, a note of yearning in his voice. "Come back."

She tossed a coy smile over her shoulder at him. "Have a little patience. I came with my friends. You can't have all my attention, you know."

He bit his lower lip. "I'd have all your attention and more if you'd give it to me."

Gisele giggled, but Cora simply rolled her eyes. "Desperate much?" she muttered, earning a warning glare from Gisele. Maiya snorted a laugh.

James narrowed his eyes at Cora, then returned his gaze to Gisele. "Come with me tomorrow."

Gisele chuckled. "He's already in love with me," she whispered to her friends.

Cora had other words to describe him. "He's a creep."

"He knows nothing about you," Maiya added.

Gisele lifted chin. "You two are just jealous."

"I know what would make you want to come with me," James said, drawing their attention back to him. "If I showed you what I have waiting for you back at camp, you'd be impressed. And I promise you, there's more where that comes from at our next stop. It would blow your mind."

"Is that so?" Gisele waggled her brows, her gaze dipping to the surface of the pool that hid his bottom half. "I like having my mind blown by a handsome man."

"It would blow *all* of your minds."

That earned a sharp scowl from Gisele, but Cora gave a dark laugh. "I doubt that very much."

"Have you ever seen a unicorn?"

Gisele's expression turned perplexed as she whispered to her friends, "Is he still talking about what I thought he was? He's referring to his..."

"If so," Cora said, barely able to smother her laugh, "I daresay it's a little lacking in girth."

"I'm being serious," James said, tone affronted. "Have any of you seen a unicorn before?"

"No one's seen a unicorn, James," Gisele said. "They're fae creatures. They went extinct with the dragons and sprites and all the other mythical fae nonsense."

"You're wrong," James said, eyes hard. "If I could show you..." He snapped his mouth shut, then turned his back on the girls with a shake of his head.

"Do you have any clue what he's talking about?" Maiya asked.

"He never mentioned unicorns before." Gisele cast a bewildered glance at her lover. "If he had, I probably wouldn't have agreed to meet him here. He might be out of his mind." The girls fell into a fit of stifled laughter, only to have it broken by a bellowing sound. They went quiet, whirling to face the entrance to the tunnel.

The sound came again, clearer this time. "James!" It was a male voice. Although it was distant, it echoed through the tunnel.

James cursed under his breath and scrambled out of

the pool. "I wasn't expecting them to notice I'd left," he muttered. From the corner of Cora's eye, she could see him shoving his legs unceremoniously into his trousers, then hastily donning his shirt and coat.

Again, Cora was reminded of the sigil, and of the fact that James' companions undoubtedly belonged to the duke as well. And they were close. So close. She breathed deeply to reel in that itch for revenge, forcing it to dissipate. In its wake, something far more pressing remained —a sensation that made the skin prickle behind her neck.

A clairsentient warning.

Fully dressed, James raced to their pool and planted a kiss on the side of Gisele's forehead. "I'm sorry our rendezvous is cut short but I must get back. Stay here for a while. Don't...don't come out yet." With that, he stormed into the tunnel and out of sight.

Gisele stared after him. "What was that about?"

"I don't know." Cora rose from the pool and marched over to her clothes, her pulse kicking up. "We should go, though."

"Why?" Gisele pouted. "There's still wine left."

Maiya didn't hesitate to follow after Cora. She pulled her shift over her head. "Is it...a feeling?"

Cora nodded. "I don't know if it means anything, but...I think we need to leave." She was a little ashamed that she couldn't elaborate. With offensive skills taking such a high place in her priorities, she'd neglected training her Art defensively. She knew how to shield, how to extend her senses to read others' emotions, but there was so much more to clairsentience that she hadn't valued enough to train. Ways to analyze feeling and sensation and know exactly what each subtle difference meant. For all she knew, she could be overreacting. Regardless, the skin continued to prickle at the back of her neck, bringing with it a dark and hollow feeling in the pit of her stomach. She at least knew enough to consider it a sign of danger.

"Oh, all right," Gisele said, reluctantly leaving the pool and meandering over to her pile of discarded clothes.

Cora had on her shift and petticoats. She bent down to retrieve her bodice—

That was when the echo of footsteps reached her ears, pounding down the tunnel toward them. She glanced over at Maiya, who was fully dressed aside from the undone laces of her bodice. Gisele quickly threw on her shift.

Just then, three figures entered the cave. James brought up the rear, a frantic look on his face. The men stopped when they noticed Cora and her friends. The tallest stepped forward, a cruel grin twisting his lips. "Well, now, what pretty beasts do we have here?"

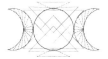

8

The three newcomers were dressed in the same style of greatcoat James wore, with Duke Morkai's sigil marking their right sleeves. All but James appeared at least ten years older than Cora. Their appearances were far more rugged too, with mud-splattered boots, bushy beards, and wild, unkempt hair. One carried a spear while another held what looked like a coiled leather whip covered in metal barbs. The tallest —who Cora assumed was their leader—palmed the hilt of one of the daggers sheathed in his bandolier.

James shuffled to the front of the group and faced the three men with raised palms. "Gringe, it isn't what it looks like."

The man named Gringe scoffed. "And what exactly do you think it looks like?" James stammered for words, but Gringe cut him off before he could reply. "You left your post. Not only that, but you left to dally with three women and didn't think to share." His cold eyes wandered from Cora to Maiya, then Gisele. Cora's heart hammered against her ribs, her stomach roiling as the man assessed them like livestock.

"I'm sorry I left my post," James said. "I shouldn't have, but I figured it was safe to come for a quick soak. And they..." He cast a helpless glance over his shoulder at the girls before returning his attention to Gringe. "They were here by coincidence."

"So you don't know them?"

"No."

"Then I suppose you won't mind if we...get to know them ourselves."

James stiffened. The three other hunters erupted with laughter. With their attention on James, Cora took the opportunity to dip down and retrieve her belted dagger. As soon as her fingers met leather, she stood and pulled it behind her back, just as Gringe's eyes shot to her.

His expression hardened. "You. Where are you from? The closest village is miles away."

Cora's mind raced to come up with an answer, but Gisele spoke first. Batting her lashes, she said, "We're from Palovore, sir. We made the trip here just for Beltane. These caves are famous, you know. Everyone comes to the hot springs during the holidays."

"Then why are you the only ones here?"

Cora stepped forward, purposefully edging closer to Maiya. "We're just the first to arrive," she hurried to say. "Dozens more are coming. My...my husband will be here. My brother too." She hated having to use the threat of another male for protection, but right now she was willing to say anything to keep the hunters at bay. Besides, better they thought she was a helpless female who needed a man to fight her battles than a girl with a dagger in her hand. If only she could retrieve her bow without them noticing.

"Dozens," Gringe echoed. His smirk said he wasn't falling for her bluff.

"Please, just leave them be," James said.

Gringe sneered at the man. "Who are you to give me orders?"

James shifted from foot to foot. "It was...more of a suggestion."

"Did you tell them?"

"Tell them?"

"About our...prey?"

James shook his head. "They know nothing, I swear."

Cora stepped closer to Maiya until their shoulders brushed. "Count to thirty," she whispered, "then take Gisele and run for the tunnel."

"What? No! We're not leaving you."

"I'm just giving you a head start."

"Are you crazy?"

"Count to thirty."

"Cora—"

"Just do it!"

Maiya made a pleading sound but took a step toward Gisele.

Gringe's gaze snapped to her friend. "Here's a suggestion," he said with a dark laugh. "Tie them up. We take them back to camp and figure out where they really came from."

With that, the hunters surged forward. Cora's heart leapt into her throat. "Thirty!" she shouted at Maiya, who'd frozen at their approach. Cora took her dagger out from behind her back and threw it at the nearest man. It glanced off his chest hilt first and fell to the ground. She wished she'd actually practiced throwing daggers before attempting that pathetic spectacle. Cora lunged for her bow instead and nocked an arrow. This gave the hunters a moment of pause. "Thirty, Maiya!" she shouted at her friend. Finally, Maiya's feet flew into action and she grabbed Gisele's arm. They darted for the tunnel. One of the hunters lunged at them, but Cora shot an arrow. It skimmed his wrist, making him pull up short.

Her next arrow grazed his neck. It would have hit dead center if not for her erratic breathing, sending her aim wild. This was nothing like practice where targets stood still, where her only threat was being mildly distracted by her own thoughts.

"Go after them," Gringe barked at the man she'd narrowly missed. He obeyed and darted after Cora's friends. Cora nocked another arrow. "You too," he said to James. "Clean up this mess you made and I'll consider not delivering your head to the duke."

Mention of the duke had Cora's blood burning with rage, clearing her mind just enough to remind her to breathe. One more hunter was still approaching—the man with the barbed whip. Gringe remained near the mouth of the tunnel, grinning as if he expected an entertaining display of theatrics. The hunter flicked his whip. She shot her arrow. Just as her fingers left the fletching, searing pain sliced down her arm. One of the barbs had torn her flesh. Her shot went wild.

The man closed in.

She kicked, she flailed, she bit, but it was to no avail as he crushed her in his grip.

Bound, gagged, and blindfolded, Cora no longer regretted neglecting her understanding of defensive magic. Now she wished she'd spent twice as much time honing her skills with weapons. Perhaps then she wouldn't have been in such a position that left her hauled over a hunter's shoulder like a sack of grain. She struggled in vain, wishing she could at least pound her fists against the hunter's back or slam her feet into his chest, but her wrists were tied behind her back, her ankles bound together. No matter how she wriggled, he paid her no heed. She heard the shift in sound as her captor's feet left the stone cave to the forest floor. "I'm going to do horrible things to you," he said, a dark chuckle in his voice.

"We question them first," she heard Gringe say from up ahead. "See if they were lying."

"But after?"

"They won't be leaving alive," Gringe said, "so do what you will."

She shouted into her gag, cursed them both with every vile insult she could think of. None of it reached their ears, as muffled as her words were.

"Gringe!" A new voice came from just ahead.

"What is it, Sam?"

"I saw it."

"Saw what?"

"The white. The one we were tracking earlier. It waltzed right into camp as if it wanted to be caught. I tried to catch it on my own—"

"Damn it. We can't let it get far. Not on our last night

here. Erwin, leave her at camp and take the south. Sam, go north. I'll signal James and Velek to head east. I'll take the west."

The hunter carrying her, Erwin, kicked up into a jog, jostling Cora with every step. From behind, she heard a low bellowing sound—a horn being blown—that ended in three sharp bursts. That must have been the signal Gringe had mentioned. Other horn blasts echoed back from farther away. A few minutes later, her momentum shifted. Erwin heaved her off his shoulder, and her back met hard earth as she landed on the ground with a thud. His retreating footsteps followed. Cora held still for a moment, straining her ears for any sign that she wasn't alone. Nothing but a crackling fire answered. She took a few deep breaths to steady her nerves—as well as she could—and cut a window through her mental shields. Extending her senses, she opened herself to nearby emotion. At first, she felt nothing. Then...*something*. Or was it nothing as well? An unfamiliar sensation filled her bones, bringing with it a quiet sorrow. And yet...it didn't feel like anything human. An animal? The hunters' horses, perhaps?

Another thought came to mind as Cora remembered what James had said about unicorns. He couldn't have been telling the truth, could he? Unicorns hadn't been seen in hundreds of years. Legends stated that all had become horses by now, leaving nothing of their ancient fae origins intact.

Rolling onto her side, she pressed her face to the ground beneath her, feeling dirt grate against her cheek as she worked to lift the cloth from her eyes. Finally, she managed to shove it over her brow.

Blinking, she took in her immediate surroundings. First, she saw the light of a campfire several feet away. Closer and just out of arm's reach—had they not been tied behind her back—laid her bow, her quiver of arrows, and her belt. Her dagger had been returned to its sheath. She glanced around the rest of the camp, seeing no one else in sight.

She wriggled across the ground, making a haphazard line for her belongings. Sweat beaded across her brow with every inch she drew near. Soon the items were within reach. Rolling to her other side so her back faced her weapons, she fumbled for her belt. Her fingers only had the slightest reach beyond their bindings, and she struggled to gain proper leverage. Finally, her pinky looped around her leather belt. She stretched her hands to get a better grip, then moved her fingers down the length of it. One hand met air as she reached the wrong end. Gritting her teeth, she reversed directions until she felt her sheath. Excitement sparked in her chest as she then walked her fingers up the sheath until they came around the hilt—

Footsteps pounded toward the camp. Gripping the dagger, she wriggled a few feet away from her belongings and rolled halfway onto her back, hopefully obscuring her weapon in the folds of her skirt. James came into view, face strained as he hauled a female form over his shoulder. Far more gently than Erwin had been, he laid his burden next to Cora. Her heart lurched as she saw Maiya's profile, her temple marred with blood. Her hands were bound in front of her, but she was neither gagged nor blindfolded.

James glanced around the camp, then met Cora's eyes

with a frown. "I let Gisele get away," he whispered. "And don't worry, this one is just knocked out."

Am I supposed to thank you for that? Her words, stifled by the gag, sounded only like a string of mumbles. She cut him with a glare that probably looked anything but threatening in her bound state. Then her eyes landed on a strange marking she hadn't noticed before. Just below his ear was a patch of raised skin in the shape of an *R*.

Cora's blood went cold. She knew what that marking was. It was a brand reserved for criminals set for execution. That *R* stood for one of the most heinous and violating crimes she could imagine.

His gaze turned steely as if he could see the realization in her eyes. "I wasn't going to hurt your friend," he said, tone curt. With that, he darted away, grabbing a spear off the ground before he left the clearing.

Alone again, Cora shifted her attention back to her dagger. Angling it toward the knot between her wrists, she sawed the blade against it. It was painstakingly slow, and for a few moments, Cora thought her efforts were futile. But then she heard a satisfying snap as part of the rope was severed. With some mobility freed, she redoubled her efforts. Another snap. Then freedom. She brought her arms in front of her, wincing at the strain on her muscles. Her forearm still seared from where Erwin had lashed her with his whip. Pulling herself to a seated position, she quickly cut through her ankle bindings and tore off her gag.

Her chest burned with anxiety, lungs contracting as she scrambled over to Maiya. She cut her friend's bonds, setting her hands free. Maiya remained limp. Cora set down her dagger and framed Maiya's face in her hands.

She whispered her friend's name. Nothing. She sought her pulse at the base of her neck, relieved when she felt a soft beat. "I'm getting us out of here," she said, then cast her gaze around the camp. She needed a safe way to flee. Steal one of their horses, perhaps. But she saw no sign of one, heard no evidence of a nicker or a neigh.

Subtle movement caught her eye from the opposite side of camp, drawing her attention to two metal cages. Both were composed of six barred panels assembled into a large box, their corners and sides tied together with rope. One stood gaping open, empty, the front of it slightly askew on its roped hinges. The closed one, however, held a single occupant—a male equine creature, brown and nearly skeletal. He wavered on hooves that seemed overlarge for his too-thin body. He blinked sleepily at her, his head dipping low, as if too heavy to hold upright. That was when she noticed the slim, white, spiral-ridged horn protruding from the center of his head, aglow with the light from the fire.

A unicorn.

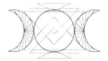

9

S hock rippled through Cora like a shuddering current, nearly taking her breath away. Without meaning to, she rose to her feet and took a few steps closer to the creature before her, her eyes fixated on the white spiral horn. Her pulse thrummed wildly.

"Mother Goddess," she muttered under her breath.

Before her was a fae creature. A unicorn. It was like he had walked straight from legend. Like the stories had said, he was larger than a regular horse, his neck sinuous, his hooves massive. That was where the comparisons ended between the faerytale descriptions and the creature before her. For his brown coat was dull, not shiny. His body was emaciated, not broad and strong. His eyes seemed more lifeless than keen.

The unicorn wavered on his legs again, head dipping, eyes blinking slowly as he took a swaying step back. His rear came up against the bars of the cage. With a sharp equine cry, the unicorn jolted away, but the movement brought his flank against the other side of the cage. Another piercing sound, one of pain.

Cora stepped closer again, squinting as she studied the cage to identify what could be hurting him. All she saw were plain iron bars bound together with rope. Such an assembly suggested the cages were used for travel, with the ability for the sides to be cut loose and reassembled with ease. The enclosure was obviously too small for a creature of his size, but it seemed otherwise benign. There were no sharp edges, no nails, no barbed corners—

Cora's breath hitched, her eyes narrowing on the seemingly innocuous metal bars.

Iron.

A metal that—if the legends were to be believed—was harmful to the fae. Deadly, even.

Her heart plummeted and with it went her control over her mental shields. They crumbled around her. Before she could gather her senses enough to replace them, she was struck by an onslaught of emotion, so powerful it made her legs quake. Hunger, pain, fatigue, terror, sorrow. The feelings enveloped her, permeating her blood and bones. It was all-consuming, all-penetrating—

"Cora." Maiya's strained voice startled her. It was enough to help her get control, to breathe, to push back against the unwanted emotions.

Taking a stumbling step back, Cora tore her gaze from the brown unicorn, breathing deeply until she felt the remnants of the emotions fade. In their place her chest was tight, her throat dry. She ignored it and whirled toward her friend, finding Maiya wincing as she tried to push herself to sitting. Cora ran to her and kneeled at her side. "Are you all right?"

"Where are we?" Maiya asked, squinting as she looked around the camp.

"Somewhere dangerous." Cora left her friend's side only to retrieve her belt, bow, and quiver. She sheathed the dagger and shouldered her other weapons. Then she squatted back down next to Maiya and put her arm around her. "We need to get out of here. Can you stand?"

Cora tried to lift her, but Maiya let out a hiss of pain. "My ankle," she said, voice quavering. "I fell. Twisted it. That's how they caught up to me."

Dread filled Cora's stomach. If her friend couldn't run, they'd be at an even greater disadvantage. Their only hope now of making it back to camp was if the hunters remained distracted long enough. "It's all right," Cora said, more to herself than to Maiya. "We're going to make it."

Shifting her stance so she could help Maiya rise on her good leg, she attempted to pull her up again. Finally, they were both on their feet. With one arm secured around Maiya's waist, Cora led them toward the edge of camp. Each step was slow and hobbling, sending a spike of panic through Cora's heart.

"You should leave me," Maiya said, hissing as she nearly tripped with her next step. "I wouldn't blame you."

"I'm not leaving—" Cora's words died on her lips as the sound of thundering steps came tearing through the woods. The hunters. They were coming back.

From the sound of it, they were heading straight for them.

"Goddess above," Cora muttered, part curse, part

prayer. She angled them to the side, attempting to flee to the other edge of camp, but they were too slow.

Too late.

The pounding steps tore into the clearing.

But they didn't bring a horde of angry hunters.

The steps belonged to hooves, not feet. The thundering rhythm had belonged to a gallop, not a run. And the creature that now reared up before Cora...

Maiya's hand flew to her lips to cover her gasp. "Is that..."

Cora swallowed hard. "Yes."

Another unicorn stood before them, but he was nothing like the emaciated brown one. This creature was enormous, muscular, his white coat splattered with mud. His russet eyes were wild as he bared his teeth.

They took a staggering step back, one that sent Maiya sprawling to the ground. Cora tried to dive for her friend, but the unicorn darted between them. He stomped his hooves, sidling toward her and shoving her back from Maiya.

A feeling slammed into her. With her shields still down, she had no defense against it. Desperation, rage, fear, struck her one after the other. She froze in place as the feelings grew, rippled, changed. Soon the sensation shifted into a sense of need, bearing a weight she'd never felt before when reading anyone's emotions. The weight undulated, multiplied, divided. Cora could do nothing but feel it unfold inside her until it settled into something new.

A word.

A voice not heard but felt. Understood.

Help.

Cora's eyes went wide. Never before had she experienced anything like this. Never had emotions become thoughts, become words. It felt strange, invasive, and utterly terrifying.

She looked to Maiya on the other side of the white unicorn. Her friend scrambled back on her forearms, struggling to stand. Cora's eyes darted between the creature and Maiya. She dove to the side to skirt behind the unicorn, but he skittered back, blocking her.

Help, came the feeling-turned-to-word again.

"I don't understand what you want from me," she said between her teeth. She tried to outmaneuver him in the opposite direction, but it was no use.

He stomped his hooves, nearly connecting with Cora's feet. She danced back to avoid having her toes crushed, but the unicorn pursued her, sending her backward again and again.

Cora's fingers flew to the hilt of her dagger. She unsheathed it and brandished it before the creature. The unicorn tossed his mane, releasing a frantic whinny.

Help.

Help.

Help.

He stomped toward her again. Cora cast a glance over her shoulder in search of trip hazards, but her gaze settled on something else.

The caged unicorn.

The white beast was forcing her toward the cage.

She faced her pursuer. "You...want my help. As in... you want me to free the other unicorn?"

He tossed his mane again. Her heart raced as she looked at Maiya. They didn't have time for distractions.

Not with Maiya's injury. If they didn't get free of the camp before the hunters returned...she didn't want to consider what would happen then.

Still, the memory of what it had felt like when she'd connected with the brown unicorn's emotions made her heart sink. There wasn't a doubt in her mind that the unicorn was being kept in a too-small iron cage on purpose. The hunters *wanted* the creature to hurt. If she had a chance to set him free...

"Fine," she said to the white unicorn. "I'll help release your friend, but after that, you need to get out of my way."

As if in answer, he sidled back and put space between them.

Cora cast another glance at Maiya. Her friend's brows were knitted either with concern or confusion. Then Cora whirled toward the cage and closed the remaining distance. The brown unicorn inside the enclosure only blinked at her, each flutter of his lids slow and heavy. She brought her dagger to the ropes binding the bottom left corner of the cage and cut through them. Then the bottom right. The upper corners were more of a challenge as they were high above her head. Standing on her tiptoes, she extended her arms and cut as much as she could reach, starting with one corner, then moving to the next. The process was slower than it had been with the bottom bindings, but soon the ropes began to fray and snap. She sheathed her dagger and wrapped her hands around the iron bars, tugging at them until the front frame began to tilt on its own, snapping what remained of the ropes. Cora darted back just as it swung down and landed in the dirt with a thud.

"Go," Cora whispered when the unicorn inside made

no move to claim his freedom. She pointed to the perimeter of the camp and infused her voice with a warning edge. "Go. Now."

Finally, he took one wavering step. Then another. His bony legs trembled as he left the cage, his hooves trodding quickly over the iron bars as if they burned. As soon as he was fully upon the dirt floor, he kicked up into an uneven trot and darted into the dark woods.

"Cora," came Maiya's voice, quivering with warning.

She turned back to her friend, but the white unicorn reared up before her. A lashing sound shattered the air, followed by a guttural neigh from the unicorn. Cora lurched back as the creature returned to all fours, but she heard the lashing sound again. This time she saw a flick of something slice the unicorn's hide. As it withdrew, a red mark welled up in its place.

Erwin, the hunter who had hauled Cora into camp, stood behind the unicorn, lashing out again with his barbed whip. Only now did Cora understand its true purpose.

The barbs were made of iron.

It was a weapon designed for wounding fae creatures.

"Run and I'll find you," Erwin said. Although he kept his eyes on the unicorn, Cora was certain he was speaking to her. The angle of his head revealed a mark under his ear, just like James' brand. This one was shaped into *TR*. She tried to recall what crime that stood for. *T* represented treason, but the two letters were too close together to stand for two separate charges. "I won't hesitate to use this on human hide. You've only had a taste so far. With another lash, I could cut through your flesh like a knife through butter."

Now she recalled what his brand meant. *TR*. Torture. He slashed at the unicorn again. Again.

The unicorn bared his teeth and tried to dance away, but no matter which direction he tried to flee, the whip found him, sliced him.

Cora jumped with every snap of the whip, but she slowly edged around the fire toward Maiya, trying to put as much distance between herself and Erwin as she could. The hunter continued to pursue the unicorn toward the cages, much like the creature had done with Cora mere minutes ago.

Finally, Cora reached Maiya, who was halfway to standing on her good leg. Cora helped her the rest of the way up, then shifted toward her bow. She paused as Erwin's eyes locked on hers.

He angled his body to the side so he could keep her in his sights. Watching her from the corner of his eye, he continued to snap his whip at the whinnying creature. "Don't even think about trying anything clever," he growled. "This whip can reach you from here."

She believed it could. The portion he held was still coiled, suggesting its length was far more expansive than it was now.

Without warning, the unicorn charged Erwin. The hunter darted back and lashed out with his whip. The leather circled the unicorn's neck, its barbs digging into the creature's skin. The unicorn tried to rear back, but Erwin tugged, tightening the whip's stranglehold.

Cora lunged for her bow and swiftly nocked an arrow. Her heart pounded a thundering rhythm but she told herself to breathe. Just breathe. She planted her feet firmly beneath her, imagining the soil steadying her, holding her. Then, pulling the fletching to her cheek, she narrowed her focus to Erwin. He continued to struggle with the unicorn, weaving back and forth as he tried to get the creature under control.

The unicorn calmed.

Stood still.

Erwin took a confident step closer.

Cora shot her arrow, felt in her bones that it would hit its mark.

It did. Slamming through the center of his throat, it tore through his flesh.

Erwin's mouth fell open as he staggered back, clutching at his ruined throat as blood poured from the wound.

Cora's stomach bottomed out. A ripple of disgust crawled up her spine.

Disgust in what she was seeing.

Disgust in herself.

She already knew the wound was fatal, knew—as Erwin slid down to the earth, still clutching his neck—that he was going to die.

Her first human kill.

And she wasn't sorry for it.

Disgusted. But not sorry.

She whirled toward Maiya. Her friend's face had gone pale, her eyes locked on the dying man. "We need to go. Now," Cora said.

Maiya nodded, the movement erratic, and let Cora guide her toward the edge of the clearing. A face stared back at her, appearing from behind the trees—it was James. He hesitated, gaze shifting from Cora to the camp, landing an extra beat on something behind her. She had no doubt it was his dead companion.

His lips peeled back from his teeth as his eyes locked back on hers. Then he put a curved horn to his lips and blew. The sound fractured the night. Rage coursed through Cora's blood as James blew the horn again. An echoing blast sounded from not too far away. With a parting, murderous glare, James fled.

Cora cursed, and Maiya let out a cry as she tripped on her injured leg. Maiya's panic seeped into Cora's awareness. Or was it her own panic she felt? Gritting her teeth, she tried to bear more of Maiya's weight to help them quicken their pace.

Four more horn blasts surrounded the camp, coming from every direction. Cora paused, eyes darting about as she tried to discern which way to go. She shifted their course slightly to the left and hefted Maiya forward—

The white unicorn blocked their path.

"I don't have time for this again," Cora said through her teeth.

Danger, came the unsettling invasion of feeling-thought.

"I know."

Danger, he said again. This time, the unicorn lowered his head and sidled closer. *Mount. Safety.*

Her eyes widened at the creature's marred flank. "You want us to...mount you. Like a horse."

He scraped a hoof in the dirt in an agitated gesture. *Safety. Now*.

She exchanged a glance with Maiya, who could only seem to nod. Then, squatting down, she hefted her friend with all her might until Maiya took hold of the unicorn's mane. "Sorry," Maiya said with a wince as she pulled the creature's hair harder to aid her efforts in climbing the rest of the way. Then Maiya extended an arm to Cora. Gripping Maiya's palm with one hand and the unicorn's mane with the other, she hauled herself up. She was hardly seated in front of her friend before the unicorn took off. Maiya encircled her arms around Cora's middle while Cora wrapped the creature's white mane around her fists.

They took off into the night, swallowed by the dark forest.

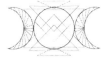

10

Prince Teryn Alante had witnessed his share of preposterous things in his life. His father's attempt to replace the queen with his mistress topped the list, as did the time Teryn and Larylis snuck out to Dermaine City dressed as palace guards to watch the traveling mummer's troupe. Only to realize he and his kingdom were the subject of their play. It hadn't been flattering. But nothing—absolutely *nothing*—compared to being sent by his fiancée to hunt down mythological faerytale creatures in exchange for her hand.

Even now, hours later as he stood on the balcony outside his guest bedroom at Verlot Palace, he still harbored the hope that it had all been said in jest. This was the Heart's Hunt, after all. The tradition was meant to be symbolic and the quest itself was supposed to be relatively simple. A scavenger hunt that could be solved in a single evening. Of course, Teryn knew nothing about this particular Heart's Hunt was symbolic.

"Where the bloody hell am I going to find a unicorn?"

Teryn asked for probably the hundredth time that evening. "And not just a single unicorn, mind you. *Three.* Do you think it was a riddle?"

Two round black eyes stared back at him, but he received no answer. Not that he expected one.

"You don't think so?" Teryn said to his peregrine falcon perched on the balustrade next to him. He slipped her a strip of raw duck he'd had brought up from the palace's kitchens. His hosts hadn't been thrilled that Teryn would be bringing the falcon, but where Teryn went Berol went too. The falcon had bonded to Teryn as a hatchling, injured and nursed back to health by the prince's own hand. Berol obeyed Teryn as much as a bird of prey could. So, to appease his hosts, Teryn promised to keep her from hunting on palace grounds during his stay and would hand-feed her instead. He could tell the bird was a little restless, but at least they'd be heading home by tomorrow. "You're right, Berol. This is absolutely hopeless. Ridiculous. Insane."

"Your choice of words suggests you must be talking about Princess Mareleau again." Teryn glanced over his shoulder and found his half brother standing in the doorway to the balcony. Larylis leaned against the doorframe with a smirk.

"Right you are," Teryn said.

Their father came up just behind Larylis and stormed onto the balcony. "I've talked to Verdian," King Arlous said. His tone alone was evidence enough that he didn't bear good news. Hands on his hips, Arlous shook his head with exasperation. "He suggests his daughter's request is sound."

Larylis frowned and pushed off from the doorframe.

"Seriously? Everyone saw his face during Mareleau's speech. He was furious."

Teryn nodded and gave Berol another strip of duck. His brother was right. Anyone with eyes could have seen that King Verdian had been taken by just as much surprise as everyone else when his daughter brought up unicorns. Not to mention the way he stormed after Mareleau when she left the balcony. Or the muffled shouts that slipped beyond the closed glass doors not long after that.

King Arlous ran a hand through his dark hair. "If King Verdian revokes his support of the Heart's Hunt, he'll be admitting he has no control over his daughter."

Larylis threw his hands in the air. "So he's going to let her send our crown prince, Mareleau's legitimate fiancé, on an insane quest. Did he make any apologies? Bring up their marriage contract even once?"

"You know he doesn't have to apologize," the king said through his teeth, cheeks flushing either with rage or shame. "He knows we don't have the funds to fight him. And he knows that *we* know exactly where we stand in his eyes. We're lucky the marriage contract hasn't been torn up entirely. If it weren't for our exclusive trade agreement with Brushwold, it probably would be."

Lucky. Teryn internally scoffed. He had several choice words to explain his pairing with Mareleau and *lucky* certainly wasn't one of them. Still, he knew what his father was getting at. He turned to fully face the king and his brother, propping his back against the rail as he slouched into it. "I have to go through with this farce."

King Arlous nodded. "There's a chance Prince Helios and Prince Lexington will back out. Either way, I'll send informants to gather intel on whether there's any truth to this unicorn nonsense."

Teryn opened his mouth to ask if they could afford informants but stopped himself. While he knew information didn't come cheap, he also knew his father couldn't be persuaded against a course of action when he had his mind to it. Hence his kingdom's current financial state. So instead, he gave a reluctant nod.

"Arlous, my love, there you are." The king's mistress stepped onto the balcony. "I've been looking for you everywhere. You promised we'd attend the Beltane feast tonight."

The king's expression softened although his posture remained tense. He met his lover with a soft kiss to her forehead. "Apologies, Annabel. We were just discussing... important matters."

Her face brightened. "You mean about the Heart's Hunt?" She faced Teryn with a simpering smile. "Unicorns! Aren't you just...so excited?"

Teryn wanted to roll his eyes but he forced himself to mutter a curt, "Thrilled."

As much as Teryn resented Annabel Seralla for nearly usurping his mother, he knew the blame didn't lie entirely with her. His father was the one who'd risked the stability of his kingdom in the name of love...and failed. Lady Annabel had been the king's mistress since before Teryn was born. He'd been raised alongside his half brother, fully aware that their mothers were two different women. They shared the same father but not his surname. It took him nearly thirteen years of life to understand the taboo undercurrents of his familial ties. That was when things got complicated. When his parents' fights grew louder, more frequent. When his mother demanded Teryn's brother—a boy who'd become his best friend—be sent away to be raised out of her sight. For three years, Larylis lived as a ward to Lord Ulrich until, without explanation, Ulrich suddenly sent him back home to Dermaine Palace. Teryn's mother was furious at his return and demanded he be sent away again. What followed was the scandal that nearly bankrupted the Kingdom of Menah.

Lady Annabel turned back to King Arlous. With a pout on her lips, she straightened his lace neckcloth. "Can we go to dinner now? You know Verlot's feasts are far better than ours."

Teryn's father smiled down at his mistress. "Of course, darling." Then, turning back to Teryn, he added, "We will make this work, Teryn, I promise you. If there's a way for you to win the Heart's Hunt, I'll find it."

Teryn tried to give his father what he hoped was a confident smile, but he'd learned years ago not to put much weight in his father's promises. Not that his father didn't try. He did. He was steadfast and tenacious when it came to those he loved. Often, though, love wasn't enough.

No, if Teryn wanted to see this ridiculous Hunt through, he'd have to do it himself. The question was how. He was a skilled hunter, so that wouldn't be an issue. He'd gone on royal hunts since he was old enough to walk. He'd felled his first beast at age ten. It was the same year he not only developed a keen love for the spear—his weapon of choice—but found Berol. Ever since, he'd spent his summers honing his craft, learning to hunt larger and rarer beasts. But never a legendary beast. This wasn't the age of unicorns and dragons. This was the age of reason. Something Princess Mareleau clearly lacked.

Annabel gave Larylis a casual wave as her only acknowledgment of her son before the couple left the balcony. That wasn't unusual behavior for Annabel. She'd borne two more children after Larylis—both boys —and had sent them away to boarding school as early as she could. Teryn could surmise it was to keep them out from under the queen's ire, but he'd always thought Annabel seemed far more interested in being a lover than a mother.

Teryn fed Berol the rest of the duck and stroked a finger over the top of her head.

Larylis came up beside him. "I don't know how you pet that thing without fearing loss of a finger."

"Fear is for the weak," Teryn said in jest. "Besides, you've petted her plenty of times before."

"Yes, with a healthy dose of fear." Larylis reached out to lightly scritch the back of the falcon's neck. Berol extended her wings and ruffled her feathers, making him jump back. Then, stuffing his hands in his pockets, he leaned against the balustrade. "So...how are you really feeling about all of this?"

Teryn ponded his answer. In truth, he was frustrated. Irritated. Absolutely perplexed. And yet he was resigned to do what needed to be done. His kingdom was running out of time to repay their debt to Cartha. If they waited much longer, the bank would escalate their efforts from sending pirates to hiring mercenaries. The latter wouldn't simply raid their trade ships. They'd collect Menah's debt in lives.

The most reasonable solution was to wed Mareleau.

Her dowry would be enough to settle their debt with the bank. If his engagement with the princess fell through, well, they'd be left with very few options. Sure, another marriage alliance could be made, but what were the chances another kingdom would be willing to risk allying with them? He knew it could take years to draw up an agreeable contract.

The Kingdom of Menah didn't have years. Not where the Bank of Cartha was concerned.

With his brother's question still hanging unanswered between them, Teryn planted a crooked grin over his lips. "You want to know how I'm really feeling? I feel like today has been the most humiliating spectacle since we visited that mummer's troupe. Remember that? They had us played by literal dogs while Father's impersonator went about humping a woman dressed as a sow."

"I'm serious," Larylis said, although he couldn't hide his laugh. "Hunting fae creatures, competing against two other princes for a woman's hand that you've already been promised...it's a lot to do for someone you don't love."

There was trepidation in his tone, which brought Teryn's attention to his brother's face. That same pained look he'd noticed earlier had returned. "Are you truly concerned about me doing too much for a woman I don't love? Or for her because I don't love her?"

Larylis stiffened.

"Wait." Teryn took a step closer to his brother, startling Berol, who sidled down the balustrade. "Do you... have feelings for her?"

"Of course not," Larylis rushed to say, pushing off

from the rail to straighten. Despite his words, there was a sudden flush in his cheeks. "I don't—"

"You knew her. Back when you were a ward to Lord Ulrich. Did the two of you—"

"No, Teryn, it isn't what you think." He shifted from foot to foot, then slouched to the side. "Oh, all right. We kissed."

Teryn's eyes nearly bulged out of his head. "You *kissed*? Are you telling me I'm engaged to someone you've kissed? And that you've never found it pertinent to mention until now?"

"It was three years ago. I was sixteen. It meant nothing." His voice dipped with a note of regret, one that wasn't lost on Teryn.

"Larylis, if you have feelings for her—"

"I don't." This time his tone was firm. Certain. "You know I dislike her."

"Yes, well, I hadn't known you disliked her after having had your tongue in her mouth." Teryn's last word quavered with a chuckle. That was when he realized something. He wasn't mad at his brother. Disturbed, perhaps. A little indignant that Larylis hadn't trusted Teryn enough to tell him the truth until now. But Teryn was neither angry nor jealous.

Which probably wasn't a good thing. Not where his future romantic prospects were concerned. However, Teryn had always known he wouldn't marry for love. Unlike his father, he was determined to do what was right for his kingdom. He'd stay true to his word. His duty.

Unless...

"Promise me you don't have even the slightest feelings for Princess Mareleau. Or...if you do, just...just be honest." Teryn held his breath as Larylis stood frozen, shoulders tense. He didn't know what kind of answer he expected, or what he'd do if Larylis did in fact harbor a secret affection for his fiancée. Part of him wanted to hear his brother proclaim a deep love for the woman, to beg him not to marry her. Teryn knew Larylis couldn't wed Mareleau, though. She was a princess and Larylis was illegitimate. Even so, it would be the one thing that could set Teryn free, the one thing that would fix his heart firmly against the unwanted match for good.

And, as a result, would send their kingdom into further peril than it was already in.

Finally, Larylis' posture relaxed. "I have a lot of feelings about Princess Mareleau, and I guarantee none of them are good." He punched Teryn lightly on the chest. "I feel bad for you. That's all."

Teryn wasn't sure if he believed his brother, but the sense of calm settling in his gut reminded him that any other answer would have brought nothing but turmoil. "I feel bad for me too," he said with a smirk. "She must be a terrible kisser."

Larylis threw his head back with laughter, shattering every last remnant of tension between them. For a moment, Teryn felt like they were boys again, enjoying each other's company without a care in the world. Without knowing the weight of a kingdom would one day fall upon Teryn's shoulders. And that Larylis wouldn't be allowed to share the burden with him.

Once they sobered from their mirth, Larylis took his leave, insisting he wanted to visit Verlot's library before they headed home in the morning. That sounded like his brother, all right. Larylis had never met a library he didn't like.

No sooner than Larylis left did a knock sound at Teryn's door. With a frown, he opened it, finding a palace servant on the other side. The man handed Teryn a small envelope. It bore no emblem, just an unmarked wax seal. "Your Highness," the servant said with a curt bow.

Teryn dismissed him and brought the mysterious envelope inside his room and out onto the balcony. Berol immediately tried to take the envelope from him.

"No, this one isn't for you," Teryn said, pulling it out of her reach. While Berol wasn't a messenger bird, Teryn had trained her to carry letters on occasion. Mostly to his mother or back home to his father while visiting his mother's palace.

Teryn opened the letter and removed its contents—a single sheet of paper with only four sentences scrawled across it. None of them bore the name of the sender.

Meet me in the garden at midnight. Water nymph statue. The busty one with the ample breasts. It will be worth your while.

Teryn read it five times over, then flipped it back to front. Who the hell had sent such a strange missive? And what could they possibly want?

It will be worth your while.

Teryn realized the letter could have been sent by an emboldened chambermaid hoping to get Teryn alone on Beltane. It was almost tempting enough to excite him. He'd entertained numerous liaisons of a similar nature in the past. That is, until he started to feel too much like his father. Breaking hearts. Spending time with women he knew he could never wed. Should he seek pleasure now, he had to do it with predetermined detachment. Not on a whim with someone who very well might expect to become his mistress. Besides, if he were to enjoy a meaningless tryst, it wouldn't be in the home of his betrothed. Still…

He read the letter once more, snorting a laugh over the *ample breasts* line. If the letter wasn't sent in the name of seduction, he hadn't a clue to its purpose.

What he did know was—come midnight—he'd be damned if he didn't find out.

11

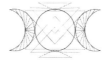

Larylis Seralla didn't have his father's name. He wasn't an Alante like Teryn, nor was he a prince. Instead, Larylis went by his mother's surname. Seralla. And yet, it didn't matter whose name he'd been given or whose blood flowed in his veins. For he had neither of his parents' fickle hearts. They'd nearly started a war over their love. Larylis was determined never to be so foolish. To never forget his place.

So when Teryn had asked him if he had feelings for Princess Mareleau, he'd lied. Sort of. While Larylis no longer kept love in his heart for the princess, he hadn't been telling the truth when he'd said their kiss had meant nothing. And there hadn't been just a single kiss, but several. However, only one had felt significant. It was their final kiss. At the time, it had meant the world to Larylis because it had sealed their mutual expressions of love. Of course, that was before he'd learned what it really meant to be the illegitimate son of a king. Mareleau must not have understood it either at the time. Not until they were caught kissing in the stables by her uncle. That was when Larylis had been sent back to Dermaine Palace. By the time he'd arrived, he'd learned Mareleau was already engaged to Teryn. Whether the arrangement had been made before or after they'd been caught kissing, it mattered not. For the letter he'd received from her that day told him everything he needed to know.

I could never love a bastard.

Meanwhile, Teryn had been sent a letter too, one chronicling her excitement over their upcoming nuptials and professing her undying love.

Larylis knew then that Mareleau wasn't who he'd thought she was. Despite the way he still caught his heart lurching at the thought of his former flame, Larylis was determined not to get in the way of her and Teryn's union. Not like his mother had done, driving a wedge between the king and queen until Arlous did the unthinkable—broke vows, severed royal bonds, and nearly drove his country into chaos in an effort to make Lady Annabel his new queen. His father had insisted it was in Larylis' best interest too, for if Annabel was queen, Larylis could be named a prince. His mother had whispered far more devious suggestions—that it could also mean he might have a stronger claim to the throne after Arlous passed.

A claim he never asked for.

Never wanted.

His jaw tightened at the memory. A sour taste lingered in his mouth as he left his brother's door and headed for the library. Seeing Teryn struggle with the burden of having to right their father's wrongs reminded Larylis exactly why being a prince was far less admirable than storybooks made it sound. Sure, were Larylis a prince, he could have wed the girl he'd once loved. Then again, considering how cold and duplicitous she'd proved to be, he was willing to bet he'd dodged a dagger in being born a bastard.

Larylis reached the end of the hall before he realized he'd passed the turn that led to the palace library. After a week of dining and dancing, he craved the quiet solace of books. Besides, the library at his home palace was starting to get out of date, with his father approving fewer purchases to stock it.

He looked back the way he'd come, down the length of polished marble floor, the elegantly papered walls, the gilded frames and oil lamps interspersed every few steps. At this end of the hall, the lamps were dimmer, the bustle of servants far less frequent. He looked to his left, finding an unlit corridor. Even after three years away from the palace, he remembered it. Knew where it led. Perhaps he'd had a subconscious reason for bypassing the library.

His feet began to move before his mind caught up. Soon the corridor opened to a circular alcove. He stood at the center of it, remembering how many times he and Mareleau had met there in secret. A half smile tugged his lips as his eyes roved the four enormous windows, each with a cushioned seat built into the sill with a view that overlooked the garden, perfect for reading on a blustery day. Three of the floor-length velvet curtains remained tied open, while one on the far right was pulled closed, obscuring both the window and its sill. He recognized that window, even with the drape drawn shut. It had once been his and Mareleau's favorite place to hide.

Feeling a nostalgic pull, he approached the curtain and tugged it open.

His heart climbed into his throat.

For a moment, he felt as if he'd stumbled upon a tableau from the past. There sat Mareleau, curled on the cushion with her knees pulled up to her chest, just like how she used to sit when they were younger. She startled and whirled away from the window. If this truly were a scene from memory, Larylis knew what would happen next—she'd give him her secret smile, take his hand, and drag him down next to her. His breath would hitch, his heart would race, and his lips would burn with their desire to claim hers...

"What are you doing here?" she blurted out in a rush, eyes wide.

It was enough to shatter the illusion, to remind Larylis this wasn't a tableau and the woman in the window wasn't the girl he once loved. "Sorry." Larylis dropped the curtain and turned away, but before he could take more than a few steps, he heard her rush out from behind the velvet drape.

"Larylis."

The sound of his name on her lips sent his pulse racing. It was the first time he'd heard her say it since the day he'd been sent back home. That was the last time they'd spoken. The last time they'd stood close enough to touch. Slowly, he turned to face her.

She was still dressed in the same silvery blue gown she'd worn during the poetry competition, but it hung a little looser off her curved frame, as if she'd undone her laces for comfort. Her hair too hung differently, with pearls and flowers dangling haphazardly from the ends.

A portion of her pale tresses had been pulled into a crooked braid, one she anxiously fumbled with now.

It was a braid Larylis had seen many times before. She always braided her hair when she was nervous. Or happy. There was a time he'd fantasized about unraveling that braid himself, unraveling the laces of her gown, trailing kisses down her—

He shuttered his eyes, forcing himself back to the present so he could gather his composure. He sketched a stiff bow. "Princess Mareleau."

She stood silent, her fingers winding around the ends of her braid. Her expression flickered with uncertainty, her lips darting between a frown and the barest ghost of a smile. She opened her mouth as if to speak but quickly snapped it shut. Releasing her braid, she folded her hands demurely at her waist. She stood tall, chin lifted, features schooled behind a haughty countenance. "I said, what are you doing here?"

He averted his gaze as if she wasn't worth looking at. If there was one thing he'd learned about being a bastard, oftentimes on the receiving end of insults and mockery, it was how to pretend things didn't bother him. "I certainly wasn't looking for trouble," he drawled, "but it seems I've found it. Good evening, Your Highness." He made to step away, but she only drew closer, forcing him to halt in place. The aroma of jasmine invaded his senses, making his lungs feel tight. It was a scent he'd thought he'd forgotten. He'd been wrong. Now that she stood so close, he found himself unable to keep his eyes off her.

Seven gods, she was beautiful. More so than he remembered.

It was an observation better left forgotten, one he

banished before it could breach his lips in the form of a compliment.

"Is there more you wanted from me, Highness?" His words came out far rougher than he'd intended. But when he saw Mareleau stiffen and take a step back, he was grateful for his inadvertent gruffness, if only to place more distance between himself and that intoxicating jasmine.

Her gaze turned cold. "How did you like the poetry competition?"

"You mean the way you publicly insulted my brother by allowing eight other men to compete for your hand?" He pulled his lips into a humorless smile that didn't meet his eyes. "Charming."

Her cheeks reddened, her eyes narrowing as she put her hands on her hips. "You can't blame me for not wanting to marry your brother." Her voice trembled, her chest rising and falling rapidly above the bodice of her gown.

Larylis was surprised at how flustered she was. Finally, he managed to look away from her again, keeping his gaze fixed firmly over her head. "Do you enjoy torturing your suitors?"

She lifted a delicate shoulder. "A girl must take pleasure where she can."

"Because a man's sincere admiration isn't pleasure enough for you."

"Sincere." She scoffed. "I haven't met a sincere man in my life."

Larylis jutted out his bottom lip in a mock pout. "What a shame. At least you can settle for riches and a title, which I'm sure you value far more."

Her mouth fell open in indignation.

That prompted a wicked grin to form on his lips. He knew he shouldn't take any joy in irritating her. It wasn't like he blamed her for rejecting him all those years ago. He understood her position. Her duties. What he couldn't forgive was her treatment of Teryn. Her flagrant mockery of their engagement. The one she'd once insisted by way of letter that she was so excited about.

He brushed a piece of lint off his silk waistcoat, then assessed his nails. "If we're done here, I have far more entertaining matters to attend to."

She crossed her arms. "Oh? Are you going to dinner then?"

"That depends. If you'll be there, I'd rather clean the stables."

She blinked at him, and her lips once again darted between a frown and a smile. He couldn't fathom why she'd consider smiling after such an insult.

Unless...

Did she *enjoy* his teasing? Did it remind her of when they'd first met? How he'd tease her relentlessly and she'd return lighthearted insults just as fiercely? How their first kiss had been sparked after exchanging verbal blows only to wind up tangled in each other's arms? In fact, it had happened in this very alcove...

His heart thudded at the memory, but he shoved it away. Taking a step back, he gave her another bow. "Goodnight, Your Highness."

"Larylis, why did you never—" Her words were cut off by another voice.

"Mareleau Harvallis." Queen Helena's tone rang heavy with reproach as she stormed down the corridor toward them, followed by four young women who he assumed were Mareleau's lady's maids. Three were around the princess' age, while the fourth he knew was a few years younger. It was Lurel, Mareleau's cousin. He'd met her several times when he was their uncle's ward. She gave him a surprised half smile, which he wasn't able to return under Queen Helena's furious scrutiny. "Where have you been? You're supposed to be at the feast."

Mareleau lifted her chin. "I wasn't hungry."

"I don't care if you're hungry. Tonight is the last night your guests are here. You *will* attend." The queen faced the four girls. "Sera, Ann, Lurel. Return to Mareleau's room so you can prepare to make the princess... presentable again."

The three girls ducked into curtsies and quickly scurried away. Larylis quietly edged down the hall, hoping he wouldn't draw the queen's notice.

"Breah," Queen Helena said to the remaining woman. "Escort Lord Seralla back to his room so he doesn't get *lost* again."

He bristled at the queen's unspoken demand—that he was not to attend tonight's feast. It wasn't as if he'd planned on going anyway. Gritting his teeth, he turned back to the queen and offered her a bow. As he let Breah lead the way, he couldn't help but wish he'd gotten to hear what Mareleau had started to say.

Mareleau stared after the man she'd once fancied herself in love with, torn between relief over being rid of his aggravating presence and regret that they hadn't been able to speak longer. Their interaction hadn't been even remotely enjoyable. Or—more accurately—it shouldn't have been. And yet, for reasons Mareleau couldn't comprehend, she found herself invigorated by the inter-action. Perhaps because, beneath his casual composure and coarse words, she'd sensed something. Maybe it was all in her mind, but she could have sworn Larylis Seralla still had feelings for her.

It shouldn't matter to her. He'd ignored her when she'd needed him the most. Refused her letters. Sent back silence for every tear she'd cried after being forced to part with him. Left her standing alone before the altar in a rundown Godskeep several miles from home, watching the door for hours. He'd never shown up.

She knew now it had all been for the best. A fifteen-year-old girl had no business eloping. Still, he could have at least replied to her letter. It would have saved her many tears and a whole lot of embarrassment.

Queen Helena angled her body so she blocked Mare-leau's view of the hall—and Larylis' waning figure. The queen had been in a dark mood ever since Mareleau made her announcement, and she didn't seem anywhere close to being rid of it. Her mother was like that at times, drifting between maternal kindness and cold fury without anything in between. "What were you doing alone with that boy?"

"That boy? You know who *that boy* is, Mother."

"And your father and I have forbidden you from speaking to him, much less being alone with him. He nearly soiled your reputation once before. Had anyone but your uncle caught the two of you in that stable—"

"Reputation," Mareleau said with a cold laugh. "I

don't recall you caring much for my reputation when you left me alone with Prince Augustine."

Her mother's expression softened at that, draining some of the fury from her eyes. She put a hand to her forehead, then swept a curl from her brow. When she next met Mareleau's gaze, she wore a sympathetic smile. "I just don't want you to do anything you'd regret."

Mareleau wanted to say that marrying any of her current suitors would lead to more regret than anything else would, but she held her tongue. So long as her mother was trying to control her temper, Mareleau would too.

"Darling, I understand what it's like to be in your position," the queen said. She took Mareleau's arm and linked it with her own. With leisurely steps, she led her out of the alcove and down the dark corridor. "I too had to give up my own desires in the name of duty. However, I held far less responsibility on my shoulders. I wasn't the heir to my father's crown like you are. Even so, I had to relinquish my dreams to marry Verdian."

Mareleau sighed. She'd heard this all before. Whenever the queen wanted to prove just how much she sympathized with her daughter, she'd go on and on about *abandoning her dreams* and how grateful she was to have done so.

Queen Helena's tone turned nostalgic. "I had perfect pitch, you know."

Mareleau *did* know, as she was forced to hear about it again and again. Helena, in her youth, had been a talented musician. She played the harp and piano and had the most pleasant singing voice. She could play any song by ear after hearing it only once and composed new music from thin air.

"The audience used to weep when I'd play. My father nicknamed me his *Little Siren* after the creatures of fae lore."

Mareleau nodded along as if she hadn't heard this a thousand times.

Then, as if coming out of a daze, the queen turned to Mareleau with a warm grin. "Speaking of fae lore, I apologize for not trusting you when you announced the goal of the Heart's Hunt. I'd assumed you hadn't been taking the competition seriously."

Mareleau studied her mother's profile, startled by the unexpected apology. "That means...you've changed your mind? You think I *am* taking it seriously?"

"Your father and I spoke to Lord Kevan. He confirmed he had, in fact, seen a unicorn with his very eyes, as did several of his men. They hunted it for a week before it crossed the border from Selay into Khero."

Mareleau pulled up short, her heart leaping into her throat. "He...he really said that?"

The queen nodded.

"So...Lurel's earrings..."

Queen Helena gave a dismissive shrug and nudged Mareleau to start walking again. "Your uncle purchased those earrings for her, which were only rumored to be made from unicorn horn. Still, it gives added legitimacy to your Hunt."

Mareleau bit the inside of her cheek. While she'd needed her uncle to carry the blame for her ridiculous request, she hadn't expected his tale to be so convincing. Could he have been telling the truth?

The queen's tone turned sharper. "I'd have preferred it if you'd picked something far easier and hadn't delayed the Heart's Hunt for a week. But I can't blame you for being a romantic. You always were."

Mareleau wanted to gag. Seven gods, her parents didn't know her at all. She wasn't a romantic. She simply wanted freedom from cold courtships, from groping hands and loveless declarations. She wanted to be respected as heir to her throne without needing to marry. Was that so much to ask? At the very least, she wanted to avoid marrying Larylis' brother. If it ever came down to a forced alliance, she could handle marrying just about anyone but Teryn.

Despite how much she'd hardened her heart after Larylis had shattered it, she would never be able to reconcile living in the same palace as him, dining at the same table, bearing his brother's children while the boy she preferred—

Fiery rage bubbled inside her, but she forced it down. Right now, there were more pressing concerns to worry over.

If Uncle Kevan hadn't been lying, if unicorns truly had returned from extinction…

That meant her suitors might successfully complete the task she gave them.

And she'd promised to marry whoever did first.

The thought made her want to crawl out of her skin. At least she had one small comfort. For the time being, no matter how short it might be, she was free.

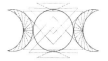

12

J ust before midnight, Teryn made his way to the palace garden. The evening's festivities were still underway, so no one paid him much heed as he slipped through the halls, past the bustling ballroom, and out to the garden courtyard. From there, he began navigating the twists and turns of the walking paths flanked by elegantly manicured shrubs and flower beds. He came to the first statue along the path, but it was a marble likeness of King Verdian, not a busty water nymph. He chose another branching path, discovered a few more statues, but none resembling the description in the letter.

The deeper he went into the garden, the more wary he began to feel over the possible intentions behind this meeting. Nearly every twist and turn brought him stumbling upon lovers stealing covert kisses, couples locked in passionate embraces meant only to be witnessed by shadows. He supposed he shouldn't have expected less on Beltane.

Teryn reached a portion of the garden boasting impressive water features—ponds and fountains as well as several artistic arrangements utilizing pumps and pulleys that almost seemed like magic. The sculptures here looked far more like water nymphs than the previous ones had. And yet, there wasn't much to distinguish the characteristics of one statue from another, nor was there any sign of someone waiting for him. Not until he entered a quiet courtyard with an enormous fountain standing at its center. Only now did Teryn understand the emphasis on ample breasts in his letter, for the figure atop the fountain was heavily endowed indeed, plus a rounded swell of belly and curved hips. Even more telling was the hooded figure standing before it, back facing him.

Teryn took a few tentative steps forward, but the figure didn't seem to notice his approach. He stepped closer again and realized the rush of the fountain was likely drowning out the sound of his steps. With a deep breath, he closed the remaining distance and placed his hand on the figure's shoulder.

The figure lurched back and whirled around, revealing a man several inches shorter than himself dressed in plain black clothing and a rather conspicuous cloak.

Teryn blinked a few times to ensure he was seeing whom he thought he was. "Prince...Lexington?"

"Seven gods and demons," the man cursed, clutching his chest. Prince Lexington was one of the three champions Teryn was competing against in the Heart's Hunt. Which meant he couldn't have been the one to send him the letter.

Could he?

Lexington let out a low whistle. "You scared me half to death." His eyes flicked from Teryn's face to his brocade waistcoat and formal jacket. "You don't look incognito."

Wait, did that mean...

Teryn kept his voice neutral as he said, "Your letter didn't say I should."

Lexington shrugged, confirming that he, in fact, was the letter's mysterious sender. "Well, I suppose it doesn't matter, so long as I can say what I came here to say."

Teryn stood tall and crossed his arms, narrowing his eyes with suspicion. If they were to be competitors, he assumed this meeting wasn't going to be a friendly one. "What exactly did you come here to say, Prince Lexington?"

"First of all," he said, raising a finger, "call me Lex. I despise the name Lexington. Second of all..." He cast his gaze around the small courtyard and motioned Teryn closer to the fountain. Lowering his voice to a whisper, he continued. "I'll make this quick. I'm here to offer you an alliance to help you win the Heart's Hunt."

Teryn tilted his head back. "Why the hell would you help me? We're supposed to be adversaries."

"How can we be adversaries when we both want the same thing?"

Teryn narrowed his eyes again. "Are you telling me you want me to win? Why?"

"Because you're going to let my kingdom in on your trade agreement with Brushwold."

"Our trade agreement is exclusive." He did not add that—before the Bank of Cartha had started sending pirates—it was the only thing keeping his kingdom afloat. Brushwold was a small country but had something no one else had—Aromir goats. The animals produced the most coveted wool, famed for both its warmth and softness. Since Teryn's kingdom specialized in clothing manufacture, the trade alliance had been a natural one. Anyone on this side of the Balma Sea who wanted Aromir wool had to purchase it from Menah. It had been just enough for Teryn's kingdom to get by. Until Menah stopped receiving Brushwold's shipments, that is. And if they started sharing that trade...

Teryn nearly blurted out a *no* until he considered an alternate perspective.

If Teryn won the Heart's Hunt and secured his marriage to the Princess of Selay, Menah would have Mareleau's dowry. His kingdom could finally pay off their debts to the Bank of Cartha and turn their financial situation around.

Teryn brought a hand to his chin, considering the man before him. "Why do you want to help me, Prince Lexington?"

"Lex."

He rolled his eyes. "Why do you want to help me, *Prince Lex*?"

The man gave him a bewildered look as if the answer should be obvious. "Because I've no desire to marry that spoiled harpy of a woman."

Teryn pursed his lips to keep them from quirking into a grin. "If you don't want to marry her, then why are you here?"

"My father wants me to marry the princess for Selay's

trade with the Southern Islands. However, if I can get us Aromir wool, Father will be satisfied."

"Why me? Why not offer an alliance to Prince Helios?"

Lex's lips pulled into a grimace. "Have you met him? He looks like he strangles puppies for fun. And that's after he's finished drinking the blood of virgins and kindly grandmothers."

Again, Teryn had to force himself not to grin. His own impression of the brutish prince hadn't been much different. He lifted his chin and posed his next question. "How exactly do you propose to help me?"

"By forfeiting to you, obviously."

Teryn expected more to follow, but only silence stretched on. "Wait...are you saying you have no plans to physically aid me in any way?"

Another perplexed look from Lex. "Of course not. I'll stay here, you'll go frolic through the woods in the name of love, and when you return with the princess' gifts, you'll brag about what fierce competition I was."

"Is that so?"

"It's a solid plan."

"I don't see the benefit to me."

"Less competition," Lex said with a shrug. "Better odds."

"I automatically have better odds because you just revealed to me you have no intention of winning."

"Damn. Fine, I'll come with you. I'll help you...kill magical creatures and such." He said the last part with a flourish of his hand. "Then we'll return with the gifts, and you'll spout on and on about my hunting prowess and how you beat me by only the narrowest margin.

We'll dine, we'll dance, we'll celebrate your nuptials, and you'll grant the Kingdom of Tomas access to your trade arrangement with Brushwold."

"I'll *try* to include your kingdom in the agreement," Teryn amended, "and if I can't, I'll arrange a special discount on the purchase of Aromir wool. And that's *only* if I win."

Lex's mouth fell open. "Only if you win? That's hardly fair."

"Take it or leave it." Teryn honestly wasn't sure which option he'd prefer. While aid would be welcome, especially since Mareleau's terms forbade her three champions from hiring help or bringing guards, was Lex going to be *that* helpful? Helpful enough to put his kingdom's greatest asset on the line?

If I win, he reminded himself, *Menah won't have to rely so heavily on said asset.*

Lex shook his head as if the whole arrangement were a personal affront. "Fine." With a resigned smile, he extended his hand and took a step toward Teryn—

And halted as a steel blade blocked his path. The sword was held by Prince Helios.

Lex stumbled back from the sword, its edge glistening beneath the moonlight. Prince Helios didn't pursue him. Instead, he grunted, "Dead." He whirled toward Teryn, whose hand was already flying to his hip. It came away empty. Teryn cursed under his breath. Why hadn't he thought to arm himself before meeting a stranger in a shadowed garden? "Dead," Helios said again, pointing his blade at Teryn's heart.

"Very cute," Lex said in a mocking tone. "We're all good and dead. Mind telling us what in the name of the seven gods you're doing here?"

Teryn took a cue from Lex and tried to pretend he wasn't at all intimidated. He forced himself into a casual posture, eying Helios through slitted lids.

Prince Helios sheathed his sword and stared stone-faced at them. "I'm here to join your alliance," he said in a gruff voice.

Lex's face went conspicuously pale. "What alliance?" he uttered too fast.

"The one you invited Prince Teryn to join but not me."

Lex's gaze shifted furtively from Teryn to Helios. "I... don't know what you're talking about."

"At eight this evening, you sent a servant with a message for Prince Teryn. At a quarter to midnight, you left your room and entered the garden. At ten until midnight, Prince Teryn entered the garden. And here you are."

Lex's eyes bulged. "How do you know all that?"

"The servant you paid a single gold *sova* to deliver your message only required two *sovas* to tell me exactly where the message had been sent. The chambermaid who brought your dinner this evening, Lexington, only required five *sovas* to watch your room for the remainder of the evening. Meanwhile, one of the hall servants watched Prince Teryn's room for the cost of six."

Teryn scoffed. "Are we supposed to be impressed?"

"Everyone has a price. Every piece of information can be bought if you know the right currency."

"Do you like speaking in riddles," Teryn said, "or is that just an aspect of your glowing personality?"

Helios' jaw tightened as he slid his gaze to Teryn. "I don't know why the two of you chose to form an alliance, but your terms have now changed. The three of us will be working together."

Lex huffed a laugh. "Why would we agree to work with you?"

"I've already demonstrated my knack for gathering information," Helios said. "It just so happens I already know much about the prey we seek."

"How do you know we don't too?" Lex said, puffing his chest in a way that was not at all convincing.

"You don't."

"How do you *know*—"

"Answer me this," Helios cut in. "How many hunting parties are currently seeking unicorns?"

Teryn and Lex said nothing.

Helios' lips curled into a smug grin. "Who are they hired by? Where are the unicorns most commonly spotted? When did the first sighting occur? How thick is their hide? What's the best weapon to use against them?"

Teryn's fingers curled at his sides when he really wanted to send a fist to the other man's face. It took all his restraint to appear unflustered. "What's the best way to shut you up?"

Helios glared at Teryn. "Have you any clue how to most effectively skin a unicorn?"

"No, because I'm not a complete psychopath," Teryn said dryly.

He turned to Lex. "How does one dehorn a unicorn?"

"You pay someone to do it," Lex said with a nod.

Helios shook his head. "The two of you are clueless. You'll never find the unicorns without my help."

"If we're so clueless, why bother making an alliance with us?" Teryn asked.

"Unicorn hunting is not a solo endeavor. Even with three of us, it would be hard."

"All right," Teryn said, entertaining his line of reasoning. "What are you proposing then? We team up, help each other seek the prizes? Each champion must find three unicorns. One for its pelt, one for its horn, and one as a pet. That's a total of—" He was about to say six, since Lex had already forfeited his place as champion...but what if that was a piece of information Helios didn't have? Even if he'd been spying on them a while, could he have heard their hushed conversation over the rushing fountain?

Teryn watched Helios closely as he continued. "That's nine unicorns total if we agree to help each other complete the Heart's Hunt. How do we know you won't take advantage of our aid to steal the first three unicorns all for yourself and abandon us? And if not, what do we do once we're done helping each other? Make a mad dash back and see who gets here first?"

Helios showed no sign that he knew Teryn was withholding anything. "We aren't going to find nine unicorns. We're going to find two."

Teryn's stomach dropped, but he tried not to let his surprise show. It still didn't mean Helios knew. "Why only two?"

"We'll take the horn and the pelt from the same

unicorn. Mareleau will never know the difference. It's impossible to tell. We'll bring back the second unicorn as her pet."

Teryn waited for him to elaborate but he didn't. "That's your plan? We hunt only two unicorns to collect one of every prize...and then what? Are we supposed to duel to the death to see who gets to keep them?"

"We're all keeping them," Helios said. "We find the unicorns together. Gather the pelt, horn, and pet together. We bring them back to her together. Her terms stated that he who returns first with what she demands will prove he loves her most and will, in turn, earn her hand in marriage. This way, all of us return as equal victors."

Teryn frowned. "Then she'll owe her hand to all three of us."

Lex raised his palms in a defensive gesture. "No, thank you. I'm not sharing a bride with the two of you."

"No, you fool," Helios growled, "she'll be forced to *choose* one of us."

"And if she refuses?" Teryn asked.

Helios let out a dark chuckle. "What, afraid your fiancée won't choose you once her hand is forced? I'd be scared too. Rumor has it she's already courted half the continent since your so-called engagement began."

He bristled at that but kept his voice calm. "I'm serious."

"If she refuses to choose, that's when we'll duel to the death."

Teryn waited a beat, expecting his words to have been in jest, but Helios made no attempt to take them back. "This plan is madness."

"Everything about this situation is madness," Helios said. "I don't know about you, but I have neither time nor patience to play the princess' game. I say we beat her at it. Use her own terms against her. Force her to simply choose a husband like a sane person. My kingdom wants the marriage alliance, but not at the cost of me doing the impossible alone. With the three of us working together, we'll be finished in two weeks tops. If the two of you try and attempt this without me, I'll be walking down the aisle before you so much as catch a whiff of a unicorn."

Teryn narrowed his eyes. "Is that a threat?"

"A fact. The things I know..." His smirk widened. "I'm honestly embarrassed just thinking about you attempting the hunt without me."

Lex crossed his arms and squinted at Helios. "Prove it. Give us one reason to believe you know anything about what we're up against."

Helios reached for his belt. Teryn stiffened as he unsheathed a dagger. Lex launched a step back, almost tripping as his calves collided with the lower ledge of the fountain. Helios chuckled at Lex's reaction and aimed the dagger at Teryn.

It took Teryn a moment to realize he was handing it to him hilt first.

He assessed Helios' arrogant expression before taking the weapon from him. As soon as his eyes landed on the blade, his breath caught. It was pale white, its tip sharply pointed, its edges curved in a sharpened spiral. He angled it, studying the strange knife beneath the moonlight. It was unlike anything he'd ever seen before. The blade seemed denser than bone, lighter than steel. He met Helios' eyes. "Is this..."

"Unicorn horn," Helios said, taking the blade from Teryn. He sheathed it, not even bothering to offer it to Lex. "Taken from a unicorn by my own hand."

While there was every chance the prince was lying—the blade could have been a fake, or Helios could have purchased it—Teryn couldn't help but feel a spark of awe.

"What do you say?" Helios asked, his face brimming with confidence. "Do you agree to this alliance, or do we part ways tonight knowing you will fail without me?"

Teryn's blood boiled at the indignity of the situation. He hated to admit Helios could be right. Teryn knew plenty about hunting but nothing about unicorns. He could fell an enraged boar and take down the largest stag in the woods, but what if there was something to what Helios had hinted at—that unicorn hunting had its own nuances Teryn wasn't aware of?

Lex edged closer to Teryn and whispered, "This is probably a good time to inform you that I know nothing about unicorns. Or killing. Or hunting. Or...forests."

Teryn suppressed a groan. If he had any chance at securing his engagement to Mareleau, he had to put his trust in Prince Helios. At least there was one thing Helios didn't know—Lex had already forfeited to Teryn. That had to count for something, right? If he could find a way to use Lex's support to gain the upper hand...he just might be able to win this.

"Fine," Teryn said. "But first—"

"See you in a week then," Helios said, not waiting for Teryn to finish before he turned on his heel and stalked out of the courtyard.

"A week," Teryn called to his back. "Don't we need a plan?"

"I have a plan," Helios said over his shoulder. Then he was gone.

Lex stared straight ahead, eyes unfocused. He blew out a heavy sigh, making his ruddy cheeks puff out. "I'm going to regret every word I've said today." With that, he too walked away.

Teryn was left alone by the fountain, wondering if pirates, financial ruin, and an unfulfilled engagement contract were about to be the least of his worries.

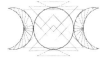

13

Cora had only gone out riding a few times since coming to live with the Forest People. The commune normally reserved their horses for pulling wagons when moving to a new camp or when going to trade with local villages. A few times, though, Cora and Maiya had been allowed to ride for leisure, to explore the nearby landscape outside a new campsite, or to simply exercise the horses. Before that, she'd ridden many times as a girl.

But never bareback.

Never racing through the night, her cheeks whipped by branches.

And never, of course, on a unicorn.

The ride was equal parts exhilarating and terrifying. She had to fight to keep her seat, and her inner thighs were burning within minutes. Maiya clung to her waist with all her might, her head tucked behind Cora's shoulder. Their speed was a near neck-breaking pace. She'd never ridden so fast, not even on her most daring leisure ride as a girl. She was confident there was no way the hunters could keep pursuit.

Cora was breathless by the time the unicorn slowed his pace to a canter, then a trot. Finally, the unicorn stopped. Cora looked around, seeking signs that they were anywhere familiar. She knew the areas between camp and the hot spring caves, but other than that...

A fresh wave of panic climbed up Cora's throat.

What if she couldn't find her way back to the Forest People?

What if she and Maiya were lost?

The unicorn stomped his hooves in an agitated gesture, telling Cora he was ready for them to dismount. She hated the idea of being lost while the hunters could still be searching for them, but she had no right to expect anything more from a fae creature. She was lucky enough the unicorn had bothered to save their hides at all. Shifting in her seat, she climbed down and nearly fell over in the process. Once she had her feet beneath her, she helped Maiya come down far more gracefully, careful not to let her land on her injured ankle.

The unicorn backed away a few paces.

Cora turned to him with a grateful nod. "Thank you for saving us."

Help, he relayed to her.

"Yes, you helped."

Help, he repeated, the feeling-word tinged with urgency.

Cora shrugged. "What are you trying to tell me?"

"Cora, are you...talking to the unicorn?" Maiya asked, coming up beside her.

"Sort of," she muttered, feeling somewhat self-conscious. "It's more like a feeling of his that I'm picking up, and it...somehow turns to words in my mind. He keeps saying *help*. The same isn't happening to you?"

Maiya wrinkled her brow and closed her eyes. She was silent for a few moments as she breathed deeply. Her eyes flew open, and her expression went slack. Maiya was accessing her Art—claircognizance. After a few moments, she gave a solemn nod.

"Did he speak to you?" Cora asked.

"No," she said softly, "but I did pick up on something. There are more like him."

"Unicorns?"

"Not just that. Caged ones. They're...they're being harmed in a way I don't understand. All I know is they're in danger."

Cora looked back at the unicorn. "You want our help rescuing more of your kind?"

He tossed his mane and Cora felt an approving emotion from the creature.

Cora and Maiya exchanged a look. "We...can't help you," Cora said, feeling her vengeful side rebel at her words. "We barely survived what just happened."

The unicorn's energy turned aggravated as he raked his hoof into the earth.

Maiya sighed and faced Cora. "I wish we *could* help. We were raised on tales about fae like him, raised to believe we'd never see them with our own eyes. Now that we know they aren't extinct, it makes me sick that they're being hunted."

Cora could sense her friend's sorrow, her desperation. Cora felt something similar herself. She remembered Gisele mentioning that James and his companions would be leaving in the morning to join the rest of their hunting party. She recalled how he'd boasted about the impressive *thing* awaiting at camp, and how there were more at his next destination. Cora hadn't taken his words as anything more than a poor attempt at seduction, but now it all made sense.

There were more captive unicorns. More tormented fae.

And they were likely all working for Duke Morkai.

Her enemy.

A spark of fiery vengeance—the same she'd felt when she'd first glimpsed the duke's sigil—roared through her.

She tamped it down. Her conclusion was the same now as it had been then. There was nothing she could do that mattered.

And yet...

"Maiya."

"Cora."

Two voices sounded through the trees, one male, one female. Maiya's hand flew to her heart. "Is that..."

"We're here," Cora called back.

Their names echoed again, not too far away, and they ran toward the sound, Cora and Maiya calling back with every step. Soon two figures emerged from between the trees and bounded forth.

Roije stopped as soon as they came into view, his face slack with relief. Behind him was Gisele, trails of tears marking her cheeks, sparkling beneath the light of the moon. She ran forward, breaking into a sob as she gathered Cora and Maiya in her arms. "It's my fault. It's all my fault," she cried.

While Cora couldn't help but agree, now didn't seem like the time to say so. Instead, she said, "We're safe."

Gisele released them, which in turn made Maiya hobble back before she caught her balance. Roije was at her side in an instant. "You're hurt." He framed her face in his hands, his expression hardening when his eyes landed on the blood at her temple.

Even in the dark, Cora could tell Maiya was blushing. "I'm fine," she said with a bashful smile.

"I can carry you," he said, and was halfway to scooping her up before she put a hand on his chest to still him.

Just as quickly, she snatched her hand away. "It's just a sprain. With help, I can walk."

"You're sure?"

"Yes." She waved at Gisele, who wordlessly obliged, putting her arm around her like Cora had done.

"Come on then." Roije angled his head in the direction he and Gisele had come from. "We're not too far from camp."

They started off, keeping a moderate pace for Maiya.

"Thank you for finding us," Cora said. "How—"

"The Magic of the Soil led me here," Roije explained. "Gisele sprung upon camp looking half dead with a wild tale about getting attacked by hunters. A dozen of us went out looking, and Gisele insisted on coming with me."

"I knew if anyone would find you, it would be Roije," Gisele said. It was a solid bet, considering his renowned magic-aided tracking skills. Gisele's lip quivered. "I'm so, so sorry. I never should have been so reckless."

"Let's just get back to camp," Cora said, still uneasy with the thought that the hunters were still out there. She knew the unicorn's speed had helped them outrun them—

Remembering the creature, she whirled around.

Her heart dropped when she realized he was nowhere to be seen.

Roije turned too. "What is it?"

She looked deep into the dark woods, searching between the trees for any sign of white fur. Nothing. She was surprised at the pang of disappointment that tugged her heart. Releasing a sigh, she caught back up with Roije. Gisele and Maiya were now several paces ahead.

"What happened out there?" he whispered.

She nibbled her lip, uncertain what to say. Would he believe the truth? She remembered the idea that had begun to form before Roije and Gisele had found them.

"Can you track...*anyone*? Even someone you haven't met?"

He considered that and shrugged. "It depends. I'd never met my father, but the Magic of the Soil led me to him. His blood called to mine."

"So, you couldn't track a stranger?"

"If I could track them for a while by usual means, I'd perhaps be able to tune in to their essence enough to utilize magic as well."

"How fresh of tracks do you need?"

He turned to face her, eyes narrowed with suspicion. "What is this about?"

She looked from him to her two friends. Cora returned to walking while keeping a slight distance behind them. Maiya looked over her shoulder with a questioning glance before casting her gaze ahead.

"Gisele told you we were attacked by hunters."

He nodded.

"They weren't just any hunters, Roije. They'd captured..." She gulped a few times, gathering the courage to say what she knew would sound crazy to him. "They had a unicorn in an iron cage. It looked starved. I witnessed one of the hunters lash another unicorn with an iron-barbed whip."

Roije made no outward sign that he was surprised. Or perhaps it was only that he didn't believe her.

"I'm telling the truth, Roije. You can ask Maiya. We both saw it. We—" She almost confessed they'd ridden the unicorn, but that seemed too unbelievable to admit. "I know it sounds crazy, but we have to do something. We need to stop them. We must tell the elders."

He halted in place and faced her. "No." His tone was neither sharp nor unkind. It was more...tired.

"What do you mean, no? This is a matter of the fae. If anyone should care, it's the Faeryn. The Forest People might no longer be of pure Faeryn blood, but their heritage is fae, just like the unicorns. It's a matter of magic—"

"No, Cora," he said, expression sagging with grief. "While it may involve fae creatures, it is a royal matter, not a Faeryn one."

Cora took a step back, taking in his posture, his feelings of defeat that began to seep into her. "You already know."

He nodded. "I spied the hunters on my way to camp. I saw them with their...their prey. I also saw whose sigil they bore on their coat sleeves."

Ice filled Cora's blood, battling the heat of her rage that always sparked when she thought of Morkai.

"Duke Morkai is too powerful. Facing him or his agents would be equal to facing the king. You know why we can't do that."

Cora swallowed back every argument. She knew he was right. The Forest People served no crown, recognized no king. If King Dimetreus—or anyone loyal to him—learned of the commune's existence, knew that a group of nomads lived on the king's soil paying no taxes, no dues... the Forest People would be hunted. Forced into modern society at best. Exterminated at worst. That was the very reason the commune swore never to get involved with royal matters. Never cross paths with agents of the crown. Never engage in anything that could draw the crown's attention.

"Did you tell anyone?" Cora asked.

"I met with the elders this morning and told them what I'd seen. They won't directly interfere."

Tears pricked Cora's eyes as she remembered the skinny brown unicorn. She could still feel his sorrow. Then there was the white unicorn, who turned his grief into rage, fought against his captors, and risked getting caught just to free one of his kind. Risked his life to save Cora and Maiya. "There must be something we can do."

He shook his head. "You need to forget what you saw. You more than anyone need to stay away from those hunters."

It took a few seconds to feel the weight of his words. Echoes of his earlier warning pounded through her head. "What do you mean by that? Why me more than anyone?"

He started walking again. "You know why."

Cora stared after him. He was halfway back to

catching up with the others when Cora tugged his sleeve. "Tell me what you mean."

He rounded on her and stuffed his hand beneath his coat. When he brought it back out, a crumpled piece of paper was crushed in his fist.

"What is that?"

Without a word, he handed it to her.

Cora felt the blood leave her face as she unfolded the paper. Once she'd smoothed it flat, she squinted at what she beheld. It was hard to make out at first, with the night so dark, but soon her eyes followed the lines of black that formed the sketch. It was a female face. Long hair. Lightly rounded jaw. Almond-shaped eyes.

The paper shook violently in her hands as she stared at her own face, the likeness as accurate as her reflection. Above her head, bold letters spelled *Wanted* while the script below the portrait read: *For the murders of Queen Linette and Princess Aveline. Reward: 500,000 gold* sovas.

Sovas were the highest form of currency on the continent. The sum was considered a fortune. Her eyes fell on what was written beneath that. *Wanted alive and turned over to the crown.*

Cora dropped the paper and lurched a step back. "Where did you get that?"

He picked it up and stuffed it back in his coat. "In Kubera. The signs were...everywhere."

"Has anyone else..."

"I don't know, Cora. If these signs are papered around the other villages, I suppose it's only a matter of time."

She took another step back, her heart racing. She felt as if the ground were about to swallow her up.

"It doesn't matter," Roije said, reaching for her. "I

don't believe what it says about you. There's a chance the others won't either."

She wanted to take his word for it, but she could feel the weight of everything he left unsaid. They both knew the truth. Once word got out that she was wanted by the crown, she wouldn't be allowed to stay. Sure, Salinda would defend her. Try to protect her. But what of the others? If the Forest People were so determined to stay out of royal affairs that they'd refuse to help captive fae creatures, then they'd certainly refuse to harbor a fugitive. Worse...what if they turned her in? It would go against the Forest People's rules, but the likeness...it was too close. When she'd first been condemned for the crime, she'd been a twelve-year-old child. No one could have guessed her current appearance so accurately. Could someone in the commune be a spy? Could they have discovered Cora's identity and...and...

A far more reasonable explanation came to her, one that filled her with the darkest shade of dread.

No one had spied on Cora. No one had run off telling her enemies of her appearance. For if they had, why not turn her in right away? Why not reveal where to find her? No, this was a matter of magic.

Dark magic.

A mage's magic.

Duke Morkai could somehow *see* her.

And if he could see her...

She glanced at Maiya and Gisele, almost at the edge of her vision. If he could see her, he could see *them*. All of the Forest People. If he didn't know their location yet, he soon could. She could handle the thought of being personally targeted by the duke. In fact, part of her relished the thought. Relished the prospect of getting her chance at revenge. What she could not tolerate was putting the Forest People at risk in turn. Suddenly, her fear over her own fate shifted to that of her friends. Of the few amongst the commune who'd become as close as family.

It wasn't enough to avoid villages. To hope her identity wasn't discovered.

Her throat burned, eyes prickling with unshed tears, even as she forced her heart to harden. To do what she knew she needed to do. "I have to go," she said, voice strained.

"What do you mean?"

"You said it yourself, Roije. The Forest People don't get involved in royal matters. *That*," she pointed at his coat where he'd stuffed the Wanted poster, "shows just what a danger I am. What a danger I've always been."

"It's different with you," he said. His voice held so much conviction she almost believed him. "Salinda—"

"Salinda deserves better. You all do. I can't...I can't endanger you." She took another step back, then glanced at her two friends again. "Tell Maiya I'm sorry."

Before he could say another word, she turned and ran.

THE SUN WAS JUST BEGINNING TO RISE BY THE TIME SHE made it back to the hot spring caves. Progress had been slow in returning, as every step was haunted by the threat of hunters, not to mention the threat of hope. Every snap of a twig, every hoot of an owl sent her stomach into a roiling mess. Half of her was terrified she'd see one of the duke's hunters, while the other part hoped Roije was just behind the next tree—that he'd tracked her, had come to stop her.

To take her back home.

To comfort.

To safety.

She shook the thought from her head as she took a tentative step inside the cave. The commune was never her home, she reminded herself, no matter how much she'd wanted it to be. She could never be truly welcome, not with a bounty on her head. She'd been naive enough to think her past was only a threat if she confessed her identity, or if someone else was clever enough to figure it out.

She made her way into the tunnel, finding it empty. The hot spring cavern was thankfully empty too. Tension unraveled from her gut as she made her way to the boulder where her discarded belongings remained. With a sigh, she sat on the boulder, resting her feet as she donned her bodice, overskirt, and cloak. She was tempted to curl up right there and sleep, but she had to keep moving. It was already a risk to return here, but she knew she wouldn't get far without her cloak. It had been a mild spring so far, but nights still carried a chill. As to where she'd go next...

Her lack of options nearly overwhelmed her.

She knew how to use her bow. Skin smaller animals. She could survive in the woods and feed herself, but... was survival enough?

The duke's sigil flashed through her mind, heating her core with fiery rage.

This time, she didn't tamp it down, didn't shove her vengeful thoughts away. As she left the hot springs and returned to the mouth of the cave, she let her anger unfurl, let it heat her blood until a reckless, wild idea took root in her mind.

Because now she had nothing left to lose.

So what if she was only one girl against a pack of hunters?

So what if her efforts had to be small?

At least they'd be something.

If Duke Morkai could somehow see her, then it was only a matter of time before he found her. He might as well watch her destroy his machinations. And when he found her, she wouldn't cower. Wouldn't run. She'd send an arrow between his eyes. Show him she was the killer he'd made her out to be.

She walked through the woods, idly seeking shelter. It took her a while to realize she was no longer alone. Glancing to the side, she caught a flash of white between the trees. She stopped in place and the unicorn stopped too. They held each other's stare until the creature emerged and stood before her.

Help, he said.

Terror surged through her, tinged with an unsettling excitement. Both emotions were wholly hers. "Yes," she said to the unicorn. "I will help you."

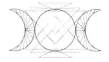

14

King Arlous slumped into the chair behind his desk, posture defeated. "Three more ships have been sacked by pirates. We'll lose our contract with Brushwold by fall at this rate."

Teryn's stomach plummeted at his father's words, although he wasn't sure how much farther it could sink. Today was the official start of the Heart's Hunt. A week had passed since the Beltane festival, and he was now back home at Dermaine Palace. In the week since his meeting with the princes in the garden, he'd exchanged only a few brief correspondences with Prince Helios, the latest of which directed Teryn to meet him and Lex at a certain inn by nightfall. That meant Teryn had but an hour to spare before departing. A prospect that had his nerves pressed in a vise. There was still a chance Helios' offer of alliance had been a ruse. Tonight's meeting could end in sabotage.

Arlous rubbed his brow, as if that were enough to

erase his worries. Then, with a forced smile that didn't match the vacant look in his eyes, the king reached for a decanter on his desk. He poured a generous finger of amber liquid into two glasses and handed one to Teryn. "Let's share a drink. You didn't come here to listen to my woes. You came to bid me farewell."

Teryn accepted the glass and took a long pull. The burning warmth of the strong spirit was a welcome distraction from his anxiety. "As heir to the crown, your woes are mine to bear."

His father winced. "I failed you, Teryn. I promised to find information on unicorns and have nothing of value to give." He lifted one of the letters haphazardly strewn upon his desk. "One informant wrote to me with vague rumors about unicorn sightings up north. Like that's supposed to mean anything. North where? Northern Menah? North as in Khero? Northern Risa?" With a huff, he took up another letter. "This one might as well be blank for all it's worth." Another letter. "Same goes for this one." He crumpled it in his hand and tossed it toward his waste bin. It missed by several inches, which made King Arlous throw back the rest of his drink and pour another. "I'm being outbid, that's what's happening. I can't afford my own spies."

Teryn didn't know what to say to that so he took another pull from his drink. His eyes wandered over the king's desk. The letters his father had referred to appeared useless indeed, considering how brief they were. His father's frustration was his own, for that was how every correspondence from Helios had been this week. And Teryn was supposed to trust the man.

King Arlous finished his second drink and began

gathering up the discarded letters. He fumbled and lost half the stack to the desk, proving he'd already been well into his cups by the time Teryn had arrived at the king's study to say goodbye.

The topmost sheet caught Teryn's eye. He leaned forward squinting at it. "What's that?"

Arlous lifted the page in question, then handed it to his son.

Teryn assessed it closer, finding a portrait of a beautiful young woman beneath the word *Wanted*. He nearly dropped his drink when his gaze landed on the sum at the bottom of the page. "Five hundred thousand *sovas*?" It was enough to repay the Bank of Cartha and still have money to spare. "Who is she?"

The king left his desk and stood at his window. The morning was gray and heavy with fog, obscuring the view of the palace gates and the rolling hills behind it.

"A wild goose chase," Arlous muttered. "An informant brought me the poster, but no one has been able to deliver anything else on the girl since. Not her name. Not her age. Not her last seen whereabouts. All we know is that she poisoned Queen Linette and Princess Aveline. It is common knowledge that the crimes were committed by one of the queen's maids, but the murders occurred six years ago. If that's what she looked like then, she could look far different now."

Teryn studied the girl again. Her expression had been rendered neutral, her eyes small and slightly angled, her hair dark and lustrous. She didn't look like a murderer. He returned the paper to the desk. "How long have you been seeking her?"

The king shrugged. "A few months now. I've been

seeking an alliance with King Dimetreus for far longer, but he responds to nothing. This, I thought, could grant me both a formidable alliance and the funds to repay Cartha. I have nothing else to offer him. Your sisters are too young to marry."

Teryn's heart clenched at the mention of his three younger sisters. His father rarely spoke of them. Teryn only ever saw them anymore if he visited his mother's palace.

"If I could catch this outlaw," King Arlous said, "we'd have everything. Paying back the Bank of Cartha would allow us to set everything else to rights. Our trade with Brushwold would thrive. We'd never again be slighted by Selay. Verdian wouldn't dare put off your marriage to the princess any longer, knowing we had the funds to threaten war."

Teryn shifted in his seat, uneasy at the talk of war. His kingdom had already been on the receiving end of such a threat when Arlous attempted to dissolve his marriage to Teryn's mother. That was enough experience to last Teryn a lifetime. "Don't worry, Father, we'll have the princess' dowry before the next ship leaves Brushwold's shores." His tone was confident, but he knew his expression didn't match.

King Arlous turned away from the window and frowned at his son. When he spoke, his voice was uncharacteristically soft. Quavering. "I'm so sorry, Teryn. I don't say it to you enough because I can't regret what I tried to do for Annabel. I love her. You must know that."

"I do," Teryn said, although he didn't consider it a virtue on his father's part.

The king returned to his desk and braced his hands on the tabletop, his head slumped with defeat. "This burden you must bear...I fear it will only leave you a younger version of me, trapped in a loveless marriage." Teryn bristled at that, but Arlous rushed to add, "That's nothing on your mother, son. She's a good woman. I respect her."

Teryn pursed his lips to keep from scoffing. How could his father claim to respect the woman he'd once dragged through scandal? Arlous had tried to annul his marriage to the queen by accusing her of infidelity. He'd claimed she'd been intimate with his late brother before his untimely death, which meant his marriage could never be considered valid in the eyes of the seven gods. Teryn had a hunch his father's actions had more to do with the fact that his mother bore only girls after Teryn while Annabel had birthed two more boys after Larylis.

"I can't take it all back," King Arlous said. "Nor can I stop hating myself for what I'm doing to you."

He met his father's eyes, saw the remorse in them, and found his own resentment softening. Even with everything the king had done, Teryn's father did love him. More admirable than that was Arlous' standing with the people of Menah. Teryn wasn't sure how many other monarchs could try to depose their queen without inciting massive rebellion. Instead, King Arlous had the people's sympathies, thanks to Annabel's popularity with the common folk. He was certain, however, that a lot of that support would disappear if Menah's poverty were more apparent in the day-to-day workings of the king-dom. For now, the king put the people first, ensured they had jobs, food, and homes while pirates ate into Menah's profits and sent the crown's coffers deeper into the negatives. Soon, the king wouldn't be able to keep the kingdom afloat without inflicting suffering upon their citizens.

Teryn had to make sure that never happened.

"I wish you didn't have to marry that woman, Teryn. I wish you didn't have to take my failures upon your shoulders."

"It doesn't matter," Teryn said. "I'll win the Heart's Hunt. I'll fulfill my duties."

The king pushed off from his desk with a growl of frustration. "I wish you didn't have to do it alone. That fool girl."

"I won't be alone." He didn't elaborate further than that. Helios' letters may have been brief, but he hadn't failed to stress the importance of keeping their alliance a secret.

Arlous assessed Teryn with a keen gaze. "Good. I don't care what you have to do, what rules of hers you have to break. Hire a hunting party. Buy the pelt and horn. She won't know a difference."

Teryn threw back the rest of his drink and set the empty glass on the desk. "I must leave soon. I should say goodbye to Larylis."

Arlous nodded. "Safe travels, son. Send Berol with word now and then."

"I will." He turned his back on his father, hoping that the next time they saw each other, they'd both have reasons to smile.

TERYN KNEW EXACTLY WHERE TO FIND HIS BROTHER. SURE enough, as he opened the doors to the palace library, Larylis was hunched over a stack of books. It wasn't an unusual sight, as Larylis frequented the library as often as his own bedroom, either poring over poetry, historical texts, or the latest novel. But ever since they arrived home from Verlot Palace, Larylis had spent nearly every waking hour in books. Teryn knew what held his brother's fascination. Knew his extra time in the library was spent on Teryn's behalf.

He approached the table his brother occupied. Larylis didn't bother looking up from the paper he was furiously scrawling something on. "Don't get your hopes up," Larylis muttered. "Everything I've written down is rubbish."

Teryn chuckled and looked over his brother's shoulder. Several stacks of books surrounded him, as well as crumpled bits of loose parchment covered in scratched-out notes or angry-looking blotches of black ink. A book lay open at his elbow, which must have been what he was currently taking notes from. Teryn scanned the wall of text in the book. At the bottom was a black-and-white illustration of a unicorn laying next to a young girl with flowers in her hair. The creature's head was in her lap, round eyes staring adoringly up at the girl. Four pixies fluttered around them. Teryn turned his attention to the sheet of paper Larylis was writing on. It contained half a page of brief notations, one which read, *According to one faerytale, unicorns are drawn to virgins. Weird. Why?*

"Virgins?" Teryn said.

"I told you it was all rubbish. You'll see another line

about a faerytale where a fae queen had six lovers and two pet unicorns. Obviously, the virgin thing is a myth." He finished writing his latest note and leaned back in his chair with a grumbling sigh. "That's the last book on unicorns I've found."

"I told you that you didn't have to do this."

"And I told you there was nothing you could do to stop me."

Teryn grinned at that. They were similarly stubborn. He supposed they both inherited the trait from their father. "Aside from pure rubbish, did you at least read anything interesting?"

Larylis shrugged. "Faerytales, mostly. The only scientific texts I found on unicorns stated they haven't been seen in over five hundred years. Our scholars are obviously behind on their records."

Teryn's own recent research—albeit far less thorough than his brother's—had revealed the same. It made no sense. How could an entire species come back after almost five hundred years of extinction? There was a part of him that still held doubts that unicorns *were* real. Then he'd recall Helios' strange blade. It had been rather convincing in the moment, but...could he have been fooled? To what end?

"You haven't read anything about hunting them, by any chance, have you? Dehorning them? Skinning them?" Helios had suggested there was some special method only he knew, but Teryn was uncertain how much of that had been posturing. "Found any maps suggesting where they can be found?"

"No," Larylis said as he reached for a book in the middle of one of his stacks, "although, I found a map in a book that mentions unicorns. I don't think it's of here, though. It talks about Lela at the end of the book, but the map says Le'Lana."

That piqued Teryn's curiosity. *Lela* was the original name for the portion of land that was now divided into three kingdoms—Menah, Selay, and Khero. Even though the land was part of the continent of Risa, there was much lore regarding Lela and its origins. Most tales insisted Lela hadn't always been part of the continent, that one day the city of Delany was the southernmost point of Risa, and the next the coast had sprouted an entirely new portion of land. Teryn had always enjoyed tales about how Lela had risen from the ocean or formed from mist. Other stories claimed the land had always been there, hidden behind a magical veil. He didn't believe any of those tales, but they never ceased to fascinate him.

Larylis handed him a book. "The map is in this one."

Teryn gathered it up, assessing the worn brown leather cover embossed with a simple gold title that read: *The Once and Former Magic of Ancient Lela*. He flipped open the cover and thumbed past the title page until he spotted the map Larylis had mentioned. It displayed an enormous land labeled *Le'Lana* and was marked by numerous rivers, forests, mountains, lakes, and streams. As interesting as it was to study, it didn't resemble Lela at all.

"Told you," Larylis said with a crooked grin. "Rubbish. I won't be offended if you'd rather not burden your saddlebags with my useless notes."

Teryn handed the book back and traded it for his

brother's notes. "I'll take it. It'll remind me of home while I'm gone."

"You mean, rubbish notes to remind you of our rubbish kingdom that's about to be sunk by pirates?"

Teryn landed a playful punch on his brother's arm. "Exactly."

Larylis laughed but his mirth quickly fell away. "I feel like I should be going with you."

"I feel like you should too, but you heard the princess' terms. She wants her champions working alone. Besides, you're needed here. You'll have to carry the mantle of prince while I'm gone."

Larylis huffed a dark laugh. "You and I both know that isn't true. A bastard cannot be a prince." His expression fell, reminding Teryn of how he'd looked the day of the Beltane festival. That, of course, only served to recall what Larylis had said about having kissed Mareleau. He'd claimed not to have feelings for her, but Teryn couldn't help wondering…

As if Larylis knew exactly who'd sprung to Teryn's mind, he said, "Don't get yourself killed for that thorny harpy, all right?"

Teryn lifted a brow. "You clearly have no faith in my hunting skills."

"Oh, I have faith in your hunting skills," Larylis said as he rose from his seat. "It's sleeping in the dirt for nights on end that will be your downfall."

"Who says I won't be sleeping at an inn every night?" he said in jest.

Larylis squeezed Teryn's shoulder with a mock pout. "Aw, that's adorable. Looks like you'll need my notes after all."

Teryn returned the squeeze and left the library. His conversation with Larylis had momentarily lifted his spirits, but now his stomach was sinking back into its familiar state of dread. There was no denying it any longer.

It was time for the Heart's Hunt to begin.

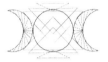

15

Cora dreamed of blood again.

The stench of it was overwhelming, the cloying tang searing her throat. She stood in the doorway of the room with the bed, a tray of tea and cookies in her trembling hands. She already knew something was wrong, for she'd begun following that tug of unease before she'd picked up the serving tray. But seeing all that blood, those sheets soaked with red, the queen lying limp with sightless eyes that stared at nothing...

Cora's scream shattered the air, and the serving tray tumbled to the ground at her feet. Only then did she notice the figure who stood at the side of the bed. Duke Morkai whipped his head toward her, his hair a slash of black tinged the slightest bit blue where it was struck by the lantern light. His face was all hard lines and sharp edges, making him appear both ancient and ageless at once. Like a statue chiseled to capture a famed faerytale hero. Or a villain, perhaps. Her breath caught when she met his eyes. His pupils were black and so large they swallowed the whites that should have framed his irises. He stood with one hand raised several inches above the body of the queen. Specks of blood rose from the sheets toward his palm. As if he were...hiding the blood. Somehow. It made no sense, but one thing was clear.

He'd done this.

Cora bit back a cry and slowly inched away from the door, hardly daring to blink as Morkai pinned her beneath his unsettling stare. Her foot hit a slick spot on the marble floor.

Blood.

No, tea from the broken teapot she'd let clatter to the floor. She staggered to right her balance, and when she next locked eyes with Morkai, his appearance had changed. His eyes were no longer black but an icy pale blue contained to his irises. Blood no longer rose to his palm, and his hand was outstretched as if in plea, not... whatever it was Cora had thought she'd seen a second ago.

"Don't just stand there," he said, waving her inside the room. His voice trembled with distress. "Help the queen!"

Cora shook the conflicting images from her mind and rushed across the threshold. Morkai shifted to the side to let her take his place. She assessed Queen Linette. Blood trailed down the woman's cheeks, her nose, her mouth, soaking the collar of her dressing gown. Nausea churned Cora's gut as she gathered the queen's cold hand in hers. "I don't know—"

"What have you done?" The voice was soft. Anguished.

A glance over her shoulder revealed King Dimetreus

standing in the doorway, eyes wide with terror. Duke Morkai stood just behind him. When had he left the bedside? The duke leaned close to the king and lowered his voice to a whisper. "You recall what she said to the queen earlier."

Cora blanched. She knew what Morkai was referring to, but...but...she hadn't meant it! She'd regretted what she'd said to Queen Linette the moment the words had left her lips. It had been an outburst, not a threat. The words had sprung from the anger of a twelve-year-old girl, nothing more. Besides, what did *that* have to do with *this*?

King Dimetreus' expression turned hard, jaw set as he burned Cora with a glare. "You did this." He stormed over to her, his voice rising to a growl. A yell. "What have you done?"

CORA JOLTED AWAKE, HER SCREAMS CUT OFF BY SOMETHING heavy nudging her shoulder. She scrambled onto her side, blinking into the dark. She expected Maiya's comforting words, the feel of her cot, the walls of her tent. Instead, all around her was dirt and the dying embers of a fire.

Where was she?

Where *was* she?

Time to wake. They move.

The words cut through her panic, helping her swallow down the terror of her dream and recall that she was no longer with the Forest People. She'd been away from them for just over a week. That was how long it had been since she'd last taken her sleeping draught, too. Not that it would have helped.

The heavy thing nudged her shoulder again, and this time she knew what it was. She angled her head and looked up at the white unicorn standing behind her. He pawed the dirt with a hoof.

We follow, the unicorn said.

In the week that she'd been traveling with the creature, she'd become better attuned to his feeling-thoughts. So much so that their communications seemed no different from any other kind of conversation. She still didn't quite understand how it was possible. Was it his magic? Or hers?

"All right," Cora said. Urgency propelled her to her feet. If the hunters were on the move, she and the unicorn had to be quick to follow. Not too quick, of course. Quick enough not to lose their trail but not so fast as to risk crossing paths and getting caught.

The sun was barely beginning to rise by the time Cora and the unicorn started off down the game trail the hunters had been following. She assessed the markings the hunters' feet had left behind. They were perhaps an hour's walk ahead of them. She was pretty sure, at least. She'd learned some tracking with the Forest People, but without much opportunity to practice, her skills were rudimentary. But after a week of following the hunters, she'd begun to understand what it looked like when the tracks they followed were too fresh. That was when the unicorn would get skittish, halting her with warnings of *danger* and *slow down*. Thankfully, his senses were stronger than hers. His scent and hearing far keener.

Or perhaps it was his magic. If that were the case,

Cora wondered why he couldn't simply guide her directly to the next party of hunters that held captive unicorns. Then again, he'd nearly been caught the last time he'd approached one of their camps.

Wouldn't have been close to getting caught, came what she'd come to interpret as the unicorn's voice, *if not for freeing brethren*. A wave of indignation rippled off the creature, echoed by Cora's own. Not only could the unicorn understand her spoken words, but now and then he seemed to pick up on her thoughts too, even with her mental shields in place. Likewise, she was always able to glean his emotions and communications, shields or no.

"Oh, and how many of your brethren did you save before I came along?"

Another ripple of affront. His lack of answer told her his grand total before she'd freed the brown unicorn on his behalf must have been zero.

"By the way, it's rude to read people's minds without permission."

Then stop listening.

Cora cut a glare at the unicorn. "I didn't mean *me*."

He gave no indication that he cared whom she'd meant. With a huff, she returned her attention to the markings on the trail before her. She was relieved there were no tracks of any captive unicorns in tow. Her companion had confirmed as much through his own senses.

They continued at a moderate pace well after midday. Cora saw no signs that they were gaining too closely on their prey. But when the unicorn halted suddenly on the trail, ears twitching back and forth, she knew they had.

They've slowed. Left trail.

It wasn't an unusual course of action for the hunters. While they were clearly following a direct path along the game trail, and their pace suggested expediency, they'd still break to hunt now and then.

Cora pulled up short next to the unicorn, and he led her off the path. They backtracked a good ten minutes and waited. Waited. Waited.

The waiting was Cora's least favorite part. Walking felt productive. Tracking busied both her body and her mind. Whenever they were forced to stop outside of evening rest, however, Cora felt caged. Restless. It made her recall James and the other vile hunters, the blood at Maiya's temple, the arrow piercing Erwin's neck. The latter stirred feelings of equal parts disgust and triumph. It made her want to do more, to hurt the hunters more. Based on their behavior and the two brands she'd spotted, she suspected the entire party was comprised of the worst kinds of criminals. With Erwin dead, there were four left. Four men she held a personal vendetta against. Four men she yearned to put down. She remembered all of their names from that night. James, of course. Gringe, the leader. Velek. Sam. All names that made her blood boil.

She wrapped her fingers around her bow, letting its familiar heft steady her. Ground her. Root her in place. She didn't draw her weapon. Didn't nock an arrow. Instead, she reminded herself why she couldn't make a move on them yet.

She needed them alive. Needed a trail to follow.

The party the hunters joined next had more unicorns. That was the reason she was out here to begin with. Once she found *them*, she could do work that mattered. She wasn't sure exactly how she'd free the captive creatures without getting caught herself, but she knew she'd need to keep her head on her shoulders. Exercise patience. Caution.

It made Cora's muscles twitch with frustration just thinking about it.

"Do you have a name?" Cora asked, keeping her voice low. The question was more to distract herself, but it was something she'd been wondering the past week.

The unicorn rippled with confusion. *You know I am unicorn.*

"Yes, but do you have a name unique only to you? You know...like how I am a human but my name is Cora."

I don't remember. His words were tinged with agitation. She got the distinct feeling he was grasping for an answer to her question...but it was lost to him.

Cora furrowed her brow. Could he be such an ancient creature that he no longer remembered his name? If so, where had he been all this time? "Where are you from?"

A pause. Then, *Forest.*

"What forest? These forests? Have you always lived in Khero?"

Again, she got the sense he was straining to find the answer. It was almost painful for him. *Not these forests. Like here but not here. Close, but not close at all.*

Cora wanted him to elaborate but his feelings of frustration were enough to tell her he likely couldn't. Theories began to buzz through her mind. What if the unicorns hadn't been extinct but in some sort of slumber? What if they'd been...trapped in some way? Of course, if unicorns were returning, then perhaps other fae creatures were too. There could be dragons, pixies, kelpies, selkies—

Only my kind, he said, cutting through her thoughts. *Only my kind are here. No others.* A wave of sorrow seeped from the unicorn, sinking Cora's heart.

"What do you think happened to the others? Better yet, what happened to you? Your kind hasn't been seen in hundreds of years."

He scraped the earth with a hoof. *Don't remember. I try. I try and try, but it's...gone. All I remember is...my forest. Then being here. Hunted.*

"How long have you been here?"

Time feels...not what I remember it feeling. Wasn't here long before I met you.

The unicorn's predicament both saddened and fascinated her. Before her very eyes was a myth come to life. A mystery unraveling. Not even the Forest People knew the creatures had returned.

Well, at least they hadn't before Roije informed the elders. And that was only if they hadn't known all along and kept the intel from the rest of the commune.

Cora's heart clenched with a mixture of anger and longing. She missed Maiya. Salinda. The comfort of her daily routine. She missed what it was like when she hadn't known just how great a danger her presence was. But mingled with those feelings was irritation at the elders' unwillingness to intervene with the plight of the unicorns. She understood why the Forest People refused to involve themselves with royal matters, but surely the capture of fae creatures was worth taking a stand against. If she had the support of the commune—even just a handful of their best trackers and hunters—they could overpower the men she followed, keep one alive for the sake of leading them to the next party, and then attack them too. She could free the unicorns and leave no one alive to tell the tale of the mysterious people who'd interfered—

So violent, the unicorn said with disdain.

Cora pursed her lips. The Forest People would likely feel the same about her bloody fantasy. They were a nonviolent people. Even hunting was done with ritual reverence. No life was taken without need. No tree was felled without blessing the soil it belonged to. No hide was skinned without gratitude for the animal that gave its life to provide food and warmth.

Another reason Cora never truly belonged with the Forest People. When she'd killed Erwin, she hadn't bothered to bless his soul or pray for his family. And she still had no desire to.

You can call me something, the unicorn said. The offer was stiff and begrudging, but it came with something that felt like camaraderie. Perhaps he too understood Cora's pent-up rage.

"You mean I can give you a name?"

Better be good.

"All right." She studied his white fur flecked with silver. His wounds left by Erwin's whip were almost fully healed, and his coat looked twice as lustrous as it had been when they'd first met. He was graceful. Quiet. "How about...Ghost?"

Rather not be named after being dead.

"Fair enough. Snowball?"

He gave a derisive whinny. *I am not a snowball.*

"Mister Cuddles?" Cora smirked.

He sidled away from her, bristling with indignation. *You mock me. I am not to be cuddled. I am strong and fearless. I am brave. Hunters tremble at the pound of my hooves.* It was the most descriptive communication she'd ever felt from him. Which meant she really must have gotten under his skin.

"Fine," she said with a soft chuckle. "Something brave then. Thunder Hoof. Rage Mane. Valorous Maximus."

He radiated with a hint of approval. *I sort of like the last one. Want it simpler though.*

"Valor? No, Valorre."

Those were both the same word.

"There was an extra *R* in that last one. And an *E*. It makes it a proper name."

Why? Your alphabet means nothing to me.

"It just does. Trust me." She was mostly teasing for the sake of entertainment, but she did like the way the name looked in her mind's eye. "Valorre. There you have it."

Fine. The word was curt but she could sense that he liked the name.

She grinned at Valorre and realized it was the first time she'd smiled since leaving the Forest People.

Valorre stiffened.

Cora's momentary mirth drained in an instant as she felt the unicorn's trepidation. "What is it?" she whispered.

The hunters. They do not pause to hunt. They pause to join others.

Fear and anxious excitement clashed in her stomach.

They'd found their prey.

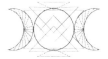

16

Every inch of Teryn's body was sore, but nowhere more so than his ass. When he'd imagined the Heart's Hunt, he'd entertained a multitude of ridiculous notions, but mostly he'd imagined, well... hunting. Stalking prey like he was used to. Moving quietly between the trees in search of mythical creatures. What he had not anticipated was five days of hard riding with only an hour or so of scouting the surrounding woods before making camp. No part of their day contained an element of what Teryn would consider *hunting*.

The first day of the Heart's Hunt had gone as he'd imagined it would. He'd ridden north until evening, met his allies at the inn Helios had specified in his letter, and —surprisingly—wasn't betrayed and left with a dagger in his chest by morning. After that, Helios had set them to riding at a brisk pace north into the Kingdom of Khero, leaving the main road on the third day only to maintain the same pace on the hunting trails through the forests.

Helios clearly had a predetermined destination in mind. One he showed no intention of sharing with his companions.

Teryn's eyes unfocused on the fire blazing at the center of tonight's camp. They were somewhere in northeastern Khero by now, a prospect that didn't sit well with Teryn. Even though he was a prince, it wasn't exactly fine manners to go hunting in another kingdom without permission from its monarch. That was yet another thing Helios claimed to have under control. Yet another secret he kept to himself.

With a grumbling sigh, Teryn leaned his head against the trunk of a tree. One glance at Prince Lex wincing as he shifted in his seat on the ground was evidence that he too found the excessive riding a bit much. Helios was currently nowhere to be seen, having stalked off wordlessly an hour ago.

"My bum has been flayed raw, I just know it," Lex said, adding a wadded-up shirt beneath his bottom, on top of four other articles of clothing and his bedroll.

Teryn let out a halfhearted chuckle. Berol angled her head at Teryn from her perch on his shoulder. His hunting vest was fitted with extra padding on each shoulder for that exact purpose. He reached into his pocket and retrieved a strip of dried venison. After taking a bite for himself, he fed the rest to Berol, who snatched it from his fingers with relish. "Lazy animal," Teryn said with a grin. "You have the entire forest as your personal buffet and yet you still come to me for treats."

"I cannot believe you have a peregrine falcon as a pet," Lex said, eying her from across the fire with a grimace. "Those talons look sharp enough to rip out my throat. And that beak. I've no idea how you can feed her by hand and still have a full set of fingers. Those are your original fingers, right? They aren't constructed of wood by now?"

"You sound like my brother." Teryn huffed a laugh and gave Berol a light scritch on the side of her neck. "She won't hurt me, though. I've had Berol since she was a hatchling. I found her injured while out on a royal hunt. Father almost didn't let me bring her home with us, but he figured it would be a proper lesson in death and the futility of fixing broken things. In the end, it only served to prove the virtues of stubbornness in the face of great odds."

"Cute," Lex said, though his expression said anything but. He shifted on his seat again, then gave up to recline on his side. "Do you think Helios actually has a plan? Or has he dragged us out here to murder us and steal your bride?"

Mention of Helios had Teryn's mood turning sour. He'd given the prince the benefit of the doubt during the week leading up to the Heart's Hunt, hoping he'd eventually share his plan with them. But after more than five full days together, he was coming to regret ever agreeing to their so-called alliance. "I don't know."

"Where is he, anyway?" Lex glanced around the camp, then shifted slightly closer to Teryn. A mischievous glint sparked in his eyes. "Should we leave him?"

"The prospect is tempting but far from rational."

Lex quirked a brow. "Nothing about our situation is rational."

"Valid point."

Lex glanced around the camp again before saying, "Our original terms still stand. You know that, right?"

Teryn was relieved to hear Lex still held a greater allegiance to him than to Helios. Although, he still couldn't figure out how that would do him much good. First, they had to find those damn unicorns. But how were they going to find a single one by riding all day and hunting so little? What was Helios' plan? Gritting his teeth, he reached into his pocket for another strip of venison, but his hand came away with only a crumpled sheet of parchment. It took him a few moments to sift through his cloud of fatigue before realizing he'd reached into the wrong pocket. Berol nipped at the paper, then gave Teryn a look that conveyed her agitation at finding parchment over treats. To further prove the gravity of such an offense, the falcon launched from Teryn's shoulder and landed on a branch in the tree above him, sending a shower of cherry blossoms to rain upon his head.

"It was an accident," he called to Berol, although he couldn't keep the laughter from his voice. He studied the paper again, smoothing out its crinkled folds until he realized what it was—Larylis' list of notes. His lips tilted into a grin as he scanned his brother's scrawled writing.

Unicorns are found deep in the forests. Obviously. Not helpful, thanks.

According to one faerytale, unicorns are drawn to virgins. Weird. Why?

Never mind the last note. I just read another faerytale that contradicts the virgin thing.

Scholars say unicorns have been extinct for over five

hundred years. Why are they back? Where have they been all this time?

Unicorns avoid populated towns and cities. Alright. That might be helpful. Be prepared to spend a lot of time sleeping in the woods, brother.

He felt a pang of homesickness then. Not for the first time, he wished Larylis were with him. Aside from the three years Larylis had lived in Selay, they'd gone on every hunt together. Larylis hadn't enjoyed hunting as much as Teryn did, preferring to admire the flora and fauna, but he had the aptitude to make a clean kill. More so, his company was second to none.

"What's that?" Lex asked, shaking Teryn from his thoughts.

Teryn refolded the paper and returned it to his pocket. "A letter from my brother. He took notes on unicorns for me."

Lex's next question came with a hint of hesitation. "Do you get along with your brother?"

"I do. He's been my best friend my whole life."

"You're lucky," Lex said with a sigh. "I don't get along with mine."

"Why is that?"

Lex's jaw shifted back and forth. When he answered, his words were ground out between his teeth. "Ben is a sniveling little troll who's constantly trying to upstage me. He's three years younger and yet he's the one who secures an engagement alliance first, and to a *proper princess*." He said the last part with clear mocking. "Well, guess what? His *proper princess* still has baby teeth. She won't be old enough to wed for at least a decade. Oh, and then he takes over *my* project to build the stupid wall between Tomas and Norun—" He cut off suddenly, his cheeks having grown red. "Never mind. I hate Ben. Let us not speak of that brat."

Teryn pursed his lips to hide his smile. "Very well."

"What did your much-less-annoying-than-mine brother's notes say?"

"Nothing helpful. Unless, of course, you're a virgin. If you are, we could test a theory and use you as bait. I saw an illustration in a book once. The virgin princess had flowers in her hair. We could weave you a nice crown of cherry blossoms." He gave Lex a teasing grin.

Lex smirked and rolled onto his back. "Your tone suggests you assume I *am* a virgin. So let me enlighten you and say that I am not."

"Really." Teryn couldn't help the note of surprise.

Lex cut him a glare. "I have a lady back home. Is that so hard to believe?"

"Oh, I imagine you're quite the bodice ripper in Tomas."

"*One* bodice. And quite the bodice it is, let me just say."

"Is that so? If you're so taken with her, why are you competing for another woman's hand?"

Lex scoffed. "You and I both know I'm not competing. Besides, participating in the stupid Heart's Hunt was never *my* idea. It was my father's. If you haven't gleaned as much already, my father wants his sons to marry princesses. Well, my lady isn't one. But once I come back with the trade agreement we spoke of, I think Father will finally approve my request to marry."

Teryn considered that. It seemed like a fair plan. Of

course, it all hinged on whether Teryn actually won. "What's her name?"

"Lily," Lex said with a dreamy sigh.

"What's she like?"

Lex waggled his brows. "You recall that water nymph statue? Lily puts her to shame."

"In what way?" Teryn tried to keep a straight face. "Her silent disposition? Her failure to respond to your touch?"

Lex rolled his eyes. "I meant her shapely form."

"Prince Lexington wouldn't know a shapely form if it fell naked onto his lap." The brusque voice silenced Teryn and Lex as Helios stalked into camp. Teryn felt as if the temperature had plummeted with the prince's arrival.

Lex said nothing in reply. It was one thing for Teryn and Lex to tease each other. Their exchange of light-hearted jabs was friendly. But there was nothing light-hearted about the way Helios teased. His every word always held a sinister edge.

Helios took a seat by the fire and set to sharpening a knife. "There are no unicorns here," he said without looking at either of them.

Teryn waited for him to elaborate, but the hope was futile. "What exactly does that mean?"

"It means we ride at dawn. Continue north."

Teryn curled his fingers into fists. It was always the same answer, night after night with nothing else to add. "Helios," he said through his teeth, "tell us the damn plan."

Helios slowly slid his gaze to Teryn. "I'll tell you the plan when I've deemed you worthy of hearing it."

Teryn shot to his feet, chest heaving with rage. "We

are in an alliance. We are not your servants. When we agreed to this arrangement, we conceded to work together. Not for you."

"I'll share my intel on a need-to-know basis."

"No." It took all of Teryn's restraint to speak with control. "You will tell us everything you know. Now."

Helios lifted his brows. "Or what?"

Teryn held his gaze. "Or we'll leave."

"You won't."

"I will. I am tired of being—"

"Tired." Helios scoffed. "Of course you're tired. You're too soft. Almost as soft as Lexington."

Lex sat upright. "How many times have I told you not to call me Lexington?"

"I'll stop calling you Lexington when you stop dressing in silk shirts. We're hunting. Not dancing."

Lex's fingers went to the silk collar of his stained shirt. Over it, he wore a brocade waistcoat that had grown equally filthy in the last week. "I like silk. It feels better on my skin than linen or leather."

"Who cares about Lex's wardrobe," Teryn said before Helios could speak again. "What matters is that this alliance has become a joke, one I'll no longer be on the receiving end of. If you need our help so badly, then tell us what you know."

"Why? So the two of you can cut ties with me and run off to finish the Heart's Hunt on your own?" He huffed a dark laugh. "Do you think I don't know? You've been planning on betraying me from the start. I'll not give you the fuel to light my pyre."

Teryn crossed his arms over his chest and watched Helios through slitted lids. He was only partially right.

While Teryn hoped he and Lex could eventually outmaneuver Helios, he seemed to think they had a solid plan
to do so. "You must give us something," Teryn said,
keeping his tone level. "Give us a reason to trust you and
we'll return the trust in equal measures."

A tic formed at the corners of Helios' jaw, but he said
nothing.

Teryn shook his head at the prince. "Is it all a front
then? Are you keeping silent because in truth you know
nothing? Have you truly seen a unicorn before? Hunted
one? Or did you buy that pretty ridged blade from a toy
shop?" Teryn waved a hand at Lex. "Pack up. Let's go."

Lex's eyes went wide. "Seriously? Oh, thank the seven
gods—"

"Stop." Helios held out a hand toward Lex, stilling
him. Keeping his glower fixed firmly on Teryn, he said,
"I'll tell you some...things. But I will not share all my intel
for obvious reasons."

"Tell us what you can," Teryn said with a shrug. "If we
deem your information worthy, we'll stay."

Helios' jaw continued to tic, his glare darkening with
rage as his knuckles went white around the hilt of the
knife he'd been sharpening. Teryn's fingers flinched, his
hand ready to lunge for his sword—

"Very well," Helios bit out and finally dropped Teryn's
gaze. "I'll answer three questions."

Teryn wanted to argue that three questions wouldn't
suit. They needed to know more. Still, at least it was
something. "Where are we going?" he asked. "And don't
just say north. You have a destination in mind, otherwise
we wouldn't be traveling at such a pace."

Helios glared at the fire as he spoke. "My destination

isn't as clear as you think, but we are heading north, for that is the only place we'll likely find unicorns. I haven't been surprised that we've yet to come across any on our travels, which is why we only hunt briefly before making camp."

"How do you know there are no unicorns south?"

"Because Duke Morkai has hired hunting parties to keep all unicorns contained in a specific area."

Teryn blinked a few times, surprised both by what he said and the fact he'd said it. It was the most detail he'd gotten out of Helios yet. Teryn pondered the information. Duke Morkai was said to be the second most powerful man in Khero, the first being King Dimetreus. While Teryn didn't know the duke personally, he understood that the man had great influence with King Dimetreus. He opened his mouth to ask another question, ask how Helios knew this and what the duke's intentions were, but Teryn was on his third and final question. He'd have to pick something that couldn't be answered by his own reasonable deductions. If he had to guess why the duke was herding the unicorns to a specific area, it would be because he sought to gain a monopoly on them. If unicorns were truly alive and flourishing, it made sense he'd try and capitalize on that. So Teryn chose a different question.

"How did you come by that blade?" Teryn nodded at Helios' hip where the strange dagger was sheathed.

Helios set down his knife and took out the weapon in question. The white blade caught the light of the fire, sending the dagger sparkling. This was only the second time Teryn had seen the dagger, and he wasn't any less awed than he'd been the first time. It served as a reminder of why he'd been immediately convinced of its authenticity. This simply wasn't a normal blade.

"A year ago," Helios said, "my father was gifted a pelt by a hunter claiming it belonged to a unicorn that was found at the southern edge of my kingdom. He claimed he'd tried to gift the horn as well, but it crumbled to ash in his hands when he removed it from the dead creature. Father dismissed the gift as a hoax, but a few months later, our spies learned of rumors about unicorns being spotted in the Kingdom of Vinias. I forged a treaty with the King of Vinias, gaining permission to hunt his lands. The rumors proved true. We caught several of the creatures just north of the border between Vinias and Khero, but like the first hunter had claimed, every attempt at removing the horn rendered it useless. We knew it was possible, for there were unicorn horn items being sold at exorbitant prices by a merchant in eastern Khero. So I sent men to find the merchant, then his supplier, and...*ask nicely* for the information I sought." His lips curled into a smirk as he shifted the dagger this way and that, sending it glittering again. "I took this from the next unicorn I found. It was, unfortunately, the last unicorn I ever saw for Duke Morkai had taken control over the hunt by then."

Teryn stared at the white blade, biting back the flurry of questions that sprang to his lips. He was relieved to finally know *something*, but it still wasn't enough. "I take it you have no intention of telling us how you finally obtained the horn without it turning to ash."

Helios gave Teryn a curt nod. "Right you are. You will know after we find our first unicorn."

Teryn gritted his teeth. "In the meantime, we head

north until we hit this *specific area* and hope we find a unicorn?"

"A unicorn," Helios said, sheathing the white blade, "or one of the hunting parties."

"What exactly does that mean?" Lex's voice held a tentative edge, congruent with the skin prickling at the back of Teryn's neck.

"I've already answered four questions. That's one more than I agreed to. I'll tell you more once we enter unicorn territory."

Teryn bit the inside of his cheek and returned to his seat under the tree. What he really wanted to do was pummel the man until he spilled everything else he knew. He wasn't sure that was a fight he'd win, regardless of whether the pummeling in question was verbal or physical. Helios had kept his promise to answer three questions, and he'd given more information than Teryn had expected. He doubted further threats to abandon their alliance would earn him more answers. And as for a physical confrontation, well, Helios was taller than Teryn, something he could say of very few people. He was bigger too. Broader. Longer reach. Teryn was trained in the art of combat and swordsmanship like any proper prince, but he'd had little practice against someone like Helios.

"Satisfied?" Helios stood and began laying out his bedroll. When Teryn and Lex said nothing, he turned a smug grin on them. "I admit, it would have been precious to see you try and leave this alliance. The two of you make the most pitiful pair. Prince Teryn, you do realize your little friend here was raised on a velvet cushion, right? He probably doesn't know how to lift a sword."

"I know how to lift a sword," Lex said, although his expression suggested he strongly preferred not to.

Helios faced Lex, arms crossed over his chest. "I'd like to see it. Come, Lexington. Show me what you can do."

"For the last time, don't call me Lexington—"

"Enough," Teryn spat through his teeth. "Both of you."

Helios rounded on Teryn, but he froze as Berol glided from the branch to Teryn's shoulder. It seemed Berol was ready to forgive Teryn for the parchment mishap. Helios eyed the falcon, some of the smug confidence draining from his expression. Finally, he said, "Get some sleep. You'll need it." With that, Helios turned his back to them and settled onto his bedroll.

Glaring at Helios' back, Teryn reached into his pocket —the correct one, this time—and pulled out an enormous strip of venison. Berol accepted it as well as a hefty dose of scritches. "Good girl," Teryn whispered. "If he tries anything in the middle of the night, scratch his eyes out."

Berol tilted her head, but Teryn had no doubt the falcon would come to his defense if needed. It almost made him wish Helios would try something. If only Teryn could be so lucky. Instead, Teryn knew that when he awoke, Helios would still have both eyes, and he'd have to face yet another day of nonstop riding. At least this time he knew relatively where they were going—and the reasons behind their destination.

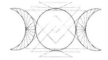

17

Cora waited impatiently for six days. Six days scouting. Waiting. Hiding. Six days watching. Learning. Listening. Six days of being almost close enough to touch the cages that held starving unicorns without being able to lift a finger to help. There were guards on duty night and day. But that didn't mean she did *nothing*. She took everything she'd learned and put her plan into motion.

Tonight, she would do what she came here for.

She'd set the unicorns free.

The sun was beginning to dip toward the horizon by the time she reached the hunters' camp for the second time that day. She'd laid the groundwork for her plan earlier that morning. Now it was time to act. She crept between the trees, her every move silent. Her skirts were tucked between her legs and into her belt to keep them from swishing around her ankles. By now, she'd discovered the quietest route to her destination—and the one that offered the most cover. She'd learned the lay of the camp, got an idea of their guard rotations, their habits. The company was made up of nine men—the four she'd followed plus five who'd already been here when the newcomers arrived. They always left two men to guard the camp while the rest went on their daily hunt from sunrise to sundown. One man guarded the perimeter while the other protected the cages.

Cora heard the footsteps of the perimeter guard drawing near, several paces away. Her pulse kicked up and she whirled behind a tree, pressing in close to its trunk. She knew which path he'd take, knew he rarely left the thin trail he'd worn through the underbrush circling the clearing. Still, it didn't keep her heart from pounding as his footsteps reached the other side of the tree. She held her breath, assessing the crunch of each step, terrified that she'd hear him pause, shift, turn. But he didn't. She released a slow exhale as the man continued past. Only then did she dare open her eyes.

Angling her body around the tree, she stole a glimpse at the guard, a man she'd learned was named Paul. He was middle-aged. Shrewd. As foul a man as the rest of them. Her suspicions had proved correct. Every member of the hunting party—both from the initial group and the one they'd joined—bore the brand of a criminal. There were no marks of simple thieves, drunks, or adulterers. They were murderers, kidnappers, or slavers. Men convicted of violent assault. Paul bore the *M* for murder. Based on what she'd overheard, his victim had been his wife.

She eyed the two flasks he carried on his hip. One was for water, the other for rum. He never drank from anything but those two flasks. However, Cora knew he refilled his rum flask every night from the bottles kept at camp, always taking his fill from the top before the rest of the men started drinking. And drink they did, night after night while she watched from her hiding place. She'd hoped she'd witness them drink themselves into a stupor, become so deeply inebriated that she could sneak into camp, save the unicorns, and leave only a mystery behind for them to wake to. But she'd had no such luck. While some of the men certainly imbibed enough to lose all mental faculties until morning, others observed moderation. That was where Cora would help them along.

She watched the guard until he was out of sight. Thanks to her observations, she knew he'd stop on the eastern edge and stay for the next half hour. Which meant it was time for Cora to move.

She stepped out from behind the tree, doing her best to ignore the hammering of her heart. She shifted her focus to her mental shields, ensuring they were firmly in place. This time, she only strengthened them in one direction—outward—while leaving herself open to receive, to sense, to pick up energies nearby. Her tattooed palms tingled as she drew on the elements, letting them weave around her like a cocoon. She called on air to muffle her footsteps, asked the earth and trees to warp her image as she approached the camp.

That was how she pictured it in her mind, anyway. She'd learned the theory of shielding and had utilized it for the practical purpose of deflecting unwanted outside stimuli. But she'd also heard tales of advanced shielding, of witches who could turn invisible simply by focusing their intent on not being seen, on merging with the elements. Cora had never seen a lick of proof that it was possible. Whenever she'd ask Salinda why there were so many tantalizing tales of magic but very little visible evidence, she'd remind Cora real magic didn't show off with puffs of purple smoke and glitter. If ever a witch used shielding for invisibility—or, more rationally put, to subtly evade notice—Cora wouldn't know. That was the whole point.

Despite having once scoffed at such a concept, Cora was willing to try it now. She was willing to try anything. Because tonight she'd need all the luck and magic she could get.

Cora crept to the western side of camp opposite from where the perimeter guard stood watch. Once there, she paused several feet back from the clearing, assessing it. She caught movement from the interior guard—James. Her fingers curled into fists at the sight of him. It took no small effort to wrench her gaze away and study the cages instead. There were six enclosures in total, all constructed of the same materials as the ones she'd seen at the previous camp—barred iron frames bound together with rope. Four of the cages were occupied, the latest catch having been brought in the day before. That unicorn was stronger than the other three. He was the only one that shifted restlessly in his too-small enclosure. She could feel the unicorn's rage at being contained, his pain whenever his flank made contact with the iron bars.

Cora itched with her desire to barge into camp and cut the unicorns free at once. She knew she could do it. She could catch James by surprise, send an arrow between his eyes, and another to Paul's heart when he came to check on the source of the commotion. Then she could cut the ropes, open the cages, and that would be the end of it.

But that was precisely the problem. It would be the end of all her efforts.

If she killed the guards, leaving clear evidence of her attack, the remaining hunters would increase their numbers, their defenses. She'd likely never get another chance to infiltrate their camp again. Never save another unicorn. Meanwhile, they'd continue the hunt.

No, she needed a strategy. And she had one. It was why she was here. Why she'd spent days spying followed by nights of stealing. She'd taken a pot here. A flask there. Harvested belladonna—a plant famous for its deadly poison. She wouldn't merely kill a couple guards and leave the rest to do the duke's bidding. She'd put an end to the entire operation in a single night. There'd be no one left to hunt unicorns.

Cora's chest carried a leaden weight, one that formed with the understanding that the Forest People would never approve of her using her knowledge of potions this way. But it didn't stop her. In her days spying, she'd only grown to revile the hunters more. If their crime brands weren't already enough—not to mention their braggery over said crimes—she also saw the way they sneered at the unicorns, how they prodded them with iron rods out of sheer entertainment. They didn't feed the fae creatures. Didn't bring them water. It was clear that these men had been selected for a reason. Not because they were skilled hunters, but because they were heartless. Cruel. Men whose only other option was the executioner's block.

If Cora had to lose a piece of her soul to put them down, so be it. She'd do what needed to be done.

Besides, it was too late to turn back now. She'd already slipped into camp that morning and laced the rum with her deadly decoction.

She crept behind the cages to a cluster of pines. There she waited until James paced to the opposite end, chuckled at something Paul said. Then she reached for the bough above her and pulled herself into the tree.

All that was left to do was wait.

Teryn Alante dipped his hands into the rushing waters of the river. The sky was a pink blush overhead, painting the river the colors of sunset. He gathered a handful of cool water and splashed it over his face, scrubbing his stubbled cheeks. Layers of grit and grime were encrusted beneath his palms. He'd need more than a splash of river water to get clean. Still, he doused his face once more, then drenched his hair for good measure.

"What do you think is worse?" Lex asked from farther downstream. Their horses stood between them, drinking their fill after another grueling day of travel. "Riding or Helios' repugnant face?"

"That's a tough choice," Teryn said. He rose from the riverbank and approached Quinne, his golden-brown palfrey. "I might have to choose riding as my least favorite thing right now, considering the repugnant face in question is out of sight for the time being. Which is unfortunate, as I used to love riding. Sorry, old girl." He added the last part for Quinne and patted her neck.

"What do you think is better, then?" Lex asked, "A warm bed or a hot meal?"

Teryn closed his eyes. "Why are you torturing me? Both. Obviously."

"You two are pathetic." Helios appeared behind them, lips curled in a sneer. Just like that, the repugnant face was back.

Lex muttered a string of insults under his breath, then said at proper volume, "I thought you were scouting."

"Unlike you," Helios said, "I don't need all day to make myself useful. Tether your horses. Then follow me."

"Tether your horses then follow me," Lex mimicked in a high-pitched voice. Teryn suppressed a smirk, but Helios gave no indication he'd heard.

"Come on," Teryn said to Lex. "Might as well see what he wants."

They met Helios near a half-visible game trail. Without a word, he led the way through the underbrush until the smaller trail joined a much larger path, this one marked with human and animal footprints alike. A few more minutes down the trail, Helios stopped.

He squatted down and pointed at something in the dirt. "There. This print is larger than the hoof of a normal horse, yet it leaves a lighter indent in the soil." His voice had taken on a reverent tone, one that almost made him not seem like a total ass. "Do you know what this means?"

"Big feet, skinny body." Lex said. "My youngest sister is like that."

Helios turned to them, and Teryn braced himself for the glare that was sure to come. His own lips were laced with venom, ready to intervene should Helios and Lex start verbal sparring like they always did. But when Teryn caught Helios' expression, the other man's eyes were wide, a tight-lipped grin stretched across his face. "It means a unicorn has been here."

That wiped all prior thought from Teryn's mind. "Are you serious?"

"Serious. Certain."

Lex shrank back a little. "You mean a *real* unicorn?"

Helios' expression shuttered, returning his dour countenance. "Why else do you think we're here?"

"What's the plan?" Teryn asked, stealing Helios' attention back to him. "Do you think we can catch it?"

"No." Helios returned his gaze to the hoof print. "This unicorn has already been caught."

"How do you know?"

"See this print next to the unicorn's? It's smaller, probably belongs to a boy. An apprentice, perhaps. These marks are about a week old but consistently show up together. This tells me the creature has been caught and is being towed along behind the main company." He pointed to a cluster of several larger footprints, these ones overlapping. "These belong to the other hunters, also a week old. The prints continue along this trail some ways. I also found fresher tracks about an hour's walk away."

Teryn had to hold his tongue to keep from expressing his shock over the fact that Helios was volunteering useful information for once. The unicorn print must have done a number on his brain.

Helios stood and faced them. "We're going to follow the tracks. The newest ones tell us the hunters have settled into a new base camp by now. The older ones will lead us to it."

"You're so certain," Teryn said, half in awe, half in question.

Helios nodded. "That's how trained unicorn hunters work. Each party is assigned a specific region. They'll hunt a small radius for a few weeks at a time, then move to new grounds once they've cleared an area. We're going to catch up to this party."

Lex grimaced. "Catch up to them and...politely ask to buy their unicorn?"

Helios grinned in a way that was not at all comforting. "Something like that."

Teryn didn't like what Helios was leaving unsaid. He had a feeling there would be no polite anything. Shouldn't that worry him?

His gaze fell on the hoof print. A *unicorn* print. Proof that everything they were doing wasn't crazy. Well, he couldn't say his mission was altogether sane, but for the first time since the Heart's Hunt began, he had hope. And he was determined to do whatever it took to keep that hope alive.

"Come on," Helios said. "We can cover more ground before nightfall."

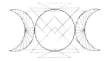

18

Cora maintained her post as the sun set and dusk turned to night. The hunters returned but not a single drink of rum was taken. She watched. Waited. The mood within the camp was strained, the silence palpable. Hardly a word was exchanged as the men sat idly around the fire hour after hour. It was eerie. Enough to make Cora's skin crawl.

Careful, came Valorre's warning. He sounded quieter than normal, but she shouldn't have been able to hear him at all.

What are you doing so close? she sent back, unsure if her words would make it through her dense shields. Not that she'd ever been so lucky to avoid him reading her thoughts before. Still, it was dangerous for Valorre to come anywhere near camp, even after the company had finished their day's hunt. She and Valorre had made great efforts not to leave tracks where the hunters would likely follow. They kept Valorre well outside their scouting radius whenever they could.

Have a bad feeling, was his reply. *Something isn't right.*

A knot formed in her stomach, but she wasn't sure if it was his anxiety or her own. There was definitely something strange happening. If the silence and solemnity hadn't already been enough, the hunters' rigid postures and darting glances were.

A horn sounded in the distance.

Hammond, a man with yet another *R* brand, who Cora had learned was the leader of this crew, rose to his feet. "Harvest," he said. "You know what to do."

Cora's throat went dry as she watched the men leap into action. Most formed a line in the middle of the camp, hands behind their backs, postures stiff, while Gringe retrieved a small chest. Cora leaned forward, bracing herself against the trunk of the tree as he opened it. Through the pine's boughs, she caught a glimpse of what was inside—two thin, white, spiral-ridged bones.

Unicorn horns.

Cora frowned. She hadn't seen these horns before, nor had she witnessed any of the hunters removing a single horn from the unicorns. So far, all they'd done was keep the creatures in iron cages, letting them grow weaker and weaker from lack of food and their close proximity to iron.

Gringe removed the horns from the chest and placed them on the ground. Hammond shot him a pointed look. "Only two? James said you'd caught three in the Ishvonn Woods."

Gringe glared at James, who already stood in the line, then muttered, "James was mistaken."

Hammond huffed a dark laugh. "If Duke Morkai finds

out you left your region while another unicorn was out there—"

"James was mistaken," Gringe repeated, more forcefully this time.

Hammond shook his head and stood at the center of the line, hands behind his back like the rest of the men. Gringe took his place next to him, then barked at James, "Get to the cages."

James' eyes bulged but he made no argument as he unsheathed a knife and approached the cages.

Cora's heart jumped into her throat. She expected him to hack open the nearest cage and slaughter the unicorn or—at best—cut off its horn. But James did no such thing. He simply stood, knife in his trembling hand.

Silence returned for several minutes, broken only by the arrival of Paul. His face was pale. "It's here," he said, then stood at the end of the line.

Anxiety swarmed through Cora. It wasn't just her own. She felt it pouring off the hunters, building and building until it was so strong that her head began to spin. She swayed on the branch and gripped the tree trunk tighter. Then, with a deep breath, she strengthened her shields both ways. The outside emotions fell away, leaving her with the much softer hum of her own worry. A worry that increased with every breath. Especially when she noted what Paul had just said. *It's here.* What did that mean?

Danger. Valorre's warning was laced with panic.

She swayed again. This time, however, it wasn't from an overwhelming surge of emotion. Her lack of foothold was aided by a rumbling in the earth below, one that sent the tree thudding. It was a rhythmic pounding that echoed the riotous pace of her heart.

Run, Cora, Valorre urged. *Run. Beast. Abomination.*

That was when she saw it. A dark form stalked from between the rattling trees a dozen feet away. It was an enormous creature, three times the width of a horse and twice as tall, resembling something between a boar and a wolf. Its head, which seemed too large for its shoulders, had a boar-like snout and tusks, but no visible ears. Its front legs bore hooves while its hind legs ended in enormous paws. It was a hairless thing with raw-looking flesh. Tiny spikes protruded from its body, lining the ridge of its back. It plodded toward the clearing, its immense hooves and paws leaving turned, loose ground in its wake.

Cora was frozen in place, unable to look anywhere but at the creature. She'd seen it before. It used to haunt her nightmares. It still did now and then, lingering just beyond that bloody room, taunting her, clashing in a place between memory and make-believe. In recent years, she'd begun waking before the Beast appeared. It had been her one solace. But seeing it now, outside the realm of slumber...

Run, Cora.

Valorre's words echoed strains of memory, but the voice of the past belonged not to the unicorn. It belonged to her enemy. The man who'd smirked when she was labeled a murderer. A man who'd dragged her to the edge of the woods outside the castle walls, drew blood from her palm, and shoved her out into the night. After that, shadows had come to life, growing paws and hooves and teeth. "Better run," he'd said—

Run, Cora! Get away! Valorre's warning roused her

from the haze of memory, but she still couldn't take her eyes from the creature. It plodded into the camp and went straight for the two horns, consuming them in a single bite. Gringe leapt back but Hammond flung out an arm and forced him to be still. Next, it swung its head toward the cages, where James was slicing loose the bindings with trembling hands.

The Beast let out a roar as he dove for the unicorn in the now-open cage. The creature moved too fast for Cora to realize what was happening. Not until she heard the halfhearted, terrified whinny, then a crunch like bones snapping, teeth gnashing. Saw a slash of blood spray the dirt at James' feet.

That was all it took to send her half falling, half climbing down the tree. She had no awareness of whether she'd been seen, whether her shields were up or down, whether the sounds she heard now were her pounding steps, her racing heart, or the crash of another cage coming open.

She knew nothing. Saw nothing through her tears.

She simply ran.

VALORRE FOUND CORA HOURS LATER. SHE WAS CROUCHED at the base of a birch tree, her shoulders heaving, legs burning from how fast and how far she'd run. He nudged her in the shoulder with his muzzle. When she wouldn't look at him, he blew a warm breath in her face and nudged her cheek. Finally, she glanced up at him with eyes that burned in the wake of her tears.

"They're dead, aren't they? The unicorns?" Her voice

came out small and tremulous. Weak. She hated it. Hated that she'd run.

The three older ones, yes. I no longer feel them near.

Cora's stomach turned as she recalled the sound of bones snapping beneath the Beast's jaws. The sight of blood. She shuddered as the vision played over and over in her mind's eye. Followed by her moment of cowardice.

There was nothing you could have done, Valorre conveyed. His sorrow was equal to her own. She could feel it in her bones.

"I could have tried to shoot it."

And get shot back by the hunters? She felt his emotions ripple with something like a disbelieving scoff.

"I could have done something," she said, but even as the words left her lips, she knew they were folly. She'd done the only thing she could have through the haze of her terror.

The haze of memory.

Valorre studied her. *You know the abomination.*

"I've seen it before. When I was twelve. Although..." She swallowed hard as near-forgotten visions surged through her. It had been the middle of the night after the queen was found dead, and Cora was locked in a dungeon cell. She'd spent all evening crying, shouting at the guards to hear her out, begging them to listen to the truth. She wasn't responsible for killing Queen Linette. Morkai was. She'd seen him standing over her dead body. She'd witnessed him doing...*something* with the blood. Something with his hands. Dark magic. It *had* to be dark magic.

But no one listened. No one came.

Only Morkai.

Cora shuddered and stared down at her palm, trying to see beyond the ink, seeking a thin pink line. A scar. But there wasn't one. There hadn't been when she'd received her first tattoo, and it had made her doubt how much of what she remembered from that night had been a fever dream. But now...

Now she knew better.

It had been real. All of it.

She remembered how the duke had pulled her from the dungeon. Bound her, gagged her, dragged her through the sleeping castle, across the lawn, through a secret gap in the castle wall, and out to the edge of the woods. There they paused in darkness, the moon nothing more than a sliver above them. "I'm doing this for you," he'd said as he cut her bindings. "I could have let you rot in that cell. Remember that. The king would see you dead for what you've done."

She bared her teeth and scrambled back from him. "I did nothing wrong. It was *you*. I know it."

He ignored her. "You murdered Queen Linette."

"You lie."

"You killed Princess Aveline."

She froze in place at the name. "What?"

Before she could say a word more, Morkai seized her hand and ran his knife over the center of her palm. Blood welled in a thin red line. She tried to snatch it away, tried to cover the wound, but he held her hand in place. With his other, he trailed a finger through the air. Ribbons of blood appeared out of nowhere, suspended in midair. With another wave of his finger, her own blood rose to meet it, weaving toward the other threads until they merged as one. It was over as quickly as it had begun.

One moment, it was as if some gruesome tapestry was forming before her eyes, then the next, it fizzled into air.

That was when she heard the pounding. That was when she saw the dark shadow tearing alongside the castle wall as if it had sprung from shadow.

His lips flicked up then, stretching into a malicious grin. "Better run."

Valorre nudged her in the shoulder, forcing her back to the present. She trembled from head to toe. Her eyes fell to her palms where her fingers had curled inward. Half moons from her nails had formed there, threaded through the ink.

"I...I'd convinced myself the Beast hadn't been real," she said. "After the Forest People found me...I didn't know what to think. I knew what I'd seen, but...surely the Beast had been a nightmare." Her dreams had been vivid back then. Constant. Worse than the new ones were. "Have you seen it before tonight?"

No. Never.

"So, you don't know what it is? It isn't a fae creature? A chimera, perhaps?"

His surge of indignation was answer enough. *No fae creature. Nothing like me or my kind.*

Cora frowned. The Beast was unlike anything she'd ever seen before. If it wasn't fae...what was it?

Vile abomination, Valorre said with a derisive snort. Then, after a pause, he asked, *Will you leave now?*

Her eyes shot up to Valorre. "Leave?"

Because of the monster. Will you stop trying to help my brethren?

Cora considered her answer. She still felt shaken from what she'd witnessed, from the memories she'd unearthed. But she remembered what Valorre had said when she'd asked if the Beast had killed the unicorns.

"You said it only took the three older unicorns."

Yes.

"Then one more is still alive. The newest one they captured."

Yes.

It hadn't eaten all of them. Only the oldest, hungriest, most fatigued unicorns. Would the Beast come back for the other once it reached a similar state? If so...why? And how did the duke tie into all of this?

The questions sharpened her mind, sent her fear scurrying. In its wake, she knew her work was not done. Yes, she was terrified to learn that the Beast was real. The thought of ever having to face it again sent her pulse racing. At least next time she'd be prepared.

Next time, she wouldn't run.

She'd shoot.

She'd shoot it again and again until its blood drenched the earth.

"No, Valorre," she said with a sigh. "I'm not going anywhere." She rose to her feet and brushed her hands on her skirts. They'd come untucked sometime between running and sulking by the tree. "Let's make camp by the stream. We can hide our tracks and I can refill my water skin."

Valorre snorted. *You could use a bath too.*

She recognized the teasing in his words, understood his attempt to lighten her mood. It worked. Her lips curled up at the corners. "Fine, a bath too, first thing in the morning. By evening, I'm going back to the camp. Sooner or later, they'll drink that rum."

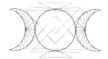

19

The next morning, Teryn Alante gripped his spear in his right hand, relishing its comfort, its familiarity. With his left foot forward, right foot back, he angled his body to the side. In one fluid movement, he raised his spear, rotated his hips, and brought his right arm down in a smooth arc. He released the shaft and sent the spear soaring straight ahead. It landed with a thud in the dirt. He wiped the sweat from his brow and retrieved his weapon, then returned to his previous spot. Set his feet. Angled his body. Threw the spear. Then again. Again.

"Are you going to do that all day?" Lex asked in a bored tone. He sat in the shade at the base of a tree, a novel in hand. The morning sun was warm with only a mild spring breeze to interrupt the heat of its rays.

"Shouldn't you be practicing as well?" Teryn asked, taking aim for another throw. "We're close. You heard Helios this morning."

"Oh, I heard him," Lex said, then returned his attention to his book. "Mostly, I heard when he told us to wait here because we're—what was it he'd said? That's right. *Bumbling idiots who he wouldn't allow to mess things up now that we're close to our prey.*"

Teryn threw his spear with extra gusto this time. It landed several feet farther than the last. Lex was only slightly exaggerating Helios' parting words when he left them after sunrise. Before that, Helios had spent an hour studying the tracks around the clearing they'd bedded down in for the night. He was certain he'd found additional unicorn tracks, no more than a day old, but was befuddled that they only appeared alongside the smaller set of human footprints, separate from the rest of the hunting party's tracks. Helios wouldn't say more than that, only that he'd spend the day scouting, convinced they were closing in on the hunters' location. That was when he'd told Teryn and Lex to stay put and added some insult over their intelligence and capabilities. It had taken much restraint on Teryn's part not to throw his spear into the other man's back as he walked away. Which was why he'd decided to funnel all that pent-up aggression into throwing practice. Spear was his weapon of choice for hunting. If Helios' observations were correct, he'd have reason to put it to use very soon.

Teryn retrieved his weapon, then stood before Lex. "You do plan on actually helping me, don't you?"

Lex looked up from his novel. "I am helping."

"Are you, though?"

"I already told you I don't hunt."

"Have you any skill with weapons?"

Lex put a hand to his chest, affronted. "Are you questioning my integrity now too?"

Teryn shrugged. "Just curious how much of this alliance benefits me at all."

Lex turned a page in his book. "You'll get your beloved princess."

His stomach turned at the word *beloved*. Planting his spear tip in the dirt, he slouched to the side and propped an arm on the end of the shaft. "Oh? And how do you suggest we do that? So far, our plan is to return with a tie."

"Don't know," Lex said absently. "Maybe we can slit Helios' throat in his sleep."

"Are you offering to do the throat slitting?"

Lex quirked a brow. "Of course not. I'm skilled with a sword, not a dagger. Besides, I'm not going to war with Norun. My kingdom has been avoiding that for a decade."

Teryn frowned. He remembered when the Kingdom of Norun conquered Haldor and Sparda, two smaller kingdoms that had been south of Norun's borders. The other Risan kingdoms, including Teryn's own, feared Norun would seek to conquer other neighboring lands. Thankfully, the conquest never went any further. Menah had the benefit of having two other kingdoms standing between them and Norun. Lex's kingdom, however, shared a border. "Don't you have a wall?"

Lex shifted awkwardly in his seat as if the question annoyed him. "Yes, we have a wall. Don't you have traps to check?"

Teryn held up his palms. "I didn't realize a wall was such a touchy subject." Even as he said it, though, he remembered Lex's rant about his brother stealing the wall-building project from him.

"Yes, well, I'm starving. I get cranky when I haven't eaten."

"You know, you could check the traps yourself."

He turned another page in his book. "And get blood on my shirt? No, thank you."

Teryn rolled his eyes, but there was only amusement in the gesture. Lex was probably the least helpful ally he could ever want, but he was entertaining in his own way. Best of all, he wasn't Helios.

"What are you reading, anyway?"

Lex glanced at the cover. "Some naughty romance. It's about an earl who falls for his sister's lady's maid."

Teryn's grin split his face. "You read naughty romance?" He wasn't even sure Larylis read such fare, and he tended to devour almost anything of the written word.

Lex lifted a shoulder. "I do now. Stole it from the library at Verlot before I left."

"You stole that. From Verlot Palace."

"Figured I'd want some reading material for the journey."

"You do realize you're a prince, right? You could walk into any bookstore and probably take any book for free."

Lex continued as if he hadn't heard a word Teryn said. "I didn't realize it was the naughty variety, but I daresay, I'm finding it rather informative." He waggled his brows at that.

Teryn shook his head with a chuckle. Then, spear in hand, he left the small clearing and entered the cover of trees. He peered overhead for any sign of Berol, but the falcon was nowhere to be seen. She'd left to hunt half an hour ago. Which was what Teryn now set out to do himself. Well, perhaps not hunt, but fetch lunch just the same. He'd set a few traps nearby for small game and one in a stream for fish. Unfortunately, the first three traps proved empty. Damn. That left the fish trap. He shifted course to the east where he'd found the stream earlier that morning. Walking along the bank, he sought signs of where he'd left the trap. He remembered a boulder that reached about waist high. And a cherry tree standing just above it, pink blossoms clinging to its boughs. It was rare to find trees with that many blossoms still intact this late in the spring, but there was one hardy variety—the Rosa Solara—that carried pink petals almost until summer. That should make it easy to find. Sure enough, a hint of pink caught his eye upstream. He took a step—

And froze.

A flash of movement snagged his attention. He turned, seeking what had fled the opposite side of the stream. There was nothing there, just ripples amongst the rushing current. He held still for several moments, keeping his breaths slow and steady. When he witnessed no further signs of movement, he continued along the bank, slower this time. He kept a more mindful grip on his spear, used his front foot to test the ground ahead before fully taking a step. Teryn should have been doing so all along. Regardless of whether his traps proved successful, any found prey would do for lunch.

The foliage grew denser around the stream the closer he came to the tree. He navigated around it with silent steps, creeping up a slight hill until he found a slim trail that led back to the stream. As he drew close to the cherry tree, it became clear it was not the one he'd been looking for. There was no boulder. No trap. Still, there was something in the music of his surroundings that kept him moving forward. A light cadence punctuated by birdsong. It was the sound of hooves. A deer, perhaps. Too graceful to be a boar. His mouth watered at the thought of venison. He'd fed the rest of the dried strips of meat to Berol last night.

He held his breath and waited for the sound again.

There.

It was coming from near the stream behind the densest patch of foliage. With slow, careful steps, he moved forward, softly prodding the earth with his lead foot to avoid snapping twigs or kicking loose stones. The hoofbeats grew clearer, approaching the stream from the opposite side of the brush. Then it stopped, replaced with a gentle splash. Then another. The creature was likely drinking from the stream. Teryn edged closer and closer until he was finally able to glance around the edge of the brush to the rushing waters on the other side. His breath caught as his eyes took in the animal facing away from him. But it wasn't a deer at all. It was…a horse. An enormous white stallion with hooves the size of—

His foot shifted, caught on a loose rock. He regained purchase, but the sound had already caught the creature's attention. It stopped drinking at once and swiveled its head toward Teryn.

He blinked several times, certain his eyes were deceiving him. Perhaps it was hunger. But no matter how he tried to battle both reason and visual evidence, there was no denying the white horn protruding from the horse's head.

It wasn't a horse after all.

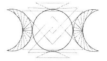

20

Teryn swallowed hard, feeling as if his throat had turned to sand. His heart hammered against his ribs like it would break free from his chest at any moment. He didn't dare blink. Didn't dare move a muscle as he waited for the unicorn to dart away.

It didn't.

It simply stared back at him, its russet eyes penetrating, probing. That was when Teryn remembered the spear in his hand. And the reason he held it.

Not the reason he'd come to the stream, but what had prompted his practice earlier that morning.

This enormous, impossible creature was the very reason Teryn was in these woods. *This* was his prey.

Sweat slicked his palms. His forearms felt stiff, as if they were rebelling against the command Teryn was trying to give. *Lift. Throw. Kill.* That was what he'd come here to do. With one throw, straight to the lungs or heart, he could win two of Mareleau's prizes. The horn. The pelt. After that, only one live unicorn to serve as the princess' pet would stand between him and victory. He tried to feel emboldened by the thought, but his stomach only clenched tighter. Revulsion crawled up his spine, prickling his skin like tiny knives. He'd hunted before. He was no stranger to killing an animal. But, for some reason, this felt different. Wrong.

Damn it, he cursed silently to himself. *You must do this. You cannot fail now, you sorry fool. Lift. Throw. Kill. Done.*

Steadying his nerves, he took three deep breaths, then slowly angled his body to the side. He paused, waiting to see if the movement would set the creature fleeing. Instead, it took another step closer. There was something defiant in its posture now, the way it lowered its head, the way its lips began to lift from its teeth. Teryn saw its horn in a different light. This wasn't simply a pretty faerytale decoration. It was a razor-sharp weapon. If Teryn missed, he'd be on the receiving end of that horn. Feeling a greater sense of urgency, Teryn lifted the spear. The unicorn stepped forward again, lips flapping with angry breaths. Teryn's muscles tensed. Sweat dripped down his forehead and into his eyes. Another wave of revulsion swept over him, sending his stomach churning. He knew what needed to be done but his body wouldn't respond. Nor would his heart.

Throw, damn it! Throw!

He lowered his arm the briefest increment, not toward the creature but...down.

A sharp pain seared the side of his neck. He flinched back and slapped his palm to the sting. The unicorn hadn't moved, hadn't charged, and yet something wet and warm dripped down Teryn's neck. From the corner of his eye, he could see an arrow protruding from the cherry tree a few yards behind him. Someone had shot at him. Before he could fully register what that meant, he felt the cold tip of a blade press against the underside of his jaw. Without moving, he glanced to the side, but only caught sight of an arm.

"Who are you?" The voice was quavering with rage, and...feminine.

Teryn slowly opened his palm, letting his spear drop at his feet. Then, raising both hands, he carefully shifted to face his opponent. His eyes widened as his gaze took in a petite young woman dressed in a linen shift and unlaced bodice, her skirt tucked between her legs and into a leather belt to form something like pants. She had a quiver of arrows at her back and a bow slung over one shoulder. Her hair was sodden, trailing rivulets down her tan arms—arms that bore black ink from palm to inner elbow.

"Got your fill or would you like to paint my portrait too?" She tapped the underside of his chin with her blade, forcing his gaze back to her face. Her cheeks were tinged pink as if his assessment had embarrassed her. Or enraged her, more like. She scowled. There was something familiar about her dark eyes, but he couldn't place why. Perhaps it was just that she was so unexpectedly stunning. In a wild and terrifying sort of way. Like a wildfire. He had no doubt she was equally as dangerous. "I said who are you?"

"You don't know me?" Too late, he realized the folly of his question. While he expected his face to be well known in his own kingdom, this was Khero. Besides, he didn't quite exude royalty in his current state.

She lifted her chin. "Why should I?"

He assessed her again, studying her grip on the dagger. Her height. Her reach. She was shorter than him by at least a foot. Even though she appeared comfortable enough wielding a blade, his reach was far greater.

She stepped in closer, angling the blade so its edge kissed the skin at the base of his throat. "Answer my question. Who are you?"

"My name is Teryn Alante," he said, keeping his voice level.

She gave no indication she recognized his name. "You hunt unicorns."

He hesitated before answering, which earned him a sharp bite from the dagger's edge. "Yes."

Her eyes roved the side of his neck, then inspected his hunting vest, as if she were searching for...something. Her expression flickered with confusion before she steeled it behind an icy mask. "Who do you work for?"

Teryn frowned. "No one."

"Who sent you to hunt unicorns, then?"

"A spoiled harpy named Princess Mareleau. Do you know her?"

Another flash of confusion crossed the girl's face. Her grip on the dagger slackened, and he took the opportunity to launch a step back. Before she could react, he struck her wrist and twisted it, forcing her to drop the blade. She unsheathed a smaller knife from her belt and slashed out at him. Her blade sliced his forearm, but he closed in on her anyway. Taking her free hand, he twisted her arm at an angle, wrenching it behind her back and spinning her around until she faced away from him. He tugged her arm close to his chest while she continued to try and slash him with her knife.

"Will you stop trying to stab me?" he growled. As she suddenly froze against him, he realized how close his lips were to her ear. He angled his face away from her, caught off guard by that realization.

"No," she said with a grunt and slammed her heel into his instep. He winced but didn't release her. She tried to stomp on him again, but he widened his stance and hooked a foot around her ankle. Her balance gave way, and he assisted her fall to the ground. He pinned her knife hand overhead to keep the weapon's tip from his face.

"Mind telling me why you're accosting a prince?" he said through his teeth as he finally pried the knife from her fingers and tossed it a few feet away.

"Like I care about pretty princes." She lifted her head and slammed it into his nose.

"Seven devils," he cursed, feeling blood streaming over his lips. He sprang back, hand to his nose. She brought the heel of her palm to his sternum and sent him falling on his back. He rolled onto his side, felt his hand come around the shaft of his spear. Rising to his feet, he swept his weapon out in an arc, then lifted it in preparation to throw. His eyes were glazed from the pain of his probably broken nose. It took a moment for his vision to clear. When it did, he found the woman several paces away, bow drawn, arrow nocked.

Their eyes locked, weapons still. Her chest heaved above her bodice while his rose and fell beneath his vest. "I'm not trying to hurt you," he bit out.

"Perhaps not, but you tried to kill my friend."

"Friend?" Realization dawned as he remembered what had happened before the woman had attacked him.

"Wait, the unicorn? That's your...friend?" He saw no sign of it now, nor had he any time during their fight.

"How many unicorns have you killed?" she asked.

"None."

"But you were going to kill Valorre."

Valorre. Was that its name? Was this unicorn not a wild creature but a...pet? Teryn recalled Helios' bewilderment over the tracks they'd found. They'd appeared alongside a small set of footprints—this woman's footprints. Not a boy's.

Teryn's spear arm was starting to ache from holding his position. He needed to de-escalate this situation. Quickly. Gritting his teeth, he said, "I'm sorry I tried to kill your friend."

"Sorry isn't enough. Give me one reason why I shouldn't shoot you where you stand."

"If you missed the part where I said I was a prince, then you may not have noticed the spear aimed at your heart either. So allow me to point it out."

"I can shoot faster than you can throw."

"Want to test that theory? Even if your arrow struck true, you'd have the entire Kingdom of Menah hunting you down in recompense."

"Only if you lived to tell about it."

"And only if you survived a spear wound to your most vital organ."

She narrowed her eyes. "Lower your weapon and I'll lower mine."

"Not a chance," Teryn said. "I'll stop waltzing when you stop leading. Lower your bow."

"Count of three, and we both lower our weapons. One. Two. Three."

Neither of them moved.

She released a frustrated groan. "I'll lower my bow if you promise me this. Never come near a unicorn again. If you do, I will kill you. I will not spare your life twice, prince or no."

Teryn almost opened his mouth to make that promise and mean it with his whole heart. He remembered how he'd stood frozen when finally faced with killing his prey. Every inch of his body had rebelled at doing what needed to be done. It was a worrying prospect, but one he didn't have time to address right now. All that mattered was getting on his attacker's better side. "I promise," he said. The words sent something like relief through his body, even as his mind screamed that the vow was a lie. He still had to win the Heart's Hunt.

She kept her arrow trained on him for several more breaths, then finally let it down. Teryn did the same. Neither severed their gaze.

"I'm going to fetch my things now," she said, tilting her head toward the weapons that littered the ground between them.

"Go ahead," Teryn said. They watched each other warily as she stomped over to her dagger, then her knife, sheathing them before striding to the cherry tree. She tugged her arrow from its trunk. Teryn's hand went reflexively to his neck where the blood was already beginning to dry. Had she shot an inch to the left, he might have been dead. "Nice aim," he said.

She tucked the arrow into her quiver and burned him with a glare. "I missed."

His lips curled into a smirk as he watched her walk away. Only when she was out of sight did he let himself skulk over to the tree and lean against its trunk, catching his breath while he pondered the notion that he just escaped death at the hands of a rather frightening girl. He brought a palm to his chest, finding the front of his shirt wet. It must have gotten damp from her sodden hair when he'd pulled her against him. Proof that he hadn't just hallucinated the strange confrontation.

He flinched as one of the boughs trembled overhead. "Berol," he said with a relieved sigh. "You chose the absolute least helpful time to show up. I could have used you a minute ago."

The falcon quirked her head from the branch above.

"You're right. I look a mess." He wiped the skin beneath his nose, finding sticky blood on the back of his palm. With a groan, he pushed off from the tree and headed back the way he'd come from. Berol launched off the tree and landed on his shoulder. He sighed. "Let's hope we don't run into her ever again."

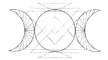

21

Cora stood in shadow, eyes trained on the man. Fury roared through her blood as she watched him recover from their fight. Part of her wanted to take aim from between the trees and shoot him down before he even knew her arrow was coming. Instead, she remained motionless, silent, waiting until he left the cherry tree—strangely, with a falcon on his shoulder—before she dared leave her hiding place. Once the man was out of sight, she retrieved her cloak from where she'd left it before she'd sprung her attack, and stormed off into the woods. She made it only a few steps before Valorre appeared before her.

"What were you thinking, Valorre?" She halted before him with her hands on her hips. "You should have run before he spotted you. That's what I did. The first time, at least." She'd been in the middle of bathing in the stream when she'd seen the man stalk down the opposite bank. As soon as he'd passed her, she'd scrambled out of the stream and donned her clothing as fast as she could. By the time she was dressed and had located Valorre, the man was about to make his kill.

I would have ended his life. You should have seen how he trembled before my might. His spear was not iron. It would have merely tickled.

She rolled her eyes and started off again. Valorre kept pace at her side. She glanced at him a few times, eyes falling on his flank where he'd been struck by Erwin's whip. The wounds had healed but it didn't stop her from remembering how his skin had split beneath the iron barbs. Her heart sank as she reached out to touch his soft hide. "You're made of flesh like anything else. You may be particularly sensitive to pure iron, but steel can wound just as deep."

I will not cower before a boy.

Cora wanted to argue that he was far from a boy. He may not have been like the men from the duke's hunting parties, but he was tall. Broad. Strong. *Very* strong. The way he'd whirled her around, pulling her against his chest when he'd tried to disarm her. The way he'd pinned her on her back and wrenched the knife from her fingers. Angry heat crawled up her cheeks at the memory. She shook her head and shifted her attention to the name he'd given.

Teryn Alante.

She hadn't realized it then, but she knew that name. Remembered hearing it when she was a child. Teryn Alante was the Crown Prince of Menah. What was he doing out here? He'd admitted to hunting unicorns but also insisted he hadn't killed one. She'd opened her senses to him then, felt the truth of his statement, mingling with conflict over what he'd almost done to Valorre. Then there was that odd bit he'd said about having been sent by Princess Mareleau. He had to have meant Mareleau Harvallis, Princess of Selay. Another name she recalled.

If you're so worried, then you should have killed him instead of letting him go.

Cora cut him a glare, but she had no argument to give. She wasn't entirely sure why she'd let him go. They'd been evenly matched once they'd faced off with spear and bow, but she could have shot him after. He was a unicorn hunter, and that made him her enemy. Sure, he was a prince, and killing him would make her an enemy to his kingdom. But she could have fled the scene and left no one the wiser to what she'd done.

Still, she couldn't fight the feeling that settled in her chest, one that told her that—despite all evidence to the contrary—he didn't deserve to die.

"I miss when I only understood you in one-to-two-word spurts," she muttered.

Valorre rippled with something like laughter. *The boy agitates you. Or interests you.*

"You're the only one agitating me. Next time you come across a human holding a weapon of any kind, you run. Understand? Otherwise, you can rescue your brethren on your own if you're so tough."

Valorre's emotions contracted with something Cora couldn't read. Then he conveyed, *You care.*

Her irritation softened. She reached for Valorre again, stroked his white fur. "Yes, Valorre, I care. You're my... friend." That was what she'd called him when she'd confronted the prince.

Friend. He seemed to take the word and roll it around in his mind before saying it again. *Friend.*

"Friends keep each other safe, no matter how tough the other thinks they are. So no more unnecessary heroics, all right? Save that for our rescue mission."

All right.

Cora's lips curled into a small smile. It had everything to do with Valorre and nothing—*absolutely nothing*—to do with stray thoughts of the aggravating prince she'd met at knifepoint.

TERYN, LEX, AND HELIOS RODE ALL AFTERNOON. BY THE time they slowed their pace, night had fallen. The sky was dark, the forest quiet. The only sounds were swooping bats and the pound of their horses' hooves. Teryn glanced up at the canopy of trees, trying to spot Berol flying overhead. If Teryn had to guess, the falcon was certainly making a meal out of the buffet of bats currently on display.

Helios made a clicking sound with his tongue, and his horse slowed to a stop. Teryn and Lex halted behind him as well. They'd left the main trail some time ago, and their current path was narrow, allowing only enough room to ride single file. Helios dismounted and crouched in front of his horse. He studied the path for a few silent moments, then snapped his fingers at Lex. "Lamp."

Lex stared at him. "Seriously?"

"Lamp," he said again, with more force this time.

With a grumble, Lex dismounted and retrieved the oil

lamp from Helios' saddle. Handing it to him, he said, "You could have done that yourself."

Helios took it from him wordlessly and continued his study, seeking signs of the hunters they'd been tracking all evening. Teryn had insisted hours ago that they make camp for the night, but Helios refused, stating he had a plan. Like usual, Teryn and Lex were not let in on what exactly this plan entailed. Teryn had only been back at camp for an hour after his encounter with the unicorn girl when Helios returned from scouting. After relentless teasing over Teryn's bloodied state—which Helios attributed to the hare Teryn had been in the process of skinning—Helios ordered them to mount and ride. He'd found the camp. "They have a unicorn," he'd said, revealing some of the excitement Teryn had glimpsed when he'd shown them the first hoof print. He'd also mumbled something about another set of prints. Prints that made no sense because—again—they did not follow the others. He'd trailed these strange tracks. Lost them in a stream.

Teryn had nearly spoken the truth then, almost told him what had happened, why he'd had to set his nose and clean wounds on his neck and forearm.

But he hadn't.

Instead, he'd kept quiet. Not even Lex knew the truth.

Now he smirked at Helios' back. It felt good to know something Helios didn't.

After studying the trail a few minutes longer, Helios gestured for Teryn to dismount as well. As soon as Teryn left the saddle, a dark shape swooped down from the trees, startling the horses. Teryn's horse calmed first, as it was only Berol, coming to perch on Teryn's saddle horn.

Quinne was used to the falcon, but that didn't mean the palfrey was immune to being startled by Berol from time to time.

"That thing is terrifying," Lex said, hand clutched to his chest.

"You mean adorable." Teryn reached up to stroke the falcon's feathers. Berol nipped affectionately at his fingers, then set to preening.

"Both of you shut up," Helios muttered.

Lex made a face behind Helios' back.

They continued on foot at a moderate pace, punctuated by Helios' observations. Finally, he seemed to find what he'd been looking for. "Stop here." Helios began to rummage around in one of his saddlebags. As he withdrew his hand from the bag, he held a piece of parchment in his fist.

"Mind telling us what that is?"

Helios faced Teryn and Lex with a smug grin. "We're going to have dinner with friends."

THE SOUND OF VOICES FELL UPON TERYN'S EARS. THAT WAS the second clue that told him they were nearing their target. The first had been a plume of smoke wafting over the trees—a campfire. He tightened his grip on his horse's reins as he walked her through the underbrush, his muscles tensing with every step. Helios seemed fully confident in the plan he'd concocted, but Teryn wasn't so sure. Helios had told them to follow his lead. Act cordial. Don't gawk at any captive unicorns as if they'd never seen one before. When Teryn had pressed him to elaborate,

Helios said only, "We dine. We sleep. Then in the morning, we take what we came for."

Lex seemed even less comfortable with what they were about to do. Time and again he tried to catch Teryn's eye with a pointed look, as if he hoped he'd intervene. But Teryn wouldn't. He only had a small notion of what it would take to steal the captive unicorn, and he assumed it meant parting camp as friends and returning as foes, perhaps while most of the hunters were off on their hunt. There was no honor in such a ploy, and the prospect made his skin crawl. Still, he wouldn't stop it. Not when he was so close to getting what he needed to save his kingdom from ruin.

Soon the light of the campfire shone through the trees. The conversation coming from inside the clearing was louder now. But as they closed the distance, the talk cut off. Their approach had been noted.

"Seven gods," came Lex's panicked voice.

Helios shot him a glare. "Act natural."

"This is me being natural," Lex whispered back, but he said not a word more as they continued forth.

Teryn's pulse raced as they approached the clearing. Helios halted just outside the perimeter, hands raised. Teryn and Lex pulled up short in turn. Four of the eight men inside the camp already had weapons drawn. Even the unarmed hunters demonstrated threat in their stiff postures, their hands fisted at their sides. Hostile didn't even begin to describe their expressions. It was enough to distract Teryn from the row of cages at the far end—and the gray unicorn inside one of them.

Helios flicked his wrist, a motion that was followed by every set of eyes, but all he held was the piece of parchment he'd taken from his saddlebag. "Easy," Helios said. "We're brothers."

The man at the center of camp, one holding a crossbow, nodded at the figure next to him. The second man approached Helios, sword in one hand, and took the paper with the other. He scanned it before returning it to Helios. Teryn caught sight of a brief letter bearing a seal etched with a crescent moon—an unfamiliar sigil. The hunter stepped back but his posture remained stiff. "Whose company?"

"Drass," Helios said with ease.

"Drass," the man echoed. "He still out in the Dorvish Pass?"

"The Cambron Pass."

The man eyed Helios through slitted lids. "What are you doing out here, then?"

Helios nodded his head back toward Teryn and Lex. "Our contract is up. We were heading to Brocken Village to refill supplies for our trip home when we were waylaid by bandits." Teryn was surprised not only by how well Helios could lie, but by the subtle shift in his tone. It was brimming with camaraderie, devoid of his usual smug brusqueness. Instead, it held a rough edge that masked any hint of royal flair.

The hunter's eyes roved from Helios to Lex, then landed on Teryn, gaze falling on his bruised nose. "Bandits, eh?" He then dragged his eyes over their horses, pausing when he caught sight of Berol, still perched on Teryn's saddle. The falcon stared back at the man just as intently, shifting her stance as if to draw attention to her sharp talons. The man's knuckles went white on the hilt of his sword, and he returned his attention to Helios.

"Aye," Helios said. "They provided us a good chase before we buried their sorry bones. Still, it took us far off course. We saw your fire and hoped for company and a meal to share."

"I'm surprised you deigned to dine with us at all. Drass and his merry band of mercenaries tend to think themselves above our ilk."

"I don't see why. We all work for the same man, don't we?"

The hunter assessed Helios one more time, then looked over his shoulder to exchange a glance with the man holding the crossbow. Teryn held his breath as the camp fell under a tense silence. He sure as hell hoped Helios knew what he was doing. His lies sounded believable to Teryn's ears, but still...

Finally, the hunter lowered his crossbow with a nod. "We'll share a meal."

The other man sheathed his sword and stepped to the side. "Brothers," he said with a nod. Teryn didn't know if he'd imagined the mocking lilt to the man's voice, but he returned the greeting just the same.

"I don't like this," Lex whispered to Teryn as they followed Helios the rest of the way into the clearing.

Teryn ignored him but he couldn't agree more. He could almost feel the dark glares burning into his back as they tethered their horses. He could hear suspicion pitched into every whisper as they approached the campfire. No, they weren't amongst brothers at all, and Teryn wondered if the hunters felt the same. If so, they might as well have stumbled into a nest of vipers.

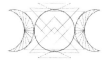

22

Teryn barely tasted his meal as he ate. Every bite of pheasant settled like ash in his stomach. But he kept on eating. Kept filling his mouth with one slow bite after the next if only to keep from having to talk. Thankfully, Helios took the brunt of that burden, joking with the men and regaling them with hunting tales so convincing, Teryn entertained the possibility that this had been his true identity all along. Whenever a question was directed at Teryn, he kept his answers brief. And when the same happened to Lex, particularly when he was caught staring at the caged unicorn, Helios interjected before he could speak. "This one's mute."

One of the hunters, a man Teryn had learned was named Sam, began to gesture with his hands.

"And dumb," Helios added. "Hunting's the only thing he's keen at."

Lex started to scowl but seemed to think the better of it, adopting a vacant expression instead. Teryn could see evidence of his indignation in the red flush that crawled up his neck.

After dinner, the mood became far more relaxed. Helios' act was so convincing that the man who'd held the crossbow—Hammond—insisted they stay the night. After that, bottles of rum were passed around, and the mood relaxed even further. Lex retired to his bedroll early, stomping the whole way there. Berol too abandoned Teryn, fleeing the incessant chatter and taking a perch in one of the trees. Meanwhile, Teryn remained at the campfire. Listening. Watching. He studied the men, their behavior, their words, trying to glean as much information as he could. He knew better than to rely on Helios alone. The hunters were all in various states of dress, most down to their tunics. Others wore heavily armed bandoliers while a few remained bundled in greatcoats. He caught sight of a sigil on their coat sleeves—a black crescent moon on an indigo background—the same sigil that was on the paper Helios had. He wondered if it belonged to Duke Morkai, the man Helios had mentioned as having a monopoly on the unicorn hunt.

As the night wore on, it was safe to say the men were the most unpleasant company he'd ever kept. Not in their treatment of him, but in the hard looks in their eyes, the sharpness of their words, their unsavory topics of conversation. Blood. Violence. Their treatment of women. It only served to further unsettle the meal in his stomach.

Teryn accepted the rum whenever it passed his way but he did all his drinking in act, determined to keep his focus sharp. Though, time and again, his attention slid to the caged creature. There were six cages in total, but only one was occupied. The unicorn inside was nothing like the enormous white one Teryn had confronted that morning. This one seemed weak, wobbling on its legs. His chest felt tight as he watched it, unable to tear his eyes away—

"I know that look." Teryn startled as the youngest man of the party, James, sat next to him. "That's envy, isn't it? I take it you didn't have the best luck during your contract."

Teryn grunted his response. He was going for a Helios-like persona. Man of few words. Gruff. It was a bit nauseating impersonating a man he so disliked, but if that was what it took to keep a low profile, he'd do it.

James handed him a bottle, and Teryn accepted it. The liquid brushed his closed lips before he handed it back. "Shame," James said. "You should've been out here last year. There were unicorns everywhere. We'd spend a month in one place and catch dozens. Now, we barely last three weeks before deeming an area overhunted. We had only five horns for harvest last night. *Five.* Can you believe that?"

Teryn gave him a sympathetic look as if he understood the struggle keenly, but his mind snagged on the word *harvest*.

"Only three were live kills because the others had been taken manually and *that one* isn't ready yet." He nodded at the caged unicorn. "Although I hope he makes it long enough for the next harvest. I hate doing it manually, you know?" He glanced at Teryn, a meaningful look in his eyes, but Teryn couldn't fathom what he was trying to convey. Part of him wanted to remain silent, but the other half felt as if he were on the brink of something important.

Infusing his tone with an air of bored disbelief, he asked, "You hate doing it manually?"

James shrank down as if embarrassed. "Yes, don't you? The way they...you know. And the noises they make." He paled and took a deep drink from the bottle.

Teryn lifted a shoulder as if the matter was no bother to him. Inside, he was bothered indeed. What noises? What was he referring to? Was it...removing the unicorn horns? Helios had mentioned a special method but had yet to elaborate.

"I'm always the one holding them down," James said, lowering his voice. "Never the one wielding the knife. I think holding the knife would offer a...I don't know. A distraction."

"A distraction?" Teryn echoed.

"Not like the monster is any better. At least then all I have to do is cut open the cages and try not to get blood on my boots."

A chill ran down Teryn's spine, one that sent his heart thudding. It took all his control to keep his composure. "The monster."

James took a deep drink of rum and handed the bottle to Teryn. Keeping his eyes fixed on the other man, Teryn pretended to drink again. James' eyes went unfocused. "I saw it today," he said, voice barely above a whisper. "No one believes me, but I did. I was checking traps when it plodded by. You know what that means, right?" James leaned in close. "It's claiming our prey outside of the harvest. Which is unfair. If we don't collect, we don't get paid."

Teryn made an indignant noise, nodding along.

James went on. "And if it can do that...why are we

even here? Why are we starving these creatures to an inch of their lives if the monster can run amok as it pleases, gobbling up the freshest fare?" He took another long pull of rum, anger written in the set of his jaw. His eyes had become glossy with drink, his pupils so wide they nearly filled the rim of his irises. He ran a hand through his hair which revealed a mark on his neck, just under his ear. It was a brand. An *R*.

Teryn didn't think his blood could go any colder. His kingdom didn't brand their criminals but he knew Khero did. He also knew what that *R* likely stood for. Add to that the way James talked about unicorns—starving them, harvesting them for some monster, holding them down, wielding a knife...

He didn't see the full picture James was painting, but the edges were becoming clear.

Teryn looked across the fire to where Helios was chatting amiably with a hunter named Gringe—the one who had questioned them when they first arrived. Helios caught his stare and narrowed his eyes. He grinned then, and there was something sinister in the curve of his lips. In the way he held Teryn's gaze without falter as he continued to chat. It was a dare of sorts. A silent confession. Teryn's fingers curled into fists, his eyes narrowing right back. He understood then that Helios knew exactly what James had been referring to, whether he'd heard their conversation or not. Helios knew whatever the harvest was, what the monster was, and what it took to manually remove a unicorn's horn.

Teryn suspected Helios had kept the information to himself less out of a need for control and more because—

had he told Teryn the truth—perhaps he never would have come.

CORA'S ANGER REACHED NEW BOUNDS AS SHE WATCHED THE prince mingle with the men he'd sworn he didn't belong to. When she'd confronted him, she'd asked who he worked for. He'd said no one. She'd reached out to him with her senses, felt nothing to suggest he'd been lying. Clearly he had.

She glared at him from her hiding place in her tree, smirking as she watched him press the poisoned bottle to his lips. He'd get his due soon enough.

She'd been waiting in her tree since before dusk, hoping tonight her plan would finally come to fruition. Her relief had been palpable when the hunters were back to their crass, rowdy selves upon returning from the day's hunt. That meant tonight the Beast would not come. However, she nearly gasped out loud when she saw Prince Teryn Alante enter the clearing, his companion bearing a writ marked with Duke Morkai's sigil. Was Teryn Alante even the man's real name? Had he lied about being a prince too? She supposed it didn't matter now. He'd sealed his fate when he drank the rum.

Her heart clenched at the thought. But why? Why did she recoil at the idea of him dying by her clandestine machinations? He may not have borne a brand like the other hunters, but was he any different on the inside? She could admit, he didn't look altogether comfortable. She only wished she could hear what he and James were whispering about. The other men were too loud, too boisterous.

The branch shuddered above her. At first, all she saw was shadow, but her breath caught as she made out the shape of a falcon amongst the pine boughs, its condemning eyes locked on her.

What do you want? she tried to convey, but this animal wasn't like Valorre. It couldn't understand her. Still, she was pretty sure she could understand *it*. The falcon curled her talons around the branch, inched down its length until she was a foot over Cora's head. A silent threat. Cora held her gaze, daring her to try anything. The bird may have had talons, but Cora was armed too. Her bow wouldn't serve her at this range, but her knife or dagger could. Even so, she had no desire to fight off a falcon at all.

"It's too late," she whispered. "I'm sorry." She doubted the bird could understand her, even when speaking out loud. The falcon made no further move. Instead, she turned her head, nestling down as if preparing to nap.

A thud struck the earth at the base of the tree. She startled, as did the bird. But as she peered into the dark, she saw it was Paul, who'd once again been on perimeter duty. Now he lay facedown in the dirt, his flask in his hand.

She didn't need to open her senses to know he was dead. Cold sweat pricked her neck as she stared down at the body. She'd done that. Her hand had brewed the decoction, poisoned the liquor. Her actions and intentions had snuffed out life in an instant.

Killing Erwin was one thing. He'd directly threatened her, attacked Valorre.

But Paul...

He's no better than Erwin, she reminded herself. Perhaps he had no personal qualms with Cora, directed no immediate threat her way. But he was not only a convicted murderer but a willing participant in the hunt. He'd captured fae creatures, trapped them with iron, denied them food and water. He'd stood by while the Beast devoured the unicorns.

Her guilt faded into a cold and deadly calm.

Setting her jaw, she returned her gaze to the camp and waited for the next body to fall.

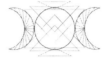

23

Teryn watched James die. He hadn't realized that was what had happened, at first. When James had begun to slump to the side in the middle of his story—something Teryn was grateful for, considering the repulsive subject matter the man favored—it seemed James had just fallen asleep. It wasn't until another man toppled over. Then another. Teryn glanced at James with renewed interest, saw the blue tinge to his lips, his open eyes that stared sightlessly ahead.

With a jolt, Teryn rose to his feet, just as two more men fell. The camp burst into fits of commotion as the remaining men ran to their comrades, checking their pulses, shouting panicked orders at each other.

Teryn's eyes darted around, then landed on Helios. Suspicion crawled up his spine. Helios, however, looked just as perplexed as Teryn. Heavy brow furrowed, Helios stood frozen as another man collapsed, fingers clawing at his throat as his face turned blue.

"What the hell is going on?" came Lex's voice as he

sprang up from his bedroll. His question went unanswered.

Only three of the hunters remained breathing. Gringe, Hammond, and a man named Sam. Gringe and Sam were distracted by their fallen brethren, but Hammond was backing away from the fire. Toward his crossbow.

Teryn palmed the hilt of his belted dagger, edging slowly toward his horse, where he'd left his shortsword and spear with his saddlebags. Lex simply stared at the horror unfolding around them, muttering curses under his breath.

One step. Two steps. The next brought him to his horse—

Hammond cocked his crossbow, loaded a bolt, and aimed at Lex. He swayed slightly on his feet before planting his legs firmly beneath him. "I thought you were supposed to be mute, boy."

Lex's hand flew to his hip, but he too had come to the campfire unarmed. Hammond squeezed the trigger on his crossbow, but Teryn already had his spear in hand. Hammond swayed again, and his bolt missed Lex by a foot. Teryn's spear, on the other hand, did not miss. It struck the center of Hammond's gut. The man looked down, staggering once more. Gringe and Sam whirled away from their companions. Gringe's sword was drawn, while Sam unsheathed his dagger. Unlike Hammond, neither man seemed affected by whatever had felled their friends.

Helios already had his sword drawn by the time Gringe rounded on him. "Did you poison our meal?" Gringe said as steel met steel. "Or our rum?"

"Neither," Helios said through his teeth as he parried Gringe's attack.

That was all Teryn could witness before Sam sprang at him. Teryn didn't have time to reach for his sword or his spare spear, so his dagger would have to do. Sam was a grizzled man, older than Teryn by at least twenty years, and his stout stature put his reach at a disadvantage to Teryn. But his confident composure was that of a man who had no doubts about who would come out the victor. Teryn dodged a lunge aimed at his stomach, then another angled toward his side. He sidestepped, turned, brought his blade beneath Sam's ribs. The other man blocked him, slicing Teryn's inner elbow. Teryn staggered back, his fingers flying open from around the hilt. Sam lunged for his throat, but Teryn dove to the ground, fighting through the pain in his arm as his hand closed around the hilt of his dagger again. Blood slicked his palm, but he blocked Sam's thrust. With a kick to the gut, Teryn sent him back a few steps. Sam staggered for only a moment before he closed in again. Teryn blinked sweat from his eyes, felt a wave of dizziness rush over him. Was it blood loss, or...

He knew the truth then. It had been the rum. Every man had shared the meal, but not everyone had drunk the rum. Not Helios. Not Lex. He hadn't realized it then, but he'd never witnessed Sam or Gringe accept the bottles either. But Teryn...

He'd let the liquor touch his lips when he'd feigned drinking. Lips that he'd surely moistened at some point during the fight. It wasn't enough to knock him off his feet, but dread filled his bones. He tried to clear the terror from his mind and parry Sam's attack—

The attack didn't come. Sam halted a foot away. Teryn shuttered his eyes, trying to figure out what had happened. In a matter of seconds, a spurt of red caught his attention, trickling down Sam's neck to stain his tunic. That was when Teryn saw the steel tip protruding from his throat. Lex withdrew his sword and they both watched Sam fall to the earth, clutching his throat until he died in a pool of his blood.

"Seven gods," Lex said, voice panicked. His sword fell to his feet. "I...I killed a man. I've...I've never killed a man."

Teryn met Lex's haunted gaze, realizing he could say the same for himself. He glanced beyond Lex at the carnage littering the camp. At Hammond, dead with Teryn's spear protruding from his gut. At the men lying lifeless around the fire. Finally, his eyes settled on Helios, who simply stood with his arms crossed, a smug smirk on his face. Gringe lay motionless against a tree, his tunic punctured with several wounds.

"Turns out Lex is the better man with the blade after all," Helios said, tone mocking. "He just saved your pathetic life."

Teryn stormed over to him. "While you just watched."

Helios shrugged. "I was curious."

Fire raged through Teryn's blood. "You did this. You poisoned them, didn't you?"

"No," Helios said, "but it certainly benefited us, didn't it?" Without another word, he stalked over to the caged unicorn. A dead man was slumped before it, and Helios kicked him to the side. The unicorn trembled within the cage, lips peeling back from his teeth as Helios brought his dagger—the one carved from horn—to the ropes binding the frame.

His conversation with James swarmed his mind, and he recalled the suspicions he'd had right before James fell. Teryn wiped his bloodied hand on his pants and strode over to Hammond. After prying the spear from the man's gut, he raised it. "Stop."

Helios glanced over his shoulder, but only let out a dark chuckle. "You wouldn't dare, princeling. Trust me, you need me for this next part."

"Tell me everything about this *next part* or I will throw this spear. If not to kill, then to maim your leg. You're not keeping any information from me for a second longer."

Finally, Helios stopped cutting the ropes and turned to face Teryn. He spun the unicorn horn blade in his palm, unfazed by Teryn's threats. "I respect your initiative," he said, though his expression revealed anything but respect. "What would you like to know?"

"Tell me what you're planning on doing to that unicorn."

His answer came out smooth. "I'm going to remove its horn."

"*How* are you going to remove its horn?"

"The only way that allows it to remain intact and not turn to dust."

Teryn narrowed his eyes, which earned him a dark chuckle from Helios.

"Very well," Helios said. "Try not to piss yourself. In order to remove a unicorn's horn, one must carve it from the creature's skull while it's still alive."

Bile rose in Teryn's throat, the image James had begun to paint now made fully clear. "And the pelt?"

"As much as possible should be removed while the unicorn breathes, although not all can survive the skinning. Unlike the horn, the pelt won't dissolve if the creature dies. Instead, it loses its texture and sheen. Any part removed while it's alive is worth a pretty fortune."

Another wave of dizziness struck him, but this time he wasn't sure if it was Helios' words or the poisoned rum. He planted his feet, forced himself to keep his spear arm steady. "What of the monster?"

Helios scoffed. "What monster?"

Teryn studied his face, seeking signs that he was lying. "You don't know about the monster?"

Shaking his head, he returned to face the cage.

Teryn took another step forward before Helios could resume cutting the bindings. "Stop, Helios."

"No."

"We aren't taking that unicorn's horn. Or its pelt."

Helios let out an irritated groan and turned back around. He wagged his dagger at Teryn. "This is why I didn't tell you. I knew you'd be too soft."

"We'll take this unicorn as the princess' pet."

"No, we won't. That's only one of the three gifts. We cannot return without all three, or else our plan will mean nothing. Three gifts. Three champions. Equal effort to meet Mareleau's demands in the cleverest, most efficient way. Do you want a chance to marry the princess or not? Is your kingdom not worth one animal's life?"

Teryn felt his resolve weaken. He glanced at the caged unicorn, saw fear in his eyes, hunger in his gaunt form, pain where open wounds marred his hide.

"That's all it will take," Helios said, a placating quality to his voice. "One unicorn, and we'll have the hide and the horn. After that, finding the pet will be easy. We can kill this one before we take its hide, if that is your wish. The horn, however...you know what must be done."

Teryn thought about his father, his kingdom, his duties as heir. The promises he'd made. His heart ached to spare the unicorn, but when had following one's heart ever served the greater good? His father had followed his heart and nearly brought war to the shores of Menah. Mareleau was supposedly following her heart by seeking a better match than Teryn, but her Hunt had now resulted in a massacre. Teryn's duty was to his kingdom. Mareleau may have had no qualms with breaking their contract, but he'd promised to marry her. Promised his father he'd do what needed to be done to secure her hand.

And if it meant killing one unicorn...

He glanced at the creature again and felt his stomach drop. Grief tugged at his bones, dragged his heart over brambles and thorns. The words left his mouth before he realized what he was saying. But they were true. "It's not worth it. It was *never* worth it." If his promised bride was so heartless as to make such a violent request in exchange for her hand, then he wanted nothing to do with her. She'd broken her promise. Teryn would break his too.

Helios' shoulders tensed. "So, you forfeit."

Teryn swallowed hard, his throat dry. "I suppose I do."

"And you, Lexington?"

No answer came.

Teryn cast a quick glance at Lex and found him still standing over Sam's body, his face pale.

Helios moved, bringing Teryn's attention back to him.

He now held his sword in addition to the dagger. Teryn prepared to throw his spear, but Helios was quickly closing in. Instead, he held the spear out before him. If he couldn't throw it, he'd fight with it. Helios continued his charge but was suddenly stopped by a flurry of feathers and talons. Berol scratched at his face, forcing Helios to shield his eyes. The falcon raked her talons through the man's forearm, sending his sword clattering to the ground. Helios slashed out blindly with the dagger.

Teryn's heart pounded as he watched Berol carve gouges in the man's flesh. He was torn between aiding Berol's efforts with a spear to the gut, or calling the bird back. Before he could consider what to do, he swayed on his feet. *The poison*, he thought with terror. He swayed again, legs trembling. Berol suddenly took off, heading straight for Teryn. He expected her to land on his shoulder, but the falcon only flapped her wings in his face, forcing Teryn back. Back. Back.

"What are you—"

His words dissolved under the sound of trembling earth. Something enormous barreled past Teryn, directly over the place he'd just stood. He heard Lex cry out, turned to find him curled on his side, cradling his arm. When he looked back at whatever had invaded the camp, he realized *this* was the monster. There was no other name for it. It looked as if two creatures had merged into one, born from flame, its skin raw and red. A ridge of spikes ran down its spine. Teryn scrambled back, but the monster paid him no heed. Its beady eyes were fixed on Helios. In the next moment, it was upon him. The creature opened its giant, salivating maw and closed it over Helios' head and shoulders. Teryn couldn't blink as

Helios' muffled screams pierced the air. Blood poured over the monster's lips and dripped to the ground below. Helios clawed, stabbed, but the monster continued to bury its teeth deeper into his flesh. The unicorn horn blade fell to the ground, and Helios' body went still. The monster released him, but Teryn knew he was already gone. He held his breath as the creature ran its nose over the earth, as if seeking something. It inched closer and closer to Helios' discarded blade.

A crash sounded. Teryn's eyes flew to the cage where the unicorn was bucking madly.

With a roar, the monster charged the cage, slamming it with its enormous front hooves. The iron bars dented but didn't break. Still, the monster relentlessly struck the cage again and again.

Suddenly, the monster reared back with a roar. An arrow pierced its neck, and Teryn saw another had already gouged its eye. A figure emerged from the trees, bow raised, arrow nocked. The girl from the stream shot the monster again, blinding its other eye. The creature roared and wailed, trampling the lifeless bodies strewn about camp as it tried to shake the arrows free. The woman shot it again, directly between the eyes. Teryn expected the monster to falter, to slow, but it didn't. Instead, it tore away from its attacker, crashing against tree trunks as it fled into the night.

Teryn's chest heaved as he struggled to catch his breath. His body trembled from head to toe. Something brushed against his temple. Berol. She nipped at him as if to test that he was unharmed. "I'm fine," he muttered, voice strained. He wasn't sure when the falcon had landed on his shoulder. He'd been too distracted by the monster.

His eyes drifted to Helios' maimed body, the blood all around him, the battered earth left in the monster's wake. Movement drew his gaze, reminding him the threat wasn't over.

The woman stormed over to him, an arrow aimed at his heart. "Why aren't you dead?"

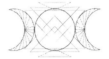

24

Cora tried to keep her bow steady as she confronted the prince, but her body was racked with tremors. It had been one thing to watch her carefully laid plans end in a bloodbath as Gringe, Hammond, and Sam turned on the prince and his friends. She'd waited in her tree for the fight to end, knowing she'd have to take down the victor. She hadn't expected Teryn Alante to battle his friend over the fate of the unicorn, nor had she anticipated the Beast. As soon as it had threatened the unicorn, she had no choice but to act. Now it was gone, but she didn't know for how long. Her arrows left it wounded. Would that be enough?

Teryn stared at her, his spear still clutched in his hand, forearm stained with blood beneath an open wound at his inner elbow. His falcon watched her with unblinking eyes, daring her to make a single move that would harm the bird's master. Or was the prince—like Cora was to Valorre—the falcon's *friend*?

Teryn's eyes narrowed. "You're the one who poisoned the rum."

"And you drank it. So why aren't you dead?"

She expected terror from him. Or rage. Anything but the weary answer he gave. "I didn't drink. It only touched my lips." He gulped. "Will I die?"

She released a sigh and let down her bow halfway. "No, but do you recall the promise you made?"

He squeezed his eyes shut and rubbed his brow. "That I wouldn't come near another unicorn."

"Or else I'd kill you," she finished for him.

His eyes were unfocused when he opened them. "It seems today is a day for breaking several promises."

She huffed a laugh. "Do you expect me to break mine?"

"I...I didn't know."

"Didn't know what?"

His gaze sharpened and slid to the unicorn. "I didn't know what it took to remove a unicorn's horn."

Cora felt the blood leave her face. Before she'd witnessed Prince Teryn's fight with the man he'd called Helios, she hadn't known either. She'd assumed the horn had to be severed, not...cut from the unicorn while it was still alive. Did Valorre know?

Teryn met her eyes. "I'll never do that," he said, tone laced with conviction. "I'll never take a unicorn's horn."

She considered his words, opened her senses to try and feel if he was lying. Not that she trusted her observations. "You lied when you said you worked for no one."

"I didn't lie."

"I saw the writ your friend had."

Teryn glanced at the dead man, then winced, as if

he'd forgotten the carnage. He shook his head. "I don't know what that was, but I can only guess it was a forgery. Why would we work for anyone? I'm the Crown Prince of Menah. Helios was the Prince of Norun. Prince Lex—"

Teryn stiffened. His spear slid from his hand as he whirled around. The motion sent the falcon launching off his shoulder to land in a nearby branch. Cora drew her arrow, following Teryn's every move as he crouched down beside a man Cora hadn't realized was alive until now. "Lex!"

Cora hesitated, watching the two, before letting down her bow.

The man named Lex lay on his side, his arm pressed to his chest. Blood stained his silk shirt, marring the gold brocade of his frayed waistcoat. "What the bloody hell, what the bloody hell..." Lex repeated over and over. Finally, he met Teryn's gaze. "What the bloody hell was that thing?"

"The Beast," Cora said.

Teryn glanced over his shoulder at her. "You know what it was?"

She nodded. "It...works with the hunters. They feed the unicorns to it."

"Why did it..." His voice trailed off as his eyes landed on the body of his dead companion. "Why did it attack Helios? It barely spared me a glance, but it went straight for him."

"I don't know." With slow steps, she approached the body. A few feet away, she found a discarded dagger. Gingerly, she picked it up, noting its white spiral blade. All at once, she sensed a dense, murky energy that buzzed against her palms, burning the ink there. The feeling was so strong, her lungs began to contract. Dropping the blade, she launched a step back.

Hide that, Valorre said. Cora startled at his sudden appearance behind one of the trees outside the camp. There he remained, not daring to take a step within the clearing. *Sheathe it. Cover the blade. The abomination is drawn to our horns.*

Her heart slammed against her ribs. She glanced at the waning campfire. *I could feed it to the flames*, she said in her mind.

It will not burn.

She considered simply leaving it where it lay or burying it in the ground. But the idea that someone else could find it, wield it...

Worse, she imagined the Beast returning, unearthing it, devouring it. She wasn't sure why the Beast was drawn to horns, why the hunters fed it starving unicorns. But there had to be a reason. Whatever it was, Cora needed to do whatever it took to keep the Beast from consuming another horn.

Without a second thought, she reached for the white-bladed dagger again and dropped it into her quiver. As soon as it struck the bottom, she felt its dark energy recede. Relief flooded through her. Now she just had to hope that her inability to sense the horn anymore meant the Beast couldn't either.

She returned her attention to the two men—only to find Teryn removing his shirt. Momentarily shocked by the unexpected sight, she could do nothing but stare at the flex of his shoulder muscles as he drew his tunic over his head and immediately set to tearing it into strips. He tied the first one around the cut on his arm, then crouched by Lex and began to dress his friend's wound.

We must go, Valorre said.

Cora shook her head to clear it and tore her gaze from the two princes. She knew Valorre was right. It was madness to linger. The Beast could be back at any moment. There was but one thing left to do.

She jogged over to the unicorn's cage. The creature within trembled as she brought her knife to the ropes and severed the bindings. The front of the cage fell open, but the unicorn did not move. "Go," Cora said, voice soft. "You're free."

A sharp sound pierced the quiet of the camp. Cora startled at the noise, as did the unicorn. In a flash, it darted out of the camp in a blur of gray. She whirled around, finding Teryn behind her, hands pressed together. That was when she understood the sound had been a clap.

Cora glared at him, keeping her eyes anywhere but below his chin. He'd donned his hunting vest again, but he'd only secured the bottommost closures. Which meant he might as well still be topless. "You didn't have to scare it like that."

He lifted a shoulder in a fatigued shrug. "Perhaps fear will keep it well out of the monster's range." With that, he turned away from her and strode back to his friend.

She watched him walk away, her argument dying on her tongue. As much as she didn't want to admit it, he was right. The unicorn needed to get far away from here, no matter what. And so did she. Casting a final glare at his back, she made her way to Valorre. He remained in shadow at the edge of the clearing.

The stout one is badly wounded, Valorre said.

Cora followed Valorre's line of vision and saw Teryn and Lex walking toward three tethered horses. She noted the way Lex continued to cradle his arm to his chest. "Why should I care? Let's go." She skirted around him but Valorre remained rooted in place.

The tall one tried to save my brethren from the dead man. He radiated with something like awe. Gratitude.

"Weren't you the one telling me I should have killed him at the stream?"

Maybe I was wrong, he said with a touch of indignation. *Maybe he and I both were.*

Cora bit the inside of her cheek, urgency propelling her to leave the men behind. She owed them nothing. If anything, they owed her for warding off the Beast.

Valorre scraped the earth with a hoof.

"Fine," Cora said between her teeth. She crossed the camp, trying to ignore the dead bodies she stepped over, and approached Teryn and Lex. Teryn was trying to aid his friend into his horse's saddle, but Lex kept losing his balance. "Let me see the wound."

Teryn whirled around, brows knitted. "Excuse me?"

She ignored Teryn, addressing Lex directly. "Your arm. Show me."

He eyed her from head to toe. "Like I'd trust you. Did you not just poison an entire camp?"

"They were bad men," she said, swallowing down the guilt that crept up from her heart. "Did you not see the brands on their necks? Besides, I had to stop them from hurting more unicorns. This was the only way I could do so on my own."

Lex scoffed but said nothing more.

"Show me your arm." When he still refused to move, she added, "You'll have a much easier time riding if you don't bleed to death."

"I wrapped it well," Teryn said.

She turned her scowl to him. "You bandaged his wound with your filthy shirt. Did it never cross your mind to use a clean one?"

"Did it ever cross yours that perhaps we don't have any? We've been traveling for—"

"Then I assume you were planning to eventually stop, boil fresh strips of cloth, disinfect the wound, and pack it with a poultice. And that's only if he doesn't also need sutures."

Teryn said nothing, only held her gaze, jaw set. Finally, he relented. "Just let her see it."

Lex eyed her through slitted lids several moments before he too seemed to relent. With a roll of his eyes, Lex extended his arm. Cora stepped close and knew at once it was bad. The bandages were already soaked through over what appeared to be three gouges. She opened her senses to him and discovered just how much pain he was hiding. His arm radiated with the severity of his wound. She could *feel* it darkening her senses, could almost see it in her mind's eye as she took his arm with gentle fingers. Peeling back a corner of the bandage, she caught a glimpse at part of the wound. It only confirmed what she'd already felt. "Is that from..."

"The monster kicked me out of the way with its hind leg," Lex said stiffly.

Again, Cora debated turning her back and leaving them to their own fates, but she could feel Valorre's reproach from here. When did he get so softhearted? She let go of Lex's hand and released a sigh. "The wound needs sutures and a poultice. Come." She turned and waved for the men to follow. "Gather your horses. I'll help you."

"I don't want your help." Lex's tone was laced with venom.

Cora threw a look over her shoulder. "Do either of you know how to stitch a wound? Disinfect it? Do you know which herbs will relieve pain and calm inflammation? Which ones will stave off infection?"

Teryn and Lex exchanged a glance. Of course they didn't. According to Teryn, both men were princes. Royals had no need to learn first aid. The Forest People, however, were well versed in healing, even those whose Art didn't specialize in the craft.

"Have you any particular fondness for that arm?" she asked.

Lex huffed. "Of course I do. What kind of question—"

"Unless you want it amputated after infection sets in, come with me." She left the camp and didn't wait to see if they'd follow.

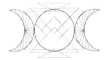

25

"I'm not drinking that," Lex said, scowling at the clay cup Cora handed him.

Teryn watched their icy standoff with a mixture of amusement and trepidation. They were seated around a modest fire in the middle of a secluded clearing by a stream. He was pretty sure it was the same stream he'd met the woman at the day before, and—from the way Cora brought out cups, flasks, and pots from behind a bush—he assumed it was where she'd made camp for the last several days. They'd trusted her enough to follow her away from the scene of the bloodbath and obeyed her instructions to start a fire, boil water, and soak fresh strips of linen torn from yet another of Teryn's shirts. She'd told them her name, briefly introduced them to her unicorn companion —much to Lex's awe and incomprehensible stammering— but that was to the extent that they knew her. Well, that and the fact that she'd poisoned nearly an entire hunting party. Teryn couldn't blame Lex for his trepidation.

"It will help calm your nerves and ease your pain," Cora said.

"Yes, being dead certainly puts an end to nerves and pain. No, thank you."

Cora rolled her eyes. "It's not poison. It's tea. Lavender, chamomile, and willow bark."

Lex gave Teryn a pointed look, drawing Cora's attention to him as well.

Teryn sighed. "Surely you understand why we wouldn't want to drink anything you offer."

She pursed her lips and held his gaze. He only shrugged. "Fine," she said, setting down the cup and taking Lex's arm. "Suffer through the pain if that is your wish."

Lex blanched a little but made no further argument.

"Are the bandages dry yet?" she asked Teryn.

He ran his fingers over a corner of one of the strips of cloth she'd asked him to dry by the fire. "Yes."

"Bring them here."

"You make demands like a queen," he muttered as he gathered the cloth and brought it to her.

"No," she said as she began untying the blood-soaked bandages from Lex's arm, "just someone who has no reason to help you but is anyway."

The unicorn named Valorre tossed his mane. The creature had maintained his distance from Teryn and Lex, keeping to the opposite side of camp. Even so, Teryn caught the unicorn watching him from time to time, likely holding a grudge over the spear incident. Berol, meanwhile, took up post as far from the unicorn as she could get. Every so often, she'd shift in the branch overhead as if to remind both Cora and Valorre that she was watching.

Cora paused her ministrations and looked at Valorre. Then, resuming her removal of the bandages, she said, "Why should I be nice? I don't see you being warm and cuddly."

Teryn frowned, eyes darting between the girl and the unicorn. "Did you just...talk to Valorre?"

Her face went slack with surprise. Perhaps she hadn't realized she'd spoken out loud. She quickly covered the expression with a look of nonchalance. "Don't you talk to your feathered companion? What's her name? Barrel?"

"Berol," Teryn corrected. "Like the—"

Her gaze darted to him. "Like Berolla, the fae queen's legendary dragon."

Teryn was surprised she knew. Faerytales were common enough, but he'd only heard about this one from Larylis. When he'd first found the falcon as a hatchling, he knew she needed a fierce name. Part of him thought it would improve her chances of survival. So when Larylis shared the tale of Berolla—the dragon who once ruled the skies in the days of the Elvyn and Faeryn —he knew it was the perfect namesake.

Cora averted her gaze and steeled her expression, as if she regretted showing interest in their conversation. She finished unwrapping the bandages and reached for a flask.

"What's in that—" Before Lex could finish, Cora poured it over the wound. The smell of strong spirits wafted into the air. Rum. Teryn could only hope it bore no poison.

He watched as she cleaned Lex's wound and began to

stitch it closed with a needle and thread she'd taken from one of the pouches on her belt. When Lex began whimpering, she wordlessly handed him the mug of tea. This time, he accepted it. Her every move was steady and methodical as she continued her work. She'd clearly done this before. After the final stitch was made, she spread a mushy paste over Lex's arm, its odor pungent.

Lex wrinkled his nose. "This is disgusting. What is it?"

"Herbs," Cora said, then held out her palm to Teryn.

He stood at her side and handed her the cloth. By the time she was done wrapping his arm, Lex looked as pale as a ghost. His throat bobbed as he cradled his arm against his chest. "Do you have more tea?"

Cora didn't hide her smirk as she poured him another mug.

Teryn expected Lex to thank her as he accepted the offering, but instead he said, "You must be a witch."

Cora simply stared back at him.

Teryn stiffened. "Oh," he said, looking at her in a new light. "You are a witch." It made sense now. Her knowledge of healing and poison. The fact that she lived in the woods. Except... "I didn't know witches were real."

She faced him with a quirked brow. "I didn't know idiot princes were real, and yet here you both are."

Teryn bristled. "What did we ever do to you?"

"Do you honestly have to ask?" She stood and planted her hands on her hips. "You tried to kill Valorre—"

"Yes, remind me why the two of you seem to know each other," Lex interjected.

"—then you lied to me about who you work for—"

"I told you," Teryn said, "I didn't lie."

"—then you lied to me when you promised never to come near a unicorn again."

She had a point about that last part. "I'm...I'm sorry about that. About all of it. It was important that I try..." He ran a hand over his face, his fatigue bone deep. "I'd *thought* it was important to complete our mission. I'd thought..." He shook his head and returned to his seat on the other side of the fire.

Her brow furrowed as she studied him, her head cocked slightly to the side. After a few moments of silence, her shoulders fell, as if she too were overcome by the same exhaustion Teryn felt. She returned to sitting. "Tell me the truth then. Tell me why you came to hunt unicorns."

"Or else..." He expected a threat. Why else should he tell her anything? Why else should they do anything but part ways now, knowing not a single thing more about one another? She hated hunters. He was one. Perhaps his intentions weren't as dark as that of the men she'd poisoned, but she was right. He'd almost tried to kill her unicorn companion. He'd broken his promise—a promise he'd made without any intention of fulfilling it— and targeted another unicorn right after. Had James not planted suspicion in his mind, Teryn might not have been prepared to stop Helios in time. If Helios had taken the unicorn's horn, Teryn would have shared the responsibility.

His stomach turned at that. *All this time, Helios knew. He knew I'd be too soft for the truth.* Teryn wasn't sure if he should feel ashamed about that. It wasn't like he'd thought they could remove a unicorn's pelt without killing it. While it had never occurred to him that the horn would need to be taken while the unicorn was alive, he'd always known the creature would have to die. Was that where Teryn drew the line? He could kill, but not make an animal needlessly suffer?

He remembered his hesitation at the stream, how his body had seized up when he'd prepared to throw his spear at Valorre. He'd felt revulsion at the thought of killing the unicorn, a thousand times stronger than any distaste he'd felt during a normal hunt. Something inside him, whether he'd recognized it or not, had known a unicorn was not just another animal. That killing them to appease a spoiled princess' vanity was wrong.

Which meant Helios had been right. Teryn had always been too soft, right from the start.

Teryn realized Cora was still watching him. There was something discomfiting about her gaze. It was too probing. Too penetrating. He felt as if his heart were made bare, laid across his face in stunning detail like one of the illustrations in Larylis' books.

"I just...I want to know." Cora's voice was softer now. "I came here to rescue the unicorns from the hunters. To keep them from being captured. Now that I know the Beast is involved..." She shook her head. "I need to know more. Do more. And I have a feeling you know more about it than I do."

Teryn huffed a dark laugh. "You'd be surprised, then. Helios kept us in the dark about almost everything."

Cora leaned forward. Her expression took on a hint of pleading. It was the first time he'd seen anything close to vulnerability in her eyes. "Please."

Rubbing his brow, he released a heavy sigh. "It's called the Heart's Hunt."

Teryn told her everything he found pertinent. He kept any information regarding his kingdom's debt to himself, telling her only that he was engaged to Princess Mareleau Harvallis, but had been slighted at Beltane when she invited other suitors to compete for her hand. She listened with rapt attention as he went on to explain his alliance with Helios and Lex. He told her what little information Helios had shared—how Helios had first come to learn of unicorns, how he'd made a treaty with Vinias to hunt their lands until unicorns could no longer be found north of Khero, how Duke Morkai had taken control over the hunt. He told her of their plan to steal a unicorn from the hunters, how they'd tracked them to the camp.

By the time Teryn was done with his tale, Lex had already retired to his bedroll and was fast asleep.

Cora, however, seemed more energized than ever. She paced before the fire. "Prince Helios said there are more hunting parties."

Teryn nodded. "I got the impression there were several more. When we arrived at the hunters' camp tonight, Helios knew exactly which name and location to say."

She stopped her pacing and faced him. "He showed them a writ as well. I want to see it."

Teryn's gaze went to Helios' horse. It was tethered next to his own, eyes closed. He hadn't had the heart to leave it at the site of a bloodbath, so he'd brought the mare with them when they'd followed Cora here. Besides, the horse was laden with Helios' bags, which could be full of any number of useful items for the ride home. But...did his saddlebag contain the writ? Or had he had it on him when the Beast attacked?

"I don't know if we have it. He could have kept it on him when we joined the hunters."

Cora started off toward the horses. "He put it back. I saw him."

Teryn blinked a few times, only realizing now just how unsettling it was that she'd been watching them the entire time. He followed after her and approached the horses. Berol launched from her branch and landed on Quinne's saddle. She nestled down as if to sleep but peeped an eye open to watch Cora step up beside Helios' horse. The mare was named Hara, if he remembered correctly. She was sleek and black, larger than Quinne. Cora opened a saddlebag while Teryn went to the one on the opposite side. Hara paid them no heed, for she clearly had a much better temperament than her former master. Teryn glanced over the saddle and realized Cora had to stand on her toes to get a look inside the bags. Meanwhile, his height provided him a clear view of the bag's contents—several knives, flasks, waterskins, leather pouches of dried meat, articles of clothing. He moved the items around until he found a stack of folded papers.

He took them out and smoothed out the top sheet, angling it so that the fire illuminated it. It was a map of the lower half of Risa, its main focus on the three kingdoms that comprised the land once known as Lela—Khero, Menah, and Selay. The forested areas were marked with either an *X* or a circle. Most of the *X*s were written over the southernmost parts of Selay and Menah, with only a circle or two drawn over their northern forests. Within each circle was a number. The ones in Selay and Menah bore ones or twos. Meanwhile, the circles drawn over the forests in Khero were marked with numbers in double digits. Could it possibly be the number of unicorns found in each region?

His eyes moved to northeastern Khero, which was the part of the map that hosted the most notations. There he found marks dividing the forests into regions, with a name next to each. These regions were contained to a radius around Ridine Castle. This must have been the *specific area* Helios had spoken of. Teryn sought out his current location. They were in northeastern Khero near the southernmost region noted on the map. There he found the word *Hammond*. Just northwest of there was the word *Drass*. Teryn remembered that name. That was whose hunting party Helios had pretended they'd come from when Gringe had questioned them.

Teryn gritted his teeth, his anger over Helios' refusal to share intel still sharp, even after the man's demise. What else had he been hiding? He moved the map to the back of the stack and studied the next paper.

His breath caught in his throat.

Two dark eyes stared back at him, keen, fierce, and intelligent.

He knew those eyes. They'd watched him from the other side of the fire mere moments ago.

Now they watched him from under the word *Wanted*.

No wonder Cora had looked familiar when he'd met her on the other side of her blade. It was because he'd seen her before, studied her likeness on the poster he'd found on his father's desk.

It made sense now why Cora was so well versed in poison. How she'd killed six men without batting an eye.

His gaze dipped to the bottom of the poster, even though he already knew what it would say. *For the murders of Queen Linette and Princess Aveline.*

He swallowed hard, his throat suddenly dry. When he'd first seen the poster, he hadn't given the murders much thought, but he remembered the deaths. Remembered how the people mourned, even in his own kingdom. The killer had left no sign of a wound on either body. Poison, it was deemed, but other theories circulated, spoken only in whispers.

A witch, they'd said. A young serving girl who'd dabbled in the dark arts and held a grudge against her royal masters. The queen was known to have been with child when she died, while the princess...

Teryn's chest felt tight. Princess Aveline had only been a young girl. He'd met her once when they'd both been children. Back when their kingdoms were friendly. Before her parents died in the plague that swept the continent for the better part of a year. At six years old, she'd been brave. Charming. Full of life and wit and beauty. She'd been his very first crush for all of the two weeks she'd spent as a guest at Dermaine Palace with her parents. She'd hardly looked his way the entire time, and yet he'd blushed and hid behind his mother's skirts whenever she was in the room. Teryn had almost forgotten. Now that he remembered, his heart plummeted with grief.

He stole a glance at Cora, her brows knitted as she read the parchment in her hands, oblivious of the truth he'd discovered.

He may not have learned much about her, but he now knew one thing. She'd killed Princess Aveline Caelan.

His eyes slid back to the poster and settled on the next words.

Reward: 500,000 gold sovas.

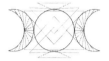

26

Teryn didn't seem to notice Cora's approach, even as she paused before him. He was too entranced by whatever he was reading. "You were right, it's a forgery," she said of the writ she'd found. The seal was almost an exact replica of Duke Morkai's crescent moon, but the word *Calloway*—the name of Morkai's duchy—was in the wrong script.

Teryn startled at the sound of her voice. He met her eyes over his stack of papers, his face a shade too pale. She opened her senses and felt his spike of alarm seep into her. But it wasn't her sudden appearance that had him so rattled. It had more to do with whatever he was looking at. She furrowed her brow. "What did you find?"

He went to hand her the top paper but ended up dropping the bottom of the stack. She bent to gather the loose papers before they could get soaked by the dewy grass. When she stood, he handed her one of the sheets. "You'll want to see this."

She took it from him and saw it was a map. Her heart

sank deeper and deeper the longer she studied it. If the markings represented what she thought they did, there were several more hunting parties. It shouldn't have come as a surprise. She'd begun to suspect as much when she'd witnessed Gringe interrogating Teryn and his companions. He'd too readily accepted that they'd come from another company of unicorn hunters. Sure enough, *Drass* was labeled over the Cambron Pass, just as she'd heard Helios say.

Her lungs felt tight as she took a few steps back, slumping against the tree that met her back. "This is so much worse," she whispered.

"Do you intend to hunt all of them down? To...poison them?" She felt his judgment then, his condemnation of her actions.

She met his eyes. "If you have something to say, say it. You insisted they were no friends of yours."

He watched her for a few moments before averting his gaze, eyes unfocused. "No, they weren't. Nor were they good men. Still...it was a bit reckless, don't you think?"

"It worked."

"Barely. Three men didn't drink. What would you have done if Helios, Lex, and I hadn't been there to take the fall? To fight them for you?"

She clenched her teeth. "I didn't need you. Had you not been there, I would have taken them down with my bow one by one."

"What if you'd been caught?"

"I wasn't."

"What. If. Just think about it."

She did. Her heart raced as she imagined numerous ways her plan could have gone wrong. She could have been spotted. Even more of the men could have abstained from the rum. She could have tried to pick off the survivors and gotten a crossbow bolt to the heart. But that was the risk she'd taken from the start. She knew she was only one person. She knew the odds were against her. That didn't stop her from trying. It was a risk worth taking if it meant saving the unicorns. Denying the Beast its meal. Destroying whatever dark plans Duke Morkai was brewing. Now that she was no longer with the Forest People, this mission was all she had.

Crossing her arms, she pushed off from the tree, feigning more confidence than she felt. "You won't stop me. I'm going to find every last one of these hunting parties and wipe them out."

"When the duke sends men to replace them, what then?"

She startled every time he mentioned the duke. It was strange that he knew Morkai was involved but didn't show even an ounce of the terror that was due. That was probably because he didn't know the man was a mage. To him, the duke was just a businessman trying to turn a pretty profit.

Then his words sank in, flooding her with an over-whelming wave of exhaustion. He was right. The duke would send more men to replace the ones she killed. Did that mean there was no end to her efforts? No way to keep the unicorns safe for good?

Her next words came out with far less conviction. "I'll do whatever I can for as long as I can."

Teryn's posture stiffened. She sensed his tangled energy, felt him fighting against the words that were poised on his lips.

She gave him a pointed look. "What?"

He rubbed his jaw, then locked his eyes on hers. "Let me come with you."

Her face went slack. Surely she hadn't heard him right. Why would he want to come with her? She'd tried to kill him. She'd threatened his life. It had to be a ploy. Indeed she felt...*something* emanating from him. Some mixture of guilt, trepidation, and fear. It was heavy and cloying. She suddenly felt like they were standing too close, the three feet of space separating them not nearly vast enough.

He must have seen her reaction in her eyes, for he took a step back as if to appease her. "Hear me out," he slowly said. "Let me travel with you to the next camp. I assume that will be the Cambron Pass, correct? It's the closest."

She considered remaining mute on her plans, but she gave him a curt nod.

"Then let me aid your efforts in rescuing the captured unicorns there. That's all I ask. With my help—Lex's too, if he's willing—we could free the creatures, maybe without nearly as much bloodshed. If you find our aid useful, perhaps we can help you further, should you choose."

"Why? Why would you help me?"

"I owe you a debt. You treated Lex's arm. You must allow me to repay you."

"I don't want you to repay me."

"It doesn't matter. I'm a prince. Chivalry is my guiding compass."

She snorted a dark laugh. "It didn't seem like it when you aimed a spear at me."

"You tried to stab me first—" He shook his head. "That's beside the point."

"No, Your Highness," she said, tone mocking. "I don't care about your chivalry or your moral compass."

"Then care about what I could help you accomplish. Faster. Easier."

She eyed him through slitted lids. Suspicion prickled the back of her neck. "You're hiding something. What aren't you telling me?"

His eyes widened for a fraction of a second before he steeled his expression. When he spoke, his words were slow. Careful. "Now that I know what I know, I can't finish the Heart's Hunt. But perhaps I can do something worthwhile while I'm here."

She shook her head, not buying any of that. "What's in it for you? You may not have won your silly Hunt, but neither did anyone else. You could simply go home and claim your bride's hand—"

"I have a duty to my kingdom," he said, tone firm, "to do the right thing." He punctuated the last two words. With a deep inhale, she let herself feel his emotions. She sensed only truth.

"And you think helping me free some unicorns is the *right thing*?"

He hesitated before answering, but when he did, he was resolute. "Yes."

She heard soft steps coming up alongside the horses. Valorre. Berol ruffled her feathers at his appearance, edging farther down Teryn's saddle.

You could let him help you, he said.

She cast him a dark glare. *You can't be serious.*

It's dangerous doing this on your own.

I never heard you complain before, she silently conveyed. *You're the one who dragged me into this, you know.*

If you recall, I asked both you and your friend.

Her heart clenched at his reference to Maiya. But Valorre was right. He had implored them both to help, and Cora had sought the aid of the entire commune, only to be denied by Roije. She'd already fantasized about how much easier her mission would be if she'd had the Forest People to help. But the commune had skilled magic users, trackers, and hunters. Teryn and Lex were just...princes.

She returned her attention to Teryn. "How do I even know you'd be a help and not a hindrance? I saved your life from the Beast tonight."

He quirked a brow. "Technically, you saved the caged unicorn's life. The Beast only went for Helios, and I don't recall you intervening on his behalf."

"The creature wounded your friend and I bandaged him up."

He shrugged. "Still, wouldn't it help to have more than just you protecting Valorre? Your arrows wounded the Beast, but the monster didn't fall. I'm skilled with a spear, while Lex..." He trailed off, some of his confidence faltering. "Lex can wield a sword. You saw how he killed one of those hunters."

She rolled her eyes. "And nearly curled up in the fetal position after."

He sighed. "Give us a chance. Let us redeem ourselves. Let us do some good after everything we nearly destroyed."

Her gaze slid to Valorre. *I still think it's a good idea*, he said. *I like him. He's very tall.*

I take offense to that.

Why? He's very handsome and so concerned over my well-being. Did you hear him? He wants to fight off the Beast for me.

Oh, is that all it takes to win you over?

Valorre had nothing else to say.

She met Teryn's eyes, reached for his emotions. Her palms tingled as she sifted through his energy. She felt strength and fear. Hesitation and conviction. Something murky lurked at the edges, which told her he was still hiding things from her. But so was she. Could his secrets be any bigger than hers?

Finally, she released a grumbling breath. "I'll think on it."

He blinked a few times. "You will?"

"I'll tell you what I decide in the morning." She went to brush past him, but his hand landed on her shoulder. Her body went stiff, her pulse thrumming. She glanced down at his hand, felt the heat of his palm on her bare skin where her shift had slipped down her shoulder.

In an instant, he snatched his hand back. Even in the dark, she could see color rising to his cheeks. He cleared his throat before he spoke, fingers curling tight. "I just wanted to implore you...please give it serious consideration."

It took a few seconds to steady her breathing. "I will," she said, her voice a whisper.

Teryn waited until Cora was fast asleep by the dying embers of the fire before he approached the horses again.

He used the same technique he did while stalking prey—prodding the earth, taking one slow step after the other—to ensure he didn't wake her. Quinne softly nickered at his approach. He paused, waiting to see if Cora would stir. She didn't. Valorre, thankfully, was nowhere to be seen. He'd caught the unicorn wandering in and out of camp during the last couple hours that he'd feigned sleep.

He rifled through his saddlebags to retrieve parchment and quill. Berol landed quietly on his shoulder and nibbled his temple in greeting. After giving her a few affectionate scritches, he quickly scrawled his message. Then he took the Wanted poster he'd stashed inside his vest when Cora hadn't been looking and rolled it together with his letter. Finally, he sealed it and lifted it toward Berol. She clasped it in one of her talons.

"To Father," he whispered. "Home."

He then offered her a strip of pheasant he'd pocketed during dinner. She accepted it as well as more pets, then launched off his shoulder. He watched her silhouette against the dark sky until she merged with the night. A pinch of worry settled in his gut. He'd never sent her away this far from home, but she'd always returned with ease before, no matter where they were. Besides, this was the only way.

He needed to get a message delivered to King Dimetreus as soon as possible. Berol couldn't simply fly to Ridine Castle—a place she'd never been—and take up perch outside the king's study. The only way to let him know that Teryn had found the fugitive was to get a note to his father first.

Teryn stepped back from Quinne.

And froze.

The moon illuminated something white between a pair of trees. It was Valorre. He watched Teryn with his large russet eyes. How long had he been standing there? Teryn smiled at the unicorn, trying to exude innocence as he returned to his bedroll. The truth was, Teryn was anything but innocent. His string of broken promises was only just beginning.

At least he had one consolation.

The girl he was going to betray wasn't innocent either.

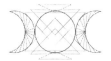

27

L ex, Teryn knew, would take some convincing.

"You can't be serious," Lex said, eyes bulging.

Teryn kept his voice far lower. "I am." They stood near the stream, watering their horses. He glanced toward their secluded camp and the tendrils of smoke that wafted above it. Cora had already been awake by the time Teryn had opened his eyes. He was almost surprised to see her there, tending the fire and boiling something fragrant in a cook pot. As much as he'd itched to ask if she'd made her decision, he dared not say anything more than a cordial greeting. The fact that she hadn't snuck away when she had the chance told him she was at least considering his offer. For now, that was enough.

He'd woken Lex after that, inquired about his arm. Trying not to be too obvious, he'd then pulled Lex away and had him bring his horse. Once they'd reached the stream, Teryn let him in on his idea. He hadn't told Lex everything. Only what he'd told Cora. Not because he didn't trust Lex to keep a secret. They'd successfully hidden their original alliance from Helios, after all. It was more that this situation felt particularly tenuous. The way Cora's dark eyes always held far too much intensity, how she always seemed to be watching, studying, reading between his words...he knew he needed to tread carefully. Letting Lex in on his secret would be a last resort.

"We only have to accompany her to the next group of hunters," Teryn said. "That's all."

Lex gave him a pointed look. "Oh, that's *all*? We nearly got ourselves killed by the last company."

"Yes, but that was when we knew nothing. Helios kept us in the dark. Cora was working against us. Now, we'll be working together."

"I don't see how this helps you get your princess."

"It doesn't," Teryn said. "If you want to return home now, I won't stop you, but I'd rather have your help. Should you come with me, I promise as soon as we return to Dermaine Palace, you can have anything you want. You want in on our trade agreement with Brushwold? You got it."

Lex made a bewildered face, but it was quickly replaced with a look of surprise. "Oh." A pause. Then another, more drawn out, "*Oooh*. I see what this is."

Teryn lifted a brow. Could he have guessed Teryn's true motive? "What?"

"You like her. Cora."

Teryn's heart did a strange thing in his chest. He opened his mouth to deny it but thought better of it. Perhaps he could use Lex's assumption—as incorrect as it was—against him. He decided to let Lex interpret his silence however he wanted.

Lex nodded, a crooked grin lifting his cheeks. "You no longer care about the Heart's Hunt because you've got a new hunt in mind." He waggled his brows. "A hunt up a certain pair of petticoats."

A flush of heat climbed up his neck, and his pulse quickened at the sudden visuals Lex's crass comment provided. It was far from the worst thing he could imagine. Cora was stunning. Terrifying, yes, but...

He recalled the feel of her skin beneath his palm when he'd unwittingly touched her bare shoulder last night, remembered the sharp heat that ignited his hand, warmed his chest—

No. He shook the outrageous musings from his mind. *She's a murderer. There's nothing enticing about that.* His blood quickly cooled, but he forced his momentary lack of composure to creep into his voice, letting his words tremble a little as he said, "Maybe it's more than that." It was almost too much for him to keep a straight face. Thankfully, Lex didn't know him well or else he would have called his bluff. Teryn was not the kind of man to do ridiculous things for love. To him, love was fiction. Folly. The breaker of peace and the bringer of wars. But Lex didn't have to know that.

Lex grimaced. "You can't want to...marry her. You're a prince, Teryn. Princes don't marry wood witches. Besides, isn't your kingdom—dare I say—broke?"

Teryn stiffened at that. They hadn't discussed Menah's financial state, which meant rumors must have spread as far as Tomas. It shouldn't have been a surprise. "Lex, I need you to trust me," he said, stripping all pretense from his tone. "Come with me or go home, the choice is yours. But there's only one option that's going to get you a contract for Aromir wool. What's it going to be?"

Lex puffed his cheeks as he considered. After a grumbling exhale, he said, "Fine. I'll do it for the damn goats."

Teryn's lips spread into a grin as he slapped his friend on the arm—the uninjured one, of course. "Thanks, Lex. One more thing. Please don't tell Cora about...you know. My feelings."

"All right," he said, "but if I see the two of you kissing or canoodling, the deal's off."

Teryn snorted a laugh. He took Quinne's reins as well as Hara's and began to walk them back toward camp. "Trust me, that's not going to happen."

"Clearly, you've never been in love," Lex muttered.

TERYN HAD BEEN SUSPICIOUSLY QUIET ALL MORNING. CORA had expected him to bring up his proposition a hundred times already. Instead, he'd said nothing about it. Had he changed his mind? An unexpected disappointment sank her gut but she ignored it. Swallowed it down. Finished making breakfast.

Teryn and Lex returned from the stream and accepted bowls of root vegetable stew. They didn't even ask if the meal was poisoned. It wasn't, of course, and perhaps the fact that Cora was eating too eased any suspicions they might have. She watched them throughout the meal and found that Lex kept shooting strange looks at Teryn—ones she couldn't quite read. Whatever it was about, it had Teryn blushing furiously and wolfing down his stew as fast as he could.

After they'd all finished eating, a heavy silence fell. Cora could feel the weight of her decision resting on her shoulders, but she still didn't know what to say. Did she want them coming with her? She could admit she'd felt slightly safer last night knowing it hadn't just been her and Valorre at camp. Not to mention they had supplies, horses, cookware, weapons. Blankets and bedrolls. Meanwhile, Cora had only what she'd been able to steal and carry on foot.

She'd never been one to allow strangers to get close to her, and these two already knew far too much. They knew she was a witch and the one who'd poisoned the hunters. Facts that hadn't seemed quite so grim last night when their lives were at stake, but now the realization sent waves of anxiety through her. They could turn her in for what she'd done. And what if they found out who she really was? Teryn and Lex may have had no allegiance to the Kingdom of Khero, but after everything Teryn had said about duty and doing the right thing...

Cora picked up their bowls and wordlessly went to the stream to wash them. After a while, Valorre came up beside her. It was the first time she'd seen him all morning. She'd felt his presence close by, but she knew he wasn't content to stay in one place. He was a restless, wild spirit. Undoubtedly fae.

I'm certain those are clean by now, Valorre said.

She glanced down at her hands, realizing she must have been lost in thought. With a sigh, she stood and began walking down the bank, her steps slow. She knew it was time to make a choice. It was already well past dawn and if she wanted to reach the Cambron Pass quickly, she'd need all the time she could get. A sudden thought occurred to her. Teryn and Lex had an extra horse. If she accepted their company, she was sure she could use the mare for herself. She could travel faster than she ever could on foot.

Valorre rippled with indignation. *I am much faster than a horse. I could carry you.*

"Yes," she said with a grin, "but riding bareback isn't the most comfortable thing, and I'd never dare saddle you."

That seemed to satisfy him. *I would never stoop so low as to wear a saddle. What a silly contraption. I'd look very foolish indeed. Very well. Does that mean they're coming with us to help save my brethren?*

She nibbled her lip. Then the sound of clashing steel drew her attention. She paused, glancing back toward camp. Teryn and Lex were sparring just ahead. It seemed Lex's injured arm was his non-dominant hand, for he parried Teryn's attacks with ease. Teryn, she was irked to note, was once again without a shirt. She rolled her eyes as she approached them.

Teryn nodded at her with a grin, one that made her stomach tighten. Or perhaps it was the indecency of him being shirtless. She kept her eyes anywhere but his broad chest, his arms roped with muscle, his pants that seemed ridiculously low on his hips—

Crossing her arms, she returned his grin with a glare. "Do you ever wear a shirt?"

He shrugged and parried a halfhearted thrust from Lex. "Thanks to Lex and his refusal to let me turn his shirts into bandages, I only have one left. I'm not going to sweat in it."

"It's hardly safe to spar without one."

"Oh really?" he said as his shortsword clashed with Lex's. "I hadn't noticed because Lex isn't trying hard enough."

"My arm hurts," Lex said, then muttered something about Teryn showing off. That was when Cora realized what this little performance was all about. Teryn was trying to prove that they were useful. Skilled. That their aid would serve her.

Oh, the tall one is very strong, isn't he?

Cora cut a glare at Valorre. *Do you have a crush on Teryn?*

What is crush?

Never mind. She returned her gaze to the boys, watching as they set down their swords and drank from skins of water. Teryn shrugged on his hunting vest just as a familiar shape veered down from the sky. Berol landed on his padded shoulder, a scroll tucked in her talon.

He sent her away in the middle of the night, Valorre said. He didn't seem concerned, but she narrowed her eyes with suspicion.

"What's that?" she asked.

He met her eyes over the paper he was reading. "A letter from my father. I sent Berol with a note telling him I wouldn't be coming home for a while."

She clenched her jaw. That meant he'd already assumed she'd say yes to his proposition. It made her want to deny him outright.

He walked toward her, a questioning look in his eyes. "Have you decided?"

She found her words trapped in her throat as he held her gaze. He held it too long. Too unflinchingly. Blinking, she averted her eyes and pondered his question. Her time was up. She needed to choose.

Her gaze returned to his and she found that his eyes were in the process of sweeping over her form. His assessment made her breath catch. She dared not open her senses to him. Dared not read too much into his gaze. For surely he couldn't find much to be desired when he looked at her. She was a mess of tangles. Of soil and stone. Of petticoats tucked around her legs like pants. He was a prince, a man used to soft women with even softer demeanors.

She lifted her chin, reminding herself she didn't care what he thought of her. Not her appearance, not her personality, and certainly not her romantic appeal. He was a prince determined to make amends where his honor had failed. She was a witch with vengeance in her heart and violence in her soul.

"Put a shirt on," she said, sneering at his bare chest as if it were repulsive to her. It wasn't, but that was one of many secrets she was determined to keep. "It's time for us to go."

"Us," he echoed. "As in…the three of us."

Valorre sidled closer to her, making his approval clear.

"Yes," she finally said through her teeth. "Now, hurry up or I'm leaving without you."

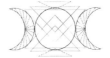

28

For two days, they traveled northwest for the Cambron Pass. They kept a decent pace with Cora riding Hara. After throwing most of Helios' personal items into the campfire, she'd kept all his useful belongings and took his mare for herself. She was surprised the animal was so amenable to new ownership. Based on the many snide remarks Teryn and Lex had made about Helios, she'd assumed his horse perhaps wouldn't respect her. Hara, however, was as even tempered as Cora could hope. Valorre took it upon himself to remind her who was the better of the two of them, and Cora always made certain to reassure him that, yes, he was the most magnificent and fearsome creature of hoof and mane.

Berol flew overhead, sometimes going so far as to become a pinprick in the distance, other times diving for prey or riding on Teryn's shoulder. She was curious about the prince's relationship with the bird. Not enough to ask him about it, of course. She made it her mission to speak as little as possible to the boys. The less they knew about her, the better, and she had no interest in getting to know them. They were temporary allies, not friends.

By the end of the second day of travel, the Cambron Mountains loomed large ahead. On the third, Cora found the first notable tracks.

She felt her nerves begin to fray the closer they came. Taking down the first group of hunters had been a harrowing enough experience. Now she was going to do it all over again. This time she had help, although it was still up for debate whether they would prove useful.

Each night, Cora's exhaustion was so deep that she'd fall asleep within minutes of bedding down on her newly acquired bedroll. Her slumber was—thankfully—deep and dreamless. But on the third night, after a day of tracking, stalking, and inching closer to her prey, she dreamed.

THE NIGHTMARE STARTED MUCH LIKE ANY OTHER. SHE walked down a dark castle hall, following the pull of some terrible wrongness. Every step sounded hollow in her ears. The smell of dust and rot filled her nostrils, tickling the back of her throat. She walked forward, for that was the only direction that existed in this strange dream. A few steps more and a serving tray appeared in her hands. Then the door. That horrible, dreaded door.

She knew what she would find inside. This time, she didn't fight it. This time, she ran for it, knowing the sooner she saw the room the sooner this dream would end. Her feet flew beneath her as she reached the threshold. Even though she'd known what she'd find, the sight of the dead queen still took her breath away. She froze in the doorway, the tray slipping from her hands. Morkai stood at Queen Linette's side, his hands drawing the blood from the sheets, from her lips, from under her nose. Blood that seeped from no visible wound. He stopped and whipped his head toward her, and the scene shifted in an instant. Morkai wasn't manipulating the blood, he was gesturing out of shock or panic. Part of Cora knew that wasn't right, knew what she'd seen was real. But another part of her doubted. Doubted enough that when he called her over to help the queen, she obeyed. She gathered Linette's cold hand in hers, uncaring that the woman's blood was now smeared over her own palms.

The voice came next. One she expected but was startled by just the same.

King Dimetreus let out a soft wail as his eyes landed on his wife. His hand flew to his chest as he halted in the doorway. "What have you done?"

Morkai whispered to the king, "You recall what she said to the queen earlier."

"No," Cora said, rounding on them. She shuddered as the word left her mouth. There was something wrong about the way it failed to echo through the room. As if her voice didn't belong there. "I didn't mean it."

King Dimetreus gave no indication that he'd heard her. Instead, he rushed to her, anger replacing his anguish. "You did this. *You*. What have you done?"

Cora trembled before the king's rage. She knew what would happen next. Knew a dark cell awaited her. A demand for her death.

"No." The word was louder this time. She pinned the

king with a glare. "No. This time, you will listen to me. I didn't do this. It was him." She pointed a finger at Duke Morkai. Her gaze shot to him, meeting his eyes. They shifted from an all-encompassing black to a blue so pale it was almost silver. His lips slid into a lazy smirk.

Returning her gaze back to the king, she was startled to find him frozen. Not just unmoving, but unbreathing, unblinking.

Morkai stepped up beside King Dimetreus. "You can't change the past by altering your dreams."

She clenched her jaw. A strange sense of duality washed over her as her hands balled into fists—fists that felt too small and too large at once, as if she were both the twelve-year-old version of herself that existed in her nightmares and her current self. The one who slept. Who dreamed. Who raged against this scene from the confines of her mind.

"You never fought against your sentence in the past," Morkai said.

"I was too shocked," she replied, her older voice mingling with her younger.

"It's useless. Besides, regardless of what you think, this *was* your fault."

"It wasn't. You did this."

Morkai waved his hand and the bedroom disappeared. Like an inkblot spreading over parchment, a new scene began to appear. Little by little, the colors grew brighter, her surroundings sharper. Her blood went cold when she realized where she was.

The dining hall at Ridine Castle formed around her. Its stone walls were decorated in intricate tapestries. The light from half a dozen candle-studded chandeliers cast everything in a warm, cheery glow. The tables were overflowing with courtiers dining, chatting, and drinking. Cora strode straight to the head table at the far wall. She knew she was late. It had been intentional. Her headaches had been coming on harder recently, and whenever she was forced to be around so many people, they became nearly crippling. No physician seemed to know what was wrong with her. There was no visible ailment. No disease of the body to treat. When she'd speak of feeling like she was being invaded by the hearts and minds of everyone around, she'd receive only unsettled stares. She'd hoped she could wait out the course of tonight's dinner, but Master Benedict had found her curled up beneath a staircase. Now she had no choice.

Master Benedict kept his hand on Cora's shoulder as she approached the table, his grip a reminder that there was no running away. She owed the king and queen an explanation, he'd said. Wincing at the pounding in her head, she lowered into a curtsy. She returned her eyes to the king and queen, bracing herself for the scolding. There wasn't one. Dimetreus was deep in conversation with Duke Morkai while Linette stared pointedly at her husband, her distaste in being ignored made clear by her pursed lips. Finally, Dimetreus turned from Morkai and gestured Cora closer to the table. Before he could say a word to her, Linette interrupted. "When shall we have a ball, my love? You promised me a ball this month."

The king claimed his wife's lips with a kiss. "You shall have a ball, darling, but not until our son is born. You are in no condition to dance. After he's made his appearance in the world, we'll celebrate. We'll have balls night after night until he's a year old. Then we'll host the finest party anyone this side of the Balma Sea has ever witnessed."

Linette's expression faltered as she shifted awkwardly in her seat.

"What is it?" the king asked.

"It's...oh, it's nothing." She batted her lashes and infused her tone with nonchalance. "It's just...I'm not very far along. Surely I can dance. I'd hate to let my newest gown go to waste before I grow too large to wear it."

The pounding in Cora's head increased, but the invasive energies shifted. They were no longer coming from the rows and rows of tables behind her but the one she stood before. Against her will, her attention focused on one person alone. Queen Linette. Cora felt a rippling anxiety turn in her stomach, a feeling that was not her own. With it came a sinking weight of guilt. Then something darker. Heavier.

"You aren't with child." The words left Cora's mouth before she could swallow them back. She hadn't yet learned which of her observations were better left unsaid. Had yet to understand why everyone else seemed blind to the things she gleaned so easily. So unwillingly.

Queen Linette's head whipped toward Cora. "How dare you say such a thing."

"It's true." Her voice came out tremulous. "You... you're lying. You were never with child."

"You wretched, awful creature—"

King Dimetreus held up a hand, silencing his wife. Master Benedict began to tug Cora away, but Dimetreus shook his head. His attention narrowed on Cora, voice soft. "Why would you say such a thing?"

Linette spoke before Cora could. "How many times have I told you, Dimetreus? She needs to be sent to a Godspriest. There's something wrong with her. She's infected by the seven devils and must have them cleansed from her soul."

Cora felt heat rise to her cheeks. "I do not need a Godspriest," she said, a frantic note to her voice. "I am not infected by the seven devils."

Linette looked around the dining hall. Cora was suddenly aware that silence had fallen over the room. She could feel the attention of innumerable pairs of eyes boring into her back. Linette spoke softly through her teeth. "Don't make a scene."

Cora's attention darted to Dimetreus. Why wasn't he speaking up for her? Tears sprang to her eyes as her blood began to boil like never before. It felt as if the energies she'd absorbed were compounding, the tightness in her skull growing sharper. She could still feel the queen's emotions the most, could feel her fear mixed with disgust, her guilt and her shame and so many things that Cora was too young to understand. "Tell him the truth," she yelled. "Tell him that you lied."

Linette rounded the table and grabbed Cora by the arm. "You rotten little witch."

Cora shrugged free, her breaths coming out in sobbing gasps. "I'm not a witch." That word had been a filthy thing then, something spoken with disdain. Cora hadn't yet learned that witches were real, that they were nothing like the storybook monsters she'd heard about.

Linette dragged her away from the table. "You are a witch," she muttered under her breath, all the while keeping a smile on her lips.

Cora glared up at her. She made no move to lower her voice as she said, "If I'm a witch, then I curse you."

Linette dropped her arm like she'd been burned. Her chest heaved, eyes roving the room and the eyes that continued to watch them. "Stop," she said, tears springing to her eyes. The queen shuddered. She was truly afraid of her. It was written in the emotions Cora sensed, writhing, contracting, spilling deeper into her until she felt like her head would explode.

She erupted with a shout. "I curse you to die."

Without another word, she kicked up her heels and ran from the dining room.

She crossed the threshold, desperate for the relief of the quiet halls.

But the doorway only led her to a room with a blood-stained bed.

"No," she breathed. The room was as frozen as it had been when she'd left it. The king remained locked in place, the queen staring sightlessly ahead. Only she and Morkai moved.

"You did that," he said.

"I didn't mean it," Cora said. This time, her voice was her own, without a hint of her younger self. "Even if I had, it wasn't a true curse. Witches don't curse people."

"How do you know? You spoke the words, sent them out into the ether. She died that very night."

"You killed her," Cora said through her teeth.

"Yes, but what if it was your fault? What if your words sparked a series of events that resulted in her death? Is it really so improbable? You killed the queen. You let Princess Aveline die. Deny it."

She opened her mouth to say she wasn't a murderer,

but the words turned to ash on her tongue. The version of her that existed outside the dream had ended seven lives mere days ago. Erwin with an arrow to his throat. The hunters who drank her rum.

Morkai took a step closer. The lantern light glinted off the sharp planes of his face, making him look both beautiful and terrifying at once. "Maybe Linette was right all along. Maybe you're an evil thing. You kill without remorse. You choose death, violence, and solitude over the safety of a new home. You lied to people who loved you. Turned your back on your dearest friend without even a goodbye."

Her legs began to tremble as she tried to put more distance between herself and Morkai.

"Maybe you're even worse than me." With a flutter of his fingers, the room began to dissolve again, this time under swirling shadows. They crawled down her throat, filled her lungs, raked talons over her heart. Black filled her vision as she struggled to free herself from the strangling dark mist. No matter how she fought, where she turned, she was pinned in place. The shadows refused to abate. They simply pressed harder. Harder. Squeezing her lips like a kiss of death.

CORA.

Cora.

"Cora!" The sound of her name made her body go still.

Her muscles ached as if she'd run for miles, as if she'd thrashed and raged in her sleep the same way she'd done in her dream. She blinked into the night, but her eyes were glazed with tears, casting everything under a blur. Something heavy was still pressed to her mouth, the smell of sweat and soil filling her senses. It was wrong. Foreign. Her mind struggled to remember.

Where am I? Where am I?

Then she remembered. Somewhat.

Her body went limp, and the heavy thing left her mouth. A hand. She waited only a beat before reaching for her belt and unsheathing her knife. With her free hand, she thrust outward, striking blindly with her palm. A gasp followed, then a thud, and she shoved all of her weight into the other body until she felt it collapse beneath her. She blinked again and again to rid the glaze of tears from her eyes. When her vision finally cleared, she found Teryn looking back at her, eyes wide with surprise. He was flat on his back while she straddled his stomach, her knife at the base of his throat. She felt a slice of wind beat her cheek. As she turned her head to the side, she caught sight of a dark shape darting for her.

"Berol, no," Teryn said.

The falcon pulled out of her dive and lifted into the sky. Cora saw Berol's shadow cross the moon as she circled overhead.

She returned her gaze to Teryn, her chest heaving as she struggled to catch her breath. Their eyes locked.

"What are you doing?" Teryn asked, voice low, calm, steady. His eyes, however, revealed a tinge of fear.

"What were *you* doing?" she said, her words uneven, frantic. "You had your hand over my mouth."

"You were screaming."

She shuddered, reminded of her dream, the shadows

that had tried to strangle her. "You had no right to touch me."

The fear left his eyes, replaced with indignation. "You wouldn't wake. Your screams nearly gave me a heart attack. I thought you were being murdered."

"So you decided to smother me in my sleep."

"I called your name a hundred times. The last thing I could think to do was muffle your shouts while I tried harder to wake you. Would you rather I let you carry on? I'm sure the hunters we're supposed to be sneaking up on would only be too happy to follow the source of a distressed woman's cries. And not to aid her, either."

That sent a spike of alarm through her. She lifted her chin, staring down at him with a glare. "Don't you dare touch me like that again."

He scoffed. "Do you think I wanted to? Do you think I took pleasure from it?"

The word pleasure sparked the memory of how his palm had felt on her shoulder. Her heart thumped heavily in her chest and sent a wave of heat to her cheeks.

His eyes landed on the very shoulder in question. When his eyes returned to hers, his lips quirked with a suggestive smirk. "Trust me, if I wanted to touch you, you'd know. And if I took pleasure from it, so would you."

Her breath caught, and something trilled low in her belly. She was stunned silent, her knife trembling in her hand. Without her permission, her eyes dipped to his lips, taking in their sensuous curve, the dimple at one corner. His smile slipped, an uncertain expression crossing his face. She was entranced as his lips parted, some word poised on them—

"Oh, for the love of the seven gods, get a room." Lex turned over on his bedroll.

Cora's eyes flew to the other man. Valorre stood off to the side, rippling with something that struck Cora like a snicker.

"No canoodling," Lex muttered, back facing them. "If I hear gasps or moans or even kisses, I'm going to throw rocks at your heads."

Cora returned her gaze to Teryn. She stiffened, realizing the impropriety of their position. He was on his back. She was on top of him. Sure, a knife's blade was between them, but...

She had to stifle her gasp of surprise when she realized where his hands were—at the base of her waist. Had they been there the whole time? He could have shoved her off him, and perhaps that was what he'd been prepared to do. But also...

Also...

It looked like so much more. For the tiniest splinter of a moment, it had—*maybe*—felt like more too.

She pushed off of him as fast as she could, nearly stumbling in the process. He rose much slower, his eyes never leaving hers. Then, trembling with rage, she stomped off, feeling his gaze follow her every step.

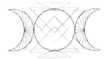

Teryn wasn't entirely sure why he followed after Cora. He told himself it was to spy, to see where she went and ensure she wasn't plucking poisonous berries to shove down his throat in retribution. But that wasn't the full truth. He was concerned. He'd heard the pitiful pitch of her cries that had roused him from sleep, had seen beads of tears clinging to her dark lashes as she'd held her knife to his throat. For a moment, it had been like she was somewhere else, trapped in her mind. He'd had every intention of pushing her off of him at the first chance, but instead...

He blushed as he recalled the look in her eyes when he'd brought up pleasure and touch. Seven gods, he'd *flirted* with her. With a woman who would sooner butcher him than bed him.

I only said what I did to shock her into calming down, he told himself. That too was a lie. He'd said it because he'd wanted to get a rise out of her. Wanted to taste her rage and test the bounds of her anger. Did he have a damn death wish? Who flirts with a woman he's planning to betray?

He shook the thought from his head as he trailed her. Valorre trotted past him, following after her too. They both disappeared into the dark. Still, he followed.

He spotted Valorre first. The unicorn stood at what Teryn realized was the edge of a rounded cliff. His white coat shone beneath the light of the moon, the ridges of his spiral horn glittering with reflected starlight. Teryn's heart leapt into his throat as he considered that Cora might be on the other side of the cliff's edge. She could have run blindly and taken a fall.

Then he saw her. Not far from Valorre, her small form was curled at the base of a tree, knees to her chest, shoulders heaving with quiet sobs. Teryn suddenly regretted coming after her. Her grief was not his to witness.

He took a slow step back, but Cora's face whipped up, stopping him in his tracks.

She rose to her feet and crossed her arms. "What are you doing here?"

"I..." He searched for words, his throat dry. "I just wanted to see if you were all right."

"Why wouldn't I be?"

Teryn knew he should leave. He was only making her more upset. If he wasn't careful, she might throw a knife at him. But despite telling his feet to walk the other way, he found himself stepping forward instead. Not toward her, but to the edge of the cliff. The Cambron Pass sprawled out before him, cloaked in darkness. Somewhere out there, the next group of hunters awaited. The thought chilled him, made him wonder if everything he was doing was reckless. He could lose his life doing what he was about to do. All so he could save his kingdom. Would the sacrifice be worth it? He glanced over his shoulder and found Cora watching him. His stomach sank with guilt. Would sacrificing *her* be worth it?

She's a killer, he reminded himself for the hundredth time. But right now, she didn't look like a killer at all. She looked...fragile. Not like a glass trinket. She was nothing like the soft women who fluttered about court. She was more like a blade, one that was forged to be mighty but still bore chips and scratches.

"I used to have nightmares." The sound of his own voice caught him off guard.

She stared at him, jaw set. At first, it didn't seem like she'd reply. Then, uncrossing her arms, she returned to the tree and leaned her back against it. Valorre nuzzled her shoulder, and Cora reached up to stroke the space between his eyes. "Let me guess," she said dryly. "You had them when you were young. Like every other child."

He gave her a weak grin. "If you'd consider me a child three years ago, then yes."

She met his eyes briefly, then returned her gaze to Valorre. "What were they about?"

He gulped before answering. "War."

"Why war?"

It really wasn't something he should talk about. Not only did he not enjoy talking about it but she had no right to know. Yet he found himself speaking regardless. "I...I don't know how much you know of my kingdom..."

She gave a noncommittal shrug.

"Well, a few years ago, my father attempted to replace my mother with his mistress." His lungs tightened. He remembered the yelling, the shouts. The way his sisters had cried. How he'd dragged them away to play games and pretend their family wasn't falling apart. "Dermaine Palace erupted with scandal. My mother fought to keep her crown while I...I was caught in the middle. Between Mother, Father, and my half brother. I loved all of them and realized I was about to lose at least one of them to some degree. My mother's home kingdom threatened war, and that's when I started having nightmares. Not all of them were truly about battles waged on Menah's shores but the familial war already wreaking havoc on my life."

Teryn glanced at Cora and found her staring, brow furrowed, hand frozen on Valorre's face. The unicorn nudged her to resume petting him. She tore her gaze from Teryn. "That sounds rough."

He released a heavy sigh and tried to make his voice sound casual. "I led a charmed life up until then, so who am I to complain?"

Her eyes flickered to his, and he saw her expression soften.

"What about you?" he asked. "What was your child-hood like? Have you always been on your own?"

Her lips pulled into a frown. "In one way or another, yes. My parents died when I was young. I was devastated when Father died, but when Mother followed...a part of me broke. I felt like there was no one left alive who understood me." Her throat bobbed, and her expression grew hard again. "It's also when my...my *gifts* started developing and I realized I wasn't like other people."

A witch, she meant. His pulse quickened at that. Even though he knew it to be true, he was still bewildered by it. People didn't believe in magic or witches. They weren't supposed to be real. And yet, he'd met both a witch and a unicorn in a single week. He hesitated before asking his next question, unsure if she'd deign to answer. "What exactly does it mean to be a witch? I've never met one before you." He rushed to say the last part.

She snorted a dark laugh. "We're certainly not about blood-filled cauldrons and human sacrifice, I'll tell you that much."

"Well, what *are* you about, then? You know, aside from rescuing unicorns, threatening princes with sharp objects, and poisoning evil men. Is poison your only magic?"

"Poison is the least of my magic," she said with an indignant scoff. For a moment, he worried he'd offended her, but she spoke again. "I'm clairsentient," she explained, "which means I experience clear feeling. Every witch has an affinity for one of the senses. There are five others in addition to clairsentience. Clairvoyance is clear seeing. Clairaudience relates to hearing. Clairalience is smelling. Clairgustance is taste. And claircognizance revolves around knowing."

Teryn tried to keep the awe off his face. He'd only heard of such abilities in myths and faerytales. "So, what does it mean to experience magical feeling the way you do?"

"It...it's kind of hard to explain. Generally, a clairsentient witch uses her own emotions, internal physical responses, and touch to connect with her magic. A certain physical sensation could mean danger while a specific emotion could mean luck. Every witch is different and it takes some time to understand how to utilize one's magic. I, however, am a little different. I tap into my magic with feeling as well, but I am also able to feel the feelings of others. One of our elders told me I might be an empath."

"An empath?" Teryn echoed.

"A witch with very strong clairsentience. An empath's senses aren't limited to her own, and she can use them to perceive outside thoughts, feelings, and energies. It's something I've been able to do since I was a child. It was nothing but a curse when I was younger. It led to some... very bad experiences. It wasn't until I met other people like me that I learned to control it and shield myself from others' emotions."

"When you say people like you, do you mean...other witches? Are you part of a coven?"

She chuckled. "Something like that."

Teryn was once again struck with awe. Could it really be that magic was real and there were others like Cora? If so, was it a good thing? Or a bad thing? A startling realization dawned on him. She could read emotions. No wonder he'd always felt so unsettled by her gaze. She was probably absorbing his feelings all the while. Did that mean...did she know...

He shook the thought from his mind. His muscles tensed. Suddenly every single thought felt dangerous. "So, your powers," he said slowly. "Can you read my mind?"

She rolled her eyes. "No, it's not like that. I still have to process what I receive through my own feelings. While I can tune in at will, the level of information I glean varies. Some things jump out at me at random, overwhelming my own senses. It can happen even when I'm shielding. Other times it's just...just an emotion I have to put a name to. It's like reading a book in another language that you've only just begun to learn."

The visual worked surprisingly well for him. He'd been tutored in several languages, but he was only fluent in three. The rest he understood in fits and starts. His eyes fell to her hands. She'd begun brushing them through Valorre's mane, revealing the dark ink decorating her palms and forearms. The designs formed esoteric symbols like moon phases and geometric configurations unlike anything he'd seen before. In fact, he'd seen very few women with tattoos at all. He had to admit they were stunning. "Do your tattoos have anything to do with magic?"

"They are a tradition amongst the—" She paused and shook her head as if she were about to say something she didn't want to. Slower, she said, "Amongst my coven. They are symbolic of a witch's experience with magic. Some think they also help us channel our magic's flow."

"*Some* think?" He quirked a brow. "Do you not believe? Are you a skeptic when it comes to your own magic?"

"No, I believe," she said but there was certainly doubt in her tone. "It's just...sometimes I wish magic were more obvious. The most common feats of magic can be explained away by coincidence, imagination, or science. I've only ever seen one kind that couldn't." Her eyes took on a distant quality that reminded him of how she'd looked after her nightmare.

"Why are you on your own now?" he asked, mostly to guide her away from what was clearly a distressing subject. "Where is your coven?"

"I lived with them until recently. I left them after I met

Valorre. I knew I needed to save his brethren, and my people...well, they couldn't help me."

"Why not?"

She stiffened, and Teryn could tell he was approaching yet another prickly topic. "I don't know how witches are treated where you're from, but here they aren't exactly considered upstanding members of society. They can't go gallivanting around the woods on crusades against fae creature injustice. Remember how you told me you've never met a witch before? That's because society doesn't treat us kindly. We stay hidden because it isn't safe for us to be found."

Teryn felt a weight in his chest, one that made him second-guess if he was doing the right thing. What if he was wrong about her? She couldn't have been very old when she killed Queen Linette and Princess Aveline. What if the crimes had been accidental? An unfortunate side effect of her growing clairsentience?

Both murders were deemed the work of poison, he reminded himself. *It doesn't get more intentional than that.*

He'd been tempted a few times now to simply ask her. But even if he did, what did he expect her to say? If she was guilty, she'd lie, which meant he couldn't trust her even if she denied the allegations. And if she *was* guilty, she'd be onto him. She'd know that *he* knew and would flee. Or try to kill him outright.

Besides, it was too late. The evidence was in the letter that was now tucked into his vest pocket. *It is done*, the note said. That was his father's response to the letter he'd sent Berol with. There was a chance this plan wouldn't work, of course. That the King of Khero wouldn't take Arlous' correspondence seriously. That the timing was terrible and nothing would come of Teryn's efforts.

The thought almost gave him relief.

Cora's voice drew him from his internal musings. "I can't imagine you think any better after what you saw me do to those hunters," she said, eying him warily.

He met her gaze, once again painfully aware of his own emotions and the fact that she might be reading them right now. With a sigh, he steeled his composure. "They were bad men and you were alone. You did what you had to do."

She seemed to relax a little at that, but her expression was cold. "I still can't fathom why you're helping me."

"I told you why."

She stopped brushing Valorre's mane. There was no jest in her tone when she said, "I don't entirely trust you."

He straightened, held her stare. "The feeling is mutual." He meant it. But for some unfathomable reason, his lips began to quirk up with a smile.

She lifted her chin and smiled back. "Good. Then we at least understand one another." She strode away from the tree and began heading in the direction of camp, Valorre following in her wake. Her back was turned to him as she paused. "Goodnight, Teryn."

His lungs felt tight at the sound of his name on her lips. *Fear*, he tried to label the sensation. *Revulsion. Hatred. Guilt.* The only one that held even the slightest truth was the last. In reality, the constricting sensation in his chest was something else entirely. It was...pleasant. Not to mention new and terrifying and highly inconvenient. "Goodnight, Cora," he replied and watched her swaying form disappear between the trees.

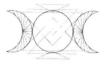

30

The next day, they followed the hunters' tracks until it was clear they'd entered their hunting radius. Which meant today was the day they'd spy on the camp itself. The prospect tied Cora's stomach in knots, but she tried to focus more on the fact that they were going to get another chance to free the unicorns. So far, she'd only saved two. Unless Valorre counted, which in that case it was three. But the three the Beast had slaughtered...

Cora steeled her resolve as she, Teryn, and Lex tethered their horses in a secluded grove at the far west of the Cambron Pass. Based on the sounds of hunting horns, the group was scouting west today. And if these hunters had similar habits to the previous group, the main party wouldn't be back until just after sundown. They only had about six hours to find the camp before it would be fully occupied.

They finished securing their horses. Cora could feel the tension radiating from Teryn and Lex, even with her shields in place. Valorre too had grown skittish since gaining so close in proximity to the new camp. He stood stiffly behind the horses, ears twitching back and forth. Even Berol seemed wary. She hadn't left Teryn's shoulder for the last hour.

"All right," she said, her own nerves creeping into her voice to give it a slight tremble, "I'll leave now and seek out the camp. Valorre will come with me, but he'll remain out of range once I think I'm close. If I find a decent vantage point to spy on the hunters, I'll stay. If I don't, I'll simply take in the lay of everything—"

"In what world did you think you were going to spy on their camp alone?" Teryn said.

His tone had her bristling. "In what world did you think I'd seek your permission?"

He shook his head. "We're coming with you."

Lex raised his hands, palms forward. "I'd rather stay and watch the horses, thanks."

Teryn rolled his eyes. "Fine. *I'm* coming with you."

Oh, yes, he can come, said Valorre.

"I don't need you," Cora said, ignoring Valorre and folding her arms. "I've done this before, you know."

"That's all well and good, but there's no way I'm waiting behind while you...endanger yourself alone."

Ah, he does have a point to be concerned, Valorre said. *I don't like when you endanger yourself either.*

Whose side are you on? she shot back.

His, obviously, he said without shame.

Cora furrowed her brow. Was that true concern in Teryn's eyes? Or something else? Suspicion, perhaps. She let down her shields just enough to sample his emotions. All she felt were conflicting elements. Fear. Trepidation.

Something that made her stomach feel warm. With an exhale, she lifted her shields again. "This is the safest part of our plan."

Lex lifted a finger. "Remind me what this plan is again? Sorry, working together as equals is a foreign concept to me, considering Helios was a royal ass."

She felt a flash of guilt. They'd told her about what it was like working with Prince Helios. How he'd kept more secrets than he'd shared. Her instincts begged her to keep the boys from getting close to her, begged her to do exactly what Helios had done. She'd only let them come along because Teryn had practically begged her. Still... she'd agreed, for better or worse, which meant she now had to suffer the consequences. Even if that meant collaborating with people she'd sooner leave behind.

Valorre came up beside her and nudged her in the shoulder. *Are they not our friends?*

No, she conveyed back.

To the boys, she said, "Today, I will scout. Gather information. Study the camp. Valorre will warn me if he senses danger. I'll try to glean as much as I can about this party's habits. I'll report back everything I find, then we'll form a plan of attack."

"By attack do you mean..." Lex mimed throwing back a drink and tipping his head to the side, eyes closed, tongue lolling from his mouth. When Cora refused to acknowledge him other than thinning her lips, he whispered, "Poison."

Her mind filled with a vision of Paul's prone form at the base of a tree, of James lying by the campfire with blue-tinged lips. The sound of bodies falling, cries of alarm—

She blinked the memories away, but her pulse had kicked up to a rapid tempo. "I don't know."

"Ideally, we'll avoid bloodshed," Teryn said. "Which is why I'm coming with you. Two pairs of eyes are better than one. With both of our perspectives, we'll have a better chance at coming up with a viable plan that puts all of us in the least amount of danger."

She wanted to roll her eyes. Of course the goodly, dutiful prince wanted to avoid bloodshed. He was a fool if he thought it was possible. Perhaps it was a lesson he'd have to learn on his own. "You can help me form a plan but I'm going to scout alone. That's final."

Teryn released a mirthless laugh. He closed the distance between them, his posture mirroring hers until only a foot separated them. Berol ruffled her feathers but remained on his shoulder. Teryn was so much taller than Cora, she had to crane her neck to meet his gaze. "Then I suppose I will too," he said. Before Cora could argue, he brushed past her, took his sword from his saddle, and left the grove. "We'll see who gets there first," he called over his shoulder.

Cora stared after him, jaw hanging on its hinge.

Lex chuckled as he walked over to his horse and took a book and apple from one of his saddlebags. "The two of you are disgusting."

She whirled to face him. "Excuse me?"

"As if you don't know." Lex settled down at the base of a tree, opening his book with one hand and bringing the apple to his mouth with the other. "You must get a kick out of riling him up, making him act all protective like that. It's cute, I guess. But...ugh, so gross."

You know what's gross? Valorre said. *Taking an apple from one's bag without offering me one. I like apples.*

Cora stroked Valorre's neck and glared at Lex. "I promise you, I haven't a clue what you're talking about."

He opened his book and began to read. "We both know he fancies you."

Cora's hand froze on Valorre's soft hide while her heart thudded against her ribcage. No, Lex couldn't be right. It wasn't possible. The concept was utterly preposterous.

The only word that left her lips was, "What?"

He took another bite of apple, muffling his next words. "I saw the two of you sneak off last night after your sexy knife play. If that's what does it for you, I'm happy for you both. Still, I'd rather keep our mission professional."

Cora's cheeks burned hotter than ever before. "This arrangement is strictly professional, trust me."

Lex shrugged and flipped a page. "If you say so. But I must warn you, I've come to like Teryn. He's a good man and a good friend." His eyes shot from his book to her, simmering with threat. "So if you do anything to hurt him, either body or heart, you'll have me to contend with."

She wasn't sure if she should be amused or impressed. Lex was hardly an intimidating specimen, but it was heartwarming that he'd defend his friend like that. More than anything, she was annoyed. Flustered. Irritated beyond belief. With a huff, she shouldered her bow and quiver and left the grove.

∾

SHE AND VALORRE CAUGHT UP WITH TERYN NOT LONG after. His smug grin was more than enough to make her second-guess not having taken an alternate route, but it seemed he'd already claimed the best path to their destination. She wouldn't inconvenience herself just because Teryn had a superiority complex.

Or was it more about what Lex had said? Was Teryn's concern over letting her go alone fueled by...

She couldn't even think it.

They followed the hunters' tracks down several different game trails until the wear in the path grew denser, fresher.

I sense them, Valorre said. *My brethren. They're close.*

Then this is as far as you can go. Stay out of sight.

Valorre rippled with worry, but he quickly flitted between the trees.

Teryn startled at the sudden movement, then met Cora's eyes. Up until now, they'd spoken only when necessary and both made a clear effort to keep their distance. "Where did he go?"

"We're too close now. It isn't safe for him to come any nearer. He'll find somewhere to hide where his tracks won't be easy to follow."

Teryn gave only a curt nod and they were on their way again.

WITH ONLY TWO HOURS LEFT UNTIL SUNDOWN, THEY finally found the camp.

Cora's palms were slick with sweat as they crept quietly toward the sound of a crackling fire. Once they caught their first glimpse of the clearing, Teryn fed Berol a strip of dried meat and gestured a finger upward. She immediately took off into the sky. Then he pointed at Cora and himself, silently conveying that they should circle the perimeter in opposite directions. She replied with a nod.

Teryn moved first, one slow step at a time. She wanted to mouth at him to be careful, but she kept the warning to herself. She was still a little peeved at how he'd insisted on accompanying her. However, she had to admit she'd come to feel comforted by his company today. Even now, having another person scouting made her feel safer than she had when she was alone. At first, she'd been worried Teryn would have no talent for stealth, but when she watched him take careful steps, prodding the earth with each foot before fully stepping down, she realized he knew what he was doing. She supposed that was one benefit to being a prince. Royal hunts were both a rite of passage and an expected pastime.

Cora circled the camp, pausing now and then to edge a little closer, stealing glances at what was beyond the veil of underbrush she kept to. No matter how many times she looked, she saw the same thing. A quiet camp. Four cages filled with unicorns. A single guard sitting by the fire. When she and Teryn met at the other side of camp— after they'd both startled at the sudden appearance of the other—she gestured for him to follow her away from the clearing.

Once they were well out of earshot, she whispered, "They have a baby unicorn." Her heart clenched just to say it out loud. She'd nearly stumbled when she'd first caught sight of it. Like the three adult unicorns, the baby was thin and frail. If she had to guess, based on every-thing she'd seen and overheard and all that Teryn had shared about what he'd learned, the creatures were close to harvest. Either the Beast would come to take them soon or the hunters would carve the horns from the unicorns' heads while the creatures were still alive.

Torture.

Slaughter.

One of the most inhumane acts of violence Cora could imagine.

They might not have days to continue spying. To brew another decoction of belladonna and establish the best way to infiltrate the camp.

"I saw," Teryn said. His lips were pulled into a frown, a disgusted look on his face that told her his feelings were much like her own.

She brought her thumbnail between her teeth to keep her hands from shaking. "And there was only one guard."

"I saw that as well." His voice held a note of concern. It probably wasn't hard to guess what she was thinking. "But he was only a boy."

That too made Cora's chest feel tight. She'd expected to find someone her own age, like James, if not a more grizzled guard like Paul. Instead, they'd found a boy who looked no older than thirteen. He bore no brand that marked him as a criminal. Had no hard look in his eye that made him seem like he was a mercenary in training. Cora would have thought they'd stumbled upon the wrong camp if it weren't for the occupied cages. Not to mention the deep reddish-brown stains that marred the earth before them.

"We have to free those unicorns," she said. "They

won't make it much longer. And this," she gestured back in the direction of camp, "is too good of an opportunity to pass up."

Teryn's brow knitted. "Does it not seem *too* easy, though?"

She had to admit it did seem too good to be true. Still, she'd looked for signs that someone else was waiting out of sight, but there was nothing. No one. Every part of her itched to act. To finally do more than watch and wait. To save the unicorns for the ones she'd failed. Perhaps she was being a bit reckless, and had she been alone, she'd probably have chosen caution. But she wasn't alone. She had Teryn.

"We have to at least try, don't we? It's not yet sundown. The hunters are still far away." The last hunting horn they'd heard had been distant.

"We can try," Teryn finally said, "but we aren't killing the boy. Instead, we do this my way."

31

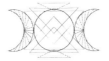

T eryn's way, it turned out, was humiliating. And yet, Cora agreed, having no better idea of her own. After stashing her bow and arrows, she circled the camp and paused just outside the clearing. The young guard was still by the fire in nearly the same position she'd last seen him—his posture slumped with an air of boredom, the side of his face resting on his hand as he poked the burning logs with a stick. Cora took a deep breath, untucked her skirts from her belt so they no were no longer wrapped around her legs, and twisted her expression into one of distress. She stumbled into the camp, feigning sobs.

The boy immediately rose to his feet. His hand flew to the hilt of a dagger at his belt, but when his eyes swept over Cora, he withdrew the hand. "Ma'am," he said, eyes wide.

She fell to her knees, her hair streaming around her. "You must help me," she cried.

He came closer. "What's wrong? What are you doing out here?"

She lifted her face, lips pulled into a pout. "I was kidnapped," she said, her voice high and feminine and breathy, "by...by...by bandits." Her words dissolved into a wail.

The boy stared at her, face pale and bewildered as if he couldn't comprehend what to do with her. Just then, a figure came up behind him. Before the boy even had a clue, Teryn hooked an arm around his throat and squeezed the sides between his bicep and forearm. The boy flailed but was out in a matter of seconds. Teryn aided his fall and settled him on the ground. With a nod to Cora, she rose, and they jogged over to the cages. Wordlessly, they got to work, severing the ropes that bound the frames. Cora opened the baby unicorn's cage first, then the one next to it. Soon all the cages were open, and all the unicorns were darting away.

We did it, she conveyed to Valorre, hoping he was still close enough to hear her. *If you can communicate with them, direct them to go east so they don't run into the hunters.*

She felt Valorre's reply as a trill of joy, one that had Cora's lips stretching into a grin.

Teryn tugged her arm, nodding his head toward the edge of camp. She followed him out of the clearing to where she'd stashed her weapons. Her pulse was a roar in her ears as she shouldered her bow and quiver. They kept their pace as mindful as they could, but Cora felt like they were running for the way her body buzzed with elation and terror in the wake of their rescue. They'd done it. They'd truly done it. She had to stifle her desire to laugh.

Teryn stopped suddenly before her.

"What—" Then she saw it.

The baby unicorn was just ahead, its body quivering. Its thin legs quaked as it tried to take a step, but it seemed too overcome with fear or confusion.

"Seven gods," Teryn cursed. "The poor thing."

Valorre, there's a baby. She's so frail. She seems confused.

There came no reply. He was likely too busy guiding the others. Which left only her.

She took a slow step toward the tiny unicorn, her tawny fur thin and clinging to her bones. The creature startled, freezing in place as her eyes locked on Cora's. Cora halted as well. Lowering her shields, she opened her senses to the unicorn. She was immediately struck by panic, a desperation to find someone very important to her. Cora's throat constricted, and she was tempted to close the link if only to free herself from the emotions. Instead, she kept her senses open and tried to move them in the opposite direction. It had been effortless to converse with Valorre, but she'd never experienced the phenomenon with any other unicorn since. This time, though, she had to try.

Easy, she tried to convey, forcing her own emotions to calm, to exude safety and protection. The unicorn's energy softened a little. Cora took another small step. *I'm not going to hurt you. I'm here to help you. If you follow me, I'll take you to my friend. He's just like you.*

She filled her mind with thoughts of Valorre, letting warmth and kindness radiate from her heart, down her palms, into the space between them.

The creature calmed further and took a step forward. Cora mirrored her every move until they were almost close enough to touch. Then, crouching down, Cora extended her hands. The unicorn tottered the rest of the way on her tiny, shaky legs until Cora's hands met her hide. Cora nearly choked on a sob when she felt how prominent the unicorn's ribs were beneath her palms. "It's all right," she whispered to her, voice thick with emotion. "We're going to help you."

Remembering Teryn's presence, she cast a glance over her shoulder. Teryn's expression was nearly painful to witness. His eyes were glazed as he stared at the unicorn. He met Cora's eyes then, and she smiled at him. She wasn't sure why, only that she wanted to erase his pained countenance and remind him that they'd done something good, something worth celebrating. He smiled back, which was perhaps an even sadder look.

Berol dove down from overhead and landed on Teryn's shoulder. There was something uneasy about the way she perched, in the splay of her wings as she nipped Teryn's cheek. Cora didn't need to be bonded to the falcon to know the bird was delivering a warning.

A hunting horn sounded, shattering the air. It was too close. Far closer than the last one had been. The baby unicorn startled and made to dart away, but Cora lifted her in her arms. She wasn't exactly a creature made for carrying, but she was so thin, her weight was hardly a burden to bear. "Shhh," Cora whispered. "Easy."

Teryn ran to her, and Berol launched back into the sky to circle overhead. He angled his head in the opposite direction of the horn, and Cora followed him. They crept away, their pace hurried. "I can carry her," Teryn offered.

"It's all right," she said. "She feels comfortable with me."

Another horn blast, this one from straight ahead.

Then another off to the side.

Cora's heart leapt into her throat. They were surrounded.

"We need to get out of here fast," Teryn said.

He was right, but no matter where they turned, another echoing horn would sound. She glanced between the boughs. It wasn't yet sundown. The hunters shouldn't be back yet. But, of course, she'd chosen risk over caution today instead of ensuring she knew exactly when to expect them back. Now Cora and Teryn could be caught. The hunters would be upon them. They'd seize the unicorn and Cora would have failed again.

Her legs begged to run while another part of her burned for a fight. Teryn was the one who'd insisted on avoiding bloodshed, while she'd only grown more furious at seeing what these hunters had done to the creature in her arms. Her heart screamed for vengeance. Her head, on the other hand, reminded her they had no idea how many men they could be facing. It was only her and Teryn—her quiver of arrows and his sword—against what would undoubtedly be insurmountable odds.

Then I fight to the death, part of her said.

No, I flee and hope I make it out alive, said another.

She felt torn in two, unsure which instinct to heed. She'd followed her impulse to stay and fight when they'd thrown caution to the wind and rescued the unicorns right away. Had that been the right choice? Or the wrong one? Regardless of what was right or wrong then, which choice would serve her best now?

A wave of vertigo seized her, forcing her to stagger her feet. But it helped her remember the soil that stood beneath her, acting as a source of stability. It reminded her of other things too. Of the air surrounding her, filling her lungs. Of the fire that was her fury. The water that was blood. The elements. Her magic.

The last thing she wanted at a time like this was to slow down and turn inward. Not when she was feeling so frantic.

But, as Salinda always said, magic was strengthened by challenge, and the simplest challenge of all was doing what felt the hardest in any given moment. If there was ever a time for magic to prove stronger than weapons, it would be now.

Fighting through her more predominant instincts, she closed her eyes and focused on her breath. She detached her emotional bond from the unicorn to focus instead on the feel of a soft wind dancing over her skin, the sensation of her hair prickling at the back of her neck. She noted the way the ground felt beneath her feet, firm and strong but with subtle give. A sense of calm went over her, telling her she'd tapped into her deepest Art. Extending her senses around her, she sought nearby feeling. At first, she felt only the unicorn and Teryn, but she brushed past them to clusters of energies beyond. She was struck by a cacophony of emotions belonging to several others—excitement, trepidation, desire, hunger. There was a darkness to these energies, a density that made her stomach turn. At least half a dozen hunters were closing in on Cora and Teryn. A spike of alarm threatened to break her composure, but she breathed it away.

Another horn sounded, and Teryn placed his palm on her back, angling her away from it. "Cora, we need to go."

She put a hand on his forearm to still him. To tell him to stay. To do what, she still wasn't sure.

Hide.

The feeling originated deep in her gut, firm and calm and certain. Opening her eyes, she saw a wide tree straight ahead, its boughs low and dense. It wouldn't hide them, not if the hunters drew close enough, but she was going to try.

She met Teryn's puzzled expression. "You're going to have to trust me," she said.

"How so?"

She tugged him toward the tree, following the internal pull she felt with every fiber of her being. The baby unicorn struggled in her grasp, but she made a soothing noise at her. "You're going to have to trust me too."

The question was...could she trust herself?

She shook the doubt from her mind and hefted the unicorn closer to Teryn. "Help me hold her."

"What are we doing?" Teryn's whisper was laced with terror, but he helped her hold the unicorn between them.

With a deep breath, she said. "Close your eyes. Whatever you do, don't say a word. Don't move, no matter what you hear. Put..." She swallowed hard. "Put your free arm around me and don't let go until I tell you to."

His eyes searched hers, his face pale. "I don't understand."

Another horn blast.

The hunters would find them in a matter of seconds.

She held his gaze, trying to convey everything she was feeling. The urgency. The hope. The gut sensation that told her *this*—no matter how absurd it seemed—was what they had to do.

Finally, he stepped closer, the baby unicorn the only thing that separated their chests. He closed his eyes and hooked his free arm around her waist.

Her eyelids closed next, and she reached out for the trunk of the tree. Her palm met rough bark, thrummed with the pulse of its life force, of the elements surging through its roots, its branches, its leaves. She drew her attention to her feet, to the firmness of the ground below, and felt another thrum. The tree's roots extended deep underground, merging with the soil, the water that fed them, the air and sunlight that helped them grow strong. Cora pressed harder against the tree, imagined she was no different. She too was nourished by the same elements. They fed her body the same way they fed her Art. She was no different from the tree, her skin so like bark she might as well be a sapling. A steady energy began to pulse through her, stilling her mind. She was aware of two distinct energies pressed close to her and extended this same feeling outward.

They were one and the same.

She, the tree, the boy, the fae.

The heartbeat of the tree was her own. Hers was the unicorn's. The unicorn's was the boy's. The boy's was hers. She could almost hear it pounding through her, vibrating up the hand that held her waist, echoing the beat in her chest. When she breathed, he did too. When they breathed, so too did the unicorn, the tree, the soil, the sky. Everything breathed.

There was nothing here but a tree.

One with vast root systems that shuddered beneath

the soil, stirring the top layer of dirt until not a footprint could be seen where once there'd been many. No longer was there a sign of the boy, the girl, and the small fae creature.

They'd never been there at all.

Just a tree.

A tree.

Only a tree.

The tree hardly acknowledged the men that stalked by. They prowled like wolves, eyes keen, but they found not what they sought. Nothing but a wood empty of everything but what should be there. The tree didn't count in minutes or seconds, but time did pass. Soon—or maybe not so soon—the men passed too, shoulders slumped with disappointment of a catch not had.

Only then did the tree unravel.

Only then did one become two, and two separated into three.

32

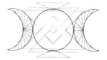

Teryn didn't know how many minutes had passed. All he knew was that he couldn't look away from Cora. He'd only obeyed her order to close his eyes for a few moments before his eyelids flew open. At first, it had been out of panic, but as her face filled his vision, calm settled over him. They were so close he could count every one of Cora's dark eyelashes, every freckle dancing over her nose. His hand felt warm on her back, and where they both held the unicorn, their arms touched. An *otherness* had surrounded them then, something Teryn wasn't sure he'd ever be able to explain. He didn't see it with his eyes or feel it with his senses. It was just there. The indescribable buzz of magic.

He hadn't known what Cora was doing, had seen nothing to explain what made the hunters walk by without giving them a second glance. He'd only seen *her*. For one strange moment, he'd felt connected to her in a way that defied reason. He'd felt her heart thrum as his own. Felt her breath move through his lungs. It was unsettling and yet completely noninvasive. He'd welcomed it. Yearned for it.

But now the *otherness* was beginning to fade with every breath. His pulse became his own, no longer entangled with Cora's and the unicorn's. He realized Cora's eyes were open now too and were locked on his. Slowly, she pulled her hand away from the tree trunk, but still, they didn't separate. She said something to him then, but his mind was too befuddled to comprehend it.

"What?"

"You're still holding on to me," she whispered, her voice unsteady.

He gulped, finding his tongue heavy as he searched for words. "You said not to let you go until you said so."

"Oh." A soft smile crossed her lips, a hint of a blush coloring her cheeks. "You can let me go now."

He held on a beat longer, then slowly slid his hand from around her waist. The baby unicorn, who'd grown surprisingly calm in the wake of such strange events, was all that connected them.

"I can carry her," Teryn said. "I think it's safe to say she feels comfortable enough with me now."

"All right." Teryn was surprised she didn't argue. She slipped her arm from the unicorn and stepped away. Teryn felt oddly cold. Empty. Whatever had happened at the tree...it had severely messed with his mind.

He wasn't even sure why he'd done what she'd told him to. He could have waited until the perfect moment and shoved her before the hunters—if that was even who those men had been. He'd been too focused on Cora when the figures had walked by, but when he'd first heard the hunting horns, he'd known his plan had worked. His father had sent word to King Dimetreus. The king knew they were heading to this camp next, knew Cora would try to rescue the unicorns. Because that was what Teryn's letter to his father had said.

I'll bring her to the Cambron Pass camp in exchange for her bounty.

He'd suspected his plan had worked as soon as he and Cora had stalked the camp and found only a young boy guarding it. Terror had surged through him then, even though he should have been pleased. He should have wanted his plan to come to fruition, right?

After that, he'd expected an ambush at any moment. It hadn't come. Part of him had hoped—as nonsensical as the hope was—that maybe his letter hadn't reached the king. Or perhaps it hadn't been taken seriously, or the king hadn't been prepared to react on such short notice. Relief had washed over him as they'd freed the unicorns, but it all fled the moment he'd heard the horns.

And now...

Now he didn't know what to think. He'd allowed Cora to hide them. Had *wanted* her to hide them. Even with his mind growing sharper, clearer, he had no desire to shout, to call back the hunters, to turn her in.

"We must go," Cora said and started off with caution.

If he took one step away from the camp, he knew what he was leaving behind.

500,000 *sovas*. Enough to save his kingdom.

All he had to do was turn in a wanted murderer.

Cora glanced over her shoulder, brow furrowed as she noticed his hesitation. She held out her hand, her tattooed palm extended his way. "Come on," she whispered. Her eyes were bright, her lips curled into a soft smile. She'd changed after what had happened at the tree. Whatever magic she'd used, she glowed with it now, radiated with it in unseen ways.

Teryn took a deep breath, knowing he was about to seal his fate. Hefting the unicorn in both arms, he returned her grin and followed after her.

CORA FELT ALIVE IN A WAY SHE'D NEVER BEEN BEFORE. HER use of magic had defied reason, obliterated coincidence, and negated any chance that she, Teryn, and the baby unicorn had evaded notice by happenstance alone. She'd made them *invisible*. Just like witch lore claimed was possible.

She understood now why it was referred to as quiet magic. Sure, her feat of invisibility was incredible to her, but to the hunters or anyone else that could have walked by that tree...to them it was like it never happened.

The aftereffects surged through her veins, pulsed in every line of ink on her skin. Resisting her instincts to run had been hard. Choosing magic over her bow had been harder. In overcoming her personal challenge, her magic had grown stronger. It still felt quiet and there was much more for her to learn, but now she believed the possibilities she'd once turned her nose up at.

Teryn too seemed changed. She'd sensed a shift in his emotions, from something dark and heavy to a lightness akin to relief. He still clung to a hint of the sorrow she'd glimpsed right after they'd rescued the unicorn, but his steps were lighter now, his smile freer. Perhaps it was just the comfort that came with knowing they'd escaped the hunters.

Valorre found them not long after. He was frantic with worry over not having warned them about the approaching hunters. Just as Cora had thought, he'd been out of range while he'd tried to direct his freed brethren to safer grounds. Thankfully, Berol had been there, even though her warning hadn't given them much of an advantage. She flew overhead now, keeping her distance from Teryn while he carried the unicorn.

What should we do with the baby? Cora asked Valorre.

The unicorn went still, ears twitching. Finally, he said, *I think her mother is near. Or...near enough. I can feel one of my kind lingering somewhere in the pass. She knows it isn't safe but she's...seeking something.*

Can you take us to her?

Valorre considered that. *No, the mother will fear you. I will take her myself.*

Cora was worried the baby unicorn might still be too shaken to walk. She turned to Teryn. "You can try putting her down."

He did as told, gently setting the unicorn on her hooves. She stumbled a little, legs splayed, but managed to keep her balance. She was no longer trembling like she'd been outside the camp.

Valorre took a few steps closer.

The baby lowered her head, posture startled. After a few moments of warily examining the much larger unicorn, she took a step toward him. Then another. Her gait was steady as she closed the remaining distance. Valorre gave her an affectionate nuzzle, then lifted his head toward Cora. *She will be fine. I will take her now.*

Cora's heart clenched as she watched Valorre guide the tiny creature away.

Teryn came up beside her. Berol was settled on his shoulder, preening. "We really did it," he said. "We actually freed four unicorns."

She turned to face him. "Thank you for helping me," she said, finding the words easier to say than she expected. She didn't want to admit that she'd been wrong in her hesitation to let him accompany her, but...perhaps she had been.

"You're welcome," he said, and again a hint of sorrow crept into the edges of her awareness. She strengthened her shields, blocking it completely. After what she'd accomplished at the tree, she needed a reprieve.

They made their way back toward camp, the sun barely a hint of light on the horizon. A comfortable silence fell between them, which was such a stark contrast to the tense quiet they'd kept earlier that day. They were nearing camp when Teryn whirled to face her.

Cora pulled up short. His expression told her that perhaps the silence had only been comfortable on her end. She frowned. "What is it?"

"We should leave this area tonight."

"What? Why would we do that?"

He folded his arms, shoulders tense. "The hunters will know someone knocked out their guard and freed the unicorns. They might try to track us. If not tonight, then tomorrow."

Cora's eyes widened, all of her pleasant feelings evaporating. "You're the one who wanted to avoid bloodshed. You only just now realize your plan has put us at a greater risk?"

"I'm sorry," he rushed to say. "Let's leave at once. Go... far from here."

She backed up a step, eyes narrowing. "My mission isn't done. You saw the map. There are still numerous other hunting parties. I can't let them continue to hunt unicorns."

"What are you planning to do? Poison all of them? What about when they're replaced with new recruits? These men are mercenaries and convicted criminals. There's no shortage of more like them."

Cora felt a crushing weight fall over her. He was right. It was too much. Still, she shook the overwhelming feeling from her heart and lifted her chin. "I will do whatever I can."

"To what end? You can't poison them all. Sooner or later, they'll catch on. They'll be waiting for you. This... this isn't sustainable. You can't do this on your own."

She threw her hands in the air. "You knew that when you asked to come with me. Is that not the very reason you begged to aid my efforts?"

He clenched his jaw, giving no answer.

She rolled her eyes with a scoff. "We ran into one close call and now you realize this isn't all fun and games. You should have known from the start that this wouldn't be some glamorous quest where you save the damsel in distress and come home the shining hero, bearing not a single scratch. I meant it when I said that I don't need you, but..." Her throat went dry. She tried to swallow her next words down, but they burst from her lips before she could stop them. "I liked having you around today."

His expression softened, eyes turning down at the

corners, but he wouldn't meet her gaze. "Cora..." His voice was soft, strained.

She took a step closer, her heart pounding in her chest. With a slow exhale, she lowered her shields just long enough to feel his turmoil. His emotions were too jumbled to untangle completely, but she identified guilt. Shame. Fear. It left a bitter taste in her mouth. "What is it, Teryn? What aren't you telling me?"

Slowly, he lifted his eyes and met hers, his expression pure agony. "Did you kill Queen Linette and Princess Aveline?"

Her breath left her lungs. She was more stunned than if he'd slapped her. For several moments, all she could do was stare. Suspicion crawled up her spine, raking claws through her heart. "How long have you known?"

He paled. "You did it then."

She took a step back, a spike of fury sending heat to her cheeks. "No, of course I didn't."

His eyes narrowed as he watched her, his arms stiff at his side. Berol too stared from her perch on his shoulder, wings slightly lifted. Teryn's fingers flinched, a subtle movement toward his sheathed sword. She went to reach for her bow only to realize she'd already wrapped her hand around it. When had she done that? Suddenly she understood *that* was why his posture was suddenly defensive—because *she'd* reached for a weapon first. And yet he kept his hand open at his side, ready to fight should it come to that, but not willing to make the first move.

It was almost painful to force her hand away from her bow, to ball her fingers into fists. As soon as she did,

Teryn visibly relaxed. Berol ruffled her feathers and nestled back down.

"I was framed," she said, voice quavering with restraint, "by Duke Morkai."

His eyes went wide. "The man orchestrating the hunt for unicorns? He framed you for murder?"

She nodded.

"So, what you're doing with the unicorns, with the hunters. It's...personal."

Another nod.

He studied her again, and she could feel the doubt pouring off of him. Of course he wouldn't believe her. How could anyone take the word of a poison-wielding witch over one of the most powerful men in Khero?

She waited for him to react. To ask her to prove her innocence. To sneer, argue, or condemn.

But he didn't.

"All right," he said, his voice barely above a whisper. Then once more, clearer, louder. "All right. Then it's even more important that we leave at once." Without another word, he stormed off.

She blinked in his wake, confused by his reaction. He was nearly swallowed by shadows far ahead by the time she started following after him. She had to jog to keep up with him when she reached his side. "What's going on, Teryn?"

He said nothing, only quickened his pace. It was enough to send Berol launching off his shoulder to follow them from above instead.

Her heart was a thundering, rioting mess as they marched into camp.

They pulled up short.

Lex stood as soon as he saw them. His eyes were wide as he searched their faces. Then his gaze swept over the five figures who stood silently around them. "I have no idea who these people are," he said, voice pitched with fright.

Cora, however, knew exactly who they were. Four of them wore black armor etched with a crescent moon. Guards. The fifth wore an elegant black coat embroidered with gold geometric designs that ran down the front and hems. Black leather gloves adorned his hands, and in one he gripped a gentleman's cane topped with an enormous amber crystal.

Cora's eyes locked on his face.

She recognized his black hair, his arched brows, and the pale shade of his blue irises. His cheekbones were sharp, his jaw sharper.

"Morkai," she said through her teeth.

The duke ignored Cora but nodded graciously at Teryn. "King Dimetreus was both surprised and pleased by your correspondence. Thank you ever so much for finding her. Your reward will be generous indeed."

Cora's gaze shot to Teryn. She saw the guilt written in his eyes and finally understood what she'd sensed all along. Her shoulders sagged as her heart crumbled inside her chest, pierced with icy talons of betrayal.

Morkai faced her, the smug tilt to his lips revealing how greatly he relished her pain. "Hello, Princess Aveline. It's been a while."

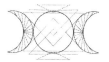

33

Cora hadn't been called by her first name in six years. Perhaps that was why—when next she dreamed—she saw not the shadowed halls of her nightmare but her childhood bedroom. She was face-down upon her bed, torn between shame and rage, when she heard her door open.

"Aveline Corasande Caelan," a deep voice said from behind her, tone pitched with warning.

Cora froze. Her brother only ever used her full name when she was in trouble. Steeling her nerves, she pushed herself to sitting and faced King Dimetreus. "I did nothing wrong."

With slow steps, he crossed the distance between them and took a seat next to her. His voice softened. "You acted brash at dinner tonight."

Her heart sank as she met his gaze. His dark eyes were gentle, a warm smile on his lips. With his shoulder-length brown hair and olive complexion, he reminded her so much of Mother. Only his nose and the stubble on his jaw resembled their father. Being reminded of her dearly departed parents made her wish he was angry instead. His sympathy only increased her guilt.

Still, she refused to back down. "Linette acted brash first and you did nothing to defend me."

"Linette is my wife and I love her dearly. I love you as well, Aveline, but you must learn to respect your sister-in-law. She is your queen. I need you to apologize to her."

She bristled. "But she's the one who lied. She's not with child, Dimi."

He chuckled. "Dearest sister, you're too young to speak on such matters. You know nothing about children or their conception. Just because her belly has yet to—"

"I know how babies are made and I know how they're born."

He gave her a patronizing look. "I assure you, sister, it isn't a stork."

"No, of course it isn't." She lifted her chin and put her hands on her hips. "When a man and woman feel desirous, a woman lifts her skirts and a man becomes engorged—"

He launched to his feet, nearly tripping in the process. "Seven devils, where did you hear that?"

She blushed, realizing she must have said something improper. She was always getting in trouble for things like that. "I overheard Lady Paulette discussing a novel with Lady Madeline."

"Banish such thoughts from your mind," he said, wagging a finger. His cheeks were as red as beets. "Regardless of what you think you know, you mustn't have acted as you did at dinner."

She stood and stomped a foot. "I didn't even want to be there. Master Benedict dragged me."

"Aveline," he said, his tone turning sharper, "you promised to attend dinner and you showed up late. To add insult to injury, you made a scene and upset Linette. She left the dining hall in tears. She's been inconsolable, sobbing in bed ever since. What you said to her was cruel."

She rolled her eyes. "I didn't actually curse her. I'm not a witch. I don't know how to curse people."

"It doesn't matter. What you said scared her. It's important that she is kept comfortable to keep the baby safe."

She had to bite the inside of her cheek to keep from arguing the fact that the queen was a liar, that she wasn't with child and had never been. She'd learned her lesson, though. Her brother was obviously never going to listen. She'd have to wait until later to say *I told you so*. Perhaps in the meantime she could try to sort out why a queen would feel the need to lie about such a silly thing in the first place. She knew queens were expected to bear sons, but she couldn't quite grasp the significance or the pressure involved. Maybe her brother was right. Maybe she was too young to speak on such complicated matters.

But still...

"I don't want to apologize."

Her brother's expression softened again as he took her hand in his. "I know, but you're a princess. The older you get the more you'll come to understand that being royal often means doing a whole host of things you'd rather not do. Please, Cora."

The name made her breath hitch. Only their mother

had ever called her Cora, and usually only when they were alone. It was a nickname taken from her middle name—Corasande—a name that represented her mother's homeland in the Southern Isles. If she was being honest, she preferred Cora to Aveline. Aveline sounded like a stuffy old queen like Linette while Cora was fit for someone wild and free. Like whom she'd prefer to be.

She knew Dimetreus was manipulating her by using that name, but she found it effective nonetheless. "Fine," she ground out, "I'll apologize. But only for pretending to curse her. Everything else I said was true."

Her brother's expression hardened, but he released a resigned sigh. "It's a start. Now, get going."

"I have to do it now?"

His only answer was a pointed look.

Shoulders slumped, she dragged her feet down the hall in the direction of the queen's chambers. Linette had separate quarters from the king. Cora was rehearsing a stiff apology when her feet stopped moving of their own accord. A dark and hollow feeling formed in the pit of her stomach. She took another few steps but the sense of wrongness increased, prickling the hair on her arms—

"Your Highness."

She startled at the voice and found the queen's youngest maid brushing by, arms laden with a serving tray bearing tea and cookies. The girl was about Cora's age. "Where are you taking that?" she asked, even though she already knew the answer.

The maid paused and blushed, shifting anxiously from foot to foot. "Queen Linette, Your Highness."

Cora walked up to her and extended her hands toward the tray. "I'll take it."

"But...but it's what I'm supposed to do." The maid stepped back, expression struck with something between terror and indignation. "A princess cannot carry a tray."

Cora cut the girl a glare, but she only blinked back at her. With a grumbling sigh, Cora unclasped a bracelet— one of many cumbersome, shiny baubles she was forced to wear—from around her wrist and held it out to the girl. "Payment."

"I...I can't take that."

"You can and you will. That's an order. Now take it and go. I need to *apologize to the queen.*" She said the last part with a hefty dose of mockery.

The maid seemed too stunned to do anything but obey, her hands trembling as she passed the tray to Cora and accepted the bracelet in return. A flash of greed lit the girl's eyes once her fingers curled fully around the item. Then, with a vibrant smile, she curtsied and darted down the opposite end of the hall.

With a proper offer of apology in hand, Cora continued to the queen's rooms. Only then did she recall the eerie feeling that had first halted her progress. It crept into her bones once more, echoed through her blood. Shadows darkened the glow of lamplight lining the corridor. Sound became hollow as the halls emptied, dimmed, and closed in tight around her.

Cora remembered she was dreaming. With that realization came a reminder of everything she knew was coming. She struggled against her dream-self, tried to force her feet to stop. But the small version of her continued on, step after step, even as her terror grew.

Her next step brought her to the door.

The bedroom.

The blood.

Duke Morkai whirled to face her. With a devious grin, he lifted the queen's blood from the sheets. It rose to meet his palm in thin red ribbons that he played like the strings of a lute.

Cora dropped the tray.

Her scream jolted her awake.

SHE BLINKED INTO DIM LIGHT, FOUND SOMETHING SOFT against her cheek. The next thing she noticed was a rocking motion. She lifted her head, saw a shaft of pale sunlight peeking between a velvet curtain and a small window. Was it already sunrise? Another turn of her head revealed a door, leather-covered walls, and a seat beneath her draped with furs. She was in a coach. That explained the constant rocking. Perhaps that had been what had woken her. Not her scream but the jostling of the carriage.

She pushed herself to sit upright, surprised to find her hands unbound. Someone sat across from her, their upper body cast in shadow, but Cora didn't bother waiting for her eyes to adjust. Instead, she lunged for the door—

The bottom of a black cane smacked into the door, an inch from where her hand had been. She reeled back as the figure leaned forward. She wasn't surprised when Morkai's face was illuminated beneath the shaft of sunlight. He watched her with his silver-blue eyes, his lips lifted in an arrogant smile. "You'll find every exit locked, Aveline. Or should I call you Cora? It seems that's the name you gave the prince."

Cora's blood boiled at his mention of Teryn. It didn't matter that he'd seemed shocked when Morkai had mentioned her true name, nor did she care about the regret that had clouded his energy when their eyes met. What mattered was that he'd betrayed her. That he did nothing when Morkai's guards surrounded her. One of them had pressed a cloth to her mouth, filling her nose with an acrid scent. It was the last thing she recalled.

Her head spun. She resisted the urge to press a palm to her forehead and instead burned Morkai with a glare. "You made a mistake in locking yourself in here with me unbound."

He scoffed, eyes falling to the ink marking her forearms. "You're no threat to me. That's why you're unbound."

She assessed his relaxed posture, the way he sat with one leg crossed over the other, his crystal-topped cane resting in his lap. One hand stroked one of the crystal's facets while his other arm was draped over the back of his seat. He was the epitome of overconfidence. Everything about him was exactly as she remembered. His voice, his smug grin, the color of his eyes, his...face.

That was when she realized he hadn't aged a day. She remembered him looking ancient in her eyes six years ago, the same way all adults looked old to a child, but that didn't explain why he looked barely five years her senior now.

"How have you not aged?"

"Blood," he said, giving no further explanation. Then he added, "It's all right if you like what you see."

"I don't," she said through her teeth. It wasn't a lie. He might look young and beautiful, but it only fueled her disgust. Her arms begged her to reach across the coach and tear Morkai limb from limb. Then she'd climb from the carriage, find Teryn, and do the same to him. Unfortunately, she'd been disarmed while she was unconscious. Her bow and quiver were gone as was her belt, taking with it her knife and dagger. That left only magic.

She breathed in deep, letting her rage pour through her, directing it down her palms, to...to...

The blood left her face. She felt nothing.

Shaking her head, she tried again, breathing in deep. Her lungs, however, felt too shallow and her mind refused to stay in one place, refused to let her focus on her breath. She breathed in again, seeking any sign that her magic was there. A light tingle ran over her palms but that was it. Her magic lingered, just below the surface, but it felt tangled. Smothered.

By what? Was this Morkai's doing?

Morkai's grin widened. "I told you, Aveline. You're no threat to me."

She bit back her retort and forced herself to mirror his composure. Leaning back in her seat, she asked with feigned calm, "What do you intend to do with me?"

His answer came easily. "I'm taking you home to Ridine Castle, of course."

She huffed a dark laugh. "To be sent back to the dungeon? To be executed at last? Why did you even bother freeing me from the dungeon six years ago if you were only going to hunt me down later?"

"Whether you return to the dungeon upon our arrival

at the castle is up to you. Should I will it, I can have you reclaim your rightful place as princess."

Her stomach flipped. She'd never dreamed of regaining her title. Had never wanted it back. Not after everything that had happened. Not after her brother had turned his back on her and condemned her. She'd let her old identity die the night she fled the castle and never said a word of the truth to anyone. Never enlightened any of the Forest People who'd brought up the poor princess' death.

"I can tell you don't believe me," Morkai said, "but I promise you it's true."

He was right. She didn't believe a word he said. "The world thinks I'm dead. How do you plan on resurrecting me?"

"That's a simple matter, for here you are breathing. Try bringing someone who's truly dead back to the realm of the living. That, my dear, is a far greater challenge but one I daresay will not be out of my reach for long."

Her mouth went dry at his words. She hadn't a clue what he was talking about, but it left a queasy feeling in her stomach. It did bring to mind a question that had haunted her these last six years.

"Who did you kill in my stead?"

"Just a maid wearing Princess Aveline's bracelet. So, in a way, you killed her. I couldn't have chosen better myself."

Fury surged through her. She balled her hands tight and considered launching herself at him. She may not have weapons, but she had fingernails. Teeth. Arms for punching and legs for kicking—

"Easy," he said. His knuckles went white on his cane.

"One move from you and I'll rescind my offer to restore your title."

She deepened her glare but forced herself to ease back against her seat. Not because she was interested in hearing his offer but because she still had many questions. "I don't understand how you did it. My brother thinks a maid killed his sister, but I'm the one he convicted, knowing full well who I was when he found me with the queen."

"He was so deep in grief, he knew not what he saw. I reminded him of that when we found dear little Aveline's body. She was so swollen from whatever poison the maid had given her that she was barely recognizable. It wasn't hard to get him to accept a new truth."

A cold shiver ran down her spine. "You brainwashed him."

"Your brother has always been a weak-minded man."

"And yet you serve him most loyally."

His eyes took on a vicious gleam. "Do I, Aveline? Or does he serve me in every way?"

She swallowed hard. In all these years, she'd let herself despise her brother. Morkai had always held the greatest fault in her mind, but Dimetreus had stood by and accepted lie after lie while ignoring every truth she'd told him. When her brother found her with his dead wife's body, he didn't hesitate for more than a second before he condemned her. He heard not a word as she argued her case. He shed not a tear as he had his guards drag her into a cell beneath the castle.

What if Dimetreus' reaction hadn't been entirely his fault? If Morkai could manipulate the king into changing his own memories...what else could he do?

"What do you want from me?" she asked, a slight tremble building in her voice. Whether it was from fear or anger she knew not.

"To talk."

"You must want to do more than talk to offer 500,000 *sovas* for my capture. How did you do it anyway? The poster. My likeness couldn't have been sketched on a guess."

He rubbed his amber crystal again. "I kept a drop of your blood."

Her eyes went wide. It took all her restraint to keep from flexing the palm he'd once cut. "Why did you take it in the first place?"

"That's not for you to know right now. Besides, I'm not finished answering your previous question. I kept a drop of your blood which was just enough to catch glimpses of you over the years."

"Why did you..."

"Why did I want to check in on you?" He barked an indignant laugh. "How can you ask that, Aveline? Do you think I released you from the dungeon to be cruel? You were a child. I was curious to know if you survived."

She noted that he said he was *curious* if she survived, not that he *cared* if she had.

"By the way, where have you been these last six years?" His gaze swept over her briefly, landing again on her tattoos. "Those are interesting markings. Faeryn *insigmora*."

Her heart leapt into her throat. She hadn't expected him to recognize her tattoos. He was a dark witch, a mage, not a...

Her eyes wandered over his face, taking in his

uncommon beauty. His sharp cheekbones. The slightest blue tinge to his black hair. And his ears...how had she never noticed the angled edge before? They weren't exactly pointed, but neither were they totally round. Could he be of Faeryn descent?

She shook the thoughts from her mind. What mattered most was that he'd asked where she'd been. That meant there was a chance the Forest People were safe from his knowledge. "Don't you already know where I've been? You confessed to spying on me through a drop of my blood."

He glanced at his nails with disinterest. "I saw your face, not your surroundings."

Relief swept over her, but she hid it behind a shrug. "I've been right where you left me. In the woods."

"In the woods," he echoed, his eyes narrowing, "where you just so happened to become marked with *insigmora*."

She held his gaze, her lips pursed tight.

The coach came to a stop.

"Ah, we're here." He leaned forward with a quirked brow. "What's it going to be, Aveline? Do I escort you from this coach as my prisoner or a princess?"

She bit her lip as a spike of panic laced through her. She still had so many unanswered questions. The hunters. The Beast. The unicorns.

"Only one of those choices will let you see your brother again," he said, a hint of taunting in his voice.

Her pulse quickened at his mention of Dimetreus. Her brother. The king. A man she'd come to hate almost as much as the duke. A man who may or may not have been controlled by a powerful mage.

There was only one way to find out. She took a deep breath and hoped Morkai couldn't hear her lie.

"I want to be a princess again."

"Well then," Morkai said, opening the coach door. "Welcome home."

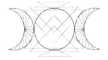

34

Teryn Alante felt like a dead man in his saddle after riding all night, but he hadn't been willing to let the duke's coach out of his sight. Not only was Cora inside it, but Teryn had yet to receive her bounty. To claim it, he'd have to meet with King Dimetreus at Ridine Castle. His reward for betraying Cora, however, was the least of Teryn's worries. He couldn't care less about it now. But that was a fact he'd kept to himself as soon as he'd realized how outnumbered he and his companions were against Duke Morkai's well-armed guards. It would have served him little to confront the duke, the very man Cora had been working against. No, Teryn would save his questions for the king himself. Perhaps he would explain why the woman he'd known as Cora was actually Princess Aveline.

He still didn't understand how it was possible. The princess was supposed to be dead, murdered by Cora's own hand. After the duke had ordered his guards to seize her and haul her into the coach, Teryn hounded him with questions. He'd been met with nothing more than an annoyingly condescending grin and the duke's assurance that Teryn could ask anything he wished once he arrived at the castle.

Which was where they were now.

It was an hour past sunrise when Ridine Castle came into view. Teryn and Lex rode through the gatehouse, following just behind the coach with two guards at the rear and two more at the fore. They entered a courtyard, which Teryn was surprised to find so empty. Perhaps he was used to the rhythm and regality of a palace, not the more practical nature of a castle. Ridine itself was a plain structure forged of stone with high walls, tall turrets, and an overall formidable appearance. Adding to that impression were the looming Cambron Mountains and the dark forests that skirted around the castle walls.

"I still wish I had any idea what the bloody hell was going on," Lex said, eying Teryn as they continued to follow the coach into the courtyard.

Teryn sighed. "I'll explain later." He'd said as much several times already, but Lex would only narrow his eyes. He had every intention of telling Lex the truth, but he wanted to wait until the duke's guards were no longer in such close proximity. Or maybe it was more that Teryn wasn't ready to admit what he'd done.

The coach rolled to a stop before the stone steps that led to an enormous pair of doors. Teryn dismounted at once and jogged toward the coach. He was stopped by one of the duke's guards. The guard said nothing, just held up a gauntleted hand and scowled through his helm. Teryn's shoulders tensed. Every part of him yearned to reach for his sword. His rational side stilled his hand. He may not have known much about Duke Morkai, but if the king had sent him to fetch Cora...

That is, if the king had sent him at all.

Teryn's chest tightened as the coach door opened. The duke stepped out first and extended his palm. No hand reached out to take it, but Cora slid out next, refusing to meet Morkai's eyes. Two more guards came down the stairs, each taking one of Cora's arms. She put up no fight as they escorted her up the stone steps.

"Cora." The word left his lips without him meaning to.

Cora froze in place, her eyes locking on his. Her expression shifted to one of murderous rage. She didn't need to say anything for him to know how she felt about him. It was there in her eyes. *Hate*. One of the guards tugged her forward and she continued up the steps, her head held high.

Like a princess.

How had Teryn not seen it before? She may not have been prim and proper like a royal, but there was a confidence to her he should have recognized. He'd seen it in the tilt of her chin, in her boldness, her refusal to apologize or follow anyone's orders but her own.

And he'd been a fool. He'd let a piece of paper and a tempting purse form his opinion of her before he'd tried to understand her on his own. He'd known she'd poisoned those hunters, murdered them without remorse, but as for what the poster claimed...

I was framed by Duke Morkai.

There was so much more going on than he understood, but nothing was going to stop him from finding out what that was.

AN HOUR LATER HE SAT IN KING DIMETREUS' STUDY. ONE hand was clenched tight around the arm of his chair while the other rubbed his brow. It was all he could do to keep from pacing around the room. He was alone aside from the guard standing sentinel before the closed door. Even so, he wanted to appear as composed as he could despite having been waiting for the better part of an hour. The duke had warned him it would be a while before he'd be granted an audience, but Teryn had refused to do anything else after he entered the castle. Lex, on the other hand, had nearly swooned at the offer of a soft bed and a bath.

Finally, the door opened. Teryn rose to stand out of respect for the king, but it was not Dimetreus who entered the study. It was Duke Morkai.

"Where is the king, Your Grace?" Teryn said through his teeth, not bothering to hide his irritation.

"The king is indisposed," Morkai said, striding over to the wide desk and sitting behind it. With slow, deliberate moves, he rested his crystal-topped cane upon the desk. He might as well have pointed a sword at Teryn for the unspoken threat the gesture carried.

Teryn held the man's gaze, studying him for further threat while he debated how to reply. He was surprised how young Morkai appeared. When Helios had spoken of the duke who'd taken over the unicorn hunt, he'd imagined a sinister old man. Not the dashing gent who sat across from him now, one who looked barely older than him. His pale eyes were uncreased, his jaw bearing not even a hint of stubble. How had this man become a duke? He certainly hadn't inherited the title, for Morkai was neither the name of a duchy nor a family surname of any prestige. Otherwise, he'd have learned the name during his many years of tutelage.

The duke leaned casually in the king's chair and gave Teryn a smile that didn't reach his eyes. "Worry not, Your Highness. The king has bidden me to settle your arrangement with him on his behalf."

Teryn clenched his jaw. "I demand to speak with the king."

Morkai cocked his head slightly to the side. "You forget yourself, Prince Teryn. This is Khero. You may have retrieved my kingdom's beloved lost princess, but you were found in the king's forest with only a forged writ of permission. A writ forged with my own sigil, might I add. I suggest you take what graciousness the king has offered you. At the moment, he's offered you me."

Teryn resisted the urge to glower and instead returned to his seat. It wasn't an ideal situation, but perhaps the duke could still shine light on some of Teryn's questions. "Your Grace, explain to me how the woman I turned in to the crown for the murder of Princess Aveline *is* the princess."

Morkai brushed a piece of lint off his black coat. "I did not grant you an audience to speak about the princess. That is a private matter belonging to this kingdom alone. Regardless, you will receive your reward. In fact, I took the liberty of paying off your debt to the Bank of Cartha."

Teryn blinked a few times. How did the duke know

anything about his kingdom's debt to Cartha? Better yet, why the hell would he pay it back?

"Oh, don't fret," Morkai said with a chuckle. "You will get your 500,000 *sovas*. Think of my settlement of your debt as a bonus. You aren't just any bounty hunter. You're a prince."

Teryn narrowed his eyes. Sure, he could feel honored by such generosity, but he had a feeling this was no favor. Instead of clearing Menah's debt, the duke had only shifted the hands of who held it. He'd purchased his kingdom's allegiance.

Isn't that what Father wanted? Teryn thought to himself. *An alliance with King Dimetreus?*

No matter how hard he tried, he couldn't see this as a blessing. "I didn't ask you to do that."

"You didn't have to," Morkai said. "Let's just say it was in my kingdom's best interest."

Teryn didn't like the sound of that. Before he could argue, Morkai spoke again.

"I understand Menah has seen its share of hardship. Scandal. Threat of war. Pirates." He paused and gave Teryn a probing look. "Not to mention an unfulfilled marriage contract with the Princess of Selay."

Teryn tried not to appear flustered by Morkai's demonstration of knowledge about his kingdom. The duke reminded him of Helios in a way, but far more subtle.

Morkai waved a hand. "Lucky for you, your strife can end with the collection of a simple bounty."

"Lucky indeed," Teryn said stiffly.

"Now that your debt to Cartha has been repaid, I

daresay your kingdom will look quite well to anyone who has scorned you thus far."

Teryn gave a grunt of agreement. He wished Morkai would get to the point already. Teryn had only known him for a handful of minutes, but he already knew exactly what kind of a man the duke was—one of smooth words to cover layers of pretense.

"Rumors run faster than horses," Morkai said. "Soon everyone will know of your kingdom's shift in status. I'm willing to bet that by the time you return home, your beloved princess will fall at your feet begging you to marry her. You'll never have to face the indignity of another ridiculous poetry contest again."

Seven gods, how much did this man know about him? Every kingdom had spies in every court, even his own. Still, it was unsettling to realize just how much more effective Khero's informants were compared to Menah's. Teryn forced a smile. "I'm sure you're right."

Morkai watched him through slitted lids. He leaned forward in his chair. "That is...unless you've changed your mind about her."

Teryn swallowed hard. His mind—for whatever strange reason—went to Cora. "Changed my mind?"

"Perhaps you're tired of being slighted by Selay. Had they wanted to sever your engagement to the princess, they could have done it with far more tact."

"They could have."

"And yet they pitted you against two other princes in a frivolous quest for unicorns. Is that why you came to Khero, Prince Teryn?"

There was no use denying it. "Yes."

"You didn't happen to have anything to do with the

slaughter of an entire company of unicorn hunters, did you? They may have worked directly under me, but I serve the king." His tone was cordial, but Teryn could hear the threat laced between each word. It told him he knew Teryn had interfered with the duke's hunt. A hunt approved by the king himself. Teryn and his kingdom could be condemned for such a crime. Morkai clearly knew Menah couldn't afford war. Meanwhile, the elegant armor worn by the duke's guards was proof enough that Khero could.

Teryn's mind spun as he took it all in. Layers upon layers of the duke's words, actions, threats. He still felt like he'd barely begun to unearth the half of it.

Morkai's lips stretched into a wide smile. "It's fantastic that we are allies now, is it not?"

"Indeed."

"An alliance is reciprocal. You finding the princess is worth even more than what the king has done for you already. Should you wish it, we could do more."

Teryn shifted uncomfortably in his seat. "More?"

Morkai steepled his fingertips against his chin, brow furrowed as if deep in thought. "I think I might know what prevented your father from demanding that King Verdian honor the contract between you and the princess."

And we're back to the expense of war, Teryn noted. "Is that so?"

Morkai nodded. "That is no longer an issue, let me assure you. King Dimetreus has a prodigious army. One that would have Selay quaking with fear. Should you seek justice rather than matrimony, say the word and Khero will come to your aid."

Teryn's mouth went dry. Once again, the duke's words were generous at face value. But under the surface...

King Dimetreus has a prodigious army.

Teryn had already assumed as much, but Duke Morkai had wanted it reinforced in Teryn's mind. Not only that but the idea that Selay would easily fall beneath said army. And if Selay—a wealthy kingdom with a more-than-adequate military force—would so easily fall...

So would Menah.

Teryn kept his expression nonchalant. "Your Grace, Menah has no desire to go to war with Selay."

Morkai tore his gaze away from Teryn and pushed back from the desk. "No, I wouldn't think so," he said with a sigh.

He and Teryn stood at the same time. It was clear the conversation had come to a close. The guard opened the door and Morkai strode toward it. As he reached Teryn, he said, "Your reward is being counted and packed at this very moment. In the meantime, the king invites you to a celebratory dinner tonight. You will attend, yes?"

"Actually, I'd rather be on my way at once." The words were untrue. Teryn had no intention of leaving until he saw Cora again, but he was curious how far the king's—and the duke's—hospitality extended. Was he truly free to leave as he wished, or...

Morkai gave him a cold smile. "Better not, Your Highness. The king does insist."

"Then I'll simply visit the stables and see to my horse after such arduous travels."

"See to it then," Morkai said. "But you should know this. Should you try and take your horse beyond the castle walls, you will find Ridine's gates closed to those who deny the king's kindness."

"His kindness."

"Like I said. He insists you stay for dinner tonight."

As the duke swept away, Teryn was certain of two things. One, that he was a prisoner, not a guest. And two, that he'd get himself, Lex, and Cora out of there if it was the last thing he did.

35

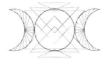

For the first time in six years, Cora was dressed in a gown. She assessed herself in the mirror, startled by her own reflection. The last time she'd seen her full reflection was in this very mirror in this very room—her childhood bedroom. She'd been shorter then. Thinner. Paler. Softer. Now her skin had been browned by the sun, her arms chiseled with firm muscle built by her archery practice.

Her eyes swept over the gown. The skirts were layers of emerald-green silk trimmed with black lace while the bodice was sage brocade. The sleeves ended at her elbows and trailed more lace down her forearms. Cora felt a sharp pang of longing in her heart. This had been her mother's dress. As soon as the gown had been delivered to her bedroom an hour before, she'd recognized it. It had come with a letter written in her brother's familiar script, insisting she wear it and join him for dinner. It was so much like something that would have happened in her youth—her brother delivering a dress and extracting a promise that she'd attend some public function on her best behavior—that she could almost pretend she'd never left Ridine.

For a splinter of a moment, she let herself imagine the last six years had been full of nothing more than mundane activity. Dances. Dinners. Greeting dignitaries, courtiers, and guests. She pretended her brother hadn't accused her of murder. That Morkai had never come into their lives after their parents died, hadn't gained Dimetreus' favor and friendship, which would eventually drive a wedge between the king and everyone close to him.

In that split-second fantasy, Cora felt peace. Joy, even. Then her gaze drifted to her eyes, and the illusion shattered. Her eyes were too haunted to belong to a princess. Not to mention her tangled hair that made a mockery of her lovely gown. She'd been delivered an ewer of hot water for a bath, but she'd need a long soak in a tub to untangle her hair. In the end, she'd settled for a messy plait down her back. Loose strands were already slipping free around her face.

A knock sounded at her door, making her jump. A guard's deep voice rumbled from the other side. It was time for dinner.

Time to see her brother.

CORA STOPPED OUTSIDE THE CLOSED DOORS TO THE DINING hall. The two guards who had shadowed her as she'd made her way down the familiar path stepped before her now, each reaching for a handle. She held her breath as they pulled the doors open. A shudder of fear ran through her.

The last time she'd been inside this room had been...

Had been...

I curse you to die.

She closed her eyes and forced the memory away. When she opened them again, the dining hall spread out before her. Her stomach sank at seeing it so empty. She'd been somewhat surprised to find the halls so vacant as she'd made her way here, but she'd assumed the servants had been busy with dinner. But that couldn't be true, for inside the dining hall, every table was empty save the head table. Only the back half of the room was lit by the lamps that lined the walls. The chandeliers overhead bore only cobwebs as if they hadn't been dressed with candles in years.

"Darling Aveline," a familiar voice said from the far end of the room.

Her eyes shot to the head table where three figures sat —Morkai, Lex, and...Dimetreus. Her heart skittered, then froze, skittered, then froze, as if it didn't know what to do as she looked at her brother. The last time they'd been face-to-face, he'd grabbed her by the arm and ordered his guards to haul her into a dungeon cell. But his voice was so warm and kind now. So much like the brother she used to love. Her throat constricted as she forced her trembling legs to move. Her eyes never left her brother's as she drew near, but with every step, concern began to darken her heart.

Dimetreus Caelan looked at least twenty years older

than the version that existed in her memories and nightmares. His eyes were rimmed with shadows, lined with creases, his lips pale. Uneven blotches of color marred what used to be his golden-tan skin. His hair, once thick and black, was now sparse, shot with white beneath his crown. He was dressed in his violet royal coat, but she noticed how it hung loose on his frame as he rose to his feet. Morkai, outfitted in the same black and gold coat he'd worn earlier that day, stood as she approached the dais. Lex belatedly followed. Dimetreus spread his arms wide and gestured for her to take a seat next to him. Her breaths were sharp and shallow as she claimed the chair, and the men returned to their seats. Morkai sat at the king's right while Lex was at Cora's left.

Lex leaned in close and frantically whispered, "If someone doesn't explain what the hell is going on, I'm going to go mad."

She looked over at him, surprised to find he must have had a full bath. His blond hair was clean and brushed away from his face. His clothes were clean too but showed obvious signs of wear from his travels. The ruffled front of his shirt was tinged yellow while his waistcoat and jacket bore several frayed seams.

"Music," Dimetreus said, snapping his fingers.

Cora startled as strains of harp emanated from the back corner of the room. She hadn't noticed the woman sitting there until now, but the harpist began to play, a serene smile on her lips.

"That's better," the king said. "Ah, and here's our final guest. Just in time, for I'm certain dinner is soon to arrive."

Cora's eyes shot to the figure entering the room. Her heart hammered, fluttered, hammered, fluttered. Again, the fickle organ seemed confused. She supposed it wasn't the only thing confused, for even her feelings shifted from fiery rage to an absurd sense of relief as Teryn walked toward the dais. She blamed her confusion on the unexpected change in his appearance. He was no longer dressed in leather britches and his hunting vest. Instead, he wore evening attire—black pants, white waistcoat, a ruffled shirt with a white neckcloth, and a black frock coat. She assumed the outfit had been borrowed from her brother, based on how the coat strained across his broad shoulders. His hair, like Lex's, was freshly washed and neatly styled, a slight curl to his dark tresses. She couldn't suppress her shock. It had been easy to ignore that he was a prince when they were in the woods, but now... there was no denying what he was.

Cora resisted the urge to smooth out her hair.

"Prince Teryn," Dimetreus said in greeting. "You are a true hero."

Teryn's face flashed with confusion before he bowed. "King Dimetreus." His eyes slid to Cora, and she realized she was still staring at him. He bit a corner of his lip as if he was desperate to say something. She only narrowed her eyes to a glare.

"Come," the king said, "join us."

He kept his gaze locked on Cora's a breath longer, then strode up to the table and claimed the only remaining seat—to the right of Morkai.

Soon after, a pair of servants entered, far fewer than she'd ever seen attend one of the king's meals before. Where was everyone? Where were the maids? Where was

Master Benedict, the castle's steward? The servants' faces were slack, eyes dull and glossy as they filled the plates with food and the glasses with wine. Lex dove in at once, but Cora could hardly bring a bite to her lips. Her stomach was tied too tightly in knots. There was so much she wanted to say, so much she needed to ask her brother, but she could do none of it with Morkai sitting so close. She'd have to find a way to get him alone.

She glanced at Dimetreus and found him looking right back. "Eat, sister. You must be starving after everything you've been through."

His expression was so kind, so full of concern, that she couldn't help but bring a spoonful of soup to her mouth just to appease his worry. She hardly tasted it, for her mind was wrapped around what he'd said. It was the first indication he'd given to suggest her appearance at dinner was anything but a pleasant-yet-not-unusual surprise. He'd expressed no shock over seeing her alive, shed no tears over how she'd aged, harbored no residual scorn over having once thought she'd murdered his wife.

She finished another sip of soup before facing Dimetreus. "After everything I've been through?" she asked, infusing her tone with only mild curiosity. She chose her next words carefully. "How much do you know?"

She could almost feel Morkai's stare burning straight through her brother, but she kept her gaze on the king. Dimetreus' expression fell. "A grave injustice was done to you, Aveline. I hope you believe that, had I known you were still alive, I would have come for you. Even when I thought you were lost along with my dearest Linette, I worked to avenge you. I *still* work to avenge you."

Her blood went cold with dread. "How are you working to avenge me?"

"Don't you worry, sister, Selay will pay for what they've done."

"Selay." Cora and Teryn uttered the word in unison.

"Yes," Dimetreus said. He took a deep drink of wine and turned toward Teryn. "If not for you rescuing my sister, I would have still thought Menah was involved."

"Involved with what?" Cora asked, drawing her brother's attention back to her.

"Involved with..." His throat bobbed. When he spoke next, his voice was strained. "I hate to even think about it. How Selay sent a spy into our midst, someone I unwittingly let get so close to my wife while I..." He slammed his fist on the table, making Cora jump. "That wretched maid. She took them from me. Linette and our unborn baby. I hadn't known. I hadn't...hadn't..."

Morkai put a placating hand on the king's shoulder. "At least your sister is alive."

"Yes," Dimetreus said, collecting his composure. "It's a miracle you managed to escape them. Thanks to Prince Teryn, our new ally." He raised his cup to Teryn.

Cora caught Teryn's eye. His expression was bewildered but she could sense that he simmered with a suppressed rage that almost matched her own. Who could he be so angry with? This whole ordeal was his fault. Wasn't he exactly where he wanted to be?

Teryn raised his glass in return, his gaze sliding to Morkai. "I helped her escape." It was a question without a question mark.

"Yes," Morkai said. "You rescued her from Selay, where she'd been held captive for six years."

Dimetreus nodded along. Cora's stomach turned.

"Am I the only one who feels like they woke up on the wrong side of reality?" Lex said, setting down his fork with a clatter. "Nothing that any of you have said tonight makes a damn lick of sense."

Dimetreus furrowed his brow and studied Lex as if seeing him for the first time.

Cora took a deep breath. "He's right, Dimi, I wasn't—"

"I wouldn't try and confuse him," Morkai said, pinning her with a warning glare. "He gets very upset when he's confused."

Dimetreus blinked a few times, then shook his head as if to clear it. He downed another drink of wine and released a dark chuckle. "He's right. I've been having... struggles with my memory as of late. I can't handle too much information or excitement at once. Which is why His Grace has been such a boon to me these last several years. He might as well be my whipping boy, but you won't hear him complain."

Cora's eyes slid to the duke's, taking in his smug grin. She remembered what he'd said in the coach after she'd mentioned how loyal he was to her brother.

Or does he serve me in every way?

"I don't like how grim the mood has become," Dimetreus said. "This is supposed to be a celebration. A joyous reunion. I've missed you dearly, Aveline." He faced her with a wide grin. There was a sweet quality to his expression that almost made him look like the version of him she remembered. But the closer she examined, the more she saw his facade fraying at the edges. His eyes were glazed over with a shimmer that nearly obscured the brown of his irises. She opened herself to his emotions, sensed a low hum of something...muffled. Suppressed. Confused. She could hardly make out a clear emotion, just a clash of vague impressions.

"I've missed you too," she said over the lump in her throat.

He clapped his hands, the sound far too loud for the quiet room. "I want to see my sister dance." Cora opened her mouth to protest, but Dimetreus shouted to the harpist, "A waltz."

"Dimi, please," she said, heat rising to her cheeks. "I can't. It's been too long."

"I insist," he said, oblivious to her discomfort.

"But—"

"Do not deny His Majesty," Morkai said. "You wouldn't want to upset him. Who knows what it could do. He might wake up and forget you were ever here."

Dimetreus chuckled. "I would do something like that, wouldn't I?"

Cora knew full well Morkai's words had been said in threat. If the duke wanted, he could make Dimetreus forget she'd come back. He could turn her back from princess to prisoner.

"Go, sister," the king said, gesturing at the floor before the dais. "Who will dance with her?"

Morkai stood easily from his chair.

But another voice spoke first. "Might I have this dance?" Teryn rose to his feet in a rush, sending his chair legs scraping against the stone floor.

Cora looked from one man to the other. Either way, she'd have to dance with an enemy. The decision, however, wasn't hard to make. She hated the thought of dancing with Teryn, but letting Morkai put his hands anywhere near her was far more repulsive. It didn't matter that he looked hardly older than Teryn. She'd rather die than dance with him.

Lifting her chin, she met Teryn's gaze with a glare. She spoke through her teeth. "Yes, Prince Teryn. I'd be honored to dance."

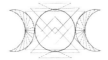

36

Cora's eyes locked with Teryn's as they left the dais on opposite sides of the table. His expression was neutral, unreadable, while hers was burning with malice. She felt as if she were meeting him for a duel rather than a dance. They met at the center of the floor, and Teryn gave a stiff bow. She offered an even stiffer curtsy. Her heart thudded wildly in her chest as the harpist began to play. Teryn stepped in close. He held one hand out to the side while the other came to her back. She stifled a gasp. Then, deepening her glare, she alighted one palm on his shoulder and draped the other over his waiting hand. She was grateful for the dinner gloves they both wore, creating barriers between their flesh. Even so, she could still feel the heat of his skin beneath them.

Teryn began to move. She stumbled, and her animosity was replaced with a flash of panic. While she'd been trained as a child in every sort of formal dance, she'd never been old enough to dance with a partner a public manner. Besides, her lessons had been years ago.

Her breaths came short and sharp as she tried to keep up with Teryn. Thankfully, it wasn't long before her feet seemed to remember what to do. Teryn must have foreseen that her dance skills would leave much to be desired, for she soon noted that they were moving far slower than the harpist's tempo. Teryn had probably enjoyed plenty of balls with plenty of capable partners, and yet he was keeping their waltz slow. Simple. For her sake.

It only enraged her more.

She lifted her eyes, realizing they'd fallen to her feet. It nearly made her lose her newly found rhythm when she took in just how close he was. They'd been this near before, primarily at knifepoint or perhaps when she'd hid them under the tree. But this, somehow, was different. She tried to keep her attention on the lower half of his face, noting how the bruising had faded from his nose, leaving only a slight yellow tinge where she'd once broken it. Then, against her will, her gaze inched up higher and higher until she met his eyes. For the first time, she noticed the emerald hue of his irises, a stunning shade even in the dim lamplight. They were turned down at the corners, brimming with unspoken apology that echoed the heavy waves of regret she sensed from him. She averted her gaze over his shoulder and raised her shields.

"Aveline," he whispered, his voice a deep rumble between them. It made her pulse quicken to hear him use her true name.

"Don't call me that," she muttered back.

He sighed. "Cora. Please believe me when I say I'm so sorry."

He led them into a turn, and she caught sight of the table. Her brother watched with a sappy expression while Morkai's stare was dark. Assessing. Lex, at the other end of the table, simply downed his wine and poured another glass. Teryn turned them again, leading her away from the table toward the unlit end of the dining hall.

"If I were armed, I'd kill you right now," she said through her teeth.

"I know."

She returned her gaze to his. "You think an apology is enough? What are you sorry for, anyway? That you've seen me in a dress, heard me called *princess*, and now realize you should respect me?"

His expression hardened. "I respected you the moment you held a knife to my throat. This was never about a lack of respect."

"Then what was it about?"

He shifted his jaw. "Desperation."

His emotions struck her again, and she felt their crushing weight. Desperation was indeed one of them, as was duty. Responsibility. Regret. Shame. It was a tangled burden of feeling, and an effort to breathe away. Her shields felt like they'd grown weaker ever since she'd been captured by Morkai. She shook her head. "Your desperation cost me my freedom."

He sighed. "You're not safe here, are you?"

She gave him a pointed look. "What do you think?"

His gaze slid over to the table. "I think there's something very odd going on here."

"Odd is one word for it." They turned, and now she

had a view of the dais. Her brother still stared with a giddy grin, his eyes glazed and vacant. There was so much she didn't understand about what was happening. It was safe to assume her brother was indeed being manipulated by Morkai through means of dark magic. She could feel the duke's influence writhing through the castle, creeping into every corner and cobweb, dampening the air she breathed. But what exactly was he trying to accomplish? What reason did Morkai have to convince the king that Selay had been responsible for Queen Linette's death, not to mention Cora's supposed captivity? And where did the Beast and the hunt for unicorns fit in?

Her thoughts shifted to Valorre. He'd been helping the baby unicorn find its mother when Morkai had come. She hadn't felt his presence once since then. Hadn't heard his thoughts. His absence made her chest feel tight but she knew it was for the best. If she couldn't feel him, then he was far enough away to avoid whatever danger she was in now.

"We can escape," Teryn whispered, bringing her attention back to him.

She quirked a brow. "Escape? Why would you need to escape? You're the honored guest. My brave rescuer, remember?"

"No, I'm not."

"Have you received your precious bounty?"

His whisper turned sharp. "I don't want it. All I want is to get you and Lex out of here. Tonight. I've seen to our horses. All three are saddled and ready, but we can't use the main gates. If you know any other way out of the castle, any weaknesses in its walls, tell me."

A memory rose to the forefront of her mind from the night Morkai had set her free from the dungeon. He'd taken her not through the gatehouse, not out one of the patrolled exits, but a portion of the wall that stood closest to the woods. Ivy had covered most of that part of the wall, and somewhere hidden behind tangled green vines had been an opening. A passage.

"You know of a way," Teryn whispered. "Please, Cora. Tell me and I'll get you free."

There was so much conviction in his tone, she almost believed him. Almost. She scoffed. "You expect me to trust you?"

"I'm trying to help."

"I don't need your help." She stepped away from him. That was when she realized they'd stopped dancing. The music had come to an end. It must have been the song's natural conclusion, for she heard her brother break into applause. Only she was aware of her and Teryn's abrupt parting.

"Cora." He reached for her hand and grasped her fingertips.

She stared down at their gloved touch before wrenching her hand away. Then, without bothering to curtsy, she marched back toward the table.

Dimetreus waved his hands at her, shooing her away from the dais. "No, let's see another dance." He snapped his fingers at the harpist, who began another song.

Morkai's gaze burned into Cora while he spoke to her brother. "I think we've had enough dancing tonight, Your Majesty."

"Nonsense. Let the young people have fun."

"My feet are tired, brother," she said, painfully aware

that Teryn had caught up to her and now stood by her side. "I can't possibly dance again."

Dimetreus gave her an indulgent grin. "You must forgive me, then, Aveline. I have just missed you so. Seeing you dance brought back the best memories. Besides," his grin took on a sly quality, "the two of you make quite the pair. Perhaps our kingdoms can take on a more formal alliance before long."

Cora's breath caught, her cheeks burning. She opened her mouth to speak but not a word came out.

Teryn, on the other hand, didn't share in her struggle. "I am honored at what you suggest, Your Majesty," he said with ease. "I am fond of your sister."

She whipped her head toward him, lips pursed to keep from emitting a string of curses. *The nerve. What a joke!*

"You forget, Majesty," Morkai said, his voice cold, "that the prince has yet to prove himself our ally."

Dimetreus gestured at Teryn. "He...he rescued her. It's quite romantic, Your Grace."

The duke's attention shifted to Teryn. "Romantic indeed. Still, he must demonstrate the extent of his heroics."

"He'll march on Selay with us," Dimetreus said. "Won't you, Prince Teryn?"

"March on Selay." Cora wasn't sure whether it was just her who'd said it because she, Teryn, and Lex were all staring bewilderedly at the king.

"Yes," Dimetreus said. His expression hardened, an edge creeping into his tone. "We must avenge what was done to my wife. We must make them pay for keeping my sister captive. For six years, I've been planning for this moment, building toward it. We will lay waste to the capital city, seize Verlot Palace, and make King Verdian regret that he ever lifted a hand against us."

A shudder ran down Cora's spine as she recalled the rumors of her brother's growing army. How Roije had to fight his way out of being recruited. All this time...the king's motive had been to build an army big enough to take down Selay? She narrowed her eyes at Morkai, but he only smiled back. This wasn't her brother's plan. It was *his*. But why?

She balled her hands at her sides and strode up the dais until she stood opposite her brother. "Selay didn't send a spy to kill your wife," she said, her words coming out with a tremor.

"Aveline," Morkai said, tone pitched low.

"I wasn't kept captive there for the last six years."

Dimetreus blinked a few times, his face going a shade paler. "What is she talking about, Your Grace?"

She expected Morkai to answer, but he didn't. Amusement danced in his eyes, which should have been warning enough to keep her from saying another word. Still, she had to try. Had to test the bounds of Morkai's control. "I've been hiding for six years because *you* sentenced me to death for the murder of Queen Linette. A crime I didn't commit. A crime *he* did." She pointed at the duke. "He framed me for it, let me take the fall, and you believed him. You believed him when he told you I'd died, but now you see me standing before you. You believed him when he said it had all been a mistake and I'd been captured by Selay, but I promise you that is untrue. Brother, do not believe another word he says."

Dimetreus trembled and closed his eyes. At first,

Cora thought he was crying. Then he stood from his seat and pounded his fists onto the table, sending the dinnerware rattling. Lex scrambled back from the table while Morkai took a sip of wine, watching the spectacle with a grin.

"Lies!" the king shouted. "You lie! You are not my sister." He reached across the table for her, but she launched back—only to recall she was upon the dais. Her foot slipped on the top step, and she began to fall.

A steady arm encircled her waist, catching her. She didn't care that it was Teryn. Didn't care that he kept his hand on her lower back once her feet were planted firmly on the ground. She only cared about the rage distorting her brother's face. He looked so much like he had the day he condemned her to die.

"She speaks the truth," Teryn said. "Every word she says is true."

Dimetreus began to round the table toward them. "You're both spies. You aren't my sister, and you aren't the prince." He whirled toward where Lex stood plastered against the wall. "Who even are you? Who are any of you? Guards!"

The door opened at the end of the dining hall, and in strode several guards. Cora noted that not one bore the king's sigil, only the duke's crescent moon.

"Get them out of my sight," Dimetreus said as he stormed away from the dais.

"Dimi," Cora called after him, but he didn't give her a second glance before he left the dining hall entirely. She pressed in close to Teryn as the guards surrounded them in a half circle. There was no getting to the door without going through the guards first. Cora waited for them to start forward, draw their weapons, and attack. They didn't.

Slow footsteps drew her attention to Morkai. He sauntered down the dais, cane in hand, and addressed his guards. "The king is having one of his fits again. He'll be right by morning. For now, ignore him."

The guards obeyed, making no move to close in.

It didn't ease the feeling of dread that had crawled into her heart.

Morkai approached Teryn and Cora, eyes narrowed to slits.

Cora felt something squeeze her hand and realized Teryn had been holding it. Gritting her teeth, she wrenched it away and took a step back. Teryn remained rooted in place. He met Morkai with his chin held high. They were nearly the same height, although Teryn was of a much broader build. In contrast, Morkai was lithe and lean, which only somehow added to his terrifying beauty.

"Prince Teryn," Morkai said, a hint of mocking in his tone, "I do believe it's time I showed you the garden."

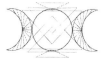

37

Teryn knew Duke Morkai's words were not to be taken as a request. It was a demand, and not just for him. The duke motioned Lex forward. Teryn found his friend against the wall, shoulders nearly as high as his ears. Lex's eyes darted from Teryn to Morkai, then to the guards. Teryn still hadn't had a chance to speak with Lex alone. He'd tried to call upon Lex earlier but had been turned away by a guard. The duke clearly had every intention of keeping them from communicating outside his presence.

Lex slowly pushed off from the wall and joined Teryn and Cora.

"Come," Morkai said. "We shall all visit the garden together." He started off toward the door and the guards gestured for Teryn and his companions to follow.

Cora didn't hesitate before she marched after the duke, which was all it took to get Teryn and Lex moving too. Teryn saw no point in arguing. No point in facing off with the guards—heavily armed ones, he was quick to note. He'd been disarmed upon arriving at the castle, which meant he had absolutely no defense but his fists. His consolation was that visiting the garden meant going outside, which would offer Teryn a chance to scope out the castle grounds. All he needed was to find an empty part of the wall. A gate left unattended. He'd done more than simply tend his palfrey when he visited the stables earlier. He'd tended all three of their horses, gathered their belongings, hid them inside each pen in anticipation of a hasty escape. He'd meant to convince Cora to agree to work with him, but it seemed their dance had only widened the chasm he'd regrettably created. Regardless, Teryn was determined to get her out of the castle. Princess or no, she was in danger here. Her brother was a madman, and the duke...Teryn wasn't entirely sure what the duke was just yet, but he had a feeling he was going to find out.

Lex leaned in close as they wove through the halls. "Care to share what in the name of the seven devils is going on?"

"We need to speak alone," Teryn whispered back. "For now, know we aren't safe here. None of us are. Don't trust a word the duke says. I'm getting us out of the castle tonight."

Lex opened his mouth to reply, but one of the guards gave him a shove between the shoulders, forcing them apart. Teryn bristled, his hands curling around air while yearning for a weapon. He'd never known a guard of any rank who'd consider laying a hand on a prince like that. In any other situation, the guard would lose his position, his hand, perhaps even his life.

Lex cut the guard an affronted glare but kept silent. He'd probably come to the same conclusion Teryn had— that these weren't regular guards. They didn't respect royal hierarchy. They followed Morkai, a duke, a man who stood below their king.

No duke should have the authority Morkai did.

The party came to an empty courtyard. It stood beneath a black sky, the sun having already set before dinner. Cool night air brushed Teryn's skin as they crossed the stone floor and funneled through a door in a low stone wall at the other side. Morkai stopped just beyond it and beckoned the rest of them to come forth.

Cora halted as soon as she took a step beyond the wall. She released a gasp, her body going rigid. Teryn and Lex quickened their pace and came up beside her.

"The garden," Cora whispered, but Teryn could see nothing resembling anything close to a garden. Instead, he found a charred field riddled with black stumps of gnarled trees. Nothing stood beyond the field save for the castle wall. He studied the towering perimeter, noting the many silhouettes of sentries atop it. It didn't bode well for his escape plan.

He scanned the sky out of reflex, but he knew he wouldn't find Berol. The last thing he'd done after preparing their horses was to scrawl a note that simply said, *Ridine Castle. Not safe. Trying to flee.* He'd left the rolled-up parchment on a bale of hay outside the stables, careful not to let any of the duke's guards see. Before he'd returned indoors, he'd caught a glimpse of Berol diving from the sky, then flying away with the scroll clutched in her talons. She'd known better than to fly inside the stables or the castle before then, just like she'd understood to keep her distance while he'd traveled with the duke's entourage to Ridine. The less Morkai knew about Teryn's assets, the better. Now he just had to hope Berol brought it to his father at once. He hadn't been close enough to convey where he wanted the letter delivered, but he trusted her to understand he was in trouble.

"This is not at all what I'd call a garden," Lex whispered.

Cora faced Morkai. "Why did you bring us here to show us *this*?"

Morkai chuckled. "This isn't what I brought you to see, but I'm glad you're impressed."

"This was my mother's garden."

"Everything comes at a price, Aveline."

"Do you have a point or do you simply like hearing yourself make vaguely ominous statements?"

Teryn nearly barked a laugh. If Cora was afraid of the duke, she was doing a damn good job of hiding it.

Morkai planted his cane in the earth and rubbed his thumb over the amber crystal. "You might have gleaned that King Dimetreus will soon be declaring war."

"I gathered," Cora said, "although I've yet to understand why. Selay is no enemy to Khero. Everything you've told my brother is a lie."

"Everything the king believes is true to him," Morkai said with a wry grin. "When he said we've been planning this for six years, that was true. And I've been planning even longer in ways you couldn't comprehend. We have the means to wage a very fast, very bloody, and very successful war. Harbor no doubts that our enemies will fall."

Teryn's blood roared in his ears. He may not have had the greatest respect for Selay and its rulers, especially after King Verdian had allowed his daughter to publicly snub their engagement. But that didn't mean he relished the thought of the kingdom falling to war. "Aside from the story you've fabricated over Princess Aveline's captivity, what reason does the king have for marching on Selay?"

"I too would like to know," Lex added, although his tone held far less fire. "I visited Verlot Palace recently, and the king and queen seemed rather...nice..." His words dissolved into nothing as Morkai pinned him with a glare.

"My reasons are not for you to concern yourself with," the duke said.

Teryn noted that he'd said *my reasons*, not the king's.

Morkai's lips lifted in a taunting grin. "But it may serve you to know that Selay is not our only enemy."

Teryn's blood went cold. "Are you suggesting the threat holds true for Menah as well?"

"I'm suggesting you choose your alliances well, Your Highness. Whether the king's army marches on one kingdom or two is in your hands."

Teryn knew the duke was baiting him but he had to know the truth. "What does that mean?"

"It means you can either act as a voice of reason or serve me as a mute pawn. Your presence here is a gift."

"Is that so?"

"Quite. I'm sure you are well acquainted with the costs of war. Not only in coin but in lives. Time. Resources. Like I said, Khero is fully prepared for battle but that doesn't mean Dimetreus wouldn't settle for a peaceful resolution instead."

"What are you getting at?" Cora said. "Stop talking in circles and tell us what you brought us here to say."

Morkai ignored her, keeping his eyes fixed on Teryn. "You, Prince Teryn, create the possibility for negotiation. Instead of marching for war, the king will demand surrender. Tomorrow morning I will send messengers to both Selay and Menah. I will call for a meeting at Centerpointe Rock in two weeks' time where we will discuss the terms for both kingdoms' surrender."

"Two weeks' time," Teryn echoed. "You're only giving them *two weeks* to prepare for a war meeting?"

"Two weeks will be more than enough time for all three parties to reach Centerpointe Rock. There will be no need for any of us to come with heavy forces in tow. For this is not a war meeting but a meeting of peace."

Teryn scoffed. "*Peace*? Not once have you demonstrated anything resembling peace. Instead, I've watched you present lies as truths, wield threats like knives, and cast a princess as a common criminal. Not to mention treating me and Prince Lex like prisoners."

Lex's eyes widened. "Wait, we're...prisoners?"

"Of course not," Morkai said. "Until you expressly refuse the king, I'll consider you allies. Anyone who'd rather not stand opposite Khero's army in the future will choose to *remain* allies."

Teryn's neck prickled beneath the threat, but he kept his expression stony.

"You know what?" Morkai turned and marched closer to the charred field. "Enough chit-chat. I think what you need is visual proof."

Teryn's eyes sought Cora's. She met his gaze and he saw all of his own fears and confusion reflected back at him.

Morkai crouched at the edge of the field and pressed his hand to the charred earth. At first, nothing happened. Then movement at the far end of the field. One of the charred stumps...was growing. A shape formed from the shadows, creating a silhouette of an enormous head on a hulking body. That was when Teryn realized it hadn't been a stump at all. It was the Beast.

Lex edged closer to Teryn, as did Cora, her hands fumbling at her back, her waist, searching frantically for the weapons that weren't there. She froze when Teryn's hand alighted on her shoulder. This time, she didn't glare or pull away.

The Beast paid them no heed as it plodded forward, showing no sign that it had ever been injured by Cora. Both of its beady eyes were intact and its raw-looking red skin hid any sign of puncture. It stopped next to Morkai and sat back on its haunches. The creature towered over the duke, but Morkai patted its hide as if it were only a dog. Then, keeping one hand on the Beast, he lifted his other palm to the sky.

Teryn didn't dare blink as he watched a fog slowly creep over the field. Little by little, the misty patches began to grow brighter, reflecting the light of the moon. Soon shapes began to solidify and disperse, forming something akin to bodies. Teryn saw a hand here, a leg there, heads with dark holes where eyes should be.

Cora stepped back, flinging out a hand. Her gloved fingers came around his wrist and she made no move to let go. "Wraiths," she whispered.

Teryn's heart slammed against his ribs at the word. The longer Teryn stared at the humanlike shapes forming on the field, the more he realized there was no other word to describe them. There were hundreds of the semi-translucent figures all clustered together over the charred soil, and in each of their hands was an equally translucent weapon—swords, spears, axes, bows. They wore armor the same color as their ghostly bodies but the style was outdated. Ancient.

"What...who are they?" Cora asked.

"Spirits from a nearly forgotten war," Morkai said. "They died trapped between two realms and have wandered the planes between the living and the dead ever since. Now they serve me. I sacrificed the garden for them, traded death for life. Or something like it at least."

Lex's voice rose a few octaves as he muttered, "What the bloody hell."

Morkai stepped away from the Beast, and the creature plodded off to lie down a few paces away. The duke turned to face Teryn and his companions, his eyes lighting up with satisfaction at seeing the three of them huddled together. "Come, Aveline," he said, waving Cora forward.

She remained in place, her fingers still clasped around Teryn's wrist.

Morkai's gaze slid down to their hands, and his expression turned hard. Cora seemed to realize the source of his attention and stepped away from Teryn, releasing her grip and fisting her hands in the folds of her silk skirts. "I have no desire for a closer view." Her eyes darted from Morkai to the wavering forms of the wraiths.

"Oh, I'm not inviting you over just to look." He

gestured to someone behind them, and one of his guards stepped forward carrying Cora's bow and quiver. "You're to participate in the demonstration." To the guard, he added, "Bring them."

Teryn tensed, assuming Morkai meant him and Lex. Instead, two more guards entered the garden from the courtyard. They hauled two bedraggled men whose hands were cuffed in iron, and shoved them before Morkai. The older of the two stumbled to his knees. His face was bruised, and an open cut seeped above his eyebrow. The younger man tried to help him up, but the duke held his cane between them.

"Monster," the younger man bit out. "Usurper. Filth—"

In a flash, Morkai snapped his cane against the side of the older man's face, opening his wound further.

Teryn started forward, his fists curled so tight he felt his nails dig straight through his dinner gloves to his palms. He halted in place at a sharp look from the duke. Another guard stepped forward, hand on the hilt of his sword. *Damn it.* He hated being unarmed. He hated himself for getting into this mess.

"Enough," the duke said to the younger man. "One more word and I'll break your father's legs."

The younger man's throat bobbed. His eyes burned with rage but he pursed his lips against further argument.

"Now," Morkai said, "walk eight paces onto the field. Refuse and your father dies. Take one step after your eight paces are complete and he dies. Go."

"Don't do it, Bradley," the older man begged. "Obey not a word the usurper says."

Bradley only hesitated a moment, just long enough

for Morkai to slightly lift his cane. On trembling legs, he strode eight paces forward.

Toward the waiting wraiths.

Only a dozen or so feet stood between Bradley and the apparitions.

The guard bearing Cora's weapons handed her the bow and quiver. She took them with a wary expression that echoed the dread Teryn felt inside. Arming Cora felt too good to be true. She kept her eyes trained on the duke as she slung her bow over her shoulder, creating an odd contrast with her elegant gown. "What is this about?"

Morkai gestured at Bradley. "He will face my wraiths while you, Aveline, defend him. If he still lives after one minute, both he and his father go free."

Teryn glanced from Cora to the wraiths, then the two prisoners.

Before anyone could argue, Morkai's voice bellowed across the field. "Attack!"

The wraiths surged forward at a run. Their moves were neither silent nor loud but something in between. Something hollow and wrong and unsettling. Cora bit back a cry of alarm and nocked an arrow. She sent it flying into the heart of one of the first wraiths. The wraith disappeared in a puff of mist. Teryn watched as her arrow shot through the ones behind it as well, carving a line through the oncoming hoard. For a moment, Teryn thought the duke's plan had backfired, but just as Cora shot another arrow, clearing yet another line through the translucent bodies, wisps of mist filled the previous gap, and the bodies reformed. They stumbled, paused, but soon the reanimated specters were running again. Cora shot another. Another. But there were too many. No sooner did she obliterate one did another take its place. They couldn't be killed. They could hardly be slowed.

Too soon, they surrounded the handcuffed man, their ghostly weapons slicing through his flesh as if they were made of steel. Cora continued to shoot, tears streaming down her cheeks as her efforts proved more fruitless with every arrow.

Until there was nothing left to defend.

"Stop." Morkai's voice no longer bellowed but caressed the night, a whisper against the not-quite-soundless slaughter on the field. The wraiths stopped at once and retreated to their previous positions, leaving the body crumpled and alone.

The older man cried out, wailing for his son.

Cora angled herself toward Morkai, but a guard was already at her side, wrenching the bow from her hands. He made no move to take her quiver, however. The prisoner continued to weep for his son as Morkai strode over to the body. Stopping just before the corpse, the duke lifted his hands, palms level with his waist. Teryn could hardly breathe, hardly blink, as he watched Morkai's strange posture. Then something began to move over Bradley's body. It started as a strange undulating motion, like snakes sliding over the dead man's skin.

It was blood.

Teryn's throat went dry as he watched a ruby pool gather in the hollow of the man's collarbone, then—against all impossibility—began to rise into the air. Crimson tendrils lifted from the body to the duke's hand, forming an orb. The ball of blood remained suspended midair, following Morkai's palm as he rotated it upward.

The duke turned away from the corpse and

approached the weeping prisoner. "I'm sorry Princess Aveline failed you and your son."

Cora made a strangled sound.

The duke kept his attention on the man, still sprawled on his knees, cuffed hands clasped together as if in prayer. He muttered something too quiet to be heard. "What did you say?" Morkai said gently.

The man lifted his head, his wounded temple still seeping. There was not grief but defiance in his eyes. "I said, I pray the seven devils drag you to hell."

Morkai looked down his nose at him. "They can try." Then, with the orb of blood still hovering over one palm, he raised the other toward the man. A thin tendril of blood lifted from the man's open wound, then snaked through the air and wove between the duke's fingers. The first orb of blood stretched out until it too resembled thread. The two sources of blood began to connect, swirling around one another, bending, twisting, weaving, until they merged as one.

The prisoner made a choking sound.

Morkai fluttered his fingertips, and the tapestry became solid. Then, with a snap of his fingers, the blood-weaving disappeared.

The man dropped at the same moment, sprawled limp on his side.

Lifeless.

Sightless.

Dead.

Teryn's gaze shot to Morkai. "You're a..." His words were trapped in his throat. It seemed an insult to call him a witch. Cora was a witch. Witches used magic. The duke, on the other hand...

This was something else. Darkness. Sorcery.

"I prefer the term blood mage," he said, "but someday you will call me your king."

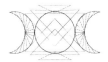

38

Cora stared at the two bodies, her mind reeling over what she'd seen. He'd taken their blood. The same way he'd taken Linette's. And her own. He'd woven the prisoners' blood between his palms, just like he'd done with hers the night he freed her from the dungeon.

What did it mean?

Teryn's voice stole through her thoughts. "You seek to be king?"

"Let us not get ahead of ourselves," Morkai said. "You must first bow to King Dimetreus."

Cora swallowed hard, seeking her voice through the tangle of emotions that threatened to crush her. "What are you implying?"

"Dimetreus shall become King of Lela," he said.

She furrowed her brow. The three kingdoms of southern Risa hadn't been called Lela in hundreds of years. If Morkai sought to reform Lela...

"That's the reason for the war," she said. "You want to

conquer Menah and Selay to rule over all three kingdoms."

"Dimetreus wants to conquer Menah and Selay. I am simply helping him execute his plan."

She shook her head. Regardless of what Morkai tried to insist, she knew better than to attribute any of this to her brother. He may have been signing the documents and approving the plans, but every seed was being planted by Morkai. "You just said you'd one day be king. How in the name of the Mother Goddess is that possible?"

Morkai lifted his chin and pinned her with a sly grin. "I am Dimetreus' heir."

"No. No, you're...you're a duke. My brother gave you that title. You didn't inherit it. You hardly earned it. You've no royal blood. I..."

"Oh, did you think *you'd* be his heir? Think twice, Aveline. To the rest of your kingdom, you're still dead. There is only one way you will ever be considered his heir again, but that's a conversation better left for when we're alone."

Cora shuddered at the thought of being alone with him. The coach ride had been enough.

Morkai turned to Teryn and Lex. "Let's get things moving, shall we? Prince Lexington, my offer to you is simple. You've seen my power. You've met my wraiths. I assure you the king's living army is equally as impressive. Dimetreus' reign over Lela will come swift. Unless you leave Ridine Castle as an ally, we will come for Tomas next. We will wipe out your pitiful kingdom in a single day and put an end to every life you cherish."

Lex's face was pale as he fumbled with the hem of his

waistcoat. When he spoke, his voice was a trembling whisper. "What must I do to be an ally?"

Teryn stiffened.

"Go home, gather your father's army, and send them to me," Morkai said.

Lex's eyes went wide. "His...army."

"I'll even take half," Morkai said with a smile that didn't meet his eyes. "Believe me, you will get far more out of an alliance with King Dimetreus than you will with Prince Teryn. Whatever belongs to Menah will soon belong to Lela instead. It's a simple choice, really. Life or death to put it plainly."

Lex took a step away from Teryn, his eyes on his feet. "When...when can I leave?"

"You can leave tonight if you wish. It seems someone has taken the liberty of readying your horse." Morkai shot a glare at Teryn at that last part. "However, I will send you home in the king's own coach. You can stay at the finest inns along the way."

Lex lifted his head at that. "Will the king pay for my meals too?"

"Anything you like," Morkai said, an edge creeping into his voice.

"All right," Lex said.

Teryn turned slowly toward him. "Lex."

"I'm sorry," Lex muttered. At first, he couldn't seem to meet Teryn's eyes. Then his expression shifted, turning to steel. "You know what? I'm not sorry. You dragged me into this and I've still yet to understand how or why."

"Lex, I wanted to tell you—"

"No, it's too late for that. I've been asking you to explain what the hell is going on ever since we met

Mister Scary over here. All I've come to glean—on my own, mind you—is that you're a liar." He jabbed a finger toward Teryn, then pointed at Cora. "You're a lost princess, and you..." He shrank back as his eyes landed on Morkai. "Well, you have ghosts, an army, and a monster and I'm terrified of all three."

"The only sensible one of you all," Morkai said under his breath.

Lex returned his attention to Teryn. "From what I understand, you already made a deal with the king in exchange for some bounty. I'm only following your lead."

"It's not like that."

"It doesn't matter," Lex said with an exasperated shrug. "I understand duty as well as you do. I also know how to identify the losing side in a battle. You forget, Tomas has watched two kingdoms fall to Norun. We've already done too much to keep from falling next."

"So you'll help him destroy my kingdom instead?"

"I'll do whatever it takes to save those who are important to me. Trust that."

Teryn's throat bobbed, his expression pained.

Cora tried to take pleasure in that look, knowing he was feeling a fraction of what Cora had felt when she'd learned what he'd done. Instead, she felt empty. She was still struggling to process everything Morkai had said. Everything he'd still left unexplained.

"Escort Prince Lexington to the royal coach," Morkai said to a pair of guards. Lex went with them willingly, offering not a single parting glance before he was out of sight.

Morkai angled away from Cora to face Teryn. With his back to her, she studied her surroundings, her assets.

The guard with her bow watched her through the slit in his helm, while another stood a few feet away. She noted more guards standing in the shadows along the wall between the garden and the courtyard. They were all heavily armed while all she had was a half-empty quiver. The rest of her arrows littered the charred field. Her fingers flinched, begging her to reach for one of the arrows anyway, if only to have something solid and potentially lethal in her hand.

"What about you, Prince Teryn?" Morkai said. "Will you play the hero or the fool?"

"If I agree to be your ally, will you let me leave tonight too?"

Morkai let out a dark laugh. "No. I've already told you. You are a gift, one too valuable to part with. So long as you are in my custody, I have the upper hand, and I will play that hand in the name of peace. As heir to Menah and the fiancé of Selay's princess, you make a most effective bargaining piece. Your survival will be contingent upon both kingdoms' surrender. Should you value your life, you will convince your father to accept my terms for a peaceful resolution. When I send word tomorrow about our forthcoming meeting, I will include a letter from you written in your own hand. In it you will sincerely implore Arlous and Verdian to meet King Dimetreus with surrender in mind."

Teryn held Morkai's gaze without falter. "If I refuse?"

"If you refuse, then you will be a silent hostage. The result will be the same. Either you speak and urge your father to see reason, or you remain silent, captive, and hope your father has the foresight to know—should he refuse to surrender and enter war with Khero—he will not win."

Cora's heart raced as she watched Teryn's face. She tried to open herself to sense his emotions, but she found her shields had already crumbled. Her nerves were raw, her senses frayed. She was already feeling everything at once and hadn't even realized it. With a deep inhale, she focused on her breath, on the solid ground beneath her feet. Little by little her mind began to clear.

"What will it be, Prince Teryn?" Morkai said.

Teryn narrowed his eyes. "I will not encourage my father to yield to you, regardless of your threat to my life. You made a mistake in telling me you sought to inherit Dimetreus' crown. You made a mistake in showing me your dark magic. I would never let Menah bow before a blood mage."

Morkai took a step closer, his tone icy. "No, Prince Teryn, the mistake is yours." He lifted a hand. "Take him."

Four guards surged forward but Teryn immediately put up a fight. Cora watched his hand come around the hilt of one of the guard's sheathed swords. That was the last thing she saw before she plucked an arrow from her quiver and charged the guard who held her bow. The guard was surprised by Cora's sudden attack and stumbled a step back, arms spread for balance. Cora closed in and plunged her arrow into a gap in the guard's armor, burying it into his armpit. The guard dropped Cora's bow to remove the arrow, taking several more steps back. He tripped again, this time over the body of the old man. The guard went down on his back, his helm tumbling off in the process. Cora gathered up her discarded bow in one hand and took another arrow from her quiver with the other. Without hesitation, she straddled the guard and thrust her arrow through his throat. Only then did she see the guard's face. It was...a girl, not much older than Cora. Her pupils were unnaturally wide with an odd sheen over her eyes. As she choked on her own blood, the sheen began to fade, her pupils constricting to a more regular size. The girl died with tears streaming from the corners of her eyes.

Cora leapt off the guard, bile rising in her throat. She didn't know why it should matter that the guard had been a girl. And perhaps that wasn't what had Cora feeling so rattled. It was more that the guard wasn't what Cora had been expecting. She'd assumed Morkai's guards were of the same ilk his hunters had been. Rugged criminals. Mindless killers. But this guard, her eyes...they held the same sheen she'd found in Dimetreus'. These guards weren't vile monsters cloaked in armor but *people*. People he was likely controlling in the same way he was Dimetreus. And she'd just killed one of them.

"Well done, Aveline," Morkai said.

She whirled around, an arrow nocked in her bow. The only guards around were the ones who stood by the wall. Her eyes shot to where she'd last seen Teryn but he was nowhere to be found. She'd been so distracted with the guard, she hadn't noticed when his fight had ended. Or *how* it ended. Was he...

She shook the question from her mind and drew her arrow. Morkai lifted a palm, and she felt a sharp pain strike her chest. Her shot went wild as she heaved over, grasping her heart. The pain disappeared, but her lungs felt tight in its absence. Her gaze flew to his upturned palm. A tiny ball of crimson floated above it.

"I still have a drop of your blood." Morkai strode closer, the red bead suspended over his palm. She held her breath, eyes locked on his hands. His grin widened. "Let's have a private chat, Princess Aveline."

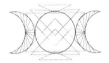

39

Every muscle in Cora's body was coiled tight, every limb poised for attack. Yet Morkai simply sat in a wingback chair opposite her and sipped his tea. They were in what used to be the North Tower Library, which seemed to have become Morkai's personal study. It was a wide circular room lined with bookcases, save for one wall that bore an enormous hearth. She and the duke sat before it, a fire blazing in its core.

Cora tried not to let her eyes leave Morkai's, but she couldn't help noting all the changes he'd made to the room since she'd last seen it. Every window had been sealed with a tapestry. Every shelf bore far more books than there was space for, every spare inch brimming with unfamiliar volumes, some boasting unsettling titles on their spines. *The Art of Blood. Grimoire Sanguina. Mastering the Ethera.* A desk was pushed up against one of the bookcases, its top strewn with parchment and several enormous leather-bound tomes. A table sat at the center of the room, littered with more parchment, more books, stoppered indigo bottles, and a crystal bowl filled with some dark liquid. The most terrifying thing of all was the enormous shape of the Beast dozing next to Morkai's chair. The creature took up a good portion of the room, its rumbling snores filling the air with a grating sound. This was the closest she'd been to the Beast. Her eyes fell on the ridge of spines running down its back. Spines she now realized weren't spines at all but unicorn horns. Valorre came to mind again, sending an ache to her heart.

If the Beast is here, Valorre is safe, she told herself.

But what of the hunters? If they find him...

With a shudder, Cora returned her study to the duke. He sipped his tea again, then tipped his chin at the cup and saucer she held in her shaking hands. "I promise it isn't poisoned," he said. "Besides, that's more of your realm of expertise, isn't it?"

She set her tea on a small table next to her chair and gripped her armrests instead. He'd let her keep her bow and quiver. Another gesture to show how little he feared her. Her weapons lay next to her chair, tempting her to reach for them. Each time she considered the action, she remembered that ball of blood Morkai had. He'd summoned it so quickly. So easily. Where was he even keeping it?

"You said you wanted to talk," she said, her voice coming out far shakier than she liked. "So let's talk."

"You have questions. Ask them."

"You're truly going to answer?"

"I have nothing to hide from you. It is my deepest wish to make you my strongest ally. I already know it is folly to lie to you, what with your Art. I can only imagine you've honed your talents these last six years." His eyes dropped briefly to the ink on her forearms, once again eying them without even a hint of reverence. "So ask. I'll answer."

Cora pored over everything she'd yet to make sense of. A vision of the dead guard's glassy eyes flashed through her mind. She closed her eyes against the guilt, banishing the sight of her hands on the arrow that killed the girl—

"How are you controlling people?" she managed to say. Forcing her eyes open, she focused on her breath to steady her. "How are you able to get people to follow you and blindly obey?"

"Not everyone who works for me follows me blindly, Aveline."

Cora thought of his hunters. No, she supposed some wouldn't take much convincing to do his bidding. "But I know you utilize magical influence for control. You've changed my brother's memories. You've convinced him Selay and Menah are his enemies." She didn't mention the guard. Couldn't mention her.

"It's called a glamour. Do you know what that is?"

She nodded. She'd learned about glamours from the Forest People. Similar to her feat with Teryn and the baby unicorn, a glamour was a way to shift another's perception to make them see what one wished for them to see. Cora had never witnessed it in action. Or, if she had, she hadn't known. Still, it seemed to have very little in common with what Morkai was doing.

He seemed to pick up on her train of thought. "What I do goes beyond the realm of a common glamour. My specialties lie less in changing what people see and more in changing what they believe. I weave thoughts into one's mind, give them images, impressions, and beliefs. It only works on the minds of the weak or willing."

"Are you saying my brother is weak?"

"I'm saying your brother has always been quick to accept exactly what I've offered him. He's always wanted an explanation for his wife's death. An enemy to blame other than himself. My explanations suit his sphere of plausibility. He's never wanted the enemy to be me, which is why your efforts to convince him otherwise fall on deaf ears."

"And what of others who work for you? Others you control?"

His lips curled into a smirk. "Like the guard I watched you kill? She had ambitions. People she wanted to prove her worth to. I merely helped her along. Impressed upon her a vision of what could be accomplished in my service."

"How do you do it? How do you keep your illusions constantly in place?" As far as Cora knew, a glamour lasted only so long as one was focused on it. Expending that kind of magic on multiple people at once for any extended length of time...it shouldn't be possible.

Morkai glanced at his sleeping Beast. "That's where my Roizan comes in."

"Roizan." Cora echoed the unfamiliar word. "What is a Roizan?"

"A creature made with the forbidden Arts—the magic of the sanguina and ethera. A Roizan is forged from death and given new life. It is no longer a natural being. No longer susceptible to mortality. Its life is bound to mine and my powers to it. A Roizan is a living vessel. It can hold unimaginable power that I am able to channel from without expending any of my own vitale."

She was unfamiliar with some of the terms. *Sanguina. Ethera. Vitale.*

Morkai continued. "Because of my relationship with my Roizan, I can maintain hundreds of glamours at once. All I have to do is weave them."

"What does the Beast—the *Roizan*—have to do with the unicorns you're hunting?"

He set down his teacup and placed his cane in his lap, caressing the crystal like she'd seen him do many times now. Was it simply an idle habit or did the crystal hold some significance? "The unicorns are a complicated subject," he said slowly.

"You said you'd answer my questions."

"I mean to. But where to start?" He gazed at the fire, but his expression was not one of deep thought. His face was smug. "There's an ancient prophecy I've spent most of my life fighting against. One that mentions unicorns, a mother, and a child. Three things I should have no reason to fear. And I don't, for there is but one element of the three that all the others hinge upon, and I've already taken an action against it that has nullified the prophecy in its entirety."

She felt cold despite the warmth of the fire. "What action have you taken?"

"You asked about the unicorns, so let us remain on topic. The unicorns are part of the prophecy, which as I've said, is null. And yet, the prophecy itself doesn't seem to know that. The appearance of the unicorns is a personal affront to my efforts, so I've made it my mission to be rid of them."

"That sounds rather petty."

Morkai shrugged. "Petty, perhaps, but quite beneficial to me. Unicorns hold some of the strongest fae magic that exists. Harnessing that magic creates a well of power. I need sources of power to work my magic, for every feat expends it."

Cora's stomach churned. "That's why you feed the unicorns to your Roizan. It...holds their magic."

"Which I, in turn, draw from at will."

"Why do you starve them? Torture them?"

"Unicorn magic is pure light, Aveline," he said, a condescending lilt to his tone. "It has been known to heal, to burn away darkness."

Cora huffed. "That's supposed to be a bad thing?"

"It is neither a good thing nor a bad thing because darkness isn't evil. Darkness is simply an aspect of light the same way death is an aspect of life. My Art deals in darkness, which makes light magic detrimental. But light can turn to dark the same way day turns to night. Unlike the natural passing of dawn to dusk, light magic needs help to transmute itself into darkness. Starving the unicorns, trapping them in iron, and letting the deadly metal drain their vitale...it corrupts their magic. Changes it. No unicorn would ever wield corrupted magic themselves, but I would. And I do. You saw my demonstration. Saw how easily I drew living wraiths from dead, scorched earth. You've seen how I can change the minds of the weak. Saw how easily Prince Lexington accepted my offer. Menah and Selay will fall, as will anyone who stands against us. Dimetreus will become King of Lela. Your only choice is to stand at his side."

Cora squeezed the arms of her chair until her

knuckles turned white. "To what end? You've implied that you intend to usurp my brother once he's claimed rule over the three kingdoms. Why? My brother has already given you more than you deserve. He made you a duke. Set you at the head of his council. How is that not enough for you?"

He scoffed. "The title of a duke. I'm already a prince of two kingdoms—a kingdom of men and a kingdom of fae. If neither of those titles are enough, what makes you think I'll settle for being a duke?" He shook his head. "I'll settle only for King of Lela."

Cora frowned. Since when was Morkai a prince? Not only that but a prince of fae? She'd already suspected his fae heritage when she'd studied his features in the coach. But...there were no living fae aside from the Faeryn descendants. No fae kingdom left to rule. As for the human kingdoms he sought to overthrow...

She gritted her teeth. "You have no right to rule all three kingdoms of Lela. Not even Dimetreus has that right."

Morkai's silver-blue eyes flashed with indignation. "I do have that right. My blood is the blood of an Elvyn king. My claim is to Lela's magic, and I will inherit it."

"What are you talking about?"

"Lela is more than it seems, Aveline. It is not a human land, but the heart of the fae realm. Fae magic seeps through every blade of grass, every root, every tree, but it does nothing but dissipate into thin air. The magic must be harnessed, and the person to harness it will be me." He shifted in his seat, some of the fire leaving his words. "First, though, I must *inherit* the land itself. Not just a portion of it. Not just Khero. All of what was once considered Lela."

"That's why you're having my brother conquer the other two kingdoms."

He nodded. "I cannot conquer Lela myself, I can only rightfully inherit it. That is a condition of the prophecy I cannot fight. Your brother, on the other hand, can claim rule over the three kingdoms through battle, brutality, lethal force—whatever means necessary. Then he will pass his crown to me after his death."

Cora bristled. "You're going to murder him."

"He's going to die," the duke corrected, lips quirked into a sly smile.

She shook her head. "You can't be his heir. Your rule will be contested—"

"Who will dare stand against me?"

Cora wanted to say her brother's other councilmen, but she realized they were likely already under Morkai's thumb. If they were even still alive. Based on the two prisoners she'd met today, it seemed Morkai didn't let those who stood against him live.

"It won't matter," Morkai said. "By the time anyone thinks to contest my rule, I will have control over fae magic. Not just the Elvyn magic that lives in my blood but the magic of the Faeryn too. Whatever magic you've seen and studied, whatever magic you think you know, it pales in comparison to what I'll have once I'm king. I will direct the flow of magic in this land, whether it's the Art of witches or the Magic of the Soil. I will give power where it is due and take it from where it is not."

Cora's mind reeled at the hidden implications. He hadn't admitted to knowing about the Forest People, but he knew about the Faeryn, the Magic of the Soil. He claimed to be an Elvyn prince. If he attained the power he sought...what would happen to the Forest People? Their magic? To witches like her and anyone who refused to bow to his control?

Keeping her voice level, she asked, "Why do you want this power so badly?"

He lifted his chin and studied her for a few silent moments. "I will do great and wonderful things, Aveline. My allies will be blessed. My enemies will be vanquished. I will shape the future of the world as I see fit. My magic will allow me to accomplish feats you can't imagine. I will put an end to death for those I protect." His expression took on a fierce quality as something dark flashed in his eyes. Slowly, he stood from his chair, planting his cane firmly before him. "You could be one of those people."

An end to death. What was he talking about? She recalled what he'd done with the prisoners' blood. What he'd done with *her* minuscule drop. She recalled the wraiths, heard their ghostly blades carving apart living flesh. If Morkai could do all that, what else could he do? What could he do to an army? What could he do during a bloody battle? Even more frightening was the thought of what he could do if his powers were increased by the magic he sought.

Cora knew in the depths of her heart, blood, and soul that—should Morkai succeed—he would destroy the world.

"You're right about one thing," he said, voice gentle. "Some will contest my right to the throne after your brother dies, and I will deal with them swiftly. I will spill their blood without remorse. You, however, can stop that from ever happening. You can save others from blood-shed by helping me strengthen my right to the throne."

"How?" she asked, although she dreaded the answer.

His pale eyes locked on hers, devoid of warmth. "Marry me."

She rose from her chair and took a step away, knocking the tea table over in the process. Her teacup and saucer clattered to the floor, but she refused to take her eyes from Morkai's. "You're out of your mind."

He took a step closer. "I can give you half my heart."

She barked a laugh as she stepped back again, feeling porcelain crunch beneath her shoes. "*Half* your heart? Is that what you consider a proper proposal?"

"The other half doesn't belong to me," he said without inflection. "But you could. I think my heart would like you. It's a jealous heart, but it could come to understand."

Another piece of porcelain crunched under her foot. This time she slipped. She caught herself on her hands and knees, making an effort to heave a few breaths as her fingers stretched toward her quiver. Her hand came around the fletching of an arrow. She rose to her feet and rushed Morkai, colliding with his torso. Her arrow slid through flesh as she angled it up beneath his ribs—

She gasped as a surge of pain struck her chest. Her vision blurred, but she refused to collapse. Clutching at her heart, she took a wavering step back, her lips curled into a wicked grin. Morkai held her drop of blood over his palm, but Cora didn't care. So what if he killed her, as long as she took him with her. His black coat was already darkening around the shaft protruding from his torso. He stared down at it for a moment. Then, to Cora's horror, he smiled. Tucking his cane beneath his arm, he brought his free hand an inch from his wound and began to gather tendrils of his own blood.

He met her eyes as her tiny drop stretched thin and began snaking toward his. "I could bind us by blood, Aveline. I could wind our fates together, force you to be my bride."

She stumbled back, her chest still throbbing with pain as she doubled over. Her vision was nearly black now.

Then the pain abated. She lifted her eyes and found Morkai frowning down at her. His blood no longer hovered over his palm and hers had returned to a tiny drop. He lowered his palm and the ball of blood disappeared.

"I won't bind you to me," he said, voice barely a whisper. "Weavings of fate take more power than I'm willing to expend. Instead, I will give you time to choose me. And you will. You will choose one half of my heart willingly, or you will take the other half unwillingly." He said the last part through his teeth as he wrenched her arrow from his flesh and threw it into the fire. Then he took his cane from under his arm and pointed it at the sleeping Roizan. He pressed his other hand to his seeping wound. In a matter of seconds, he stood straighter.

He'd healed himself.

"I will give you time to think."

"I don't need time to think," she spat out. "I will never choose you."

A tic formed at the corner of his jaw. "Is it the boy then? The prince?"

Her pulse kicked up. "Teryn? He's...he's nothing to me. He betrayed me."

Morkai scoffed. "I see the way you look at him. I've been on the receiving end of looks like that. I know what it means."

"You mean hatred? Yes, I imagine you've received many looks like that."

"You could never be Teryn's queen. Do you know what the prince's father did to *his* queen? He tried to have her replaced with his mistress. Teryn would only do the same to you."

She clenched her teeth. "I never said—"

"Haven't you figured out why I took your blood all those years ago? Why I wove it with Queen Linette's?"

Cora's breath caught. All she could manage was a shake of her head.

"I bound your fate to the queen's. It took all the power I'd stored in my Roizan up until that point, but I succeeded."

"Then why am I still alive? What are you waiting for?"

"Death was not the bond I wove. A death weaving doesn't take nearly as much power, for it is an immediate sentence, not a long-term curse. It was your fate I wove, one that guaranteed—like the queen—you would die childless. It was an idea you inspired. I don't have your ability to sense others' emotions. I can only give thoughts and feelings to weak-minded beings, not receive them. But you knew the queen had lied about providing an heir. I'd already known I'd have to do away with her one way or another. She'd already begun trying to turn Dimetreus against me. And letting her further Dimetreus' line would only hamper my plans. But your little scene at dinner that night made me realize I could take care of two problems at once."

Cora's stomach turned over with a wave of nausea. She resisted the urge to bring her hand to her stomach. "Why would you do that? Why would you try to keep me from having..." She couldn't even say the next word. The prospect of having children had rarely crossed her mind. She was nowhere close to ready when it came to becoming a mother. But the realization that he'd tampered with something so personal, so intimate....

Her legs gave out and she sank into her chair. Sweat beaded behind her neck, down her back. The laces of her corset felt too tight, too smothering. "Why?"

"The unicorns. The mother. The child. Who do you think you are in that prophecy?" When she didn't answer, he said, "The mother, Aveline. You are the mother and your child would have been my enemy. I knew of the prophecy long before I came to Khero, and I knew who you were the moment I met you. I sensed your magic, respected it. That's why I never wanted to kill you, regardless of the threat you posed. Weaving your fate was the only thing I could do to let you keep your life."

He said it with so much false kindness, it made her want to retch. Fury roared through her blood, and it demanded his life. She extended a hand toward her quiver, even as Morkai's eyes trailed her every move. She didn't care if he stopped her. She didn't care if she died trying—

The door flew open and a guard stormed in. "There's a unicorn circling the castle wall."

Morkai's expression shuttered. "A unicorn?"

"It's been trying to get in."

Cora was frozen halfway toward reaching for her quiver. Her mind went to Valorre. It couldn't be...

The Roizan stood and growled at the open door.

Morkai turned narrowed eyes upon her. "Do you have a friend, Aveline?" Her guilt must have shown on her face for he broke into a dark laugh. Turning to the Roizan, he shouted, "Find it." The Roizan darted across the room, sending the guard diving out of the way as the creature squeezed through the door.

Cora's hand closed around the strap of her quiver—

"Seize her," Morkai said. Cora dove for her bow, but the guard was faster. He tore the weapons from her grip and twisted her arms behind her back. Morkai gathered up her bow and quiver as the guard hauled her out the door. She struggled the entire way down the stairs, through the dark halls, but it was no use. The guard evaded her every attempt to free herself. Soon the stench of rot filled her nostrils. Panic set in as they entered an eerily familiar part of the castle. Not eerie in the same way she'd feel if they'd been heading for the former queen's chambers. This sense of terrifying recognition came from returning to a place Cora had only been once before.

The dungeon.

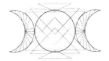

40

The fight left Cora's body. Dread filled her core as the guard hauled her over one armored shoulder. They marched past cell after cell, some doors closed while others gaped open. The dungeon hall was lit only by the occasional lamp. It was exactly how she remembered it. Dim. Terrifying. Cold. The unsettling familiarity swept Cora into memory. She was small again. A girl who'd just been on the receiving end of her brother's misplaced wrath. Tears had streamed down her cheeks as her pleas went unheard. Her brother had refused to step foot in the dungeon hall and instead stood at the doorway, watching as she was dragged away from him without an ounce of pity in his glazed eyes.

She looked at the same doorway now. It was empty this time, shrinking behind her with every step the guard took. But she remembered the sheen in Dimetreus' hollow gaze. Her brother had been under Morkai's glamour even then. It made sense now. She'd met the Roizan that night six years ago, which meant the duke had already created a vessel for dark magic, already had the ability to weave a long-standing glamour.

Her captor stopped outside a closed cell. She renewed her struggle, but the guard only squeezed her tighter. From ahead, she heard the clang of metal on metal. A door being unlocked. The guard set her roughly down and shoved her inside the now-open cell. She stumbled back into darkness and landed on the damp stone floor. Pushing herself off the ground, she whirled toward the door. Two figures were backlit by the dim light outside the cell. One was unmistakably Morkai. She hadn't noticed he'd come too.

He threw something at her feet and slammed the cell door. His voice came through a thin barred window. "If only one of you remains alive by sunrise, that person can leave."

Two sets of footsteps retreated.

She blinked into the room, willing her eyes to adjust to darkness. The tiny window provided barely enough light to see her own hands at first. But soon she began to make out shapes from the shadows. A pile of straw. A chamber pot. And a humanlike form in the corner.

She'd already known she wasn't alone.

If only one of you remains alive by sunrise, that person can leave.

Her gaze darted to her feet where she found her quiver with not even a dozen arrows left inside. That must have been what Morkai had thrown inside the cell with her. He wanted Cora to kill whoever was in here with her.

Or...he wanted the other person to kill her.

The form stirred, shifted. She bent down, grabbed an

arrow in each hand. The figure rose to standing at the same moment she did. It stepped closer while Cora stood her ground, prepared to fight. She assessed every edge of her adversary's silhouette, seeking any sign that they held a weapon too, until...

Until they stepped into the sliver of light streaming in from the barred window.

It was Teryn.

SHE WASN'T SURE WHETHER TO FEEL RELIEF OR ANGER, BUT she didn't have time to consider either emotion. He moved toward her, and she drew her arm back, ready to plunge her arrow—

He didn't close in.

Instead, he leaned against the opposite wall with a sigh. She shifted her stance so she could see him more clearly. He was still dressed down to his shirt and trousers, his neckcloth hanging untied around his open collar. His face was bruised, his lower lip split. He closed his eyes and rested his head against the wall. "He doesn't expect us to kill each other, nor does he want us to," he said, voice heavy with fatigue. "He needs me alive, remember?"

She looked down at the arrows in her hands. "Then why did he leave me with these?"

"Because he wants us to distrust each other. Either that or...or he wants to test our friendship so he can use us against one another."

She pointedly ignored the second part of his statement. "Distrust has already been well established between us, thanks to you."

"I can't keep saying I'm sorry if you won't believe it."

"You haven't said it nearly enough for me to even start to believe it. We're here because of you."

She expected him to argue, to say they were there because of *her*, because she'd lied about her identity, because she was a wanted fugitive.

But he said none of that.

"I know, Cora. I'd take it back if I could."

She felt the truth of his statement. As much as she wanted to hold on to the comforting weight of her rage, she felt some of it begin to fray. He hadn't taken Morkai's deal. Hadn't agreed to convince his father to surrender. Unlike Lex. She felt a flicker of resentment at how easily Lex had given in. Not that she could blame him. What was happening here had nothing to do with the Kingdom of Tomas and everything to do with the three kingdoms of Lela. For now, at least. What Lex had failed to understand was that if Morkai became King of Lela, he'd be a force the rest of the continent should fear. A force the rest of the *world* should fear.

She could forgive Lex for being a coward, but she wouldn't be so easy on herself.

With a deep breath, she tossed her arrows back inside her quiver and began unhooking the closures of her gown. When that didn't work, she tore her bodice and pushed her skirts down her hips until only her shift and corset remained.

Teryn straightened with alarm. "What are you doing?"

"I'm not lounging around in a dungeon cell wearing an evening gown." She turned away from him and began loosening the laces of her corset until she felt her ribcage expand. Her cheeks grew hot despite the fact that modesty was pointless in their situation. Still, she refused to meet his eyes as she marched to the cell door. There was no keyhole on this side, only solid metal. She hadn't heard the scrape of a key after Morkai had shut the door, which meant the locking mechanism must be automatic. The barred window was far too high for her to reach through and try to pick the lock. And yet, it was a lock like any other. And the door...it was just that. A door. A medley of elements.

Closing her eyes, she pressed her palms to the metal. And pushed.

NOTHING HAPPENED. FOR HOURS, CORA SOUGHT THE elements within the door. She should have been able to connect with them. In theory, at least. She'd heard tales of witches who could walk through walls, of Faeryn who could carve paths through stone with a touch. After what she'd done under the tree, she believed those stories now. Believed it was possible. The door was iron. Earth that had been heated with fire, transmuted into liquid, solidified with air. The same elements that comprised her body, animated her life force. She should be able to melt it. Move it. Seek the locking mechanism and lift it from its latch. She went through the same thought process she'd gone through at the tree, but not once did she feel a connection to her magic.

It was Morkai. It had to be him. She hadn't felt her

magic as strongly ever since he'd captured her. Not even her shields had felt as firmly under her control. The duke was blocking her magic somehow.

With a frustrated groan, she slammed her fist against the door.

"Are you going to do that all night?" Teryn asked. They hadn't spoken more than a handful of terse words.

"I'm trying to get out of here," she said through her teeth. She pressed her palms to the door, but her magic felt more muted than ever. Why had it been so much easier at the tree? She'd felt so strong afterward. Exhilarated.

Then she remembered why she'd done it in the first place.

She'd felt an internal nudge, a clairsentient *feeling* that told her to do what felt hardest in that moment. Her instincts had begged her to fight or flee but her magic had urged her to stay and hide. She'd faced a challenge and her magic had grown from it.

If that was the case, where was her magic now? Where were the great feats she'd allowed herself to believe in?

She closed her eyes and focused on her breath, stilling her thoughts until they narrowed on the feeling of air filling her lungs. The stench of rot threatened to shake her concentration, but she told herself the aroma was nothing more than air and earth and water and fire. She shifted her feet against the stone floor, letting it anchor her. She felt the damp air on her skin, could hear the trickle of water dripping in a nearby cell. She opened her eyes and studied the shaft of lamplight streaming through the barred window. With her connection to the elements made, calm settled over her. But there remained a heaviness that darkened the edges of her awareness, snagging her senses. She followed it, pursued the source, expecting it to lead her to Morkai.

It didn't.

It led her to Teryn.

From her periphery, she saw him leaning against the wall, head lowered, arms folded. The darkness she'd sensed collected all around him, but it wasn't coming *from* him. It was coming from her. She could feel it spilling from her chest in angry waves.

Morkai wasn't blocking her magic. She was.

The realization was so enraging, she felt the darkness gather even thicker. She knew then what her current greatest challenge was.

Hands on her hips, she whirled to face the prince. "Why should I forgive you?"

He looked up and met her eyes. "I never said you should, only that I'm sorry."

"Why did you do it? What great need did you—a prince—have for my bounty? Why was it so important that it compelled you to trick me into accepting your company, trick me into thinking you wanted to help the unicorns—"

"I did want to help them," Teryn said. "Perhaps that hadn't been my motive at first, but I was repulsed by what the hunters were doing. By what Helios had wanted to do. It's just that..." He stepped away from the wall and rubbed his brow. "I thought you were a murderer, Cora. I thought you'd murdered the queen and princess."

"You could have asked. You know, *before* you betrayed my trust."

"What would you have done?"

She opened her mouth but her answer died on her lips. Had he revealed that he knew who she was—knew she was wanted by the crown—she'd have fled at her first chance. And that was only if she hadn't felt threatened. If she had, well...it would have ended in a fight. Her heart sank when she imagined how such a confrontation could have ended. "You still haven't answered my question. What did you want with my bounty?"

"I told you about the scandal," he said, voice hollow with exhaustion. "About the threat of war my kingdom faced a few years back."

She nodded, trying not to think about what Morkai had said on that topic.

You could never be Teryn's queen.

The unicorns. The mother. The child...

Do you know what the prince's father did to his *queen? He tried to have her replaced with his mistress. Teryn would only do the same to you.*

The curse he wove with her blood...

"My father took a loan from the Bank of Cartha to compensate my mother and keep her father from declaring war on us. We hadn't been able to pay the bank back so Cartha resorted to sending pirates. They've been raiding our ships, halting trade between us and Brushwold. My kingdom...we were on the brink of ruin. It was my duty as heir to fix what my father had nearly destroyed. That was why I went after the unicorns in the first place."

"The Heart's Hunt," she said, remembering what he'd told her when they'd first met. He'd come to Khero to win

Princess Mareleau's hand in marriage. The thought sent an odd prickle to her heart.

"I found the poster with your face on it shortly after I realized I couldn't complete the Hunt." He ran a hand through his hair before he met her eyes again. "I regret it. I regret lying to you. I regret putting you in danger."

Again, she felt the truth of his emotions. "What about for yourself? Don't you regret getting captured?"

He let out a dark laugh. "Maybe I've gotten what I deserve."

They fell into silence. Cora nibbled her bottom lip. She could feel the darkness dissipating between them, felt something like relief lighten her chest. But she still felt a block. A challenge. One that aggravated her to no end.

"I won't let my father yield to him," he said. "I promise you, in whatever way I can, I will stop Duke Morkai."

She wanted to bark a laugh and remind him there was nothing he could do. He was a prisoner. A hostage. Morkai would send his summons to Menah and Selay in the morning. When they met at Centerpointe Rock in two weeks' time, there would be very little chance the duke would give Teryn the opportunity to speak. If the prince hadn't been such a stubborn fool, he could have lied to the duke the same way he'd lied to her. He could have let Morkai think he'd won him over only to bide his time until he could act against the duke in a way that mattered. Instead, Teryn had gotten himself thrown in a cell.

As did I, she reminded herself. Perhaps they weren't so different.

She had to admit, there was something admirable about him refusing to play the duke's game. Her admiration bloomed, softening the edges of the thorns that had embedded themselves around her heart. His betrayal still ached. She breathed it in, feeling the sensations sink her stomach, letting them thrum through her, weaken her bit by bit, crumble her, and then...*strengthen* her. Her mind grew clearer, her breaths fuller.

"All right," she whispered.

"All right, what?"

"All right, I..." She tried to form the word *forgive*, but her mouth wouldn't obey. It was too soon to feel genuine forgiveness, but she felt *something*. "I understand. I...I know why you did what you did, so...all right."

His posture relaxed. "Cora—"

She turned away from him and went back to the door. This time, when she placed her hands against the metal, a thrum of magic ran through her palm. She felt equal parts elation and annoyance. Why had her magic insisted on her making peace with Teryn? Then again, maybe it hadn't been about him at all. Maybe it had more to do with the rage and hate she'd let consume her senses. Her powers had grown when she'd hid herself and Teryn under the tree, but she'd so quickly reverted to her base instincts afterward. It was a lesson she was constantly having to revisit—the cost of ignoring the whispers of quiet magic in the face of far more tempting noise.

She could hear her magic now, though, the same way she had at the tree. It wasn't a voice that spoke but a feeling. One that guided her hand to where the door met the frame. She felt the cool metal pulse beneath her hand, echoing the rush of her blood. Once, this door was molten. Once, this door was as soft and pliable as her flesh. Once, it was but a collection of metals. Small. Separate. Movable. Even now, she could sense space in the steel, the same space that existed between her fingers, between the strands of her hair, in the pores of her skin. It moved, it buzzed, it hummed like anything else. She slid her hand slightly up, sensed movement mirrored within the door. Then she brushed a finger to the left.

A soft click sounded on the other side. She gave the metal a gentle push.

Beneath Cora's palm, the door opened.

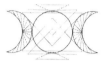

41

Cora stared at the gap in the cell door. Her body tingled with residual magic from her feet to the center of her scalp. She was so lost in her moment of surprise that she didn't realize Teryn had come up beside her until she heard the soft rumble of his voice.

"You...you opened the door."

All Cora could manage was a nod.

"You did that with your magic?" He was looking at her as if seeing something he'd never noticed before. Even to her, this was more impressive than what she'd done beneath the tree. She'd unlocked the door with clairsentient magic. Moved physical matter using sensation, feeling, connection.

If I can do this, what else can I do?

She couldn't help the smile that formed on her lips, but she reminded herself that her pride could wait. There was still a need for haste. She opened the door a little wider and glanced down both ends of the hall. One side ended in shadow where the dungeon hall led to deeper areas, more cells, places Cora had never seen. The other side revealed the closed door she'd been led through earlier—a door that would take her to the upper levels of the castle. With her magic still thrumming strong in her veins, she extended her senses and searched for nearby minds, emotions. Most of the energies she could sense were condensed in the deeper areas of the dungeon. Closer to her cell, she sensed only a few minds, their emotions dulled in slumber. She was struck with the sudden impulse to free the other prisoners but halted that thought before it could bloom. There most certainly were more prisoners like Bradley and his father, but there also could be dangerous people like the hunters. Besides, who knew how long she had before another guard would be back. Before Morkai returned.

If only one of you remains alive by sunrise, that person can leave.

Cora had no idea what time it was. For all she knew, it could be nearing sunrise already.

With a steadying breath, she took a step outside the door. She paused, waiting, feeling. When the path seemed clear, she returned to the cell, shouldered her quiver, and gestured at Teryn. "Come on. We must hurry." She took another step. When she didn't hear Teryn follow, she cast a glance back at him.

She watched his shoulders fall. Watched a flicker of hope crumble until his face was left slack. His response was strained. "I can't leave."

"What? Why?"

"You heard what he said. He needs me alive."

Cora took a step back inside the cell. "He only needs

you alive to use as a bargaining piece."

"Yes, and if he finds me gone come morning, he won't send his summons for my father and King Verdian. He won't meet with them for talks of peace."

"I thought you didn't want your father to surrender."

"I don't."

Cora took another step closer. "Then why would you let yourself be used by Morkai?"

"So long as he has me as a hostage, we know his next move. We know he'll proceed with the meeting."

"How does it help for us to know his next move if Menah and Selay don't? They don't know he's a mage. They will only know what the duke's missive tells them. I guarantee he will make terms for surrender sound favorable. Not only that, but his magic...he can influence people's minds. Change how they think."

"I've gathered that," Teryn said. "But, Cora, we're both prizes to him. He needs me for negotiations. As for you..." His fingers curled into tight fists. "I don't like the way he looks at you. The way he talks to you. The way he framed you for murder only to hunt you down now. I have a feeling he wants to do so much more."

Cora pursed her lips to keep from telling Teryn he was right. Morkai had plans for her indeed, and she wasn't sure she even knew the half of them.

Teryn spoke again. "If he finds this cell empty in the morning, discovers both his prizes are gone, who knows what he'll do, when he'll strike. I can't leave, but you can. You can warn my father not to listen to a word Morkai says. Warn him of the duke's true nature. Perhaps then we can beat him at his own game."

She felt the wisdom of his words, and yet it did

nothing to stop the ache in her chest. Now that she'd rid her heart of its icy thorns of hatred, it was left open to other emotions. His. Hers. Pain, regret, fear.

"I can't leave you here," she said, her voice breaking.

"Tell my father—"

"Come with me and tell him yourself."

"—everything you know. Everything we've seen. Tell him—"

"No." She reached for his wrist, closed her fingers around it. Her palm pulsed at their touch, no longer separated by gloves, and her heart thudded in a wild echo.

Teryn stepped in close, and for a moment, Cora thought he was going to agree. But his expression was not one of resignation. It was one of pain. "Tell him to let me go."

She felt the weight of what he meant. He wanted his father to let him die. It shouldn't have come as a surprise. She knew Morkai intended to kill Teryn if the royals refused to surrender. Only now did that strike her as something she couldn't bear. She almost wished she'd held on to her hate, for maybe then it would be easier to leave him. Easier to do what needed to be done.

She gripped his wrist tighter, took another step closer. "You stubborn son-of-a—"

Her words dissolved as he gave her a sad smirk and lowered his face to hers. In the next breath his lips were against her own, the kiss so sudden and startling she froze. Then a rush of fire swept over her, and she wasn't sure whether it was renewed rage or some absurd flood of desire. Whatever the case, she felt her lips yield beneath his, felt her hand leave his wrist to cradle the back of his neck. She buried one hand in his hair while the other ran up his chest, resting on the curve of his shoulder. His arms came around her back, pulling her tight against him, as if even the slightest inch between their bodies was unbearable. She bit back a gasp, but it only made her lips part. His tongue swept against hers and she met it with a fervor she'd never felt before. Something small inside her shouted that this was hardly the time for a kiss, but a greater part of her banished the thought, consumed by a sudden need to taste him, feel him—

He pushed away from her before she realized what was happening. She opened her eyes, found a door slamming shut before her, heard the click of the lock snapping automatically in place. Catching her breath, she stared at the closed door and realized she and Teryn now stood on opposite sides of it—she in the hall and Teryn in the cell. All previous desire drained from her body as her mind reeled over what had just happened.

"You tricked me."

"I did what I had to do," came his muffled voice from the other side.

Her hands trembled, her skin still warm from where it had been pressed against him. "I...I despise you."

"Good." His shadow shifted behind the barred window. "Then it will be easier for you to leave me here. Go. And know that if we never meet again, I think you're—"

She gritted her teeth, expecting him to say something patronizing like *pretty*, *beautiful*, or *great*.

"—formidable." The way the word rolled off his tongue with the deepest respect and admiration made Cora feel as if he'd just called her the most desirable woman in the world.

Her anger dissipated. Not fully, but enough to clear her mind. The warmth from their kiss was gone, leaving her shivering in the cold hall.

"Go," he whispered, then she heard him shuffle away from the door and shift against the far wall.

Without another word, she turned from the cell and left him behind, ignoring the tears that managed to squeeze from the corners of her eyes.

CORA BANISHED ALL THOUGHTS OF TERYN AS SHE CREPT through the dark halls in the lower level of the sleeping castle. Her steps were slow, quiet, careful, as she followed a familiar route to the servants' passage. It was the same path Morkai had taken her down six years ago. She kept her shields lowered, her senses open, stopping every time she felt guards drawing near. When they did, she pressed herself close to the walls, merging with stone and shadows until they passed her by. The servants' passage was thankfully empty. It wasn't too surprising considering the lack of staff she'd seen at dinner. She was starting to understand more and more why Ridine was so empty. Anyone who couldn't be swayed by Morkai was probably dismissed, imprisoned, or killed. Perhaps it was a good sign that the castle wasn't teeming with mindless, brainless sycophants. It could mean Morkai's influence was weaker than he'd made it seem.

Cora reached the back end of the castle. After testing a few doors, she found the one that led from the passage to the yard outside the kitchens. Enormous outdoor ovens, washbasins, and lines for drying linens stood empty as Cora crept past. She focused on her breath, on the firmness of the earth, silent beneath her soft steps. The air was cool, the sky just beginning to pale toward dawn. She fixed her gaze on the dark forests looming beyond the wall, her hope tenuous as she paused behind an overgrown shrub. With a deep breath, she turned her attention to the wall itself, seeking signs of sentries. She saw some silhouettes farther down, closer to the nearest gate, but none straight ahead. That was where the vines of ivy crawled up the wall, blanketing it like a tapestry.

That was where she hoped to find the hidden break in the stone.

With another deep breath, she drew air against her skin, earth against her feet, calling upon the elements to shield her, hide her, obscure her. Then she stepped out from behind the shrub and crept toward the wall. She kept her senses reaching outward, seeking any nearby emotions that rippled with shock or alarm.

Finally, she reached the wall and pressed herself against it. There she paused, once again assessing her surroundings for threats. The sentries remained near the gates. She tiptoed along the wall, feeling beneath the ivy for any sign of crumbling stone. Her heart slammed against her ribs, her muscles clenched in panic. Every touch revealed only solid wall. Terror nearly threatened to overtake her, but she forced herself to be calm. Breathe. Turn inward.

She closed her eyes and pressed both palms to the stone beneath the ivy, extending her senses out along the wall. To the right, she felt only dense, solid energy, but to the left...

There was a hollow, a lightness in the wall's density.

She followed it, ran her hand to where she was guided, freezing when her fingers sank beneath the ivy. She bent down, spread the ivy aside, and found an opening only chest high. In her memories, the opening had been almost as tall as her, but she'd been twelve then. Smaller. It stood to reason that the hole would seem much lower now. She peered inside, seeing nothing but darkness beyond. A ripple of revulsion passed through her when she considered what kinds of creatures or creeping things could be hiding inside such a hole, but now was not the time to be afraid.

Biting the inside of her cheek, she slipped beyond the ivy.

Hurry. Danger.

Her heart nearly leapt out of her throat at the voice. Relief and joy and surprise flooded through her, so potent it made her quicken her pace as she squeezed through the gap in the wall. *Valorre?*

She could feel him somewhere nearby, his presence growing closer with every breath. But he didn't seem to share in her relief. Instead, his energy was panicked. *Hurry. Hurry. Hurry.*

A subtle light broke through the dark space she traversed, giving her a glimpse at where the hidden gap let out. The sound of Valorre's hoofbeats hit her ears next. He was right on the other side of the wall now.

His hoofbeats were drowned out by a sudden rumbling coming from behind her. It sent the wall shaking, sending crumbling bits of rock raining down on her head. She moved faster in the narrow space. The exit was almost in reach, just as hot, moist breath blew against the back of her head. She didn't need to look behind her to know the Roizan was there. Only a few feet remained, then she'd be free—

Shouts of alarm erupted from above. The Roizan growled into the gap, setting her teeth on edge, but then it was gone. She broke through the ivy on the other side of the wall and nearly stumbled into Valorre.

Danger. It's coming. He sidled closer and lowered his head, inviting her to mount.

One of the sentries called for someone to open one of the gates. Cora gripped Valorre's mane and hauled herself onto his back. She barely had her seat before he took off. They darted through the trees behind the castle. Cora kept her head lowered as a defense against the branches that reached out to graze her flesh while they tore across the forest floor. A rumbling followed behind. Valorre wove, dodged, shifted direction, but the Roizan was persistent.

She reached for her bow but all she had was her quiver. "Damn," she muttered and retrieved an arrow anyway. Should the Roizan gain on them, she wouldn't go down without a fight. A wary glance over her shoulder revealed trees trembling, a flash of red skin in the distance.

Worry only a little, Valorre said. *I spent most of last night learning to evade the abomination. I run faster. Longer.*

"You...you found me. You've been waiting for me."

You're my friend, he said, as if that explained everything. Explained why he'd been battling a unicorn-eating demon creature when he could have kept himself safe instead. *But where is the handsome one?*

Her chest constricted with thoughts of Teryn. Heat

rose to her cheeks as she replayed the kiss he'd tricked her with. "I had to leave him behind."

Valorre rippled with disappointment. Or was it Cora's own that she felt?

Where do we go next? he asked. His words were calm despite the breakneck pace he kept. Their pursuer still followed.

Cora considered the question. Her first instinct was to flee far from Khero, away from Lela, away from Morkai and his war to rule fae magic. They could keep to the forests and hide at the far north of the continent, leaving all of this behind them. But the thought was only a fleeting fantasy. No matter how much she wished to escape what was coming, she felt in her blood that she was already entangled.

The unicorns. The mother. The child.

She knew Teryn wanted her to warn his father, but how could she hope to convince a king of anything? Now that she'd run away, Morkai would not be spreading tales of the princess who'd returned from the dead. That meant she was once again a fugitive. Still, that didn't mean she could do nothing. Her meager existence had been such a threat to Morkai's plans that he'd intervened with her fate. She didn't know much about prophecies, but the faerytales had always insisted upon their persistence. Maybe her role wasn't over yet. Maybe it had only changed.

It was a daunting thought. A terror. A burden.

But she'd faced terrors and she'd carried burdens. She could carry this one too.

She gripped Valorre's mane tighter, her blood burning with resolve. "It's time for me to go home."

42

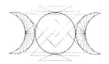

Teryn had no concept of day or night in his cell, but he knew the sun had risen when he heard footsteps marching down the hall. They were too swift to be a guard's. Too confident to belong to anyone but Duke Morkai.

He rose to his feet as his cell door opened. Morkai strode in, a smug smile stretched across his face. It fell when he found only Teryn inside. Morkai's gaze rested on Cora's discarded gown. In a flash, the duke surged toward Teryn, bringing his cane against Teryn's throat. "Where is she?"

Teryn fought to keep his composure despite his constricted airways. Even if he'd wanted to answer, the duke's cane made it impossible.

Morkai seemed to come to the same conclusion and shoved away from him. His pale eyes flashed with rage. "Tell me."

Teryn rubbed his throat, taking in heavy gulps of air.

He shot the duke a smirk. "You said only one of us could remain alive by sunrise."

Morkai took another step back, a vein pulsing in his temple. "She isn't dead."

"She could be," Teryn said with a halfhearted shrug. It took all his effort to hide the truth of his feelings—the emptiness he felt at not knowing how Cora fared after her escape. His only consolation was that Morkai had no clue where she was. Which meant she *had* escaped.

"What. Happened." The duke said each word through his teeth.

"She walked straight through the wall and left me behind."

Morkai froze.

"Oh, did you not know she's a witch?"

"She's more than a witch," the duke ground out.

"Then did you underestimate her powers?"

Morkai lifted his chin, jaw clenched tight, but Teryn could see the hint of fear in his eyes. He *had* underestimated her. The duke had expected to enter the cell and find them sitting at opposite ends, not daring to trust one another in light of Morkai's bargain. Or perhaps he'd thought to find them huddled together, cowering with fear over what the duke would do to them come morning. Not once had Morkai considered Cora would use her magic to break herself out. The fact was written plainly across his face.

The realization filled Teryn with such satisfaction, he couldn't stop the grin that spread over his lips. Teryn had never underestimated her. Had never seen her as anything but what he'd called her before she'd left.

Formidable.

She was a force to be reckoned with, a storm wind, an inferno. She was a wind-tossed sea and a snow-capped mountain. Beautiful like the edge of a blade.

Morkai didn't see that, but Teryn did.

"Don't look so smug, prince," Morkai said. "Like you said, she left you behind."

Teryn shrugged.

Returning to his carefully curated composure, Morkai planted his cane before him and folded his hands over the crystal. "Never mind the princess. I will find her again, have no doubts. My business is with you. Have you reconsidered my offer?"

"A night in the dungeon has done nothing to convince me to ally with you."

"Are you certain? This is your final chance. I will send out my summons this morning. Ally with me, send a letter for your father, and I'll award you with a personal guarantee that I'll let you live even if your father refuses to surrender."

"Can my letter say anything I choose?" Teryn already knew the answer but he couldn't help baiting the duke with his own words.

"Of course not. Your letter must be penned in favor of surrender."

Teryn leaned against the wall. "Then I refuse."

Morkai's jaw tightened. "I will make you pay, then. Should Menah and Selay surrender as they should, I will make you grovel at my feet. Should they choose war instead, then I will flay you alive before your father's eyes and make him watch as I cut you apart piece by piece."

Teryn swallowed hard. He knew standing against the duke meant his death, especially if his father made the choice Teryn wanted him to make. That didn't mean he didn't dread his fate. It also didn't mean he was resigned to it just yet. There were two weeks until the meeting at Centerpointe Rock. Two more weeks in the duke's company. Two more weeks to find a way to undermine him. Two more weeks to hope his father would make a plan. One that didn't involve bowing before a blood mage.

Morkai narrowed his eyes. "Perhaps I could start carving you apart right now. A finger would work nicely in my summons. Perhaps fill your father with a sense of urgency."

Teryn felt the blood leave his face. Despite the revulsion that turned his stomach, he forced himself to extend his hand. "Take your pick. It's a sure way to turn my father firmly against you."

The duke assessed him, eyes flicking briefly to Teryn's outstretched hand. Then, with a dark huff of laughter, he took a step back. "No, let us save the theatrics for the meeting."

"If we must."

Morkai's lips pulled into a sneer before he swept out the door. A guard closed it behind him. The duke's voice rumbled from the other side. "I'll see you at the meeting, Your Highness."

Teryn listened to the sound of footsteps receding until he could hear them no more. Only then did he let his guard down. He slumped against the wall and slid down it, his arms trembling as he draped them across his knees.

The meeting at Centerpointe Rock loomed in his mind like a dark cloud. It felt both too soon and too far away. His skin crawled with the thought that he'd be trapped in this dark cell until then. He was desperate to move, to act, to fight.

Instead, all he could do was wait.

KING DIMETREUS' DEMAND FOR SURRENDER ARRIVED AT Dermaine Palace two days later. Another day had passed since then, and yet Larylis Seralla held firmly on to his disbelief in what the letter had said. Refused to accept his brother was being held hostage. All evidence pointed to it being true, however, starting with the hastily scrawled note Berol had delivered a few days ago.

Ridine Castle. Not safe. Trying to flee.

Now his father had been summoned to meet at Centerpointe Rock in less than two weeks' time to discuss terms for a peaceful surrender. Peace—while Teryn was being kept as a bait.

Larylis was sick with worry over his brother's fate. He paced across his balcony, which he'd been doing for the better part of the morning, stopping only when he heard wings beating the air. He turned to see Berol diving toward the balustrade. Larylis rushed to her as she landed, his pulse leaping as he saw something clutched in her talon. He hoped against all hope that it was a letter from Teryn, proof that he was all right. Proof that their world hadn't been turned upside down.

His heart sank as he saw Berol carried not a piece of parchment but a charred tree branch. Larylis took it gingerly from the falcon and fed her a strip of meat he'd set aside in anticipation of her return. This was the third time she'd come back without any communication from Teryn. When Larylis had gotten Teryn's letter about being unsafe at Ridine Castle, he'd sent a note back asking for more details. Berol had returned with it still clutched in one of her talons, no sign that it had been read.

Larylis ran his thumb over the charred branch, watching it blacken the tip of his finger. Wherever Teryn was, Berol couldn't reach him. He fled the balcony and went to the bureau inside his room, surprised when Berol followed him. She rarely came inside, spending most of her time on Teryn's balcony or in her mews. The falcon landed on the top of Larylis' bureau, wings splayed as she screeched her distress.

"I know," Larylis said as he placed a fresh piece of parchment over his desk. He knew it was fruitless to send another letter, but he...he had to try.

He reached for his inkwell, but in his haste, he spilled it over the parchment. Cursing under his breath, he righted his well and sopped the ink with the paper, then began rummaging through the drawers of his bureau. Empty. Damn. He had to have more ink somewhere.

With quick strides, he went to his bookshelf, shoving aside books and stacks of paper. Finally, he found a stoppered bottle of fresh ink beside a stack of old letters and a pile of his favorite novels. He moved the books aside and reached for the ink. When he pulled it from the shelf, the letters came with it, spilling all over the floor. Larylis bent down to gather them up. He was halfway through retrieving them when one caught his eye. The letter was open, its familiar script flowing over the parchment. Gingerly, he picked it up, scanning words that had already been branded on his heart.

> *Larylis,*
>
> *We cannot see each other anymore. I can't explain. All you need to know is that I can't love you. I could never love a bastard.*
>
> *Mareleau*

Whatever had possessed him to keep the letter was beyond him, for even now, three years later, the words still stung. Perhaps more so with his brother being held captive after running off to fulfill *her* Heart's Hunt. Resentment boiled in his blood, a much more welcome feeling than fear. He crumpled the letter in his fist, strode to his desk, and tossed the princess' letter in the hearth on the way. His chest felt tight as he caught sight of it igniting beneath the flames.

"Good riddance," he muttered and poured the fresh ink into his inkwell. Berol screeched at him, her wings still splayed with agitation. He grabbed fresh parchment and his quill and began to write. "I know, Berol. I'm trying again."

The falcon hopped down from the top of his bureau to the desktop, nipping at his fingers to stop him.

"Berol, I need to write to him—"

She nipped again, forcing him to drop the quill.

He glared at the bird, prepared to shoo her off his desk, but there was something in her eyes that made his shoulders sink—a deep sadness that echoed the emotions he was trying to shove aside. A heart-wrenching possibility dawned on him, one too unbearable to consider. He ran a hand over his lower face and took a step back. "Seven gods. Berol, is Teryn...is he..."

She seemed to calm down a bit and flew back to the top of the bureau. Her shift in countenance sent him some small relief. He didn't know how to communicate with the bird like Teryn seemed able to, but he wanted to believe she was trying to tell him his brother was alive. It was clear she was also trying to convey that writing another letter would do nothing. But what else could he do? His father had shut himself in his study ever since the missive arrived from King Dimetreus. Arlous had immediately blamed himself for what was happening to Teryn, saying it was all his fault because he'd told Teryn about some outlaw's bounty. A bounty Teryn had attempted to collect, thanks to their father sending a communication to the king a while back. Never mind the fact that their father had only acted because of the letter Teryn had sent Berol with in the first place.

Larylis didn't understand the full story, and the fact that he couldn't talk to his father about it was driving him half out of his mind. He slammed a fist onto the desk. "We have to do something."

A heavy knock sounded at his door. He whirled to face it, finding it swinging open before he could grant the caller permission to enter. He may have been a bastard but the palace staff knew better than to treat him as such.

But it wasn't a servant on the other side of the door. Instead, Prince Lexington of Tomas charged into Larylis' room, a mortified guard following in his wake.

"He wouldn't take no for an answer," the guard said, her eyes brimming with apology. "Your father wouldn't see him, but I can't turn him away. He's a..."

"A prince, yes," Lexington said, although his appearance was the opposite of regal. His cheeks were smudged with dirt, his hair a blond windswept mess, his clothing torn and stained. "And yet no one seems to respect that fact nor how long or how fast I've been bloody riding."

Larylis blinked back at the man, uncertain what to make of his presence. The guard gave Larylis a questioning glance, one hand on the hilt of her sword. "It's all right," he said to her, then turned his gaze to the prince. "To what reason do I owe this pleasure, Prince Lexington?"

"Call me Lex, and—" He held up a finger, then doubled over, hands braced on his knees. "Seven devils I'm out of breath."

Larylis watched as Lex took several deep breaths before straightening.

"Teryn is being held hostage by Duke Morkai," the man said in a rush.

"I know," Larylis said, then paused. "Wait...Duke Morkai? Not King Dimetreus?"

Lex gave a flippant wave of his hand. "They're basically one and the same, but the worst part is the duke is a bloody blood mage and he's the one who really wants to become king. You cannot surrender to him."

"If we don't, he'll kill Teryn—" He shook his head. "How do you even know this?"

"It's a long story, but I was captured with Teryn. Duke Morkai offered me a deal in exchange for my father's allegiance. Little does he know, my father would rather build a wall to hide behind than join forces with a conqueror. Which left me one choice—to warn you about the duke's monsters and wraiths and try to find a way to save my friend."

Blood mage. Monsters. Wraiths. His words made no sense, but Larylis only questioned the one that seemed at least partially grounded in reality. "Your...friend."

"Teryn," Lex said as if that was supposed to be obvious from the start.

"Since when are you friends with Teryn?"

"Another long story, and if you don't mind, I'd rather only tell it once. Which means we should speak to your father." Lex turned on his heel and marched down the hall like he owned it. "In fact, we should probably head for Selay straight away. They'll want to hear this too. Besides, I've got a Heart's Hunt to forfeit."

Larylis followed after Lex, unsure whether the prince was a hero or a madman.

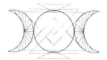

43

Cora could feel her destination drawing near. Her heart grew warmer with every racing step Valorre took across the forest floor. He'd hardly slowed his pace after escaping the pursuit of the Roizan three days prior. They'd stopped only to rest and eat, although without Cora's bow or belt of necessities, she'd been limited to whatever she could harvest with her hands or an arrow. She was weak. Hungry. But at least she had Valorre. He carried her to the Ishvonn Woods where they first met. Where she hoped beyond hope that the Forest People had remained since she'd parted from them. Thankfully, it was not yet summer, so the commune had little reason to have departed.

As Valorre galloped past the hot spring caves, weaving along the familiar path she'd trod mere weeks ago, she felt the call of home. Of family.

Of people who might turn her away the minute they saw her face.

We're here, Cora thought to Valorre when she sensed

the commune's proximity. He slowed his pace and paused near a thicket of trees. Cora dismounted, wincing at the soreness in her thighs, the ache in her legs, the hollow in her stomach. She felt a sudden stab of self-consciousness when she realized what she must look like. Dressed only in her corset and shift, no petticoats, no overskirt, filthy, her hair a mass of tangles...she imagined she appeared half mad.

I'll stay close, Valorre said and trotted away.

She felt cold without her friend, but she knew it would be best to enter the camp alone. Her mission would be much easier if the others weren't gawking at a unicorn. Then again, perhaps if they had him to gawk at, they wouldn't do so at her.

With a deep breath, she made her way toward the camp.

Familiar smells of herbs, food, and campfire invaded her nostrils, sending her stomach growling. What she wouldn't give for one of Chandra's stews. The yearning almost sent tears to her eyes, along with a hefty dose of regret. What would it have been like if she hadn't left? If she hadn't even gone to the hot spring caves at all that night? Remorse sank her heart, but she was surprised that it didn't linger. If she hadn't gone to the caves, she wouldn't have met Valorre or Teryn or been captured by Morkai.

But that would only have changed things for her.

Morkai's mission would have stayed the same. Without Teryn to hold as a hostage, without her to have brought the entire mess together...no one would have a clue the duke's war was coming.

Which is why I'm here, she reminded herself. Not for comfort. For war.

The clearing became visible between the trees just ahead. She slowed her steps and halted as she heard a soft step behind her. Just as she'd expected, her intrusion was detected.

"Cora?" She knew the voice before she saw him. Slowly, she turned to face Roije. He lowered his bow, brow furrowed, but there was something knowing in his expression. "Maiya said you were coming."

Her chest constricted at her friend's name. "Maiya...knew?"

He nodded, then shifted his feet as if he wasn't sure whether to block her path or welcome her back. She opened herself to his energy and found it cloudy. Hesitant.

"What is it?" she asked.

He lowered his voice. "The last group that went out to trade with the village...they brought back your poster."

Her stomach took a dive. Perhaps she'd left the commune at the right time after all.

His expression turned apologetic. "I don't think it's the best idea that you're here."

"Nonsense." Salinda stepped from between the trees. Her face was so warm, so kind, so motherly and familiar that Cora's throat felt tight. She wasn't sure who reached for who first, but the next thing she knew, they were wrapped in a tight embrace. Cora found herself sobbing on the woman's shoulder despite her every effort to compose herself. "It's all right," Salinda soothed, rubbing her back like she'd done every night during the first inconsolable weeks after the Forest People had found her. "You're home. You're home."

Cora wished they could stay like that forever. That she could forget what Roije had said about the Forest People's knowledge of her Wanted poster, about the dark tidings she carried on her shoulders. She wished she could pull away from Salinda and promise her she'd never leave again. But that was folly.

Once she managed to rein in her tears, she gently unraveled from Salinda's comforting arms and delivered the words she needed to say. "I need to speak with the elders."

Salinda frowned, her mouth falling open. No words came out, but Cora knew what the woman was poised to say—that Cora had no right to call such a meeting. Only another elder could, and Cora had lost that right when she refused to take the path Salinda had offered. Furthermore, she'd lost her right to even sit amongst the elders when she departed from the commune without a word. Even more so now that they knew she was a wanted fugitive.

A flash of panic struck her. If Salinda turned her away now, her visit would be all for naught. Her plans would be foiled.

Salinda's lips curled into a sad smile. "You do have much to tell us, don't you?" Then, with a heavy sigh that seemed to share the weight of Cora's burden, she said, "I'll gather the elders."

TEN MINUTES LATER, CORA SAT IN THE TENT OF THE elders. It had taken some work sneaking Cora into camp without being seen, but Roije had brought her a cloak and used his connection to the Magic of the Soil to navigate the clearest path there. It was past midday, which meant most within the commune were busy with their daily tasks, leaving very few idle enough to stare. Now she just had to wait for Salinda to return with the elders.

She wandered the tent, focusing on her breath, on the aromas of herbs and oils filling the air, on anything that could distract her from the anxiety that plagued the back of her mind. The tent of elders was the largest in the camp, used for celebrations, elder meetings, and *insigmora* ceremonies. Cora stared down at her forearm, remembering the last time she'd received a new design several months ago. She frowned as she stared down at her inner elbow crease. A dark spiral was there, an inch above her most recent tattoo. Surely that hadn't been there before—

Cora froze as the tent flap opened to reveal Salinda. She held the flap for the twelve other figures who followed. Nalia, the Forest People's High Elder, brought up the rear. She was thin, hunched, and wrinkled, as ancient-looking as the oldest tree in the forest, and— surprisingly—without a single *insigmora*.

The silence was stifling as the thirteen elders took their places in a circle around the tent. Cora didn't need to use her Art to know the elders weren't pleased about being called into a meeting with her. It would have been one thing if she were simply *Cora, Salinda's foster daughter*. It was another now that she was known as a murderer. She doubted they'd be any happier to learn the truth.

Once they were seated—six elder witches to Nalia's left, the six elder Faeryn to her right—the High Elder motioned Cora to stand at the center of the circle. Trembling despite the warmth of her borrowed cloak, she did as told and took her place.

Nalia gave a bow of her head. "You may speak, child."

She drew a long, shaking breath. "You know me as Cora, but my true name is Aveline Corasande Caelan. I'm the Princess of Khero. Fae magic is in danger."

WHISPERS SURROUNDED HER. SHE'D DELIVERED HER STORY and now stood trembling in the wake of her truth. She kept her gaze above Nalia's head, not daring to meet anyone's eyes as they deliberated her tale. They'd remained respectfully silent as she'd explained who she truly was, where she'd come from all those years ago when they'd found her, and why she'd kept her identity to herself. She'd felt their trepidation turn to terror as she'd described the gruesome hunt for unicorns and how it was tied to Morkai's magic and his Roizan. They'd stared unblinking as she'd revealed his plans for war in the name of harnessing fae magic.

Now she breathed deep, focusing on the canvas walls of the tent to keep from being overwhelmed by the emotions growing and clashing all around her. Soon the whispers turned to much louder questions and the voices of the elders rose to match the roar of feeling. Cora closed her eyes and tried to raise her shields against the cacophony, but her fatigue was too great.

"Enough," Nalia said, her soft voice somehow cutting through the noise. "We will now peacefully discuss."

"What is there to discuss?" asked one of the witches, a man named Druchan. "We live by simple rules, one of which is to never involve ourselves in royal matters."

Salinda pinned him with a glare. "Did you not hear a word she said? This may be a royal matter, but it ultimately concerns magic."

Another Faeryn elder nodded beside her. "He calls himself Morkai. *King of Magic*. He's trying to become the Morkaius. You know what that means."

Nalia's face went slack. "High King of Magic."

Cora straightened at that. She'd never heard the term *Morkaius* before, nor had she considered Morkai wasn't the duke's true name. She'd always known him as such. Only now did it seem strange to her that he hadn't taken on the title of his duchy—Calloway—when Dimetreus named him duke.

"If the prophecy is true," one of the elder witches said, "the Morkaius cannot claim the magic without being destroyed by it."

"He has created this...this Roizan thing!" argued another witch. "A channel between his body and the magic."

Cora's eyes darted between the arguing elders. "You know about the prophecy?" That was one part of her tale she'd kept vague. She hadn't mentioned what he'd said about her role in the prophecy or the curse he'd laid upon her with his blood weaving. Her question, however, was drowned out beneath the sounds of further arguments.

"War is not our way. Let the armies do the fighting."

"There will be no fighting if the royals surrender."

"And if they surrender, the duke wins."

"It doesn't matter. We protect our own, that's all."

"What do you mean it doesn't matter? We protect the land and the Arts. If the duke becomes Morkaius, he will have control over magic. He could take our Art from us. We must act."

"What can we even do? He's an Elvyn prince. A weaver—"

"He is not a true weaver," Nalia interrupted, voice fiercer than Cora had ever heard. "He may have Elvyn blood as he claims, but Elvyn weavers need only magic. This Morkai wields blood and animates spirits because he is no true weaver at all. He is weak. He relies on curses and tricks and the forbidden Arts."

Cora wanted to argue that Morkai's powers were hardly what she'd call weak. As far as she could tell, his blood sorcery was far stronger and more terrifying than the Forest People's quiet magic.

"High Elder," one of the Faeryn said, giving Nalia a respectful bow of her head, "that still doesn't explain what we can do."

"Nor do we know if we can trust a girl who's been hiding a secret identity from us the entire time," Druchan added.

"We can trust her," Salinda shot back. "I've raised her since she was a child. She told us why she hid who she was. Can you blame her?"

"She should have left the minute she learned we don't involve ourselves with royals."

"She was twelve!"

"She could have brought danger to our camp at any

time."

"But she didn't. When she realized her presence was a threat, she left."

Druchan narrowed his eyes at Cora. "She should have stayed gone."

"This isn't about Cora," Nalia said, silencing the tent once again. "This is about magic. This is about the fate of this land that we work to nurture and protect. I assure you, nothing good can come from the Blood of Darius. He will destroy not one realm but two. He will corrupt fae magic until there is nothing left of the lives we know."

Cora felt the hairs on her arms rise. Who was the Blood of Darius? Was that...Morkai?

Druchan shrank down. "It's just...stories, though. Isn't it?"

Nalia slowly turned to look at him, her expression both hard and sad at once. "No. What you call stories are merely a fraction of the truth."

Salinda nodded. "What can we do, High Elder?"

Nalia's tone was resolute. "We must kill the duke."

"How?" Druchan asked.

Nalia turned her gaze on Cora, expression penetrating. "What do you suggest, Your Highness?"

Cora's throat constricted at the honorific. She nearly told her not to call her that but swallowed the words down. Perhaps it was time to be a princess after all. She had no desire to reclaim her title, but in coming to the Forest People with the truth, she'd already taken on that responsibility. If her brother couldn't protect Khero, that left only her.

Lifting her chin, she said, "I know where Morkai is going to be next."

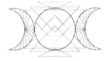

44

Two hours later, after Cora had visited the bathing wagon and thoroughly washed her hair, she went to her old tent. Her chest felt tight when she noticed her side still held all of her things —her cot, her blankets, her clothes—as if Maiya had never given up on her returning. She changed into a fresh shift, bodice, and skirt, relishing the fragrant lavender that wafted off the clean textiles. Her heart yearned to bask in the comfort of being home again, but the sinking in her gut reminded her that she wouldn't be staying for long. Druchan had been evidence enough that even though many amongst the Forest People would accept her return, there would be many others who would not. At least Salinda had promised to spread word that Cora wasn't the outlaw her poster claimed she was. It wouldn't be long before the entire camp learned what had occurred inside the elders' tent too—that some of them were going to fight an Elvyn blood mage.

She rifled through more of her belongings, finding a

spare belt, a knife, her extra bow, and more arrows for her quiver. As she began to stuff the arrows inside, something caught her eye. She peered into her quiver and saw the white unicorn-horn blade that had belonged to the deceased Prince Helios. She'd nearly forgotten about it, having not seen it since she took it from beside the dead body and tossed it in her quiver. A subtle pulse of dark energy entered her awareness, heavy and sorrowful.

"You aren't leaving already, are you?"

Cora dropped the arrows the rest of the way inside, hiding the dagger and muting its dark resonance once again, and whirled to face Maiya. They collided in a hug that included much crying on Maiya's part.

"I woke up this morning and *knew* you'd come," said her friend. "Just like I knew that poster was wrong about you when the traders brought it back last week."

They separated, and Cora studied Maiya's face, curious what else she knew.

Maiya blushed and averted her gaze with a shy smile. "Should I call you Your Highness?"

Cora gave her shoulder a playful shove. "Don't you dare." If there was one person she wanted to continue to be *Cora* with, it was Maiya.

Maiya grinned but her expression quickly turned somber. "Mother told me about the meeting with the elders, but I still can hardly believe it. Mages, dark magic, war. It's...terrifying."

Cora could only manage a nod.

Maiya nibbled a corner of her lip and said, "I understand why you did it. Why you never told me who you truly were. Still, I wish you had. I could have been there for you."

"You were there for me," Cora said, gathering one of her friend's hands and giving it a squeeze.

"Not as much as I could have been."

"What else could you have done?"

Maiya sighed. "I just...I just wish I'd known. You must have been through a lot before you came to us."

Cora wasn't sure what to say about that. She had been through a lot, but her past wasn't a topic she felt like talking about at the moment. Her mind was too wrapped up in the pasts of those she *didn't* know. She was desperate to learn more about what the Forest People knew—about Morkai, about whoever the Blood of Darius was, about the prophecy. Thankfully, she was saved from having to shift the subject when the tent flap opened again.

Roije took one step inside and froze, his eyes darting between Cora and Maiya. He seemed flustered at finding them both there. Perhaps he'd been looking for Cora to ask more details about the dark tidings she'd brought. "I'll come back," he said as he began to back out of the tent.

Cora was about to tell him they could talk about anything in front of Maiya, but her friend spoke first.

"No, Roije, it's all right." With a flutter of her lashes, Maiya took his hand.

His eyes locked on hers. The soft grin that stretched across his lips made him look more boyish than Cora had ever seen. He lowered his voice to a whisper. "I came to ask if you still wanted to go to the hot spring caves together."

Cora's cheeks burned as she suddenly realized what she was witnessing. Her eyes landed on the pair's clasped hands, the nervous, desire-fueled emotions radiating off of them in droves, the implications of Roije's invitation to the hot springs. Maiya and Roije were...courting.

Maiya glanced at Cora, brows knitted. Her energy clouded with regret. "I wanted to, Roije, but now that Cora's back—"

"It's fine," Cora said, her words coming out in a rush and with far too much enthusiasm. A strange blend of surprise and jealousy flooded through her. Her envy wasn't of Maiya. She'd never fancied Roije and had always wished the two of them would confess their feelings for each other. It was more that she was struck with a sudden longing for what her friend was experiencing. Or perhaps it was only regret over not having been there for such an exciting development in Maiya's life. Whatever the case, it brought a sudden memory of Teryn's lips against hers—

She shook her head, banishing the thought.

"Don't worry about me," Cora said, her voice back to normal. "I need to speak with your mother, anyway. Go have fun."

Maiya grinned, her cheeks flushing a deeper shade. "You won't leave tonight, will you?"

Cora had originally considered making camp with Valorre not too far away, but the pleading look in Maiya's eyes made her reconsider. She almost asked if Maiya was planning to return to their tent tonight or stay with Roije, but she quickly swallowed the question. Her friend was shy enough. She'd probably be mortified by such an indelicate suggestion. Instead, Cora gave her a reassuring grin. "I'll be here when you get back."

After Maiya and Roije left for the hot springs, Cora made her way to Salinda's tent. She found the woman sitting outside it, a quill and stack of parchment in hand. Salinda's brow was furrowed as she wrote, her energy heavy and murky. Cora realized Salinda must be recording what had transpired today. As Keeper of Histories, it was Salinda's duty to keep records of not only the past but any new events that dealt with the Arts. Salinda always put her stories to paper first before committing them to memory where she carried them thereafter. With the Forest People being nomadic, they didn't have space or the means to carry physical tomes.

Salinda didn't look up from her writing until Cora cast a shadow over her work. "Forgive me," Salinda said with a smile as she looked up at her. "I was wrapped up in words."

"You can keep writing," Cora said, stepping out of the sunlight so it could illuminate the parchment again. "I'll wait until you are finished."

Salinda shook her head and set her quill and stack of papers inside a leather sheath, then motioned for Cora to follow her inside the tent. It was the same size as the one she shared with Maiya but far messier. Furs, papers, and clothing were draped all over. Salinda's husband—and Maiya's father—had passed away some years ago. Whenever Cora had glimpsed Salinda's living space, she'd wonder if the mess helped distract her from the absence of her missing half.

Salinda took a seat on a pile of furs and poured two mugs of herb-infused water. Cora sat down across from her and took one of the clay mugs. The water tasted of mint and rosemary, two aromas she'd always associate with her foster mother.

As she lowered the cup, she noticed Salinda's gaze had fallen to the crook of her arm. "Your *insigmora* has grown since you've been gone."

Cora's eyes went wide. She'd almost forgotten the strange spiral she'd noticed in the elders' tent. "How is that possible?"

Salinda gave her a sly smile. "You didn't think all of our tattoos were inked by hand, did you?"

She blinked back at her. "Yes, that's exactly what I thought."

"For many of us, it's true. For others...well, some of us have deep enough connections to our magic that our *insigmora* grow of their own volition."

"But it's a Faeryn tradition," Cora said. "I'm not Faeryn. I'm just a witch."

"*Just* a witch," Salinda said with a scoff. "When are you going to appreciate your magic for what it is?"

Cora opened her mouth but snapped it shut. In truth, she'd been learning to appreciate her quiet magic more and more.

"You overcame a challenge that was directly related to your magic, didn't you?"

"I did. A couple of them."

"And your magic grew stronger?"

Cora nodded. "It was...frustrating," she said, remembering how difficult it had been to work against her own resistance.

"Your journey with the Arts has taken a new path, and your *insigmora* has reflected that." Her eyes crinkled at the corners. "And here I thought I'd be the one to guide you on the path of the empath."

"Empath." Cora pulled her head back. "I don't feel like my magic has grown *that* strong."

"Are you sure about that? Since you've been away, has there not been one new thing you've learned to do that no one else can?" Cora opened her mouth to deny it, but Salinda said, "Think. Is there anything you couldn't do before? Anything that has to do with emotions or sensations?"

Her ability to speak with Valorre came to mind, but she'd never considered whether that had anything to do with advanced clairsentience. If anything, she'd credited the phenomenon to Valorre being a fae creature. It wasn't like she was suddenly able to speak with every chipmunk, rabbit, and squirrel she came across. But it also didn't explain why Valorre couldn't seem to speak with anyone else but her.

Salinda nodded knowingly. "You've experienced something."

"Perhaps," Cora said slowly.

"As you step more and more into your role of empath, you will face even more challenges."

Cora grimaced at that. Not that it was a surprise. She only hoped it would get easier to accept such challenges instead of fighting against them. Then again, wasn't that the point of a challenge in the first place? For it to be hard? "Does every witch face a challenge to grow their power?"

"Every strong witch, whether they're following the path of the empath, oracle, seer, muse, alchemist, or narcuss."

Cora frowned at the last word. It was the only one she wasn't familiar with. "What's a narcuss?"

"It's a rare witch's power," Salinda said, tone grave. "One I believe this so-called Duke Morkai possesses. A narcuss is the shadow of an empath. Instead of feeling the emotions of others, taking them on, or absorbing them, a narcuss projects emotions outward. He can control and manipulate the people and objects around him. He can project what he wants others to see and feel. He is entirely focused on self-protection, self-advancement, and personal power."

That certainly sounded like Morkai. "But he said he's an Elvyn prince. You think he's part witch too?"

"I believe so. But I doubt he's faced the kind of challenge that would require him to become the strongest kind of narcuss. And Nalia was right about his Elvyn powers. If he were a true weaver, he wouldn't need to rely so heavily on the forbidden Arts."

Cora pondered that. She didn't know much about Elvyn magic, only that they wove the Magic of the Sky—whatever that meant—while the Faeryn worked with the Magic of the Soil.

Salinda continued. "What Morkai is doing is a corruption of true weaving. Elvyn magic was never used for harm, just like Faeryn magic. The power Morkai seeks is the same power that started the war that destroyed the fae several hundreds of years ago."

"Does that have to do with what the elders said about a Morkaius?"

"Yes. This duke is not the first to have attempted becoming High King of Magic. If he truly is the Blood of

Darius, then he will believe he has a right to Lela's magic."

"He doesn't have a right to it," Cora said, "does he?"

Salinda looked thoughtful for a moment. "That very question is the reason the ancient war began. It's the reason the fae were destroyed."

"But where did they go? Why are the unicorns returning? And if unicorns are back then where are all the other fae creatures?"

Salinda released a heavy sigh. "We don't know, my dear. All we have are our stories."

"What do the stories say about the Morkaius?"

"The first Morkaius was the illegitimate son of the Elvyn queen and her human witch lover. His full-Elvyn sister was chosen as heir over him, and he sought to overthrow her."

A chill ran down Cora's spine. Half Elvyn. Half witch. "You think the duke is this same man?" It should have been impossible. But was it? She already knew Morkai was ageless. When she'd asked him how he hadn't aged, he'd answered *blood*. Had he meant his Elvyn blood kept him from aging? That he'd been alive for hundreds of years? Or had he simply been referring to blood magic?

Salinda shook her head. "No one knows for sure. Our stories claim the Morkaius was destroyed in the final battle. The fight ended at the Elvyn palace in a massive explosion that turned the structure into a ruin. A ruin that stands today. A ruin that our stories claim holds the source of what little fae magic flows out into the land."

Cora furrowed her brow, wondering what ruin she was talking about. Then it hit her. "Centerpointe Rock."

She'd never seen the rock before, only knew it was a

landmark that stood at the very center of the three kingdoms, a neutral place where all three borders met. Cora had assumed that was the only reason the duke had chosen it for his meeting, but now she was starting to suspect more sinister motives.

"If Centerpointe Rock is the source of fae magic," Cora said, "and he's determined to harness the source..."

"You were right to come to us, Cora," Salinda said. "Not everyone in the commune will agree, but I do. This is a matter of magic. Of a fate greater than any of us can comprehend. Even if the meeting of the royals culminates in peaceful surrender, it will not be peace that follows. It will be the beginning of the return of the Morkaius. The beginning of a reign of darkness."

Cora's fingers curled into fists. "We must kill him."

Salinda nodded. "Thanks to the information you've given us, we stand a chance."

Cora left Salinda's tent filled with a new sense of burden and hope. This was so much bigger than she'd thought. She returned to her own tent with rest in mind, only to realize she still hadn't brought up her place in the prophecy or asked what Salinda knew about it. But as she laid down on her cot, their plans for attack buzzing through her mind, she wondered if it might be better that she hadn't confessed her role as some prophesied girl. A mother who'd been cursed to die childless. She ignored the ache in her chest when she considered what his blood weaving had taken from her and instead focused on hope.

For if all went to plan, Morkai would soon be dead.

And her place in the prophecy would die alongside him.

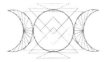

45

Larylis had figured the third time hearing Lex's description of the events at Ridine Castle would be easier to bear. He was wrong. It seemed with every new repetition, Larylis heard some new detail that flooded him with an eerie chill. The first time he'd listened to Lex's story had been in his father's study. The second time had been later that evening when Larylis had asked Lex to go over all the details yet again. Now, three days later, they sat around the elegant mahogany table in King Verdian's council room, with Lex relaying everything all over again. The day was early but the tall windows lining the far wall had been drawn shut against the sunlight, giving the meeting an even more daunting feel.

At least Larylis had finally come to accept that his brother was indeed captive, and war was looming on the horizon.

When Lex finished speaking, he was peppered with questions by King Verdian's council. King Arlous' councilmen were present too, but they'd already heard most of the tale before they'd departed Dermaine Palace.

"What joke is this?" Lord Ulrich said. He was one of Mareleau's uncles, and the man Larylis had once served as ward to. He was stout and clean-shaven with a double chin, gray eyes, and a head of brown hair cropped just below his ears. "You expect us to believe King Dimetreus is being puppeteered by a mage who uses blood magic and has a monstrous wolf-boar as a pet?" With a disbelieving scoff, he leaned back in his chair.

Larylis couldn't blame him for his doubts. He'd shared them at first. It was hard to believe in dark sorcery when no one believed in magic anymore. Magic had died with the fae. It only survived in Larylis' favorite novels. Then again, the same could have been said for unicorns, months ago.

Lord Kevan, Mareleau's eldest uncle and the head of King Verdian's council, rubbed his jaw. Unlike his younger brother, Kevan had a bushy brown beard and gray-brown hair that reached his shoulders. "No, some of the story rings true. When I spotted the unicorn last year, I sent dozens of men after it. One man came back reporting that some monstrous creature had intervened and chased the unicorn beyond the border into Khero. I took the tale as folly, but perhaps it wasn't."

"What does that have to do with anything?" Lord Ulrich said. "The rest of Prince Lexington's story could be fabricated. He could be working with King Dimetreus, weaving tales of sorcery so that we'll be more inclined to surrender."

Lex's mouth fell open. "I am not working with King Dimetreus. I risked my life in coming here. My own kingdom stands in peril because of my deception. If you surrender, Tomas is done for."

One of Verdian's other councilmen snorted a laugh. "Remind me how you supposedly got away."

"Oh, sure," Lex said. "Right after you remind me why I was in Khero hunting unicorns in the first place."

King Verdian's cheeks flushed. This was one of the rare times Larylis had seen the man without his powdered wig. His gray hair was kept close to his scalp, his blue eyes the same shade as his daughter's. "No one told you to go to Khero, Prince Lexington. If you'd had any sense, you would have kept to Selay's borders."

Lex held the king's gaze without falter. "If you'd had any sense, you would have kept your daughter from sending me on some idiotic quest without aid."

Larylis was impressed with Lex's ability to bluff so easily. He supposed it had come in handy when he'd pretended to take the duke's offer only to escape his guards when they set him up at an inn the first night of their journey. According to Lex, he'd slipped away before dawn and bought a messenger horse to take him to Dermaine.

Only Larylis and his father knew the truth—that Teryn hadn't been captured by the duke solely because of the Heart's Hunt but because of his efforts to claim the fugitive princess' bounty. The three of them had agreed to keep that part of the tale to themselves for the time being. Perhaps it was a bit underhanded to make Verdian think his kingdom was responsible for Teryn's captivity, but if it gave Menah a respectable place at the council table, Larylis was happy to carry the lie.

King Verdian glared at Lex but seemed to think he

wasn't worth arguing with. Waving a hand, he said, "Selay will not surrender regardless."

King Arlous rubbed his brow. "If we don't surrender, Teryn dies. I will not let that happen."

"Prince Teryn's fate is contingent upon both kingdoms' surrender," added one of Arlous' councilmen.

Verdian shook his head. "It is not up for debate. We weren't going to surrender to a mortal king. I'll be damned before I surrender to a sorcerer."

"So you'll have me risk my son? Your daughter's *fiancé*?" Arlous pinned Verdian with a hard stare, daring him to contradict the engagement.

Larylis shifted uncomfortably in his seat. With Prince Helios dead and Lex having forfeited, Teryn was the clear winner of the Heart's Hunt. King Verdian's guilt over Teryn's capture had been enough to solidify the betrothal between Teryn and Mareleau. Adding to that was Menah's shift in fortune. Larylis had learned of their kingdom's cleared debt in the same letter that had threatened Teryn's life and summoned his father to Centerpointe Rock. Arlous had been sure to flaunt their financial state as soon as they arrived at Verlot Palace.

Verdian spoke through his teeth. "We would be devastated by Prince Teryn's loss, should it come to that, but surrender is not on the table. I say we ignore the summons and prepare for war at once."

Larylis gripped his armrests, forcing his eyes to remain on the table instead of cutting a glare at Verdian. How could he refuse to even consider an option that saved Teryn's life?

Arlous slammed a fist on the table. "What of my son?"

"What of him?" Lord Kevan spat. "We will not surrender, therefore it is time to speak of our plans for war."

The table dissolved into a fray of arguments as the kings and councilmen began to talk over each other. Larylis' head spun, the chatter becoming a tidal wave of sound. He could hardly separate one voice from the other as they clashed with the weight of his own thoughts. Surrender. War. Surrender. War. Larylis wanted neither. All he cared about was getting his brother back. Why wasn't anyone discussing a solution that involved neither surrender nor Teryn's death?

Words burned on his tongue. He'd done his best to stay silent during the meeting thus far. His presence here today had already been met with enough scorn from King Verdian's council. No one wanted to see a bastard born of scandal at their table. But something had cracked in his father's heart after learning about Teryn's captivity. Once they'd left for Verlot, he'd refused to let Larylis out of his sight for long.

The arguments rose and crashed against each other, and still, their words remained a jumbled mess in Larylis' mind. His stomach churned, his blood turning to fire as he fought to stay quiet, stay seated—

"We must get my brother back."

Silence echoed. It took Larylis several breaths to realize the words had come from him. He stood at the table, his chair flung back behind him. He'd said nothing profound, nothing shocking, and yet the eyes of everyone at the table locked on him. It was only the element of surprise that had drawn their attention. *The bastard speaks.*

It was better than nothing, he supposed. He might as

well make use of the quiet. "We cannot surrender to a blood mage, nor can we let the Crown Prince of Menah die."

Lord Ulrich scoffed. Larylis may have been his ward once, but the man hadn't liked him then. It stood to reason he didn't like him now either. "Do you have some brilliant plan, Lord *Seralla*?" Ulrich enunciated Larylis' surname as if to remind him of his place.

Lord Kevan turned an amused gaze to Larylis. "I too would like to hear what Lord Seralla's plan is. Amongst war generals, nobles, and kings, surely a whore's son knows best."

King Arlous rose from his seat, a vein pulsing at his temple. "How dare you speak to my son that way!"

Kevan opened his mouth but Verdian held up a hand. "We'll give the boy one minute to speak," the king said grudgingly. He seemed more concerned about offending Arlous than defending Larylis. At least Menah's change of fortune had that benefit.

The eyes of the councilmen burned into Larylis. Now that they'd granted him permission to speak, he didn't know what to say. He didn't actually have a plan. Fantasies of vengeance, certainly. He couldn't count the number of times he'd imagined himself as the heroes in his favorite war novels, or perhaps General Bralish, the famed savior of the Medlon army at the Battle of Delton in 94 Year of the Wolf.

His gaze swept the mocking faces of the men at Verdian's end of the table. Then his eyes found Lex's. And his father's. Arlous gave him a subtle nod.

He released a shaky breath. "We...cannot surrender to a mage."

Lord Kevan snorted a laugh. "That has been established."

Larylis opened and closed his fists, a cold sweat breaking out behind his neck. Kevan was right. Larylis was only repeating himself. If he didn't have anything to add to the conversation, he might as well sit down.

He took a step back toward his chair but his feet refused to take another. This was his chance to be heard. There had to be something he could add to the debate. Clearing his throat, he forced himself to stand a little taller, summoning the side of him that knew how to play it cool under supercilious scrutiny. "We must get Prince Teryn back *and* refuse surrender."

"You still aren't saying anything new," Ulrich said.

Larylis ignored him, running histories, fictions, and fantasies through his mind. How had General Bralish stolen the hostages back from the Allerton Horde? His words came out slow. Careful. "We'll go to the meeting and figure out where they're keeping Teryn. He'll be somewhere in King Dimetreus' camp."

Verdian narrowed his eyes. "How are you so certain? They could keep him at Ridine Castle."

"They'll expect us to demand to see Teryn alive and unharmed before we consider surrender."

"What then?" Arlous asked, his skeptical tone in contrast with the hope in his eyes.

"Once we know where Teryn is being kept, we'll send in a covert force to break him free. Until then, we will draw out negotiations."

"Stealing a hostage is akin to a declaration of war," Kevan said.

Larylis gave him a pointed look. "Which we've

already resigned ourselves to in refusing to surrender. We will plan for war, but first we rescue Teryn."

"How do you expect to free our prince without the sorcerer taking notice?" asked one of Arlous' councilmen. From the look on his face, he was taking Larylis seriously. "We can't simply march in and search from tent to tent."

"I have an idea of how to locate him before we send in any of our men." He didn't elaborate, knowing it would take some work to convince them to put their faith in a falcon. But Larylis knew if anyone could find Teryn in an enemy camp it was Berol.

"It's reckless," Verdian said, running his hands over the ruffled collar beneath his royal white and gold coat. "But if we're already set on war, we might as well attempt to free the crown prince."

"You can't seriously consider this," Kevan said. "Larylis Seralla has no place on this council. He's a bastard—"

"Enough with that word." Arlous' voice came out hard. "Larylis *Alante* is my son and heir."

Verdian's eyes went wide. "That's taking things a little far, Arlous. Naming your illegitimate son your heir?"

Larylis couldn't argue with that. He wasn't even sure his father had meant what he'd said. He'd called Larylis... an Alante. The king's royal name. A name Larylis had been forbidden to take due to his illegitimate birth. Arlous' last attempt to legitimize him had nearly ended in war. If the queen found out, it very well could come again—

No. The threat of war was already here. It just wasn't coming from the same place it had before.

Lord Kevan scoffed. "Have you given up on getting Prince Teryn back so soon?"

Arlous held back a smug grin. "If we are to hide our plans at rescuing Teryn, we need the mage to think we've fully given up on getting the prince back when we refuse to surrender. Larylis will stand at my side during negotiations as my new heir. We won't officially refuse the king until we've received a sign that Teryn is safe."

"Dimetreus will never believe you've made your bastard your heir," Kevan said.

"Why?" Arlous met the man's gaze without any hint of shame. "I almost succeeded before."

Larylis felt sick. He'd hated how it had felt to be pitted against his brother when the scandal erupted. He didn't like it any better now, even if it was only an act. But if it got Teryn back...

"Well, Prince Larylis," Kevan said, voice mocking, "since you seem to have everything all figured out, will you be the one to organize the prince's rescue force?"

Larylis took a deep breath, forcing far more confidence than he felt. There was no use backing down now. No use revealing just how terrified and intimidated he felt. Instead, he imagined he was General Bralish, undaunted in the face of an enemy horde. Lifting his chin, he met Lord Kevan's taunting stare. "Yes, I will."

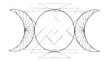

46

Mareleau Harvallis ignored the soft flutter inside her chest. It was a traitorous thing, the way her heart refused to recall that Larylis Seralla was no longer her beloved. Still, she had to admit he looked...brilliant. Brave. Standing up to her father and her uncles, coming up with a plan to save his brother.

She pushed the door open a crack wider, then resumed winding her fingers through the braid she'd been nervously plaiting for the last several minutes.

"We shouldn't be spying," Lurel whispered from behind her. They were in the drawing room that stood between the library and council room. It was mostly used by servants to stage food and libations during formal events or much larger meetings. This meeting, however, was private. Not even servants were allowed to be present. Neither was Mareleau but she didn't need her cousin to remind her that. Seven gods, the girl was annoying. Always so prim and proper.

Lurel tugged the sleeve of Mareleau's gown. "Our fathers wouldn't want us listening in. It's men's business."

Mareleau clenched her teeth. *Men's business.* So far, nothing that she'd heard had seemed particularly masculine. Why were women thought to be too soft for matters of war? Did breasts somehow make her unable to consider death and bloodshed? She had to deal with blood every month, which was more than any of the men in that room could say.

Lurel tried to pull her away again, but Mareleau elbowed the girl before she could. Doing so jostled the door, drawing the peering eyes of Uncle Ulrich. Mareleau darted away from the gap in the door. She held her breath as footsteps slapped across the floor. A second later, the door was shut the rest of the way with an exaggerated slam.

Damn her uncle.

With her view sabotaged, she spied on the remainder of the meeting by pressing her ear to the closed door, but all she could glean were snippets here and there. From what she could understand, it seemed both Selay and Menah were set on war. It was a terrifying prospect, and that was without considering the part about wraiths and mages. Her only experiences with war were secondhand accounts of battles that happened in other kingdoms. She never thought it was something she'd witness in Selay during her lifetime. Up until now, her life had been one of luxury and peace. Politically speaking, that is. Her love life was another issue all in its own.

A vision of Larylis filled her mind, for reasons she'd rather not dwell on.

Once she heard the meeting come to a close, she strode away from the door and sank into one of the chairs in the drawing room. Lurel wrung her hands before her. "Shall I call for tea, Highness?"

"I don't want tea," Mareleau said, eyes unfocused. As much as she didn't want to admit it, she felt a slight pang of guilt over Teryn's fate. He'd gone to Khero for her Heart's Hunt, after all. She'd wanted to rid herself of her suitors, but she hadn't expected it to end like *this*. Adding to that guilt was the fact that part of her *wasn't* sorry. She'd gotten what she wanted. For now, at least. If Larylis' rescue mission failed, she'd never have to worry about her unwanted engagement again.

Was it so terrible that she was considering such a benefit?

The door from the council room opened, sending her sitting upright. She expected Uncle Ulrich to come storming in to see who'd been spying on the meeting, but it wasn't him.

It was Larylis.

They both froze at the same instant, their eyes locked on one another.

His mouth hung open for several seconds before he found his words. "I...I was just heading for the library." He gestured toward the door at the other end of the drawing room. Then, backing up a step, he said, "I can use the main door."

"No," Mareleau said, keeping her expression neutral as she rose from her chair. "Lurel and I were just leaving anyway."

He offered her a bow and began to brush past, not

giving her a second glance. She glared at him, her chest bubbling with words she'd smothered in the depths of her heart for the last three years. Pursing her lips, she willed herself to say nothing, to follow Lurel out the door and back to her chambers. Larylis was almost at the opposite door when the words flew out of her mouth.

"Why didn't you ever reply to my letter?"

Larylis froze with his fingers on the door handle. He turned to face her, expression hard. "Why would I have?"

Heat burned her cheeks, her body flooding with every ounce of rage she'd held on to since he'd broken her heart.

Lurel turned a pleading look on her. "Your parents wouldn't want you talking to him," she whispered.

"Leave us," she said through her teeth.

Her cousin's eyes bulged from their sockets. "I can't leave you unchaperoned with a man. Your reputation—"

"My reputation can go to the seven hells."

"If anyone found out I left you with him, we'd both get in trouble."

She burned the other girl with a glare. "Then don't tell anyone." Lurel was right, of course. Mareleau would never hear the end of it if either of their parents found out. Still, Mareleau hated being told what to do. And her confrontation with Larylis was long overdue. "Shut the door on your way out."

"But—"

Mareleau raised her voice to a shout. "Out, you simpering fool. And if you tell anyone about this, I'll...I'll tell your friends about the time you wet your skirts last year."

She gasped, her cheeks flushing crimson. "It was two years ago and I was sick."

Mareleau only shrugged.

"You're...you're so cruel. I'm only trying to help you." Without another word of argument, she turned on her heel and fled into the council room, closing the door behind her.

Mareleau shot a withering look at Larylis, but her stomach flipped as she met his stare. He leaned against the other door, arms crossed. His gaze locked on hers, his eyes narrowed to remind her that he didn't love her anymore. Maybe he never did. She bit her lip, wondering if it had been a grave mistake to speak to him. Did she really want to know why he'd chosen to abandon her?

She wound her fingers through her makeshift braid, desperate to do something with her hands. "Then you admit you at least received my last letter."

He shrugged. "If you can call it that."

A stab of pain struck her chest. She'd poured her very soul into that letter. "Then why didn't you respond? You could have said *something.*"

"You made it clear you never wanted to hear from me again."

She blinked at him. "What are you talking about?"

He pushed off from the door and began walking toward her, his words dry and rehearsed. "*We cannot see each other anymore. I can't explain. All you need to know is that I can't love you. I could never love a bastard.*" He paused several feet away from her. "Do you deny you wrote those things?"

She opened her mouth to do exactly that, but she stopped herself. His words echoed through her mind, slamming against ones her heart had never let herself forget. "Why are you taking my words out of context like that?"

He gave her a bewildered look. "What other context was there? You wrote me three lines."

"I wrote you far more than that," she said, voice catching on the lump in her throat. She mirrored what he'd done moments ago, walking toward him while she recited her letter, every word punctuated with rage. "*Larylis, Father has said we cannot see each other anymore. I've told him how much I love you. I've told him that I will have only you. He will not listen. He thinks you're simply a fancy I'll grow out of. No matter what I say to try and explain the depths of my feelings, he tells me I could never love a bastard.*"

She paused when only a foot of space remained between them. Larylis' complexion had gone pale, his face slack. She wasn't sure what his countenance meant but it gave her no small amount of satisfaction.

She continued reciting her letter, her voice quavering with emotion. "*But he's wrong. I love you. You need to know that. No matter how they try to keep us apart I will always love you. I can't live without you, and I know you feel the same about me. Let us proceed with our plans without their blessing. Meet me at the Godskeep in Salissera at dawn on the twenty-first. I don't care if I lose my place as heir. All I need is you. Please come. Please. I'll be there.*"

Mareleau felt cold in the wake of her words. She felt empty, stripped of pride and anger alike. All that was left was truth. Vulnerability. She searched Larylis' face, aware of the way he trembled, the way his hands curled into tight fists. When it was clear he had nothing to say, she spoke again, doing her best to keep her voice level. "You never came. I waited for you for two days. I was...humiliated. Heartbroken. Mother found me."

Larylis let out a shaky sigh. They stood so close, Mareleau felt his breath warm her face. She knew she should put space between them, but she couldn't move. Finally, he spoke, voice barely above a whisper. "I don't understand. I never received that letter. I received only those three lines."

She frowned. How was that possible?

"The letter you wrote to Teryn—"

"I never wrote him a letter."

Larylis dropped his eyes from hers and ran a hand over his face. "Seven devils," he said under his breath. "Your letters were forged. Two taken from one, each word copied from truth."

A chill ran down her spine. She wanted to deny the plausibility, but the facts made it painfully clear. No letter left the palace without someone knowing about it. After she was caught kissing Larylis in the stables three years ago, which resulted in her being forbidden from seeing or even speaking to him, it made sense that her parents would do anything to keep her from *embarrassing herself further*, as they'd liked to say. She'd thought she'd been discreet when she'd sent the letter, but was it possible she'd overestimated her own cunning?

Larylis slowly met her gaze again. "Everything about that letter, from the slant of your script to the length of your loops looked exactly as if it had been penned by your hand. Teryn showed me the letter he'd received. It looked the same."

She threw her hands in the air. "Neither letter's

content clued you in to the truth? You couldn't possibly have believed I'd be so cold to you while being even remotely warm toward your brother."

"I found out about your engagement to him as soon as I returned home. I figured you'd changed your mind, that you realized he was a better match—"

"How could you believe such a thing?"

"What else was I to believe? Every word in that letter was true." His face twisted with agony.

"No—"

"It was. I am a bastard. You...you can't love me."

"But I..." She paused, debating what to say. Everything inside her yearned to reach for him, to wipe that look off his face. She didn't know what would happen if she did. If she let go of three years of hatred, resentment, and indignation...what would be left? He'd broken her heart, unwittingly or not. Then again, if she was honest with herself, she'd have to admit she'd never fully given up on him. No matter how shattered she'd become, no matter how many thorns had pierced her aching heart and split it into shards, threads had remained, connecting every fragment. She'd ignored them, burned them into rage, but despite her best efforts over the last three years, they'd come back. Every time she'd thought of him, remembered their time together, a thread would return, weaving through the hurt and the betrayal to repair the broken pieces. Now more than ever, those threads were there, growing. Piece by piece by piece, what she'd thought was broken collided back together. Her chest felt warmer than it ever had before. It bloomed into words that she rolled around on her tongue, warm and sweet with only a hint of bitter. She tasted them, tested them, before they breached her lips. "I still do," she whispered.

Larylis' throat bobbed. His brow was furrowed, eyes glazed.

She took a trembling step closer and reached a tentative hand for his chest. He inhaled a sharp breath as her fingers landed on his silk jacket. Her own breaths came hard and fast, her breasts heaving above her lace bodice. Part of her dreaded his answer to her next question, but she had to know the truth. Locking her eyes on his, she asked, "Do you? Do you still love me?"

His answer came out low and deep. "I've never stopped."

Her hands came to his collar at the same moment his wound behind her back. She claimed his lips with a greedy kiss, one of fire, desperation, and regret. They'd never kissed like this, like the other's lips were their only source of air. She arched into him, pulling him closer, parting her lips to deepen the kiss. His tongue moved against hers and hers against his. They were in perfect tandem, perfect agreement. One of his hands wove into her hair, sending pins clattering to the ground, while the other cupped the front of her bodice. She gasped against his mouth and reached for his neckcloth, untying it with frantic fingers. Once it was free, she slid her hands down his chest, beneath his jacket. He aided her efforts to free himself from it. Then she began working the buttons of his waistcoat, all the while never taking her lips from his. His palms moved to her shoulders and down the length of each arm, pausing when his hands landed on top of hers. She was still struggling with his buttons when he gave her fingers a soft squeeze. Only then did she realize he was pulling away from her. Her heart sank as her lips left his. She searched his face, saw desire still burning in his eyes. But the longer she watched him, the more his expression began to fall.

With her hands still gathered in his, he removed them from his waistcoat and took a step away. "I can't do this," he said, letting her hands slide from his palms. "You're engaged to my brother."

She gaped at him for several moments before she could find her voice. It came out breathy, still shallow in the wake of their passion. "I will never marry him."

"Your engagement is more final now than it was before."

She shook her head. "No, I will never allow it to be. I was set against it when I thought you despised me. Now that I have your love again, I won't give it up. I promise you, Lare, I will do everything in my power to end it. To be with you instead. And that's only if he returns—"

She knew at once she'd said the wrong thing. All remaining desire drained from Larylis' face as he took another step away from her.

"That's not what I meant," she said.

"It is, though, isn't it?" His voice was cold now. Empty. "That's why you sent him on some ridiculous quest for the Heart's Hunt, right?"

A spike of anger surged through her. "You can't blame me for not wanting to marry him."

He studied her for a few moments. "You've said that before. The evening of the poetry contest. I thought then...I thought it had been because of the scandal. Because of Menah's debt. All this time...you've been cruel to *him* because of *me*."

"I never chose to marry him. Our parents arranged it. But it's you I want to be with. I'm tired of letting them keep us apart. I was able to bear it these last three years only because I thought you didn't love me." She closed the distance between them, reaching for him. "Now that I know the truth, I can't—"

"No," he said, stepping out of her reach. "I...I'm not like my mother. I will not do what she tried to do."

Mareleau balled her hands into fists. "You stubborn fool! This is nothing like what happened with your mother and father, because Teryn and I aren't married yet. I'll be damned before we ever are. Besides, doesn't it matter what I want? Why has no one asked what *I* want?"

He looked at her as if seeing her with new eyes. "What do you want?"

The answer was easy. "I want the crown in my own right. I want out of an arranged marriage. And I want you. Larylis, with everything I am, I want you." She placed her hands on his chest again. "Tell me you don't want me too." His heart hammered beneath her palm. She could see his answer written in the depths of his eyes as they flickered to her mouth.

"I can't," he whispered, his words gravelly. "I can't say I don't want you. So badly I do."

Mareleau unraveled with relief. Heat spread low in her belly at the timbre of his voice. She tilted her head back, desperate to taste his lips once more.

"But I can't be with you. I...won't do that to him."

Her heart plummeted to her feet as he moved away from her once more. Without another word, he grabbed his discarded jacket and neckcloth off the floor and left.

She wasn't sure which door he'd used.

Wasn't sure she'd even watched him depart.

All she knew was she'd give anything to erase the last several minutes they'd shared—that instead of opening her heart, she'd stayed quiet. Angry. Resentful. Any of that would be better than the pain of his rejection renewed.

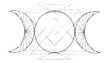

47

Cora eyed Centerpointe Rock from her vantage point on the hillside. Dawn had just broken over the horizon, illuminating the valley that surrounded the rock and casting a crown of gold upon the hills that stood sentinel around it. The rock itself was an enormous piece of weathered stone with a flat surface. It looked nothing like an ancient ruin from a forgotten war, nothing like a remnant of a fae palace. Now that she knew what it was, she couldn't help wondering what part of the palace the ruin stood in memory of. Was it once the floor of a throne room? A library? Some ancient fae queen's bedroom?

Her gaze wandered to the surrounding valley. The ground was green and plush, covered in a light morning frost. On one side sat her brother's camp, a sea of tents beneath standards of indigo and violet—indigo for the duke and violet for the king. The king's entourage had been camped there for three days—as long as Cora and her company of Forest People had been stalking the hillside—while the delegation from Selay and Menah had been camped at the opposite end of the valley since two days prior. Today was the day the meeting would commence.

She wrapped her wool cloak tight around her, chilled at the thought of what was to come. The Forest People had a plan that would end in the duke's death, but it didn't stop her from agonizing over every way it could go wrong. Cora had come to Centerpointe Rock with a small group of some of the strongest magic users among the Forest People. Roije for his tracking. Druchan for his proficiency at wards and concealing. Their elder seer. Two witches with incredible clairaudience who could listen for threats at a distance. A host of their best archers and spearmen. Several other highly accomplished Faeryn. The latter included Salinda and Nalia, despite neither having an Art honed for fighting or hiding. Cora felt a bit overshadowed by her companions' statuses, but there had never been any doubt as to whether she'd come along. This was her plan, after all. Mostly.

Cora may not have had firsthand experience with war, but her childhood education in history and warfare had been thorough. She understood what to expect from the proceedings. The meeting would begin with Khero delivering their demands and terms for the two kingdoms' surrender. If Menah and Selay didn't surrender right away, they'd be given a short time to deliberate. A second meeting could be set, at which the royals would need to deliver their final answer. If they surrendered, they'd get Teryn back. If they refused, they'd settle on terms for war.

A dark cloud of dread filled her gut. She knew Morkai

had every intention of harnessing the magic and becoming Morkaius before leaving the meeting, regardless of what the royals decided. The fact that the negotiations were taking place at Centerpointe Rock—the very source of fae magic—was proof of that. If the two kingdoms surrendered, Dimetreus would be named King of Lela. Until Morkai killed him and took his place, of course. As terrifying as that thought was, it was the outcome she both expected and hoped for. Not the part where her brother was killed but where the royals surrendered. Because—as soon as Teryn was safely returned to his people—the Forest People would act. Morkai wouldn't get the chance to kill Dimetreus or harness the magic he sought.

But if the royals refused to surrender, it would mean—

Cora shook her head against the thoughts that filled it. Thoughts of Teryn. His fate. What Morkai would do if Menah and Selay rejected his terms. What Teryn had asked of her before she'd fled the dungeon.

Tell my father everything you know. Everything we've seen. Tell him to let me go.

A pinch of guilt prodded at her heart. She knew she was working against his wishes, but her plan was better. Her plan would save Teryn's life and the fate of Lela. It didn't assuage her guilt, but she supposed it was better than what lingered beneath it—the memory of their shared kiss, of his trickery, of the way her body had so eagerly responded to his.

She bit the inside of her cheek to distract herself from the tingling warmth in her stomach and brought her mind back to thoughts of war.

Her gaze swept toward her brother's end of the valley. His party was moderate in size—about the same as the combined entourages from Menah and Selay—which boded well, for it meant Morkai might not be planning to strike immediately should negotiations turn to war. Roije and the other scouts had confirmed that no hidden armies were waiting beyond the hills, no secret reinforcements were poised to invade. Then again, the duke could summon wraiths to bolster his numbers. While she'd seen the specters contained only to the charred field, she had a feeling Morkai could conjure them elsewhere.

The plan remains the same no matter what, she reminded herself. *Get the Roizan away from Morkai. Keep him from amplifying his powers through his well of dark magic. Then kill him.*

Still, thoughts of Teryn lingered in the back of her mind. If they didn't surrender...

They must surrender. They must. It's the only way he lives.

Something soft bumped into her shoulder. She turned to find Valorre at her side, his presence immediately settling her nerves. With a weak smile, she stroked the side of his face, then rested her hand at the base of his horn. She frowned at the layer of cotton surrounding it. Even though the Forest People kept their hiding place safe behind wards and illusions, Cora figured extra precautions couldn't hurt. She'd glimpsed the Roizan at a distance a few times, stalking her brother's camp with its loping gait. She wasn't sure how far it could sense a unicorn's horn, but she wasn't willing to find out. Not when Valorre was so integral to their plans. If there was one thing that could separate the Roizan from its master, it was a unicorn. "That isn't uncomfortable, is it?"

I am not so easily bothered, he said, in contrast with the flutter of embarrassment that rippled through him. *I must look foolish though.*

"No, you look rather imposing in that pink floral pattern."

Do I? All right.

"You don't grasp sarcasm, do you?"

I...don't think so.

Cora's laugh was cut short by her sudden awareness of an approaching presence. Her walls had been kept down to allow her to perceive nearby threats. But this presence was no threat.

Salinda appeared a few moments later. She was dressed the same as Cora, in britches, a wool tunic, and a boiled leather breastplate and gauntlets. With a warm smile, she came up beside Cora and put a comforting hand on her shoulder. "Rianne has seen it. The meeting will happen very soon."

Her mouth went dry. "Did she see how it would end?"

"She saw possibilities," Salinda said. Rianne was a seer but that didn't mean she could see the future. Her magic was more about catching glimpses of possibilities. Quiet magic, not certainty. Salinda gave Valorre a reverent nod. "Speaking of seeing, I still can hardly believe what stands before my eyes. He's a faerytale come to life."

I am majestic, yes, Valorre said. *She may pet me if she wishes. One could hardly blame her. I am so very strong.*

Cora rolled her eyes. She hadn't introduced Valorre to the entire camp, only the small party she'd come here with. Not wanting to overwhelm him with a flurry of starry-eyed admirers, she'd waited until their task force had begun their journey to Centerpointe Rock before revealing him. He'd received a warm welcome and had relished their adoration. It made her think he wouldn't have minded being the center of the entire commune's attention after all.

Salinda gave him a gentle pat on the side of his neck, then turned to Cora with a more serious expression. "Are you ready?"

Cora nodded, one hand wrapping around her bow. It may not have been the bow she favored, for she'd lost that one at Ridine Castle, but it was still a bow. Her preferred weapon. A source of comfort and strength. She brought her other hand to her belt and the three knives slung there. She froze when her fingers brushed the hilt of the dagger she'd finally removed from the bottom of her quiver that morning. Repulsion shot through her, but she breathed it down. She hated carrying a weapon that had been wrought from death and suffering, but if Valorre's role in her plans became compromised, it might help to have alternate means to draw the Roizan away from Morkai. She wasn't sure if the blade was as potent as a living unicorn, but it had brought Prince Helios to his unfortunate doom.

She lifted her hand from the dagger and balled it into a fist at her side. "I'm ready."

Silence fell between them, the burden of what was to come hanging heavy like a shroud. Together they stood watching the valley.

Waiting.

Waiting.

Waiting.

Until someone strolled onto the field.

Cora's blood went cold as the figure left Dimetreus' camp. With slow, confident moves, Morkai walked toward Centerpointe Rock.

Cora met Salinda's eyes. The woman gave her a knowing nod.

It was time.

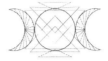

48

Teryn didn't put up a fight as he was hauled from the prison tent. He knew where the guards were taking him as they dragged him through camp, their pace too fast for him to keep his feet beneath him. His legs felt like water even when he did manage a few steps, as he hadn't been allowed to walk much since arriving at Centerpointe Rock. He'd been chained, guarded, and given only the bare essentials to keep him alive. Now he was about to see his father for the last time. His only regret was that he wouldn't get to speak with him. The gag tied over his mouth wouldn't allow him to tell his father it was all right. That he could let him go.

Hopefully Cora had. Otherwise, his father might not know enough about Morkai to reject his terms for surrender. And that...that just wasn't a possibility. His kingdom *had* to fight, war or no. They could not yield to the mage. They had to destroy him.

The guards halted just outside the camp at the edge

of the wide-open field. Teryn gathered the crisp morning air into his lungs, savoring what might be one of his last easy breaths. Several more guards and soldiers were already waiting, along with King Dimetreus. Teryn looked out at the field, seeking any sign of the opposing camp, but the valley was enormous. He could see nothing beyond the shape of the rock. Before it, however, was the silhouette of Morkai. Once the duke reached the Rock, he climbed upon it. It was brazen the way he stood unguarded, as if he were taunting the other side to act against him. Teryn almost wished they would. Any act of violence would result in retaliation. Should anyone attack Morkai now, Teryn—as hostage—would be put to death.

A price he was willing to pay.

He turned his eyes to the sky, basking in the sunlight on his skin. There was hardly a cloud to be seen, only the blue, pink, and orange hue of sunrise. It was beautiful. Perhaps the last beautiful thing he'd see.

A shadow darted over his vision—a bird. With a start, he noted the familiar flight pattern, the wingspan. His heart ached to see Berol. Of course she'd come. She'd always been able to find him. He could only hope that she wouldn't act when the time came for him to die, for if she got herself killed in the process, he wouldn't be able to leave this world free of regret.

"You played the hero well," said a mocking voice. Teryn shifted his gaze from the sky to find Dimetreus watching him with disdain. "But you ended up being a traitor. You and that...that vile girl."

Teryn bristled at hearing Cora called vile by her own brother. He started to speak but found his words muffled by the gag. Instead, he bit down on it and burned the king with a glare.

Dimetreus sneered back. "To think I let you into my castle. Fed you. Clothed you. To think I showed that wretched girl kindness when I should have sent a knife through her heart—"

Teryn lurched forward, but the guards kept him in place. He gave up his struggle and shouted at the king through his gag.

Dimetreus fully faced him and closed the distance between them.

"Your Majesty," one of the guards warned.

"I want to hear his last words," Dimetreus barked. With rough hands, he pulled the gag from Teryn's mouth. "Speak, filth. Let me hear your excuses for the last time. Fuel my vengeance and make it that much sweeter when justice comes."

Teryn held the king's gaze. "That girl is your sister." His voice felt rough in his throat. He'd been gagged since his arrival at Centerpointe Rock. "The one you call wretched. Vile. She really is Princess Aveline."

Dimetreus gave a disbelieving shake of his head. "My sister is dead. That girl was an impostor. I should have known better than to believe such a fantasy."

"If your sister is dead, then that means Selay never held her hostage. If that's the case, why are you trying to conquer them and Menah?"

"Selay sent the spy who killed my wife and sister. Menah was in on it. They sent you—"

"To do what? To claim a bounty on a woman I thought was a killer only to find out she was a lost princess?"

"No, you infiltrated my castle with a girl parading around as Aveline."

"Again I ask you, to do what? What reason did I have? What reason has anyone—Selay, Menah—had for their supposed crimes? What threats have you received? Seen with your own eyes?"

Dimetreus blinked hard several times. His glazed eyes held the same confused quality they'd had when Cora tried to tell him the truth. "You...you have no right to question me—"

"She told me her name was Cora."

Dimetreus' face went slack. He took a step back, blinking hard again.

Teryn was emboldened with the hope that he was—at least somewhat—getting through to the king. The one that existed beyond the duke's control. "It makes sense now," Teryn said, speaking carefully to keep Dimetreus' full attention. "Aveline Corasande Caelan, Princess of Khero. You watched her dance. You sat next to her at dinner. Do you honestly believe in your heart of hearts that she wasn't your sister?"

The king's throat bobbed, face pale.

"She's still alive. And...and she loves you." Teryn wasn't sure that last part was true. After everything Cora had been through, he'd understand if she hated her brother.

"The signal, Your Majesty," said a guard.

Dimetreus' lips curled away from his teeth. "Lies. Every word a lie." Just as roughly as he'd taken the gag down, he shoved it back over Teryn's mouth. This time it didn't make it between his teeth. Instead, it was pushed

only over his lower lip, something that neither the king
nor any of the guards seemed to notice.

Teryn was once again forced to move forward. As he
followed after the king's entourage toward Centerpointe
Rock, a spark of hope filled his chest. Not over his
exchange with the king, for that had served no purpose in
the end. His hope was that, if he could work his gag just a
little lower, he might be able to speak to his father one
more time after all.

LARYLIS THOUGHT HIS HEART WOULD SHATTER IN TWO AS HE
looked at his brother standing on the opposite side of
Centerpointe Rock, flanked by guards and the traitor
king. Duke Morkai stood with Arlous and Verdian upon
the rock, but Larylis only had eyes for his brother and his
shockingly awful state. Teryn's hair stood in disarray, the
already dark strands heavy with grease. His skin was
smudged with dirt, his tired eyes shadowed with dark
circles, his cheeks far hollower than they normally were.
His clothing—a pair of black trousers and what appeared
to be a once-fine shirt—was torn and stained.

Teryn met his eyes, but all Larylis could see was
Mareleau's face. Her lips. Her eyes heavy with desire. His
brother had been imprisoned, starved, and perhaps even
tortured, while Larylis had been kissing his fiancée. They
would have done more had he not regained his senses. It
had taken all his restraint to leave Mareleau, the woman
he loved, the woman who loved him back, but it had
been the right thing to do. They could love each other all

they wanted, but they could never be together. Her father would never allow it, and Teryn...

His heart ached to look at him. It only deepened his guilt knowing that Larylis now stood in their father's entourage as a false prince. Arlous' newly legitimized heir. A necessary ruse for when they'd attempt to make their refusal to surrender convincing. Morkai had to think they'd given up on getting Teryn back, all to provide enough time to spirit Teryn away and flee Centerpointe Rock before the duke learned of their duplicity.

Larylis had a plan. One that was not allowed to fail.

Larylis pulled his gaze away from Teryn to assess the proceedings on the rock. Arlous, Verdian, and Morkai stood several feet apart from each other on the rock's surface. Their respective entourages stood on the ground behind them. Arlous and Verdian had each brought their war generals and a small group of soldiers to form their retinues, while Dimetreus stood only with soldiers bearing Duke Morkai's sigil. It was no surprise that the duke was speaking for the king, both as his proxy and war general. If everything Lex had said was true, the king was merely a puppet.

The three men upon the rock kept their voices low and calm, but Larylis could still hear most of what was being said. Morkai had already reminded the two kings what was at stake—Teryn's life if both parties didn't surrender. They would not get another chance to see Teryn alive if they didn't acquiesce. Now the duke was delivering each kingdom's terms for surrender.

"Verdian, along with your surrender to your new

king, you must claim responsibility for sending the spy that killed Queen Linette."

Verdian opened his mouth, his face crimson, but he managed to hold his tongue. His shoulders tensed, hands curled so tightly his knuckles went white.

Duke Morkai gave him a taunting smile. "You may be offered a dukedom should you easily comply. Your crown, palace, fortune, and all trade agreements will be transferred into King Dimetreus' possession."

Verdian's lip curled as if he were cursing the duke under his breath. Larylis was impressed the king was able to remain silent. It had been part of their plan—hear the duke's terms, make no argument, request time to deliberate—but Verdian wasn't known for restraint.

Morkai turned his gaze to Arlous. "Along with Menah's surrender to King Dimetreus, you will confess to colluding with Selay in orchestrating Queen Linette's murder as well as sending Prince Teryn as a spy to Ridine Castle. You'll be made a viscount should you readily comply. Your crown, palace, fortune, and all trade agreements will be transferred into King Dimetreus' possession."

Arlous pursed his lips against the arguments that were sure to be brimming behind his clenched teeth. Larylis, on the other hand, felt as if his blood had been doused in ice. These ridiculous terms, confessing to crimes they didn't commit...would they not result in severe punishments for Arlous and Verdian both, regardless of any titles bestowed? He had the prickling feeling they were all being toyed with. As if the duke didn't care whether they surrendered or not.

Only that they were here.

The armor he wore suddenly felt too light. Too insubstantial. Aside from the soldiers, who wore full plates, and Teryn who had no protection, everyone present wore only breastplates and gauntlets. Anything heavier would have signaled an expectation for battle. Anything less would be foolish.

Larylis was starting to think that coming here without a full army behind them had been the foolish choice.

"Is that all?" Verdian said through his teeth.

The duke nodded. "Simple terms. A simple choice."

Larylis held his breath, waiting for his father or Verdian to deliver the next piece of their plan.

Arlous shifted his jaw and spoke, words clipped. "We will inform you of our decision at midnight tonight."

Larylis released a relieved sigh. That was what the rest of his plan hinged on. They needed the cover of darkness to act. Needed to get Morkai out of the camp while there was limited visibility. Larylis already knew how to find Teryn. Berol had located his tent before the delegation had even arrived. They'd spied on it the night before, hiding on the hillside. The only thing that had kept them from acting right away was the presence of the damn duke. He and his monster stalked the camp every hour of the night, and Larylis dared not face him head on. But tonight...

Tonight, they'd act. Larylis would stand at his father's side, drawing out negotiations and arguing over everything they resisted bringing up now. It would give Larylis' force of covert operatives the chance they needed to sneak into camp while the duke was distracted.

Arlous stood taller. "We'll meet you back here—"

"No," Morkai said.

The word sent a shard of glass through Larylis' heart, puncturing his hope, his well-laid plans.

"Excuse me?" Verdian said. "You cannot deny us time to deliberate."

"I can," the duke said, his expression devoid of shame. "You will surrender now. It is a matter of Prince Teryn's life. The choice should be easy." He slowly angled his head toward Verdian. "Or perhaps it isn't easy for you. Perhaps you don't care enough about the prince's fate to be moved. Perhaps my terms weren't gracious enough for you."

Arlous leveled a dark stare at Verdian, but he refused to meet it.

"How about I provide a royal marriage for your daughter?" Morkai said.

Larylis' veins burned with anger. How dare he bring Mareleau into this!

Verdian narrowed his eyes. "Selay will surrender if my daughter is married to King Dimetreus. Our surrender will only be made after she has borne the king an heir and you have left the continent."

Morkai let out a dark chuckle. "Your daughter will be given a marriage of my choosing, your surrender will happen now, and I will not be going anywhere."

"No!" The word erupted from Verdian's lips. "I've had enough of this farce, sorcerer. Selay will not surrender. You now have my answer." With that, Verdian stepped off the rock and stormed away, his retinue following behind. Larylis blinked after him, his body seized with terror.

To save Teryn's life, both kingdoms had to surrender.

"My...my son..." His father's anguished voice drew Larylis' gaze back to the rock. He expected to see a knife at his brother's throat, a sword over his bowed head. Instead, Morkai had stepped closer to Arlous, a mocking frown turning the corners of his lips.

"I'm a sympathetic man, Arlous. I'll give you one last chance. I will spare Teryn's life if you surrender. I will make you an ally and we will stand up against Selay together. You can get revenge for the final insult Verdian has made to your son. What will it be?"

Arlous' expression was vacant. Hopeless.

Muffled shouts came from Dimetreus' entourage. Larylis' gaze shot to Teryn as he struggled against the guards that held him back. He rubbed his chin against his shoulder again and again. Finally, he managed to get the gag beneath his mouth and his voice came out clear. "Do not surrender. Whatever you do, do not surrender. I've made peace with my fate, Father. I promise you I have. Fight him."

One of the guards backhanded Teryn with an armored glove, splitting Teryn's cheek. Another shoved Teryn's gag back into his mouth.

Morkai sighed as if the outburst had been merely a minor irritation. "What is your decision?"

Arlous stared at Teryn, his brows furrowed. Agony was etched into every crease on his face. Their father had always been strong. Stubborn. Willing to stand for what he wanted regardless of the cost or conflict. He was a steadfast ruler and a kind father. He was unflappable in all things.

Except when it came to love.

That was where his father was weak.

A strange mixture of terror, defeat, and relief swarmed through Larylis as he realized his father had only one choice. He was going to surrender. Lela would fall to the rule of a blood mage to save Teryn's life. Larylis didn't blame him. Not at all. He only dreaded what would happen to this land in the days, months, and years to come.

Arlous spoke, his voice far stronger than Larylis expected. "Very well. We will give you our final decision. First, I request an exchange of hostage."

A chill ran down Larylis' spine. Not once had they discussed a change of hostage.

Morkai scoffed. "A change of hostage? Who do you suggest to take his place?" His gaze slid slowly to Larylis.

He blanched, his legs nearly giving way beneath him. His father was going to...to sacrifice *him*. A surge of betrayal twisted his heart, but he pushed it away along with the tears that pricked his eyes. This was a sacrifice that needed to be made. If Menah didn't surrender, death would be the toll. Better to kill the bastard than the heir.

Another spike of betrayal tightened his chest.

"No," Arlous said. "I want you to take me."

Larylis froze, his mind reeling to comprehend his father's words.

Morkai grinned as if the proceedings were an entertaining spectacle. "I cannot allow you to decide your kingdom's fate and play hostage at the same time."

Arlous shook his head. "My son will take my place. His decision will be final."

"I can hardly trust the crown prince to make such an important decision on Menah's behalf," Morkai said. "He's already made his stance clear. Not that I blame him. I believe he's feeling rather sore about being a hostage."

"Not Teryn," Arlous said. "But my other heir, Larylis Alante."

Larylis looked from his father to Teryn. None of this made sense. He wasn't truly an Alante. It was only supposed to be an act in the service of a plan that had already failed.

Morkai turned his gaze on Larylis, studying him as if seeing him for the first time. "Larylis Alante?"

Larylis shook his head to deny it, but his father's voice rang out. "You are an Alante, Larylis. It is my final wish."

"I accept," Morkai said. He snapped his fingers and two guards dragged Teryn onto the rock. Everything seemed to happen in a blur as Teryn—still bound and gagged—was turned over to Arlous' war commander, General Nellman. Meanwhile, Larylis was beckoned onto the rock. Arlous now stood where Teryn had been, his wrists tied behind his back. It took Larylis a moment to realize his father had been stripped of all weapons and armor, and they now lay on the ground at Teryn's feet.

He met his father's gaze, who held his eyes with a knowing look. "I trust you. You will make the decision we've already settled on. Do you understand me? I believe in you. I love—" His voice was cut off as a guard tied a gag around his mouth. With nothing left to say, Arlous only gave him a resigned nod.

Larylis' heart hammered so hard he could hear it. It pounded in his ears, mingling with the echo of his father's words.

You will make the decision we've already settled on.

His stomach churned, sending bile rising to his throat.

Do you understand me?

Larylis understood completely.

Morkai gave him a wry grin. "What's your choice, Larylis Alante?"

I believe in you.

He swallowed hard. His voice sounded far away when he finally spoke. "We refuse to surrender."

"Very well." Morkai lifted his cane and tugged on the amber crystal that adorned the top. In a flash, the cane separated in two, revealing a long, slim dagger attached to the crystal, its hilt the same black color of his cane. Then, with a swipe, he slashed it over Arlous' throat.

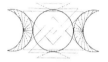

49

Teryn roared against his gag as he watched blood seep from his father's throat. The guards stepped away, leaving Arlous staggering, writhing, his bound hands preventing him from covering the wound. Teryn struggled against the arms that restrained him. This time it wasn't Morkai's guards but his father's own men. He was desperate to run to him, to save his father before he could bleed out. But all hope of that was lost when a flash of silver swept between Arlous' head and shoulders. Teryn hadn't seen the soldier come up behind his father, hadn't seen him unsheathe his sword. He only saw as Arlous' head was separated from his body before falling to the ground. Hot tears streamed down Teryn's cheeks as he renewed his struggle to get free. "No, Your Majesty. No," General Nellman kept saying over and over. At first, Teryn thought he was quietly lamenting Arlous' death.

Then he realized Nellman was talking to *him*.

He was king now.

Morkai stepped toward Larylis, who stood trembling, eyes fixed on their father's corpse. "Do you feel satisfied with your choice, Larylis Alante?"

Larylis' gaze shot toward the duke. His throat bobbed. Once. Twice. When he spoke, his words came out trembling. "We...we will now discuss terms for war."

Morkai released a sigh and extended his free hand to the side. His cane was clenched in the other, his hidden blade back in its sheath. "No, we will not."

The ground rumbled all around. A dark shape bounded over and leapt onto the rock. It was the Beast. Just then, one of the duke's soldiers blew a deep and baleful horn.

THE HORN BLAST ECHOED THROUGH THE VALLEY, ITS TONE reverberating through Cora's bones. She couldn't take her eyes off the dead king. They didn't surrender. They were *supposed* to surrender. She'd thought that was what had happened when Teryn had been transported to the other side of the rock. But now King Arlous was dead, and the horn...

It signaled battle.

She could spend no more time waiting for Teryn to get to safety. If the Forest People were going to take down the duke, they'd have to act now.

She assessed the figures who'd come to stand beside her, all dressed in the same leather armor she wore. The archers and spearmen had their weapons drawn. The Faeryn had their hands raised, ready to summon the Magic of the Soil.

A glance back at the valley showed the Roizan leaping onto the rock. It must have charged from her brother's camp when she hadn't been looking. With a spike of terror, she whirled toward Valorre and tore the cotton sheath from his horn. "Go," she whispered.

The unicorn took off running.

Cora and the Forest People followed.

〜

Teryn shouted Larylis' name, but his mouth was still gagged. His muffled cries were drowned out by the war horn, by General Nellman's call for retreat. Larylis obeyed the call and dove off the rock. One of Menah's soldiers got hold of Larylis and began ushering him away from the rock. Teryn stumbled, his movements made far more difficult with his hands still bound, but he was quickly hauled to his feet. He found Lieutenant Griff at his side, a knife in hand. He cut Teryn's bindings and gag, then hastily dressed him in a belted sword and breastplate. All of his father's soldiers—no, *his* soldiers now—formed a wall around him and Larylis against the duke's men.

Larylis sidled closer, sword raised. His hand trembled, his face as pale as a ghost as they continued their retreat. The duke's men were gaining on them. Teryn exchanged a terrified glance with his brother. Neither needed words to express how they were feeling. They were both terrified. Reeling in the wake of their father's death. "Your sword," Larylis said, voice wavering.

Teryn glanced at the sword that had been belted at his waist. Only then did he recognize it. His father's sword. His father's breastplate. Both had been stripped from his father when Arlous had taken Teryn's place. The armor was light. Not what a royal would wear into battle, but his father hadn't anticipated how the meeting would end. It wasn't how so-called *peace talks* were supposed to work .

This isn't how anything *is supposed to work.*

Arlous' death replayed before Teryn's eyes, but he forced himself back to the present. Grief lanced his heart as he unsheathed his father's sword. Morkai's men were gaining on them, and the horn had likely summoned the rest of his forces back at camp. Hopefully it had summoned reinforcements from Menah and Selay as well.

Teryn caught a glimpse of the rock where Morkai stood next to his Beast, lips pulled into a smug grin. The view was quickly obscured by a misty fog. It sprouted from the earth in patches that were growing denser by the second.

His blood went cold.

This wasn't fog.

A patch of mist turned corporeal before his eyes, forming a towering figure with a semi-translucent battle axe. The wraith swung the weapon, but not at Teryn. He was facing away from him...toward Lieutenant Griff.

Teryn's warning came too late, and the man took the axe in his shoulder. With a grunt, Griff staggered forward and whirled to face his opponent. Through the wraith's body, Teryn saw the lieutenant's eyes go wide, saw where his armor was rent open to reveal a seeping wound. The man's arm hung useless at his side, but he kept the other hand wrapped tight around his sword. The wraith swung his axe again, but Teryn dove into action. His father's sword cleaved through the specter, making it disappear into a puff of mist.

Lieutenant Griff met Teryn's gaze with a haunted look, his face already pale from blood loss.

"It's going to reanimate in a matter of seconds," Teryn said. "Be ready—"

Griff charged to Teryn's right and met the shaft of a spear that had been aiming for the flesh above Teryn's breastplate. Teryn launched back. Griff's sword knocked the spear away. Another swipe and the wraith was gone. At least the apparitions' weapons could be parried like any other, and their bodies could be vanquished by the lightest interference. Teryn had witnessed that when Cora had shot them with her bow. Her arrow had soared straight through every wraith in its path and took them out with ease.

The problem was that they kept coming back.

The axe wraith reformed before Teryn's eyes, staring down at him with two black hollows. Teryn cut through his middle before he could swing his axe, but the spear wraith was back now too. Teryn blocked his spear then swiped through his body. Turned, cut down another. Turned. Another.

They were everywhere.

Everywhere.

He turned again, watched Lieutenant Griff fall to the earth, his gut gaping open where the axe wraith had split his armor yet again. The next swing of the axe severed Griff's head. Teryn's stomach lurched. He stepped back, forcing himself to keep his nerve. Mist formed at his left but he cut it down before it could take a human shape. Another appeared on his right. Another straight ahead.

A flurry of wings stole past his vision, cutting through the bodies of the wraiths and sending them scattering into mist. *Berol.* She flew back up, her wings beating the air.

A specter holding a mace charged him. Again, Berol dove down. The wraith swung his mace. It nearly collided with her. She veered left at the last minute, missing the weapon's spiked head by an inch.

She landed on Teryn's shoulder and frantically nipped at his cheek. "Go!" Teryn shouted, waving her away. The mace wraith renewed his charge on Teryn. Berol launched off Teryn's shoulder and flew at the apparition. This time, its mace connected with one of her wings. "Berol!" Teryn saw her fall to the ground just as he cut through the wraith. As soon as it disappeared, he turned toward the falcon. She rolled on the grass and righted herself, then flew back toward Teryn. Her feathers were bent at odd angles where the wraith had struck her, making her flight uneven. She flapped her wings in his face, ushering him back. His heart squeezed tight at the sight of those twisted feathers. "Get out of here, Berol. Home! *Go home.*" She beat her wings at him a few more times, but he gently shoved her away. "Go!" he shouted as fiercely as he could. "Go away!"

She launched back into the sky and circled overhead.

"Please." The word was barely a whisper. With all his heart, he willed her away. Whether it was home, the woods, or some far off place, he didn't care. He'd rather never see her again than watch her die protecting him.

Finally, she flew out of sight.

With a bone-deep weariness, Teryn returned to the fight.

He barely noticed when a small cavalry charge came from behind. Reinforcements had arrived but it still wasn't enough. There were too many wraiths.

He swung his sword again and again, his arms aching with every slash. His father's longsword was far heavier than the shortsword he'd brought on the Heart's Hunt. Still, he fought on. The wraiths were relentless. A particularly skilled apparition pursued him, blocking every swipe and slash with his translucent sword. The sounds their two weapons made when they made contact was wrong. There was no clang of steel on steel, only a muffled crash. Sweat dripped into Teryn's eyes. His muscles screamed with every move. He parried. Stepped back. Parried. Stepped back.

His next step landed on something hard. The body of another one of his soldiers, he realized with terror. He lurched back as the wraith swung his sword, sending him tripping over the man. The wraith took his chance to close in on Teryn. Teryn lifted his sword, but the wraith was faster, his weapon darting straight toward his throat.

The wraith froze and puffed into mist. Teryn scrambled to his feet and found a thin, twisted root where the specter had been. Not too far away he saw a woman with tan skin, dark hair, and inked forearms. His heart stuttered as his first thought was that the figure was Cora. But another look revealed this woman was much older. He glanced around the battlefield and noticed a few other similar figures, their tattooed palms raised as more roots rose from the earth, tearing wraiths in two, snuffing them out before they had the chance to fully form. He saw others with spears and bows, some in direct combat with Morkai's soldiers.

Teryn wasn't sure how it was possible, but Cora must have brought her people. Her coven. She might even be there herself. The prospect wasn't entirely comforting, as he hated the thought of her being in harm's way. Still, the odds were no longer so firmly against him, especially as an infantry charge stormed into the fray.

A wraith formed in front of him, and he cut it down, ignoring the scream of his muscles. Gritting his teeth, he turned his mind away from retreat. There was one person he needed to find.

One person to kill.

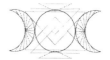

50

The air grew heavy with plumes of dirt, left in the wake of the Forest People's manipulation of roots and vines. It was some of the most impressive feats of visible magic Cora had ever seen. She couldn't gape for long, though. Not only was her vision growing increasingly obscured as she wove through the battlefield, but she had a job to do.

Salinda stayed at her side, fending off threats with her Magic of the Soil while Cora used her bow. They kept to the east side of the valley, where the field was devoid of wraiths. The specters remained to the west, the side closest to Menah's and Selay's camps, where very few of Morkai's men kept up pursuit. It didn't take long for Cora to learn why. The wraiths cut down anyone they came across, regardless of what side they served or what sigil was etched into their armor. She supposed that was the cost of employing the dead—beings whose bodies had been stripped from mind and spirit. Morkai had said they were the souls of warriors who'd served in a war long passed. They were living memories gifted with the power to kill, nothing more.

The ground rumbled beneath her feet. Cora and Salinda pulled up short as Valorre streamed past, the Roizan charging after. Cora had been too late to prevent Morkai from using his creature to summon the wraiths, but Valorre's appearance on the field had been enough to get the Roizan away from Morkai shortly after. Valorre had then begun circling the perimeter of the field, drawing the Roizan up the hillside, between the trees, anywhere to keep him out of range from the duke. But whenever Valorre had tried to lead the creature too far, the Roizan would come barreling back, forcing Valorre onto the field to tempt the beast away again.

Cora coughed into her cloak as she and Salinda moved through a particularly dense cloud of dirt. She blinked the grit from her eyes once they were past it. They were nearing Centerpointe Rock. Through the haze, she saw half of it was framed by roots, as if one of the Forest People had tried to create a cage around it. Finally, Cora caught sight of Morkai. He was battling Roije. The tracker had a spear in one hand while his other palm was raised toward the earth. He sent root after root to harry the duke, but Morkai sliced through every vine that tried to wrap around his ankle, hacked through every root that shot toward his chest. Not only did Morkai have his long dagger—the one he'd had hidden in his cane—but he now held a broadsword as well. Salinda and Cora took off toward the fighting pair. Cora's heart leapt into her throat when she passed a familiar body lying in the muddy grass.

Druchan.

He was dead.

She didn't have time to grieve or feel guilt. Only to nock an arrow and aim for Morkai. Something heavy slammed into her, and she lost her footing. Her bow skittered out of her hands as she landed on her back. A dark silhouette stood over her, backlit by the rising sun. The light glinted off a broadsword pointed over her heart.

"You," growled a familiar voice.

Her lungs tightened. "Dimi."

"Impostor," he said. As her eyes adjusted, she saw his furious glare. "How dare you come into my home and try to manipulate me. To pour salt in a wound already gaping."

"Brother," Cora said, trying to keep her voice level. "It's me. It's...it's Aveline. It's...Cora."

He froze on an intake of breath. "How do you know about that name?"

"Because it's *my* name. It's what our mother used to call me in private. You know that."

"All you speak are lies," he said, shaking his head. He continued to glare, but for the briefest moment, she thought she saw the glossy sheen over his eyes retreat.

Hope sparked inside her, and she held on to it like an anchor. "Do...do you remember when I told you how I'd learned where babies came from? How I'd overheard what Lady Paulette had been discussing with Lady Madeline? Do you remember what you said to me after? You said—"

He took a forbidding step closer, the tip of his sword pressing against Cora's thick leather breastplate, the haze once again clouding his eyes. "It doesn't matter what I said. There was a spy in my house that night. I trust nothing that was uttered where that wretched poisoner could have overheard."

He lifted his sword slightly, as if preparing to thrust.

"What about the wildflower meadow?" she rushed to say.

He paused. "What about it?"

"Do you remember when we used to have picnics on our secret cliff?" The memory played out in her mind as she said it. She hadn't even remembered it until now. "Remember how we used to watch the meadow beneath the cliff and pretend it was home to faeries? We used to imagine we could leap from the ledge and land in another world. Another realm. You took me there after our parents died." Mentioning her parents brought a lump rising in her throat. She searched his eyes, hoping to see the haze lift. It didn't. Grief snagged her heart, and rage began to bloom there. Her voice quavered, growing louder, firmer, with every word she spoke next. "You told me it would be all right. That you'd always protect me. You said you'd never let anyone hurt me. You said that, Dimi. You promised."

She no longer cared about the sword pressed over her chest, only the relief that came from uttering truths she'd let lie buried too long. "You asked me a question the night you found me next to Linette's bedside. You said, *What have you done*? I ask you the same, Dimetreus. What have you done? What have you done to *us*, to all that was left of our family? What have you done to our kingdom?"

"Enough!" he shouted. His torso heaved as he stared down at her, blinking furiously. "Enough," he said again. His voice, his posture, his expression...everything began to deflate. His sword still stood between them, but his sword arm trembled. The haze...began to lift.

She extended her senses toward him, felt his conflict, his confusion. His dulled emotions seemed to slam up against invisible walls. She swallowed hard, willing her anger to abate as she brought her palms out in a placating gesture. "It's all right—" Her words cut off as two shapes came barreling toward them. A pair of fighters on horseback locked in battle. The horse and soldier closest to them were wounded, the mount rearing back. Back. Edging dangerously near. "Dimi."

"No," he said, the word like a plea. "It can't be..."

"Dimi!" She shouted his name and began scrambling back on her forearms, her brother's sword no longer her greatest concern. She rolled onto her stomach, clawing at the earth to gain enough purchase to rise to her feet. The sound of hooves closed in, followed by a guttural neigh. A glance over her shoulder showed the wounded stallion bucking as his rider received a fatal blow. His rear hooves caught Dimetreus in the gut, sending him tumbling back. His head struck the earth. Cora was halfway to rising when the stallion bucked again. She ducked, covering her head, and caught a hoof in the shoulder instead. It sent her to the ground, several feet from where her brother lay unconscious. Perhaps even dead.

Another guttural sound came from the horse. The other soldier had opened the stallion's throat. It fell back, its body plummeting straight toward Cora. She half ran, half crawled. But when the horse landed, her legs were pinned beneath it.

～

THE GROUND WAS RIDDLED WITH ROOTS AND VINES, impeding Teryn's progress along with the relentless reappearance of the wraiths. His one consolation was that the longer the battle went on, the slower the wraiths began to reanimate. It seemed there were limits to the duke's magic. Or perhaps the wraiths' patience in following his will was wearing thin.

Teryn was nearly out of breath, his brow slick with sweat, by the time he finally found Morkai. The mage stood upon Centerpointe Rock, locked in combat with two witches, a male and female. Both had tattoos like Cora's and worked with roots the same way he'd seen others doing on the battlefield. Morkai parried every attack they threw his way, his moves swift and sure. The female sent roots crawling from the earth around the rock, snaking over the surface and weaving around his ankles while the male charged with a spear. Morkai broke free and parried the spear with his broadsword. With his dagger, he cut through the vines and kicked the tangled limbs free.

Another root erupted from the earth, this one large enough to make the ground tremble as it shot toward the rock. It wrapped around the mage's middle and squeezed. Teryn saw the duke's breastplate begin to warp. The male witch came in for another attack with his spear. With a mighty swing, Morkai hacked through the root with his sword. With his dagger, he severed the leather straps securing one side of his breastplate. He shrugged off the armor just as the witch swung out with his spear. The spearhead sliced open Morkai's side, but the duke didn't falter. He stepped forth and swung his sword in an arc.

And severed the man's arm at the elbow.

"Roije!" the female witch called out. She ran to the injured man.

Morkai pursued them both, turning his back fully to Teryn.

Teryn raced the rest of the way to the rock, determined to plunge his sword into the duke's back, straight through his ribs, his heart—

Morkai turned around and parried Teryn's attack.

"The new King of Menah," Morkai said with a smirk. Now that they were face to face, Teryn could see the blood splattered over the mage's face and neck. How many others had the duke killed? Teryn was vaguely aware of the unmoving shapes of other bodies strewn about the rock. He had a feeling most were soldiers from Menah or Selay.

"I appreciate you making things easy for me," Morkai taunted. "After I kill you, I'll kill your brother. Menah is as good as mine."

Teryn's blood boiled with rage, fueling his every move as he struggled to get under Morkai's defenses. The mage fought with surprising skill and unnatural speed. Teryn knew the mage worked terrifying feats of blood sorcery, but he hadn't expected him to fight like a trained soldier.

Teryn's eyes stung as sweat dripped into them. He blinked the moisture away, swung his father's sword. It clashed with Morkai's dagger, but the force of Teryn's swing was so hard it sent the mage's weapon flying from his hand—

A sharp pain struck Teryn's ribs. He staggered back. Glancing down, he found a gash in the right side of his breastplate. Morkai may have been partially disarmed but he still held his broadsword. Thankfully, the wound didn't appear terribly deep. Or was he simply in shock? Whatever the case, he gritted his teeth against the pain, set his feet, and strengthened his grip on his sword.

Morkai raised his empty palm.

To Teryn's horror, streams of his blood began to float from his wound to dance through the air between him and the mage.

In a matter of seconds, the duke held a ball of Teryn's blood in the palm of his hand.

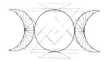

51

Cora was forced to watch the horrible scene unfolding before her. Roije and Salinda's attack. Roije's severed arm. Teryn charging Morkai. Salinda wrapping Roije's wound and helping him limp away. Cora lost sight of them in the haze, but she was close enough to see Teryn and Morkai's fight. Close enough to watch as his plate was rent open.

She could hardly peel her eyes away, even as she struggled to free herself from beneath the dead horse. At least none of the enemy soldiers had seen her, nor had anyone found her brother. With the plumes of dirt clouding the air and mingling with the bloody chaos of battle, Dimetreus looked like any other dead body.

But he wasn't.

She could feel his life force even as he lay prone a few feet away.

Her pulse thudded wildly as she watched Morkai step toward Teryn. The prince was frozen, his hand over his heart, his eyes on the ball of blood. She clawed her hands into the dirt, tried to pull her bottom half free. There was a sharp pain in one of her legs. Likely fractured from the horse's fall. Her shoulder screamed where the stallion had kicked her.

Morkai lifted the ball of blood higher and let it rotate in his hand. Teryn gasped, raking his breastplate with his fingertips as if desperate to reach his heart. She remembered that sharp pain when Morkai had used her own blood against her. But could he kill with it? She knew he could weave death by merging it with a deceased person's blood, but what could he do with just a single source?

Teryn winced. His sword clattered to the surface of the rock.

Morkai dropped his broadsword.

Cora's heart slammed against her ribs as she realized what he was going to do.

There were several bodies littered around the rock.

Gaping wounds.

Sources of blood.

Morkai lifted his free hand toward the nearest body. Tendrils of crimson rose like ribbons toward his palm.

Cora renewed her struggle, straining against the horse's weight.

Stop fighting.

The demand came from within her. Not a voice but a feeling. She ignored it.

Stop struggling.

She only struggled harder.

Slow down.

Feel.

She gritted her teeth against the urgings, raging at

them, hating them. How could she be expected to slow down and *feel* at a time like this?

A spike of resentment shot through her. Resentment at her own futility, her weakness, her stupid worthless magic—

Subtle awareness cleared a path through her anger, something soft and yielding. She continued to rage against it, but it was stronger than her resistance.

It was her magic.

She suddenly knew what this was. Another challenge.

Hot angry tears streamed down her cheeks. She didn't have time for a challenge. She didn't have time to slow down and turn inward. Not when Morkai was transforming both sources of blood into threads—threads that were now beginning to twine together.

Again, that soft, quiet urging cut through her resistance.

She hated it. Oh, how she hated it.

But she gave in. Gave in to the hate, the anguish, the panic. Let herself feel it, let it twist her heart and weaken her body. Let herself slump beneath the horse and close her eyes. Her weakness turned to calm, and calm turned to strength. Magic flooded her chest and trailed down her arms, humming through the ink that marked her skin.

She breathed.

In. Out. In. Out.

And felt.

Pain. Grief. Urgency. Fortitude.

Then something softer.

Protection. Devotion. Friendship. Love.

Open your eyes.

She followed the internal urging, saw Morkai's blood

weaving growing tighter, the strands of blood nearly fully merged. Teryn was now on his knees, still clutching his breastplate.

Allowing her quiet magic to still her mind, she followed its pull, its guidance. Followed it as it narrowed in on the space behind Morkai. She felt an overwhelming *need* to be there, to free Teryn. It was so strong she could feel it down to her bones. It tugged her palms, her body, her soul, tugged every part of her until she felt as if it would carry her there on an invisible wind.

Teryn's face warped with pain as the mage threaded another strand through his tapestry.

Her heart swelled with determination. Resolve. Conviction.

With a slow exhale, she focused on her legs, on the foot that wasn't radiating with piercing agony. She moved it against the dirt, the horse, and pictured it pressing against the very place she needed to be. Not against soil, not buried beneath a dead animal, but upon the rock—

She hobbled on one leg, suddenly upright.

Blinking at the startling shift in light, she realized she now stood directly behind Morkai on Centerpointe Rock.

His back was facing her as he continued to weave his crimson tapestry. He hadn't a clue she was there. It shouldn't be possible that she was. She couldn't have been able to move from under the horse to the rock in the blink of an eye.

But it had happened. And this was no time to second-guess what could be her last shot.

A ripple of pain shot through her injured leg as she shifted her stance. She reached for one of her daggers, stepped forward, and plunged it into Morkai's back. She twisted it as far as she could before he whirled to face her.

His eyes went wide as they met hers. His blood weaving fell to the surface of the rock. It didn't disappear like it had before he'd killed the prisoner or after he'd woven her blood with Linette's. It simply spilled as ordinary blood should. His magic ruined. His tapestry incomplete.

Cora held his gaze and unsheathed her next dagger. With a thrust, she drove it into Morkai's abdomen. She grabbed her final knife, thrust toward him, but he knocked her hand away. Unfazed, she swiped and slashed and stabbed. He backed up a few steps and held out his hand. She expected him to reveal her tiny ball of blood again. Expected to feel the searing pain strike her chest at any moment.

It didn't.

She plunged her final knife into Morkai's side and grabbed an arrow from her quiver—

Teryn gasped.

Her eyes flew toward him. He'd been halfway to standing but now doubled over. Fresh tendrils of blood seeped from his wound as Morkai drew it toward his palm.

She glanced back at Morkai, saw blood spreading over his padded tunic everywhere she'd struck. He held her gaze with a sneer and wrapped his free hand around the hilt of the knife in his side. As he pulled it free, more blood darkened his tunic.

Her lips curled into a wicked smirk. If he pulled all of her blades free at once, he'd bleed to death before long.

He narrowed his eyes as if he had come to the same

conclusion. Gritting his teeth, he pressed his open palm over the wound while the other continued to summon Teryn's blood. "I need my Roizan," he said.

"He's busy right now." She clenched her hand around the shaft of her arrow, assessing where she could strike next.

"Drop your arrow and call off your unicorn friend—"

"No."

"—or Teryn dies."

Teryn bit back a cry as Morkai drew more blood from his wound. He sank back to his knees, his face white. He was losing blood far faster than Morkai. He'd die, even without a blood weaving.

"All right." The words left her mouth in a rush. She let the arrow fall to her feet. "All right. I'll call off Valorre. Drop Teryn's blood."

"Call off the unicorn first."

She released a slow breath and sought her connection to Valorre. She sensed him on the hillside, his energy frantic, fatigued. *Run out of range.*

He rippled with defiance. *The abomination will come back to the field.*

It's all right, she said, trying to convey her certainty. Her sense of calm amongst a storm of fear. *Just do it.*

She felt the unicorn's grudging acceptance.

"It is done. The Roizan will return."

Morkai turned his palm down. She noted that the blood didn't fall. It only disappeared. That meant he still had it, the same way he still held her tiny drop somewhere. He took a step toward her, his face distorted with rage. "Stop fighting against me, Aveline. I have already won. Lela will be mine by the end of this battle. There will be no war. No surrender. It ends here. This is your last chance to choose me."

She hobbled a step back, her injured leg screaming in protest. Catching her balance, she lifted her chin and tried to exude far more confidence than she felt. "You already know my decision. I will never choose you. And you haven't already won. You've lost. You may have killed King Arlous and may think you can kill Teryn too, but King Verdian has fled to safety." She didn't know if that last part was true, only that she hadn't seen the King of Selay on the battlefield yet. No one could see far in this haze. Her chest squeezed as she pondered her next lie, uncertain if there was a chance it could be true by now. The thought tinged her voice with sorrow, giving weight to her possible deception. "My brother is dead. You have no one to inherit Khero from."

His lips tightened into a line.

"You made a mistake in keeping him on the battlefield," she said.

Morkai spoke through his teeth. "He wasn't supposed to be on the battlefield. I ordered him back to camp."

Cora frowned. If her brother had been ordered to safety...why had he been out there? Had he purposefully sought her out? If so, why? Based on the anger he'd shown during their initial confrontation, it could have been for revenge.

She remembered how his eyes had briefly cleared of their sheen. It hadn't lasted long, but for a moment she'd felt like she'd connected to a piece of his true self.

Perhaps it had been hope that had driven him after her.

Over Morkai's shoulder, Cora saw the lumbering

shape of the Roizan breaking through the dusty haze. It set the rock rumbling as it clambered toward its master.

The duke shook his head with a dark laugh. "You're wrong about one thing, Aveline," he said as he removed another one of her daggers. "I do have someone left to inherit Khero from. You."

The Roizan ambled closer and closer, panting with fatigue, lips coated in froth. Morkai pressed his hand over the freshest wound and reached for the final embedded dagger. The one she'd plunged into his lower back when she'd first found herself transported onto the rock. His face contorted as he reached behind him and wrenched the blade free.

Cora stepped back, stifling a cry as her injured leg made contact with the rock. She angled herself slightly toward Teryn. He'd managed to remove his breastplate and now pressed his palm over his wound.

With the final dagger free, Morkai locked his eyes with hers. "If your brother is truly dead, then I need you more than ever to claim the throne."

The Roizan reached the edge of the rock.

"But I don't need you alive. All I need is your body." A wild grin stretched over his lips, his pale eyes flashing with menace. He held his hand—the one still clutching her dagger—toward the Roizan. He hadn't looked at the weapon after he'd removed it. His attention had been too fixated on Cora. Too engrossed in his own wicked plans to question whether Cora had any of her own. Didn't think to wonder why Cora had stopped fighting him. Why she didn't flinch or cower as the Roizan leapt upon the rock.

Morkai's expression shuttered with relief, his free

hand still pressed to one of his wounds. A wound that was surely knitting back together at that very moment.

It didn't matter.

The Roizan's eyes narrowed on the blade in its master's hand, a blade forged from a white horn. It opened its salivating maw over Morkai's arm and snapped its teeth shut. With a cry, Morkai faced his creature, eyes wide with surprise. The Roizan didn't seem to see Morkai at all, not even as the duke swung out with his free hand, shoving at the beast's snout, desperate to free himself.

Cora edged the rest of the way toward Teryn and linked her arm through his. Together they scrambled off the rock, tumbling to the root-strewn grass. She looked back at the rock just as the Roizan opened its mouth again, this time snapping its teeth over Morkai's head. Then his body. Blood poured between the Roizan's teeth as he continued to crunch through flesh and bone. The monster devoured his master, his maker, until there was nothing left that could be called a being at all.

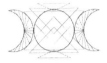

52

Larylis fought, certain that his next breath would be his last. Part of him wasn't sure he deserved another breath. Not after what he'd done. Not after the choice he was forced to make. One that ended in his father's death. Still, he swung his blade. Whether he fought a man of flesh or a wraith of mist, every cut conjured visions of father's ruined neck, his severed head, his lifeless eyes. He saw the pride, the trust, right before Larylis condemned him to die. It didn't matter that it was what his father had wanted. All that mattered was that his voice had delivered the sentence. His words had driven the blade.

Part of him yearned to quit fighting, but somehow a fire remained kindled deep in his heart. It drove his arms to move when they were too fatigued to feel, planted his feet on the slick mud when all he wanted to do was sink to his knees and weep.

He fought that urge now as he battled a wraith. Their swords clashed again and again. Larylis' reaction time was getting slower. His weapon heavier in his hand. But that ember still glowed. Still begged him to fight.

The wraith seemed to slow as well. It had already reanimated several times. Each time it reformed, its misty body took longer to condense into a humanoid form. He'd noticed it with other wraiths as well. The longer a wraith fought, and the more times it was felled, the more hampered it would become, as if the act of reanimating was too much work. The will to fight and die over and over too burdensome to bear. Larylis had already seen numerous wraiths wander off the field and disappear. Others simply refused to reanimate.

Larylis parried a particularly lethargic swing and swept his blade through the wraith's middle. As it disappeared, he took the chance to assess his surroundings. The haze was still heavy where he fought, as a few of the tattooed vine-wielders battled wraiths nearby, sending new plumes of dirt into the air with every root they drew from the ground. He'd been terrified when he'd first seen them, certain they served the mage. But his fears were quickly assuaged. They were fighting *against* the duke and his men.

Nearby, he spotted Lex facing off against a mace-wielding wraith. The prince had joined the fray with the infantry charge and had fought with alarming tenacity ever since. He heaved and stumbled, but not once did he give up. Larylis wondered if the same persistent fire that kept him on his feet burned within Lex too.

A misty shape drew his attention. The wraith Larylis had been fighting began to reform in front of him, but he slashed through it before it could fully solidify. A strangled cry rang out, pulling his attention to his surroundings once more. It didn't ring with the same tenor as a yelp of injury or a grunt of strength. It was neither a battle cry nor a shout of vengeance or rage. Instead, it was a long wail of anguish. Terror. He squinted into the haze and saw a soldier fall to his knees and tear off his helm, his posture slumped. He wore the black armor of the duke's men. His opponent, a soldier from Selay, went in for the kill. The other man held up his hands in surrender, falling on his back.

Another similar wail echoed elsewhere on the field. A man stumbled by, peeling off his plates of armor, eyes bulging as he stared at his surroundings as if seeing them for the first time.

A shiver ran down Larylis' spine.

He forced his gaze back to the place where his wraith opponent would surely rise.

It didn't. No matter how long he looked, the wraith didn't return. He scanned the field around him. More bewildered soldiers stumbled past. Some fell to their opponent's swords while others cried out to surrender. Still, others continued to fight, unplagued by whatever drove their comrades to confusion.

Larylis had no idea what was going on.

One thing was certain, though.

The wraiths were gone.

A SCREECHING BELLOW ECHOED THROUGHOUT THE VALLEY. Cora watched as the Roizan pressed its snout to the surface of the rock, sniffing, tasting. Then, with another piercing howl, it began to buck and thrash. Cora and

Teryn backed farther away from the rock, their moves hampered by their respective injuries. Cora didn't dare look away from the Roizan as crimson saliva frothed at its lips. It tossed its enormous head and scraped its front hooves over the rock. Howls turned to grunts. Grunts turned to whimpers.

Then it stilled.

The Roizan's head drooped as if suddenly too heavy for its shoulders. Its eyes closed, its hindquarters quavered. With a final tremor, it fell upon the rock with a rumbling thud. Its red skin began to blacken and char, burning everything from its snout to its tail to the ridge of white horns running along its spine. Fiery veins of red began to spiderweb through its charred flesh. The Roizan slowly opened its maw and released a deep moan. With a final breath, the body of the Roizan collapsed into a pile of ash.

Cora watched as a gust of wind stole some of the ash and sent it scattering over the field. Part of her expected the beast to reform, for Morkai to rise from his bloody remains. The longer she watched the more certain she became.

Morkai was gone.

Just as the duke had said, his magic was connected to the Roizan, and the Roizan's life was bound to his. The duke's death meant the end of the Roizan. An end to his well of magic. And—hopefully—a severing of Morkai's control. Without the duke's numerous glamours being fueled by the Roizan's magic, those he'd been controlling should now be free.

That was her theory, at least.

Teryn let out a pained gasp. She whirled toward him,

his name lurching from her lips. A spike of terror surged through her. He was badly injured and his wound was still bleeding. Thanks to Morkai, he'd already lost far too much blood. He swayed on his feet. She reached out to steady him, wincing at the pain in her leg. Her own injuries could wait. Without a second thought, she retrieved an arrow and slashed the head through the bottom of her cloak. It wasn't as effective as a knife, but all her blades were still on the rock. The two the Roizan hadn't eaten, that is.

With frantic fingers, she wrapped the strip of wool around his torso, relieved that the lesion over his ribs wasn't worse. It was a jagged cut, both from the sword Morkai had struck him with and the armor that had bitten into his skin as a result. It certainly wouldn't help that the strip of wool she'd bandaged him in was dirty. At least it would slow the bleeding before he could get to a field surgeon.

Once the wound was wrapped, she stilled her fingers and lifted her eyes to his. He stared down at her with a thoughtful expression. One that made her breath hitch. She realized now that they hadn't been this close since he'd tricked her with a kiss. Nor had they exchanged a word since then either. When she'd seen him fighting Morkai, her only thoughts had been to save him, protect him, defend him. Their last meeting hadn't mattered, nor had his betrayal or their kiss or any of the other conflicting emotions she felt around him. But now...

Her cheeks warmed as she noticed her hand was still pressed to his chest. Over the other side of his ribs. Beneath his heart. She was about to lift her palm when his hand closed over hers.

"Thank you," he said, his voice a quavering whisper. He ran his thumb over the back of her hand, his touch so soft it almost made her shudder.

"Teryn," a male voice called out from nearby.

Cora slid her hand from under his and took a step back.

Teryn slowly angled his body to face the figure that ran toward them. Cora recognized the man from his presence at the negotiation. His resemblance to Teryn made it easy to guess who he was.

"Larylis," Teryn said, voice heavy with relief. The two embraced with the affection of brothers. Cora, feeling like an interloper, took another step back. She stifled a cry as her heel caught on something in the grass. Shifting her weight more evenly over her uninjured leg, she glanced down at what had nearly caused her fall. There, almost hidden amongst the overturned earth and muddy grass, was a long, slender blade. An amber crystal lay beside it, broken off from the hilt. She bent down and gingerly lifted the crystal. Her palm thrummed against its cold facets. A murky energy pounded against her hand, turning her stomach. She nearly dropped it when she noticed red dripping from the bottom of it.

Blood.

Was the crystal where Morkai had stored the blood he'd stolen?

Swallowing down the bile that rose in her throat, she prepared to throw the crystal into the pile of ash. Then something caught her attention. Some swirling movement behind the amber facets. Her palm thrummed again, this time sensing a new energy. It wasn't dark or murky but...different.

A hand fell softly on her shoulder. She bit back a gasp and shoved the crystal into an inner pocket of her cloak. Teryn gave her a sad smile. "Larylis, this is Cora."

Larylis gave her a solemn nod. "Lex told me about you."

Teryn furrowed his brow. "What do you mean, Lex told you?"

"He came to Dermaine to warn us about the duke's true intentions, then joined our entourage when we left for Centerpointe Rock. He fought with our forces."

Cora and Teryn exchanged a befuddled glance. The last time they'd seen Lex, he'd taken Morkai's deal.

"He's apparently a master of deception," Larylis said. He gave a humorless laugh, one in contrast with the sorrow in his eyes.

It reflected her own sorrow as she looked past the two men to the field beyond, where bodies lay strewn about. Horns bellowed from the east, signaling Khero's retreat. Morkai's death couldn't be widespread yet, but it was clear the tide had turned. The duke's magic had been severed.

It's over. She felt Valorre's words. Glancing around, she sought sight of him to no avail.

It is, she conveyed. *Where are you?*

Close. Your people flee back to the hillside. Will you go with them?

She turned toward the hill where the Forest People had hidden the last few days, but the haze was still too thick to make out any retreating forms. Extending her senses, she felt them near. The survivors at least. Salinda had made it. Roije too, although she sensed him only faintly. Her chest tightened at the knowledge that some of the Forest People had died today and more still could from injuries. Because of her.

Because we had to do what was right, she reminded herself.

She imagined how the battle would have gone without the Forest People's aid. The wraiths would have overpowered Selay's and Menah's forces if not for the roots and vines that tore through the specters with ease.

"What is it?" Teryn asked, his fingertips lightly brushing against hers.

She met his eyes and felt as if her heart were suddenly torn in two. Valorre's question echoed through her mind.

Your people...will you go with them?

The Forest People had fought at her side. They'd intervened with royal affairs in the name of protecting fae magic. But were they truly *her* people? Or were the citizens of Khero—

A dreadful realization sent her heart skittering.

"Dimetreus!" She whirled toward where she'd seen him last. There were too many bodies. Too many figures still darting across the field, some in retreat, some in combat. Finally, she spotted the dead stallion. Not far from it, a cluster of soldiers stood. She began limping in that direction. An arm caught hers and helped her forward. She flushed as she glanced to the side, expecting to find Teryn.

Instead, it was Larylis. "Let me help you."

Disappointment struck her. Of course it wasn't Teryn. Teryn was injured. He walked slightly ahead of them, his gait uneven, his hand pressed against his bandaged ribs. "King Verdian," Teryn called.

A man turned around, and Cora recognized the King of Selay. His eyes widened. "Prince—" He cleared his throat. "*King* Teryn. You're alive."

"I am."

The king shifted his stance, his posture stiff. Cora sensed guilt wafting off of him. "I'm sorry for your loss."

Teryn accepted the king's condolences with a nod.

Verdian's jaw shifted side to side. Lifting his chin, he said in a somewhat begrudging tone, "It will be an honor if you'd take my daughter as your bride when we return home."

A jolt of something fiery sparked in Cora's chest. She breathed it away, forcing her attention from Teryn to the group of soldiers who still stood in a cluster near the felled horse. One turned around. "Your Majesty, the traitor king is awake."

Cora's heart leapt into her throat as she watched the men part to reveal her brother. His eyes darted wildly about as he tried to rise from his knees. A soldier had Dimetreus' arms behind his back and kicked him in the shoulder to keep him down.

A strangled sound left her brother's lips. "What's happening? Where...where..." He blinked several times and shook his head. "A nightmare. No, a nightmare."

Cora surged forward. "Dimetreus!" Another soldier stepped before her, shoving a gauntleted hand out to halt her progress. She hobbled back, eyes darting from the soldier to her distressed brother.

"Who the hell is this?" came King Verdian's sharp tone. Cora met his gaze and found cold eyes looking back at her.

"This is Princess Aveline," Teryn said, coming up beside her.

Verdian let out a bark of humorless laughter. "The dead princess brought back to life?" He scanned her until his eyes landed on her tattooed palms. His lips curled in disgust. "She's a witch. Like the others. The ones with the...vine sorcery."

"The witches fought *with* us," Teryn said, voice surprisingly calm.

Verdian spread out his arms, glancing exaggeratedly from side to side. "Then where are they now?"

Teryn's tone darkened. "Princess Aveline killed the duke."

The king gave him a patronizing look. "Princess Aveline is dead, Majesty."

"Aveline?" The voice was weak, trembling.

Cora met Dimetreus' eyes. They were no longer cast beneath a glossy sheen. They were still shadowed with dark circles and lined with creases that belied his age. Proof that Morkai's death didn't immediately return his well-being.

"Dimi, it's me," Cora said.

"She's working with the traitor," Verdian said. "Take her too."

The soldier with the upraised palm darted forward but Teryn stepped in front of her.

"Out of the way, Majesty," Verdian said through his teeth.

"She's no criminal," Teryn argued. "And she's injured."

The king raised his brows and glanced briefly at

Teryn's torso. "So are you. We need to get you to a surgeon."

"Just let Cora go."

"Cora," Verdian echoed. "I thought she was *Princess Aveline*." He said the last part with clear mocking.

"She is," Teryn said, his voice tinged with desperation. "Did Lex not tell you?"

The king denied it at the same moment Larylis said, "He told *me*."

"Just let her explain," Teryn said.

Verdian shook his head. "If she really is who she says she is, she can come with us willingly and explain during questioning." He leaned to the side and met Cora's gaze.

Fiery rage flooded her core. She spotted her discarded bow, left beside the stallion when she'd been knocked down. Her quiver was still strapped to her back. She could dive for her bow, fight her way out. Or...

She glanced at the hillside where the Forest People were waiting. Where Valorre was waiting.

Your people...will you go with them?

She could close her eyes and try to do what she'd accomplished earlier. She hadn't had the opportunity to revel in what she'd done. Somehow, she'd managed to step across time and space. One moment, she was trapped under the horse. In the next, she was on the rock.

Her body flooded with calm. Perhaps she could do it again. Morkai was dead. Her mission was complete. She could leave this all behind. If the Forest People wouldn't have her back, then she and Valorre could go out on their own—

"Aveline," Dimetreus cried out again. "What...what has happened?"

Her gaze slid back to her brother.

Questions invaded her mind. What would happen to Khero now? The other kingdoms saw Dimetreus as a traitor. An invader. Cora couldn't call him fully innocent, for she still felt the ghost of resentment clawing her heart. But he didn't know what was happening. He might not remember anything between now and when Morkai had first begun manipulating his mind. How could he defend himself and explain what Morkai had done if he didn't understand any of it?

She was reminded of something she'd said to herself only days ago.

If my brother can't protect Khero, that leaves only me.

Her shoulders slumped, her fingers unclenched to hang open at her sides. She thought not of the hillside and the freedom that beckoned her nor the bow that demanded blood. Instead, she met Verdian's hard stare with defiance. She stepped out from behind Teryn, doing her best not to limp or wince. "I am Princess Aveline," she said. "I will go with you and provide whatever proof you require. You will hear me out and you will give my brother a chance to defend himself."

Verdian's face slackened with surprise but he quickly steeled it. "Very well," he said. "Take the traitor and the supposed princess."

"Treat them as befits royalty," Teryn added, his voice firm. The voice of a king. He stared at the soldiers, gaze unflinching, daring any of them to contradict him.

Verdian released a grumbling sigh. "Get King Teryn to a surgeon." The king strode away, his final order sending the soldiers into a frenzy of movement. Two men took Cora by each of her arms.

"Treat her well," Teryn called. She could no longer see him through the commotion, and his voice sounded farther away now. As the soldiers hauled Dimetreus to his feet, she finally caught sight of Teryn. He was being escorted away by far gentler hands. Glancing over his shoulder, he met her eyes and gave her a small nod. She felt his reassurance. His worry. His unspoken apology tinged with a promise—he wouldn't let anything bad happen to her.

A voice crept into her awareness. *Shall I fight them?* Valorre's unseen nearness filled her with a steadying warmth.

No. I'm going with them willingly.

Then I'll go too.

You can't, she said. *We don't know what they'll do to a unicorn.*

His energy rippled with something like a scoff. *They will not see me. But I will follow. I'll be near. I go where you go now.*

Her lips curled into a small smile, fueling her strength as she let the soldiers lead her to the western side of the field. Despite her aching leg, her fatigue, and the storm of questions that tangled in her mind, she kept her head held high. Kept her shoulders back.

Whatever came next, she'd be the princess she needed to be.

WANT MORE EPIC ROMANTIC FANTASY?

Keep the magic alive! The next book in the *Prophecy of the Forgotten Fae* trilogy picks up right where *A Throne of Shadows* left off! Find out what happens to Cora, Teryn, Larylis, and Mareleau in *A Cage of Crystal*. There's more magic, more adventure, more romance, and more fae.

Still don't have enough epic fantasy in your life? *The Fair Isle Trilogy* is another series featuring epic magic and enemies-to-lovers romance! Set in a Victorian-inspired world, this series dives straight into all things fae romance. Start with *To Carve a Fae Heart*.

ACKNOWLEDGMENTS

For those of you who don't know, *A Throne of Shadows* is a variation of the first book I've ever written. An earlier version was originally published as *Shadows of Lela*. That first book holds a special place in my heart. Without it, I wouldn't have grown as a writer and gone on to write all the books that followed. Nor would I now have this fully rewritten (and dare I say much improved) edition that is *A Throne of Shadows*. Still, that doesn't mean the path to rewriting this book was easy. I was often flooded with doubt during the process. I tend to give birth to all my books that way. And yet, the labor continues with each new book. Thankfully, I have a lot of people in my life that make this whole writer thing more than worth it.

First of all, thank you to my readers, the old and new. I am so grateful for the readers who loved the original and are now exploring this new version. I am equally grateful for those readers who are entering the world of Lela for the very first time with this book, as well as those who chose this story as their very first book from me. You make this possible. Do not forget how awesome you are just by being you and reading books.

Thank you to my husband, daughter, and all my pets. Your support uplifts me from the lowest places and brightens my mood when I get anxious.

Thank you to my editor, Kristen, at Your Editing

Lounge. You have been a real champ at dealing with my deadline changes.

Thank you to my typo hunters and proofreaders, Claire, Emily, and Bianca. You are the keenest sleuths when it comes to hunting down those final persistent little errors!

Thank you to my writer besties, and all the Queens of the Quill! Valia Lind, Hanna Sandvig, Kay L. Moody, Joanna Reeder, Rose Garcia, Stacey Trombley, Charlie N. Holmberg, K.C. Cordell, Clarissa Gosling, Abby J. Reed, Kristin J. Dawson, and Alison Ingleby. I can't even imagine where I would be without you guys and your never-ending support.

ALSO BY TESSONJA ODETTE

ENTANGLED WITH FAE - FAE ROMANCE

Curse of the Wolf King: A Beauty and the Beast Retelling

Heart of the Raven Prince: A Cinderella Retelling

Kiss of the Selkie: A Little Mermaid Retelling

— And more —

THE FAIR ISLE TRILOGY - FAE FANTASY

To Carve a Fae Heart

To Wear a Fae Crown

To Spark a Fae War

YA DYSTOPIAN PSYCHOLOGICAL THRILLER

Twisting Minds

ABOUT THE AUTHOR

Tessonja Odette is a fantasy author living in Seattle with her family, her pets, and ample amounts of chocolate. When she isn't writing, she's watching cat videos, petting dogs, having dance parties in the kitchen with her daughter, or pursuing her many creative hobbies. Read more about Tessonja at www.tessonjaodette.com

instagram.com/tessonja
facebook.com/tessonjaodette
tiktok.com/@tessonja
twitter.com/tessonjaodette

Made in United States
Orlando, FL
05 June 2022

18503876R00321